MOURNING BLOOM
AUSTIN SCARBERRY

Copyright © 2024

Austin Scarberry

Scrolls From Scarberry

Cover Art and Design © 2024

T. Thorn Coyle

This book is a work of fiction. All characters, places, and incidents are the product of the author's imagination and are used fictitiously. Any resemblance to actuals persons, events, or locales is coincidental. No portion of this book may be reproduced in any form without written permission from the publisher or author, except as permitted by U.S. copyright law. Nothing here may be used to train Large Language Models, or AI. This book is licensed for your personal enjoyment only. All rights reserved.

1

I t wasn't a thankless job, being a Staffkeeper. In nearly every town, every village, every port, the Staffkeepers of Shaefi were welcomed with open arms and extravagant revelry. And after all, why not? Shaefi's followers brought with them peace and joy, the cessation of hostilities and the hope of a future without conflict. It was tradition in Naefja for villagers to show their respect for the Staffkeepers by yielding all iron for the duration of the travelers' visits. In this way, they symbolically gave up war and toil in favor of mirth and love. No matter where in the realm one went, this practice was well known. It was unanimous. It was sacred.

In Kichishi, of course, it was none of these things. In Kichishi, it was impractical. It was naive. It was foolish.

The boy named Baggi found these thoughts turning over in his mind, as relentlessly as the wheels of the boar-driven wagon on which he sat. His face was relaxed, small eyes closed in his pale, triangular face with a slightly upturned nose set between them. His ears were narrow and tense with concentration, twitching slightly at each word passed between his traveling companions. He ran his round-knuckled fingers lightly over the staff of apple-wood laid across his lap, as he had so many times before, and Contemplated. Baggi tugged at his long auburn braid absentmindedly, still running his other hand over his staff. *No*, he thought, *not my staff. My brother's staff*. It had been in the boy's possession for several years now, and still Compromise felt like a borrowed tool. He felt the gentle cold emanating from the runes. It comforted him.

Around him, sweet bird-song filled the ever-warming morning air, rising to energetic crescendos before joining the caravan in their lazy descent. The mountain trail was a wide and well-maintained switch-back, only a bit steep, yet even with the wagons being pulled two abreast it was slow going. Despite the pace, the Staffkeepers were in good spirits as they beheld their first view of Kichishi below. Light forest covered the ground before them for some miles, yellow and green and loud with wildlife even from so far above, and beyond that lay the prairies that covered so much of their southern neighbor's lands. There would be beasts most Naefjans had never seen, giraffes and roam-lizards and blood-beetles, creatures whose size or aggression would never be tolerated in the freezing, conservative chill of Naef-ja's mountains. Here, there was enough for even those most hungry hunters to thrive. Here, their fierce nature was respected. Perhaps they were even revered.

A shouted "halt" from the lead wagon drew Baggi away from his Contemplations. Curious, he opened his silver eyes and leaned off the wagon's left side towards the source of the command. Elder Sage Hrafn was speaking with a man in gentle tones, but the man seemed unimpressed with the Elder Sage's words. Baggi felt a puff of indigna-tion in his chest. *Doesn't he know who he's talking to?* He quickly caught himself, balanced his emotions, and meted out self-admonishment. *Looks like two hours of Contemplations tomorrow,* he thought glumly. *And just as I was getting used to the one.*

His pride dispelled, Baggi fell back to simple curiosity. The men seemed to be having trouble reaching an agreement, and although the caravan could undoubtedly force their way though, the Staffkeepers of

Shaefi were not given to forcing matters unnecessarily. Baggi pushed off the wagon and got to his feet, shaking his legs a bit to restore circulation. Staff in hand as always, he began walking in the direction of Elder Sage Hrafn.

The two were arguing, that much was clear. Or rather, the local man was arguing. Hrafn maintained the composure of a patient mother, one who genuinely enjoyed explaining the ways of the world to her child. He stood tall, posture strong even in his age, with one wrinkly, long-fingered hand wrapped around his staff. Among the many Staffkeeper Orders, Elder Sage Hrafn's composure was renowned. It was said that in a contest of patience, even time itself would concede to Hrafn. His biggest acolytes claimed, only half-jokingly, that Death had gotten tired of waiting for Hrafn's time to come and simply given up on the task altogether. The new apprentices usually got a few weeks of good laughs from this. Baggi had been one of them. Now, though, he mostly Contemplated the Elder Sage's longevity, and hoped as only a child can that his Blessing would manifest in more immediate ways.

As he approached, Baggi took stock of this local man. His hair was black and curly, and despite his short stature and lean physique, his shoulders were wide and strong. His features were hardened yet remained confidently aloof, like a panther readying itself to pounce, and his neatly square jaw was just as neatly shaved. His eyes burned fiery orange, the mark of a pure-blooded Kichishi, and despite the sweltering south-western clime, he was dressed in hard black leather and an iron cuirass. He lacked the furs Naefjans so often wore out of necessity, instead bearing a sort of wide, platform-like mantle. Crimson material, so fine as to be nearly transparent, flowed over his shoulders and cloaked the man, dancing delicately in the wind. The mantle itself was adorned with round symbols hewn from opal, signifiers of status: one bore the sigil of a roam-lizard, saddled and fierce, another a flower with six flame-shaped petals. Baggi had never seen garb like this before, but he had heard of it; the Staffkeepers had called it a *korta*.

"Ah, Baggi! Just in time," said Hrafn, a serene smile further wrinkling his round, weathered face. The sparse remains of his pure white hair fluttered limply in the wind. "Perhaps a more youthful approach is what we require."

Baggi's eyes widened. "Are...are you sure? Maybe one of the Staffkeepers would be better at this. I mean, I'm just an apprentice..." he mumbled, glancing around at anything but the two men before him.

Hrafn took three steps closer to the boy and laid a hand on his shoulder. "No," he said, silver-white eyes twinkling like snowflakes, "you're exactly who we need. Just remember your lessons."

Baggi gulped, took a deep breath, and nodded. Turning to the local man, he approached and bowed respectfully in the Shaefini tradition. *Eyes closed, both hands on the staff, bow to connect the staff and forehead,* he coached himself. The cool energy twisted through Compromise and into him, filling his head with supernatural calm. *Yes, that's it. Feel the flow of knowledge between the staff and mind.* Still bowing, he fixed an image in his mind of the rune he wished to invoke. When he could see it as clearly as if written in ink, he spoke its name and called upon its power.

"Ansuz," he said. The magic swam towards his vision and he knew he had been successful. *Now,* he thought, *open your eyes and...* he nearly lost the link right away.

The man was rolling his eyes! *Rather,* thought Baggi, *the boy is rolling his eyes.* For now that he had linked to the Ansuz rune on his staff, Baggi saw through the uniform, the adornments, and the attitude. He saw a boy not much older than himself, a boy who had seen hardship and bore the weight of many lives on his *korta;* a boy who saw a caravan of foreign Staffkeepers descending the mountains into his home; a boy who would rather die than concede this pass to strangers who might harm his brothers and sisters. *Now I see why the Elder Sage needed a child,* thought Baggi, *this one will likely never trust an adult again. Including himself.* The boy in uniform was glaring at Baggi expectantly.

"Well?" he demanded. He spoke in the Base Tongue, presumably for the travelers' benefit. "Are you planning to change my mind? To tell me what harmless folks you northerners are? Save your breath and both of our time. Turn around now. Your caravan is not getting through." His accent was substantial and carried the spark of competition.

"I am Staffkeeper Apprentice Baggi. Who are you?" replied Baggi in the Kichishi language.

The boy cocked an eyebrow and huffed. "What do you care?" He crossed his arms and glared once more, but with Ansuz Baggi couldn't miss the spark of curiosity. He waited for the boy to lose patience. Baggi knew he wouldn't be waiting long. He was right.

The boy rolled his eyes once more. "Amund is my name. I guard these lands by order of Jarl Gunni himself. And those orders include keeping out dangerous foreigners and questionable magical organizations, like Staffkeepers!" He hissed.

Baggi tilted his head innocently. "Questionable? Dangerous? You must have been misled. We are Staffkeepers of Shaefi, she whose domains are peace, life, and mirth." Seeing the boy eying him suspiciously, Baggi continued, "I understand your distrust. Many Staffkeepers represent the goddess of conquest; some even represent Death! But you can trust me. Those Orders have naught to do with us. In fact," he leaned in conspiratorially, "I could do without some of those other

Staffkeepers myself. But alas, there's only one Solabell, and we're all stuck living in it. The best we can do is try to coexist and lend each other a hand when necessary, right? It's tough when you have no one to rely on."

Baggi felt a small pang of guilt as he weaved the persuasion with Ansuz; the rune granted him insight, and with it the apprentice was able to glean the other boy's loneliness, his desire for a comrade he could trust, his desire for a friend. When Amund's gaze met his own, an unspeakable exhaustion cried out. This was too much. With an invasive snapping sensation, the link to his staff was broken, but the rune had done its work.

Amund sighed and waved on the rest of the caravan. "Fine. I am trusting you." He whirled on Baggi and prodded him on the chest. "Do you know what that means? It means that if you betray that trust, I will then be responsible for finding you and bringing you to justice. I hope you will not put me in that position." It was spoken as a threat, and if not for the insight Ansuz had granted him moments before, it may have worked. But Baggi knew that the boy called Amund was no threat; he reminded him of his elder brother.

Still reeling from the broken link, it was all Baggi could do to smile weakly, bow once more, and retreat to the wagon as it prepared to resume the descent. He sighed and plopped down in the hull, his entire body vibrating as the last dregs of magic withdrew. Crossing his legs and closing his eyes, the apprentice dutifully resumed his Contemplations.

***

The caravans had reached the foot of the mountain trail some time later, and the lightly forested valley floor offered just enough light through its canopy. Its warmth fell on Baggi as he splayed out on the wagon's roof, settling over him as slowly and effortlessly as a sheet of falling parchment. Chattering monkeys and buzzing insects surrounded the travelers, the boldest among them daring even to approach until forced away by this or that Staffkeeper wielding insincere threats and feigned staff-strikes. The noise was louder than Baggi had anticipated, and it seemed every creature in the woods was out this afternoon, each chasing each other in and around the treetops and bushes, biting and flapping and screeching, vying for a spot in the sun to rest only until they were able to find an apparently choicer patch, at which point the whole frenzy would be renewed. Sunlight so intense and so soon after arriving in a new land was an unexpected treat, yet the local fauna's covetousness indicated that this was more than just a fair-weather day; it was a sign of approval from Shaefi. *A good omen,* the apprentice thought. Apparently, however, the travelers themselves were susceptible to the same irrational avarice as the animals.

"Move, Baggi! Leave some sun for me!"

From his left side, Baggi felt his limbs being playfully shoved aside as a girl with short, even-cut blonde hair claimed the space.

"That is, unless you're more important than the rest of us now." The girl looked at him askance. There was a teasing tone in her voice, but Baggi recognized a flash of real worry.

"More important? I can't imagine where you got that idea, Kettil."

"Me? You brought it back with you after your little tutoring session with the Elder Sage."

"I was just the one who happened to be there," he snorted.

Kettil crossed her arms and shot him a suspicious glance. This was no cause for alarm, of course. Regardless of the girl's intelligence, she was still a child, and children questioned many things that adults wouldn't give a second thought.

Baggi had met Kettil three months into his apprenticeship, when she had arrived with the latest batch of potential apprentices at the Temple at Enton. A wide-eyed little girl of no older than ten, she made it her mission from the moment she stepped inside the entrance hall to see everything there was to see, a habit which had landed her in heaps of trouble on more than one occasion. She had a large forehead that she might someday grow into, and on occasion a loose tooth might show itself between her oft-pursed lips. Her eyes were large and dark with precociousness. In posture, she was two heads shorter than her fellow apprentices; in alchemy, she stood head and shoulders above them all. Normally, apprentices at her stage in the program would still be confined to Temple for another six weeks, but with her skill, it hadn't taken much convincing for Hrafn to make an exception.

"Sometimes I wonder about you, Baggi. Playin' the bumbling apprentice one moment, then rubbing elbows with Sages the next. Is this some kinda play for early advancement?"

"Of course not! I'm not 'playing' anything! Runic magic is difficult, and I get lucky often."

"More lucky and more often than anyone else," Kettil grumbled.

"And what about you?" Baggi shot back. "With all your talk of my ambitions, you seem to have forgotten that you shouldn't be here in the first place."

Kettil smirked. "That's different. Luck has nothing to do with it. I'm just the best Alchemist Apprentice."

"Maybe so," he admitted, "but that's an exception, and you like being an exception. Believe me, I'm only trying to follow the rules, no ulterior motives involved. I hate when things don't go as planned."

"Alright, alright already," said Kettil, rolling her eyes. "Staffkeepers and their rules. I swear, you get less fun by the day."

"Ah, yes, I often forget that alchemists have no rules. 'Just throw it in the pot and hope for the best,' isn't that your motto?" he jested.

He was surprised when she pursed her lips and turned away, surveying the woods around them. The playfulness was gone, replaced with a melancholy edge Baggi had come to expect when she was in a philosophical mood. *Looks like something serious is on her mind,* he thought. He decided to wait it out; she would open up when she was ready.

"Baggi?"

"Hm?"

"Do you think they'll hurt us here?"

There was a long pause before he responded. "I don't know what pain these people have been through. I don't know what their Staffkeepers are like. I don't know what they think we are, and I don't know if they care to learn." He paused for effect, watching Kettil carefully as she absorbed his words. She was a deceptively good listener. "What I do know is that these lands and these people are no strangers to war. I know that they can be reasoned with. I know that they have families, and loved ones, and feel fear and love just as we do. And, most importantly, I know that we are here to help them. Even if they hurt us."

Kettil watched the space between the trees, the shade bending and stretching here and there with the branches. She chewed on his words, slowly examining the composition, dissecting the philosophy. Baggi was struck, not for the first time, with the gravity of her expression. Not many children could wear the face of a scholar, yet she did so without even realizing it. *She would probably make a great Staffkeeper too. Contemplations come naturally to her.* Baggi felt a pang of jealousy, and quickly balanced it with admiration. *Such talent.*

"Yeah. I guess that is why we're here." Kettil turned back to him and smiled slightly. "You really are gonna make a great Staffkeeper."

Baggi smiled back and tussled her sandy locks. "Thanks. Perhaps someday. Now get going! I know for a fact you haven't finished your daily formulae."

"What? How?" she demanded.

"Because you always put off formulae until the last minute, right before bed."

Kettil grinned mischievously. "Well how else am I gonna have time for the important stuff, like sitting in the sun and talking to you?"

Now Baggi was the one rolling his eyes. "Flattery? Really, Kettil, I thought better of you. Now go on! We'll talk later, after we make camp."

"Oh, fine." Kettil stuck out her tongue at him. "I'll see you later." She clambered down the side of the wagon and skipped back to her own, dolor dispelled and every bit a little girl once more.

When she was out of sight, Baggi finally allowed the worry to show. In truth, Kettil's fears were not unique. Baggi hadn't been with the caravan long, but this was a lesson quickly learned. As he crossed his legs and began Contemplations, the memories floated to the surface of his mind. It had been a mere two weeks into his journey, at a border city between Naefja and the Melenno Valley, where Baggi had first seen a man die.

***

It was a wet, muddy, and altogether miserable day. Snow had long ago turned to sleet, pelting and soaking the Shaefini as they navigated the mountainous trail. *Worst day yet,* Baggi thought, already an expert in feeling sorry for himself. *At least at Enton, we had hot meals and dry beds. Alas, such is the life of a Staffkeeper!* He knew the sentiments, had heard the grumbling. It seemed that complaining was an unofficial sacred rite in the caravans, and Baggi had taken to it with a zeal. It was part of the fun, after all. Constant complaints meant that the journey was going well, that the most dire challenges they faced were those of inconvenience.

Their travels through the Eastern Great Pass hadn't been wholly uneventful, but neither had the excursion proved hostile. Most folk in the region were goatherders and shepherds, able to carve out a comfortable if quiet living in the mountains surrounding Geluwam. There was no more opportune place to harvest wool than so near the Soft City, and the relative affluence of their region was felt in the local hospitality. The Staffkeepers had been spoiled on mutton and cheese at every stop, despite the Elder Sage's polite protestations, and local crofters asked only for the usual services in exchange: perhaps it was a doe who wasn't producing ample milk, or the limp that had rendered their herding dog near-useless. Regardless, the requests were humble and the Shaefini were happy to serve.

Geluwam, Baggi reflected as they approached, *fashion capital of the world.* Geluwam was immense, a multi-leveled city carved into the side of the mountain. The city loomed over them, huger and more foreign than anything the boy had ever seen. Its architecture was assertive, pointed roofs and tall, narrow structures from ground and ceiling both belying the image of sharp teeth, yet the countless foot-paths and bridges between them tempered the city's aggression with a healthy measure of grace. He knew they were in no danger besides; the guild-tribes of Melenno Valley relied on traders and caravans such as theirs to purchase their crafts, being largely sedentary people themselves. Still, this proved little issue for the crafters of the eastern realm. Wealthy and influential folk across the world boasted Geluwam fashions; like all goods produced by the Melennese guild-tribes, the quality was unparalleled – as was the price. Baggi had dreamed of wrapping a Geluwam cloak around his shoulders for years, until he had become a Staffkeeper Apprentice and received his uniform. Now he settled for the innocent lie he told himself, that his own Shaefini cloak was far more valuable.

The wagons splattered mud furiously as the caravan proceeded into Geluwam until finally the overhanging rock provided them respite. The locals wore refined garb that made clear their station: those with wealth were dressed in clean white wool indicating they were safe from the mud and grime of the lower levels, keeping mostly to the walking paths far overhead, while those with smaller fortunes hid the filth of their surroundings in darker tones and layered garments. These protected the poorer folks' inner finery as they made their way about the lower levels where merchants and travelers would arrive and conduct most of their business. Baggi, a villager himself, felt the sudden desire to make himself seen as well, to seize some of the airs that even the humblest of city folk wore in easy excess. He puffed himself up, hood drawn over his face in what he assumed to be a mysterious manner. Overtaken by excitement, Baggi forgot all sense of humility. *I can't wait to see how the guild-tribes receive us!* He thought, *Perhaps with a parade? No, no, the streets don't allow for it. Must be a feast then. Such a hospitable people!* The wagons groaned and the boars grunted loudly, the sounds echoing through the cavernous streets as they carried trails of thick mud over the polished multi-colored cobblestones. An inn towered before them, an imposing three-story block with a pointed cap and a sign hanging from the front entrance that read 'Black Wool Boarding House' in calligraphic Melennese script. *The stables alone are bigger than every house in Jolk put together,* Baggi thought, the memory of his village bringing an unexpected pang of homesickness. He shook it off and focused instead on his excitement. There was well enough room for the caravan.

When they arrived at the stables, Baggi and the other apprentices immediately began tending to the mighty boars that pulled their wagons, unhitching them and checking them into stalls while the Staffkeepers went inside and made payments for their lodgings. Even this task was not yet menial to Baggi. He was in the perfect sweet spot between learning a new job and growing bored of it, where the work was still fresh enough to make him feel knowledgeable and important, yet not so new as to be intimidating. The others finished and hurried inside towards the promise of a warm hearth, but Baggi lingered to scrub the wheels. It was difficult to find time to be alone in a caravan, and he relished the opportunity.

He was finishing up and wiping the mud off his hands when something caught his eye: in a stall at the other end of the stable, a dull white horse was watching him. Baggi approached and, unthinking, reached out a hand to stroke the horse's nose, only to yelp and retreat as the creature took a bite at his fingers. He saw now that its teeth were unnaturally sharp. *Has your rider filed your teeth? It's no wonder you're so surly,* he thought. Baggi chuckled nervously as he realized how close the beast had come to his fingers. *I might have lost a hand,* he thought. Baggi glanced at the saddle hanging in the stall and his heart stopped. *No. Please, no.*

There were skulls dangling from the sides, precisely arranged and curated by type. All of them featured the same ominous sigil carved between the eyes. Baggi saw a bear skull, a wolf skull, a cat skull, and many others from animals he didn't recognize. Some were angular, with narrow cheeks; some were squat and wide, and must have once housed an enormous amount of flesh; others were in exotic, asymmetrical shapes Baggi couldn't even imagine framing a real creature. Yet these only drew his attention for a moment, for most of the skulls were much more easily recognized. Most of the skulls were human.

Baggi was shaking. He couldn't focus. *Please, not one of them,* he silently pleaded. Images flashed through his mind faster than he could keep up with: the bones, worn like jewelry; the pitch black robes, flapping in the wind; a woman wearing horns and carelessly tossing him an oblong white orb from her saddle. It had looked like a giant egg for just a moment.

His brother's smiling face. His brother's skull. The sigil carved between his eyes.

He stepped backwards, halting, his legs stiff with fear. All he could think to do was squeeze his eyes shut, clasp one hand over the other, and pray desperately. *Shaefi, I implore you. I beg you. Let it be a bandit. Let it be a beast-slayer. Let it be a bounty hunter or even an eccentric collector. Please,* he prayed, *don't let it be a Staffkeeper.*

Baggi finished his prayer and forced his eyes open once more. The stables were full of an eerie quiet, a quiet living in the pit of Baggi's stomach and making him feel as if he were about to fall from somewhere high up. *I must go tell the Elder Sage. We cannot stay here,* Baggi resolved, and yet his feet would not move. *I must warn them. I must save them. I'm the only one who knows what danger we're in.* And yet, his feet would not move.

A clamorous procession saved him from his own fear. The apprentices were rushing back into the stables, screaming, crying, shouting as they re-hitched the boars in record time. The Staffkeepers of Shaefi followed, yelling orders and getting mud on their sky-blue and white raiment as they took to the work usually reserved for the youths. The last of the travelers to emerge were the Sages of Shaefi. They were calm and focused, each command clear and each movement smooth, yet their every gesture carried the strength of a wave accelerating towards shore. Baggi flushed, shame coursing through him. *I'm too late. It's already happened.* He blinked back tears and threw himself into the fray, working through blurry vision.

After mere minutes, the caravan was ready to depart. Baggi looked around as he clambered into his wagon. *Five apprentices and myself,* he counted, *nine Staffkeepers, two Sages and one...wait, where is the Third Sage? And where is Elder Sage Hrafn?* Come to think of it, Baggi realized that he hadn't seen the Third Sage or the Elder Sage emerge from the inn at all. The First and Second Sages were standing closely together, locked in fierce debate. Baggi knew that a disagreement between Sages could take hours to resolve. If the missing company was still inside, with that other Staffkeeper, then they didn't have hours. Baggi let himself weep openly as he made one last prayer. *Queen of Peace, don't let me die.* Then he grabbed Compromise, jumped off the wagon, and sprinted through the mud towards the inn.

In the confusion Baggi made it to the doors before the others could stop him. He heard a Staffkeeper shouting his name, but there was no time to listen, and besides, he could hardly hear their voices over the pounding of his heart. Then, suddenly, there was calm. It seemed the entire caravan had frozen, and Baggi felt a faint reassuring presence, like a gentle hand on his shoulder. *Either Shaefi heard my prayer,* Baggi thought, *or this is the eye of the storm.* He took a deep breath, stifled his sobs, and pushed open the door.

The Black Wool Boarding House was, on first impression, calmer than the stables. A long staircase spiraled upwards to his right, hugging the wall all the way to the spiraled ceiling. Every few feet, the stairs turned to platforms, evening out to offer level entrances at each room. Ignoring this eye-catching feature, however, allowed one to perceive the actual danger Baggi had willingly walked into. The common area was populated by some locals and travelers, all of whom remained tightly pressed against the walls as if hoping to pass through the stone and thereby escape the room's perilous stillness. For in the middle of the common room stood three men: the Third Sage, Ove, stood clashing with a Staffkeeper dressed in pure black attire sewn with bones while the Elder Sage watched sadly. Their bodies were still, yet Baggi could feel their auras pushing against each other. The outsider was standing with one hand atop the crown of his staff, and from the door Baggi could see blood flowing from his palm. It ran down the dark wood, filling and coloring the runes, drawing out their power. If not for Ove's own magic, the aura alone would have made Baggi vomit. The man had a crazed look in his eyes, a hunger from which Baggi involuntarily shrank back. Just as he had feared, a Staffkeeper of Death was here.

He bumped into the door behind him, shaking himself out of the stupor. Though the strain was clearly great, Ove yet held his own. The Sage of Shaefi was on the defensive, completely occupied in repelling his opponent's advances. Baggi watched with great concern as the two Staffkeepers fought, opposing clouds of magical essence snapping and diving at each other like dancing flames. The men's bodies may have been still, but the energy crackling between them belied the truth; they were clashing with their lives at stake. To Baggi's great concern, Ove did not hold the advantage.

Usually, a Staffkeeper of Shaefi's strength was based in love, joy, and serenity. If a Shaefini lost control and allowed themselves to be tainted by hostility, the link to their staff would considerably weaken and eventually snap, leaving them defenseless. In a clash, this could mean death or worse. Compounding this danger were the efforts of the opposing Staffkeeper, who would likewise try their utmost to overwhelm the opponent with their own aura and personality. When the opponent's aura was so steeped in violence and death, even a sliver of that aura breaking through could prove damning. Thus, clashing with other Staffkeepers, and especially Staffkeepers of Death, was something the Shaefini avoided. It was not only immoral; it was extremely dangerous.

Ove was a Sage, but even a man of his station was not infallible. The hands which lovingly caressed his staff were beginning to tense. It was only a matter of time before the Staffkeeper of Death prevailed. After Ove fell, the Elder Sage would be next. Baggi had to do something, and quick. *But what can I do?* He wondered in a panic. *I can't even link to my own staff. No, I can't get involved like that. My only hope is to distract Ove's opponent. Maybe that will give him the opening he needs.* Baggi prepared to run towards the clash, prepared to scream or stomp or wave his arms, but then Hrafn turned and met his gaze.

The Elder Sage wore an expression Baggi had never seen before. *Like a peaceful pond envious of the stormy sea*, the apprentice thought. Hrafn approached, and while the two Staffkeepers clashed, unmoving, blood and sweat pouring freely, stood shoulder to shoulder with the apprentice. They watched in silence for what may have been seconds or may have been minutes. Too soon, Ove began to waver, and the clash was decided.

The Staffkeeper of Death's crimson aura descended on the opening in Ove's own light blue. It fell on him, rending him apart, devouring him greedily and rapturously. The smoky red suffused the Sage's skin, purging the light of Shaefi and rotting his body in an instant. He wailed in pain, but only for a moment. Before the torture could be prolonged, Ove was rent in two, blood and viscera spraying over the bar and tables, painting the garments of the onlookers an uneven red. Both sides of his body sloughed to the ground in a wet heap. Somebody screamed. Baggi hardly realized what had happened, and then it was over. The Staffkeeper of Death turned towards him, features relaxed in ecstasy.

The Elder Sage had seen enough. He raised his legendary oaken staff, Mischief, and before the other Staffkeeper could even open his mouth, Hrafn spoke a sentence heavy with the weight of many runes. It met the man in the middle of the room, and with a slight bow, the Staffkeeper of Death withdrew. He walked out the front door, never looking back.

The Elder Sage heaved a woeful sigh. Baggi felt a wetness on his lips and wiped it away. His hand came back red and pink. Numb, he stared at his own palm. *Ove's brain?* he pondered. *It's a good brain. How did it get there?* The apprentice was still. Both stood, silent and somber, for a long time. Then Hrafn invoked another rune and touched his index finger to the boy's head, and the dam broke.

Baggi wept fiercely, clinging to Hrafn, screaming for terror and loss, but most of all screaming for rage. Hrafn would need to address this with the boy later, but not now. Now was the time to weep. He embraced Baggi, wordlessly, and allowed him this small comfort.

***

As his Contemplations ended, Baggi opened his eyes. It was early evening, and the walls of a Kichishi village were within sight. Kettil's words returned to him unbidden.

Do you think they'll hurt us here?

Baggi unconsciously wiped at his lips, finding nothing there. It had become habit since that day. *I wonder what kind of Staffkeepers they have here,* he thought. Then he dismounted the wagon and prepared to unhitch the boars.

2

T he settlement was unlike anything Baggi had ever seen. After a fresh-faced guard opened the gates and allowed the Shaefini to enter, he found that the buildings were irregularly shaped, with hastily added rooms and ramshackle sheds accompanying most. The roads weren't paved or cobbled; rather, they were like his own hometown's during the summer, rustic and packed down through frequent use alone. Nearly everywhere he looked was painted in bright yellows and reds, with a few splashes of purple here or there, and above many doors hung signs depicting juvenile perceptions of business. One showed an ecstatic baker using a peel to pull bread from a domed clay oven; there was another featuring sprites of some sort, laughing and affixing shoe buckles; still a third depicted a stocky man with an apron and one grotesquely muscular arm, holding a smith's hammer and winking at the viewer. For all that he saw of the town's curiosities, not a single villager made themselves known as the caravan made its way to the center of town.

The inn wasn't hard to spot, as it, too, bore a cartoonish sign. The man on it was apparently in awe, starry-eyed and slack jawed as he admired a pint of mead and a well-made feather bed. Although it was not huge, the inn did house stables, and luckily for the Shaefini, the space was currently unoccupied. The building was single storied save for a poorly constructed crow's nest on the roof that added another two or three. Baggi marveled at the oddity. There appeared to be a guard keeping watch from the vantage point, but only their triangular cap was visible from below. Baggi heard faint snoring coming from above, and he smiled despite himself. Since they had lost Third Sage Ove, the caravan usually exercised great caution when arriving in a new settlement. Still, the town was infused with such color and character that Baggi couldn't imagine the people being anything but pleasant. In his admittedly limited experience, evil folk didn't often make silly paintings.

The apprentices got to unhitching the wagons, no rush among them today. The sun was setting beautifully, and no one seemed in a hurry to get inside. Kettil set to work beside him, doing her best to help despite her stature.

"Strange place, isn't it?" Baggi asked conversationally.

"I like it. After a week of nothing but white snow and grey rock, it's nice to see some color."

"Mm. A bit ramshackle though, don't you think? And that lookout post on the roof?"

Kettil squinted up at the crow's nest. "Maybe they just like to keep a sharp eye around here. That's what that man in the pass was doing, right?"

"Yes," Baggi frowned, "but keep a sharp eye for what?"

"Probably for scary ol' foreigners like us!" Kettil giggled.

Baggi chuckled as well. Perhaps she was right, and it was simply a case of misplaced caution. After all, Amund had mentioned "questionable magic" or some such. As anyone who had ever met a Staffkeeper of Shaefi could attest, they were harmless to a fault. *Still,* Baggi admitted, *they don't know that. And something must have happened to make Amund so distrustful.* He began his final task, dispensing apples to the boars as thanks for a long day's labor. Kettil sat on a stool much too tall for her, swinging her feet while she waited.

"I just can't shake the feeling that something is off here," he pondered aloud. "It's not an ill omen, exactly, just...it's different. What do you think they're like?"

Kettil shrugged. "As long as they're human, it doesn't matter to me. My potions will fix them just the same."

"That much we know, at least," he agreed, wiping his hands on his pants. "Now, let's get inside and have some supper, shall we?"

The duo circled the building back to the front entrance and pushed through the door. Inside, the decorations were just as frantic as the rest of the village. Each chair seemed painted a different shade of red, and the dozen or so "tables" were in actuality tree stumps that had been clumsily nailed to the floorboards. An open archway on the far wall served as the intersection of a hallway where the rooms could be found as well as the kitchen and, on the other side, a backdoor to the inn itself. The Staffkeepers were gathered around the bar where Elder Sage Hrafn was speaking to the innkeeper. Although he could not see the local through the crowd, Baggi felt relief. *It's not a ghost town after all,* he thought. A chalkboard hung above the bar, with scrawled lettering that read: "WELCOME TO THE FLAMEBUD INN! PEPPER CIDER, ONE YELLOW-ODD. MEAL, TWO YELLOW-ODD."

The sign was written in the Kichishi variant of the Base Tongue, colloquially known as Sparktongue. It was an energetic and hard-angled script, the very antithesis of the Naefjan's own soft and gentle Flowspeak. Every apprentice learned the regional variants of Base Tongue as part of their training at the Temple at Enton, but most of his peers held a mild distaste for Sparktongue, viewing it as too aggressive or even crude. Baggi, though, had a soft spot for it. Sparktongue represented a passion in its speakers, an ambition and drive that he couldn't help admiring. He had spent most of his free days at Enton with the Temple's language tutor, refining his Kichishi accent, learning the minor modifications to syntax and rhythm and the subtlety of its rigid, multitudinous tones, then spent countless nights studying and practicing at it until he found himself at times thinking in the language. As a result, he was perhaps the most comfortable Sparktongue speaker in their caravan, and certainly the most practiced. *Probably why Hrafn made me do the talking with Amund earlier*, he realized. His admiration for the Elder Sage deepened. *He's always two steps ahead of the rest of us.*

"Come on, Baggi, I wanna see who they're talking to." Kettil pulled him by the hand and circled around the congregation before he could protest in favor of supper.

The other apprentices were already running about, claiming tables and complaining proudly at an offensive volume. Kettil usually had a good sense of being in the right place at the right time, so if she was forgoing the fun and games then Baggi knew it was best to trust her. They approached the far end of the bar, opposite the crowd, and Kettil clambered onto a stool. Baggi followed suit, claiming his own stool and admiring the counter before them. It was L-shaped and made of milky amber-colored timber with a glassy finish he could nearly see his own reflection in. *Petrified wood?* He marveled, *This would cost a fortune back home.* He thought uneasily of what meager finances the caravan possessed. *Now I understand what's taking so long.*

"Huh? But she's just a kid," Kettil said, confused.

Baggi tore himself away from admiring the petrified wood and looked to the far end of the room. His brow furrowed as his eyes confirmed the girl's words. There was, indeed, a child, around Baggi's own age, behind the bar. Her hair was wild, the color and temperament of an erupting volcano, and its tight curls bounced around her face as she spoke with great animation. Her cheeks were strong and her chin a bit square; the nose, too, was even and somewhat wide. The girl's eyes, same color as her hair, curved nobly even as the brows above pressed down with annoyance and narrowed them. Like most Kichishi, her skin was pure black. She leaned forward aggressively on toned arms, a bartering technique that seemed to be providing the Elder Sage great amusement. This, in turn, caused the innkeeper even more irritation. She puffed herself up and began speaking quicker in heavily accented Sparktongue.

Baggi nudged Kettil in the side, motioning subtly for her to move within earshot. She nodded, and they began hopping stool by stool toward the exchange, pausing a few moments at each new seat so as not to attract attention and disrupt the conversation. Theirs was a tried-and-true method, if unnecessarily surreptitious, which they had used to great effect several times before. Or so the duo thought.

"What are you doing?" demanded a familiar voice from behind them as they were perched awkwardly between two stools. Baggi and Kettil froze, looked at each other, and with as much tact as could be afforded in the situation, turned around to face the speaker. It was the boy from the pass, Amund. He stood, arms crossed, with an eyebrow cocked, and began tapping his foot. "Well? Only just arrived and already displaying suspicious behavior?"

"Amund! So good to see you again," Baggi replied. "But how are you here? As you yourself say, we only just arrived."

Amund rolled his eyes, a habit which was beginning to annoy. "Your caravan wasted time on the main road, Staffkeeper Apprentice Baggi." There was a hint of mockery in the young soldier's voice when he spoke Baggi's title. "There is an easy shortcut from the foot of the mountain to Flamebud. A straight line, rather than the horseshoe trail you took."

The apprentice forced a smile and tried not to lose his temper. "If so, why did you not think to share this information with us, my friend? It would have saved the boars a lot of work."

"Because you are Staffkeepers. I wanted to arrive before you so everyone could be warned."

So that's why we didn't see anyone on the way in, Baggi thought, *they were hiding from us.* "My friend, I thought we had resolved this before," he said. "You can trust us."

"No," Amund retorted, "I agreed to trust you as far as Flamebud. Here your actions will speak for themselves, and you will either be allowed to continue towards the capitol or, more likely, will be deported. It all depends on you, *my friend.*"

Baggi was too tired from using Ansuz earlier to link to Compromise again, and a long day of travel had exhausted his remaining patience. He would much rather not have this conversation again, but Kettil was displaying unexpected bashfulness. He knew the intimidation act was required of Amund's position, but that didn't mean he had to like it.

"Oh, thank Shaefi! Without you watching our every move, I was worried we would give up that whole "systemic pacifism" routine and get on with the depravity!" Baggi snapped. He regretted it immediately, seeing Amund's face harden and a hand move toward his sword belt. Before either boy could open their mouths again, Baggi felt a finger shoved roughly against his lips, silencing him. Baffled, he looked over at Kettil. She glared at him intensely for a moment, before turning to Amund with a sweetness he had never seen from her.

"I'm so sorry for my friend here. He means well, but you know Staffkeepers," she said. "They always think they know better." She smiled ruefully at Amund. Baggi began to protest and was immediately shushed once more. "My name's Kettil. You can actually trust me. I'm an alchemist, see? No staff here except Compromise," she reassured him, gesturing to the tool in Baggi's hand.

Amund seemed taken aback momentarily, before nodding. "I do understand Staffkeepers can be this way. Just keep an eye on him." He began to step away before pausing and looking back over the *korta* on his shoulders. "'Compromise'? A little naïve, is it not?"

Baggi pursed his lips and regained his calm before responding. "No. No, I don't think so at all."

Amund regarded him with a mixture of wariness and intrigue. Then he chuckled quietly and departed. Kettil stared after him, transfixed, as if he had been a specter drifting through the inn. Baggi briefly considered taking offense but, ultimately, couldn't find it in himself. Instead, he chuckled as well.

"So, you're keeping an eye on me now, huh? That's different," he teased.

Kettil giggled and elbowed him playfully. "Sometimes, you talk too much for your own good. And usually it works out, since you're so good at talking. But for the times it doesn't, I'll be ready to shut you up," she replied. "Besides, did you see that guy's weapons? A sword *and* a spear! He must be some kind of hero or something!"

Baggi snorted. "Yes, or something."

***

Elder Sage Hrafn had made many deals in his exceptionally long life. He had brokered countless agreements, ended hundreds of feuds, and buried more hatchets than any Staffkeeper before him. He was known far and wide as The Benevolent Sage and had published several texts on the subjects of empathy and diplomacy. These texts had become required reading in the apprentice curriculum at Enton, had already influenced generations of Staffkeepers. His name was spoken with awe, that of his staff, Mischief, with wonder. If one wanted to arrange a truce, one went to Hrafn.

As Staffkeepers of Shaefi, the caravan's finances were limited. This was nothing new, nor was it cause for alarm. The Shaefini had relied on donations from citizens who attended rituals or received treatment from their alchemists for hundreds of years, living humble but comfortable lives. They charged nothing, of course, but folk could be trusted to express their gratitude in whatever meager means were available to them. Sometimes, this donation came in the form of cold, hard odd. More often, it meant two dozen eggs or a pound of pork. Yet, in recent years, Naefjans were not as affluent as they once were. The Alchemist Guild famously underpaid their laborers whilst their exports via the port of Yngmuth brought in massive profits, creating a wealth disparity that only grew day by day. Compounding this misfortune were increasingly emboldened Staffkeepers of Death, who had in recent years been much braver in their attacks. As a result, folk clung to whatever paltry wealth they possessed. Naefjans could no longer afford healing brews, the Alchemist Guild rate being so exorbitantly expensive, and few could afford the time and expense to make pilgrimage to the Temple at Enton. For a time, it seemed potions were reserved for the rich and noble born.

So Elder Sage Hrafn had decreed a change in his Order's structure. No longer would the Staffkeepers of Shaefi stay in Enton, treating whoever may visit. Instead, the Staffkeepers would visit the folk across the realms, providing their services to those folk who were unable to make the pilgrimage themselves. A portion of the Order would always stay at Enton, to maintain the temple and provide service to those who lived in the region. The remaining Staffkeepers, alchemists, and approved apprentices would join caravans and spread the services of Shaefi far and wide, healing and enchanting whoever was in need. The Elder Sage himself would lead a caravan, accompanied by three of the Nine Sages of Shaefi. The other two caravans would be led by two Sages each, along with any number of Staffkeepers they deemed appropriate. Two Sages occupied Enton, and every year the caravans would return and the groups would cycle. Each and every apprentice's first assignment was Hrafn's caravan. This was a deliberate arrangement, of course, so that the Elder Sage could take the time to observe and guide them individually. When he declared an apprentice ready, he would convene with the Sages, request their approval - which had never been denied to date - and arrange for the ritual which would make them a full-fledged Staffkeeper of Shaefi.

Four hundred years had passed since then with little progress made toward breaking the Alchemist Guild monopoly, and in all that time and despite all his expertise, Hrafn had rarely struggled so to broker an agreement as he did now with the innkeeper of the Flamebud Inn. Several minutes of back and forth, the girl snapping and huffing all the while, left the two no nearer to agreement than when they had begun. If Hrafn had been a younger man, he may have reached impatience by now. But of course, Hrafn didn't lose patience. The closest he got these days was mild confusion.

"Come now, dear girl, surely there is someone in need of healing? Someone who can't seem to get rid of that cough, or perhaps one who was born crippled? We freely offer treatment to any such people, as a gift on behalf of Shaefi. I can't guarantee successful treatment, of course, but we will most certainly do what we can. And all we ask in exchange is a warm hearth and a hot meal," Hrafn gently cajoled. "Although," he laughed good-naturedly, "a lukewarm meal would do the trick just as well!"

The innkeeper was not impressed, but neither was she offended. "Look, old man, I get it. You want a place to stay, and we have rooms. Trouble is, without the odd, you're asking me to trust your word. And nobody around here trusts an outsider's word, not without Amund saying so."

"Excuse me, miss," came Baggi's voice from behind Hrafn, "did I mishear? We require Amund's approval?" The boy gently pushed his way through the assembled Staffkeepers. "If so, you have nothing to worry about. He has given it freely, mere moments ago. Did you not see him standing there just now, warmly welcoming my friend and me to your village?" Hrafn observed the boy tilting his head slightly, a common disarming technique that Baggi was especially good at. He smiled proudly, turning away to avoid offending the innkeep.

"Uhh...who are you? And how do you know Amund?" she asked, looking lost in her own inn.

"Oh! Of course, please forgive me. I am Staffkeeper Apprentice Baggi. Who are you?" he replied, bowing formally as he had with Amund. Then he turned to the assembled Staffkeepers and gently motioned for them to leave. Hrafn tactfully led them to a stump table on the other side of the room.

"Torny," she replied curtly, before looking proud and blurting out, "that is, I am Flamebud Innkeeper Torny."

"What a lovely name, Torny," Baggi smiled. "I'm shocked that Amund didn't mention you, given that your inn is so breathtaking. Of course, the inn pales in comparison to its proprietor."

"What's a proprietor?"

"One who owns or operates a place like this."

Torny's scarlet eyes went wide and her face turned bright to match. She scoffed inarticulately and looked away for a moment before responding.

"Okay, look, you guys can stay here for now, but you better be ready to pay up! Go see Amund and he'll tell you where the sick kids live. Then send him here after, so I can have a good yell at him!" She crossed her arms and shooed him away. Baggi, not wishing to push the issue, bowed respectfully and retreated to give the other Staffkeepers the good news.

I can't believe that worked, he marveled. *If only I could be so confident with my own people.* Baggi began wonder to why it was always easier to talk to strangers than those he knew, but the thought was cut short when he felt a clap on his shoulder and nearly yelped aloud. He turned and offered a prayer of thanks for his restraint when he saw the culprit.

A young Staffkeeper with long black hair and a heart shaped face stood grinning widely at him. She slouched casually, and her long eyelashes implied an expression of constant, pleasant surprise. As was the fashion among the more youthful Staffkeepers and apprentices, she wore as uniform only the Shaefini cloak, a sky-blue to white gradient coloring it from hem to hood. Underneath, she wore traveler's pants and a white tunic. The silver brooch clasping her cloak was fashioned in the shape of a boar, proof of her status as a Staffkeeper of Shaefi. Baggi felt the usual nervousness that speaking with his superiors brought and struggled to rebalance his emotions. *Calm, Baggi,* he urged himself, *today favors you! Don't say anything foolish and it will stay that way.*

"Well done, Baggi. Turns out you're quite charming, huh?" she said, wiggling her eyebrows suggestively. Baggi blushed and cleared his throat.

"Hello Hjordis, I didn't see you there."

"Naturally; I was behind you."

"...Right. So, uh, you saw that? Yeah, well, I would've used Ansuz, of course. But they say repetition breeds remorse, and since I already used it earlier today to get us past the guard in the mountains," he boasted, trying to look as casual as possible while watching Hjordis' reaction intently, "I thought I would challenge myself."

Hjordis smiled at him. Baggi liked the way she showed her teeth and narrowed her eyes. It reminded him of a wolf, and was equally intimidating, albeit for different reasons. Staffkeeper Hjordis was Baggi's assigned mentor, charged with guiding his development as a Staffkeeper and guarding him from the dangers of the road. She took a stern stance on neither, by his assessment, but this did not bother him. Rather, he liked that she trusted him to provide for his own well-being, only invoking seniority when teaching him how to conduct this or that ritual or otherwise advising him during their day-to-day assignments. It made him loathe to disappoint her, anxious to live up to her expectations.

"Wow," she said now, "you were going to link twice in one day? How is it that Hrafn hasn't made you a Staffkeeper yet?"

"I'm sure the Elder Sage has his reasons. If he says I'm not ready yet, then I believe him," Baggi replied, not quite modestly.

"Well, if the Elder Sage is saying you're not ready yet," she replied, coy, "then he's not saying it to me. Keep up the good work."

Without further ado, she strode off to rejoin her peers, twirling her beech staff dexterously and whistling as she went. Baggi watched her go, and when she was out of sight, finally allowed himself to relax. *I can't believe it. Hjordis was impressed! She even thinks I should be a Staffkeeper already!* Baggi beamed as he waltzed back to rejoin Kettil at their stump. Even her unimpressed expression couldn't sour his mood. *Today really does favor me!*

***

Amund was tired. After nearly two years as Chief of Flamebud, he was beginning to worry for the future of his village. All chiefs in Kichishi had worries, naturally, but Amund envied them. Their problems were simpler, the stakes were lower. *Who cares if Jarl Gunni is raising taxes on imports? Who cares if the wildcats are aggressive this year? Those are nothing compared to what we face at the border.* Amund didn't trust or even like outsiders, true. But in all fairness, he didn't like or trust most of his countrymen either.

The early evening sky was infused with a rich crimson hue, and Amund took a rare moment of respite to sit on the edge of the town well and watch. *Red,* he thought, resentful, *always red. No matter where you look, red.* He thought of the other villagers, all of them children. He thought about the day that had made them all orphans. He remembered smearing red paint on the buildings, tables, wherever the blood needed to be covered up. It had been a shortsighted solution. A childish solution.

Across the square, an apprentice with a shaved head evoked a rune to create the image of a dancing pixie in his palm. His friends laughed and applauded this frivolity. Amund rolled his eyes, though in truth he envied their innocence. *At the very least, these ones do not seem cut from the same cloth as those monsters,* he thought.

Amund heard the door to the inn swing open with a soft jingle. Turning, he saw a group of four emerge. Two he recognized, of course, as the apprentices Baggi and Kettil. *His little sister or helper or what have you. Are they not apprentices? Why are those two involved in every-thing?* The other two were older, though not by much, and carried a bit more authority. The first, a girl, had long black hair and silver-white eyes, signs of a mixed Kichishi-Naefjan bloodline, and looked to be similar in age to Amund. She twirled her staff in circles, the movement quick and energetic. *She is fast,* he noted, *but has no control. An unsure grip and poor balance. It would be an easy disarm.* The other was taller and ganglier, an awkward and fidgety man in round spectacles with a pointy, clean-shaven jaw and eyes wrinkled in the corners from frequent squinting. His light brown hair was put up in a frazzled bun, and his expression was even more manic. Moment to moment, he jerked his head about here and there, seemingly caught off guard by the sights and sounds of Flamebud. Like Kettil, he bore no staff, and instead wore a huge rucksack and several leather belts affixed with various pouches and vials. The contents were vibrantly colored and glowed faintly in the dimming light of the evening.

To Amund's consternation, the procession spotted him straight-away. Amund sighed as Baggi pointed a finger and the group approached him at the well. *At least he has the courtesy to look unhappy about it as well,* he thought sourly. When they were still several paces away, he hailed the Shaefini.

"Apprentice Baggi, what is it now? I thought I approved your stay already," he said, deliberately using Sparktongue.

"I assure you, Amund," Baggi replied as they drew near, "I would be overjoyed to leave it at that, but we have arranged a deal to treat your sick in exchange for lodgings and it seems nothing gets done in this village without your say-so."

The nervous man stepped forward and took Amund's hand without warning, shaking it vigorously and bowing. His glasses jounced on his nose as he did so.

"I am Shaefini Alchemist Elof. Well met," he said in a shaky voice.

Amund was too stunned to react, which was just as well. *These people have no tact! You don't lay hands on someone you've never met, with no warning, and expect not to be struck in retaliation!* He seethed at the insult but forced the anger into his lungs and pictured his inner flame enveloping it, just as his mother had taught him. The fury burned down to naught but ashes, and as he exhaled Amund visualized the dust dissipating as it was carried off in the wind. *I am chief now. I must maintain my composure,* he told himself, *even when suffering fools and vagabonds.*

"You are outsiders, so I will grant you this advice," he forced out. "In Kichishi, you do not touch a stranger unless they proffer a hand. To do so without this sign of approval is a grave insult and may require a peace offering of blood. Do you understand?" he demanded.

To Amund's surprise, Elof scampered backwards. *Is...is he hiding behind that girl?* The chief marveled. Even she seemed embarrassed by this display; she shot him a rueful glance and shrugged. Kettil was struggling to contain her guffaws, and Baggi just closed his eyes and pinched the bridge of his nose, looking exhausted. His was the exasperation of an unprepared father, an exasperation which Amund was intimately familiar with. *Common ground with a Staffkeeper?* He thought. *A remarkable day.*

"I apologize on behalf of Alchemist Elof," sighed Baggi. "He's a touch jumpy, especially in new places."

Amund furrowed his brow. "You travel in a caravan, yes? Are you not always in new places?"

"Yes," Baggi replied flatly. Hjordis strode forward, the man behind her jumping a bit at the unexpected movement.

"I am Staffkeeper Hjordis. Who are you?" she inquired politely. Despite her apparent ancestry, her Sparktongue was slow and deliberate, like a child just learning to speak. Amund rolled his eyes. *At least Baggi is fluent in our language.*

"You all speak the same words" he said, full of derision. "I am Amund, Chief of Flamebud. What do you want?"

"You're the chief?" Baggi balked openly, before recovering his composure. "But you're just...that is to say...aren't you a bit young?"

"My father was chief before me, and he taught me all that I needed to know to be chief after him. Besides, I am the eldest in our village. It is only proper," he replied, caring little how smug he sounded.

"In that case, forgive me," Baggi said, bowing like he had when they first met. "I owe you greater respect than what I have given you. Please, accept my apologies."

Amund narrowed his eyes and waited for the boy's mockery to reveal itself. Yet it never did. After several moments, Baggi was still bowing and his friends were looking at him with expectation in their eyes. Kettil coughed loudly and pointedly. *What are they waiting for?* He wondered, somewhat flustered. *Am I supposed to say something?*

"Ah...well...that is fine," Amund managed. "You knew not. Now stop bowing to me. That goes for all of you! It makes me uncomfortable." Baggi raised his head and laughed a bit.

"As you prefer, Chief Amund."

Amund smiled without thinking. "Very well Baggi, I will show you where you are needed. The smith and the baker could both stand to be examined, but the tailor is probably more urgent. We will go there. Will your little gang be coming too?" He eyed them coolly.

"Oh yes, naturally," Baggi replied. "Actually, Kettil and I are mostly just observers. Alchemist Elof and Staffkeeper Hjordis will be administering treatment. The Elder Sage thought that we would be best suited to the job," he told Amund as the older boy led them through the village's uneven, curving streets.

"And why is that? Surely a twelve-year-old cannot be more adept than your Staffkeepers?"

"Surely," agreed Baggi. "But I handle Sparktongue better than most Shaefini, and most Naefjans at that. As for Kettil, she needs practical experience to supplement her theory. And for the record," he added, bristling, "I'm fourteen."

As chief and host, it was Amund's job not to make his guests feel foolish. This was proving especially hard, but he bit off a retort before it could leave his lips. *Ah, fourteen. What a terrible age. Then again, fifteen is not much better. Nor sixteen. Now that I think about it,* he mused, *fourteen may actually be as good as it gets.* After fourteen, the world rapidly started becoming more complicated. After fourteen, the responsibilities started piling up. Amund shook himself out of self-pity before it could swallow him.

The village did not take long to navigate, and in no time the group stood before a garish red and blue home. A plank swinging above the door displayed a young dandy with noodle-like arms, striking a fashionable pose while his ensemble sparkled. The foreigners seemed vaguely impressed by the sign. Amund hid his smirk. *Brilliant work, Talia,* he thought, and a local idiom occurred to him: *An eye once drawn is yours to release.* Baggi alone was staring at the splattered red paint on the front and sides of the house, confused by the slipshod pattern. Amund did his best to ignore his questioning glances. *That one is perceptive. He will ask about it eventually.* In the meantime, though, the chief cleared his throat.

"This is the home of Talia the tailor," he said, "a villager in need of healing outside of our ken. Follow me closely and be respectful of her home."

The Shaefini nodded in acquiescence. He knocked five times, waited a moment, and announced their intent to enter. Upon hearing no response, he gently pushed open the door and led the group inside.

As they stepped inside, he heard soft gasps from the Shaefini and smirked. Foreigners always reacted this way, and for good reason. All over the room, from wall to wall and floor to ceiling, stood hundreds of beautifully arrayed *kortas* in a breathtaking variety of shades. While Amund's own *korta* was the scarlet hue of ibis down, these encompassed cooler shades as well. Some were narrower, with dark blue or black material, while others were shorter but stouter, in shades of muddy green and brown. Precious few of them were the same scarlet as Amund's, and a mere two were on proud display over the counter, gold and silver threads dancing lithely in the breeze from the front door. None of them had yet been affixed with opal, but even without the gems the material shined brilliantly. *Of course they are impressed,* thought Amund. *Everybody loves the kortas.* He drew himself up, full to the brim with pride in his people, then cleared his throat curtly, snapping the visitors out of their reveries. They stared at him with wide, admiring eyes.

"She will be resting in the back. Follow me," he said, and led them around the counter to the living quarters.

In the back room, a girl laid on a bedroll, shivering violently. Her eyes were closed, seemingly unconscious, which was all for the best. *Perhaps she will sleep through the whole procedure,* Amund thought, failing to convince himself. A blanket covered her up to the neck, and aside from the shivers there were no immediately visible symptoms. Baggi and Kettil made way for their elders to approach. Amund eyed them skeptically but was both surprised and relieved to see that both had adapted more business-like expressions. The jumpy one (*Elof, was it?*) still looked a bit shaky, but his jaw was set and his eyes belied a seriousness of intent. Hjordis knelt with him at the girl's side as Elof checked her temperature and pulse. Then he turned back to Amund.

"Would it be alright if I...well, if it's not offensive to you...if I removed the blanket? It is most necessary to conduct a thorough – " he abruptly stopped talking as Amund held up a hand, then nodded.

Elof nodded back, then, with shaky hands, carefully removed the blanket. Talia's shivers intensified, and an eerie stillness suddenly fell over the Shaefini. Amund's heart skipped. *What is it?* He wondered in distress, *What is amiss?* Underneath the blanket the girl bore a gruesome wound, an eerie depiction of a skull carved with brutish abandon. The marking covered most of her collarbone. Elof and Hjordis whispered something close together, speaking intensely. After a few moments, Hjordis nodded and Elof motioned for Kettil to draw closer; he murmured something to her, and Kettil's face went white. She nodded and began measuring ingredients, passing them to Elof afterwards as the elder alchemist began setting up his alembic and crucible. Meanwhile, Hjordis and Baggi both held their staffs in one hand and knelt with the other stretched towards the tools. Slowly, the alembic began bubbling, the ingredients Kettil measured now being carefully monitored and treated by Elof. Amund gawked at them. *Is this what alchemy looks like? I anticipated it would be more...thrilling.* He watched them work together, communicating softly and con-stantly in their liquid language. *Their teamwork is admirable. I am not impressed,* he stubbornly insisted, *but still, admirable.*

Hjordis whispered something to Baggi, who nodded once, lowered his outstretched hand, and rose. He stood next to Amund, speaking now in hushed Sparktongue.

"How did she receive this wound?" he asked.

Amund suppressed the urge to shudder as the recollection washed over him, focusing instead on the flame in his chest, as his mother had taught him. Once more he carefully bundled the fear and pain and fed them to the fire, melting them to ash and releasing the dross in a long, measured exhale. Only then did he answer.

"A Staffkeeper did it."

Baggi nodded sadly, looking unsurprised; perhaps he had known all along. Amund was unsure how to feel about that, so he burned in silence. After a moment, Baggi whispered to him once more.

"Staffkeepers of Death. Do they come through these lands often?"

"Once was enough for them," Amund muttered. "They took what they needed."

Baggi was quiet once more, thinking hard. "So that's what happened. That's why there are only children here. But why spare you?"

Amund barked a hard and humorless laugh. "It was not their choice. I took who I could and fled west, seeking aid in Takkin. We returned to a village in ruin."

"And Talia? She did not escape with you?"

"No. I failed her in that way," he answered, a flash of remembered shame coursing through him. "We arrived in time to chase off her attacker, but too late to shield her from this wound."

"Were there any noticeable symptoms associated with it?"

"Not immediately," Amund replied, his voice betraying concern as he went on. "She recovered well, with only occasional pain around the mark. So it was for nearly two years. But in recent weeks, she has been getting worse. The pain has increased, sometimes so bad that she cannot move. Some days are better, but most are like this." He waited for Baggi's response impatiently. "Well? Can you do anything about it?"

Baggi looked surprised. "Of course we can. This is our specialty," he replied, and Amund was surprised to find that he believed him.

Baggi bowed and rejoined Hjordis. He relayed the information to her, and she began discussing the details with her companions and devising a treatment plan. Amund was able to parse an occasional word here and there, but he had never learned Flowspeak and was mostly limited to the universal words that made up the Base Tongue. *Probably ridiculous magic jargon anyway,* he told himself. *Who cares? All that matters is that they are capable.* Judging by the precision and speed of their movements, this was a safe assumption. Amund felt an unfamiliar awkwardness. *What now? Am I expected to stand here and do nothing?* He was not used to watching others work; it made him feel old.

Soon, the results of their work were distilled into a tempered glass flask. Elof held it aloft near the window, checking it for purity and shine in the light. Kettil, too, examined the potion intently, even taking notes on a scroll procured from her sleeve. *She is diligent. It is good that Baggi has her to look out for him,* Amund thought. After a moment, Elof judged the potion satisfactory and approached Talia's bed mat. He bade his apprentice tilt their patient's head, then opened Talia's mouth with one hand and slowly trickled the mixture down her throat with the other. Amund watched in equal parts amazement and anxiety as the pink liquid glowed, lazily flowing like a stream of honey in sunlight. Hjordis, standing next to Elof, touched her staff to her forehead like Baggi had done earlier, then invoked a foreign name Amund had never heard before. Even from across the room, he felt a soft wave break over him and a tingling in his body. He raised a hand and realized it had gone numb.

Hjordis was concentrating hard on Talia. Her aura, a soft purple cloud with twirling, twisty texture, slowly settled over the younger girl's body, fitting itself to her size before gradually sinking into her. The Chief of Flamebud was not a total stranger to runic magic, yet never before had he seen such a procedure. He looked to Baggi for reassurance; the other boy held up a placating hand. The apprentice touched his forehead to his staff as well and closed his eyes. He stood still for several moments, seemingly lost in thought. Then his eyelids raised as he laid a hand on Talia's wound and he invoked his own rune. This one Amund recognized from the ancient tales.

"Yngwaz," Baggi breathed, and the room was filled with life.

Talia started tensing up sporadically, as if something inside her were kicking. The spasms gradually intensified, and Amund noticed

Hjordis biting her lip as she concentrated on her patient. Sweat was pouring down her face already. Talia began groaning slightly, and then Baggi pressed on the wound. Suddenly, Talia's moans became painful screams. Elof held her down and spoke reassuring words in her ear. Then, too slowly for comfort, a dark inky cloud began streaming out of the sigil on Talia's collarbone. It issued forth, cloaking Baggi's face in darkness as he kneeled over the girl. Amund began to panic, stepping forward to pull him out of the cloud, but then he caught a brief glimpse of the boy through the smoke and stopped short. The apprentice did not seem alarmed. In fact, he seemed determined, almost relieved. He began applying more pressure, a process made evident by Talia's increasingly tortured wails. Amund gritted his teeth and contracted his hands into tight fists, fingernails digging into his palms. *A citizen of my village is in pain*, he thought, *and all I can do is watch.*

"Now, Baggi," Hjordis urged, "settle it!"

Baggi hesitated for the briefest of moments, a cocktail of wild emotions flashing across his face. Amund recognized them from his own reflection: fear, self-doubt, righteous fury. Then the boy set his jaw and pressed down harder on the sigil. Talia released one final wail, then there was a perversely gentle popping sound as the residual smoke burst out of the wound and drifted out the open window. Immediately, the Shaefini collapsed on the ground, breathing heavily and regarding each other with wild, adrenal eyes. Then they began to laugh, slowly at first, and then more and more enthusiastically as the result sank in. Amund assumed this was a good sign.

"You did it! I knew you were ready and you did it! Do you know what this means?" Hjordis gushed to Baggi after the tension had left.

"I did it. I really did it," Baggi managed with mild disbelief. "It really worked," he said, then leaned against the back wall and hugged his staff tight to his chest. "I couldn't have done it without you," he said, seemingly speaking to the tool. Amund cleared his throat.

"I, for one, have no idea what this means. Did the treatment work? Is Talia to recover?" he asked impatiently. Hjordis beamed at him, sweat still pouring down her face.

"It worked all right," she said, slipping in and out of Sparktongue in the excitement, "it worked like salt and butter!"

Amund wasn't sure if this was a translation error or merely Naefjan idiom. He didn't care either way. He knelt by Talia's side and opened his canteen; she would be wanting for water when she woke, and this, at least, he could provide.

"I am glad to hear it," he sighed.

3

The infant laid perfectly still as Njal the goatherd approached. He doffed his cloak without thought for the blizzard and clumsily swaddled the child as snowflakes fell upon his hairy arms, melting at first but then piling up as the skin chilled and tightened. Njal held the infant close to his chest and rushed down the path toward his cottage. *For one to leave a baby out in the blizzard,* he wondered, *how desperate must they have been?* He thought to shelter the child only until its parents could be found. Its skin was beginning to turn blue, yet its eyes were awake with interest. Silent as the falling snow itself, the infant made not a sound as it was borne towards its new home.

***

The baby turned out to be a girl. Njal held her in his arms near the hearth until she had thawed and then he placed her in the cradle of willow that he had never quite been able to part with and left to put the kettle on. She waved her arms vaguely back and forth, rocking herself. Njal watched from the other side of the cottage, knowing that any further affection would only multiply the pain of their imminent parting. He mused on the years he and his late wife had spent trying to conceive a child, of the various enchantments and blessings the

Staffkeepers of Shaefi had offered and the humbling array of potions and salves their alchemists had provided, all in vain. *Weren't much use to begin with, but for that matter they were even less help when Helga took ill,* he bitterly ruminated. The scream of the kettle shook him from revery. He poured the water into a teapot and sat by the hearth while it steeped to await the girl's parents.

Yet they did not come that day, nor the day after, nor the weeks that followed. And all the while, Njal fed the girl goat's milk with a pinch of Shaefi-Sugar and a dash of skepticism. The alchemical powder seemed by Njal's reckoning to satisfy the child's hunger, but then it was difficult to tell as the infant so rarely made noise. Occasionally she would hiccup or cough, and of course she would wail often during the deep of night, but mostly the girl laid in her cradle and waved her arms and looked around in curious silence.

Njal named the child Valdis, meaning goddess of Death, because she had done what so many of the legendary heroes could not: she had bested Death, and in her newborn days at that. The child's hair was dark blonde, like honey, but she had the emerald eyes of the Valley. *Must be a half-breed,* thought Njal without malice. It was not uncommon in the Eastern Great Pass, so close to the border. He watched the infant grow into child and taught her his trade, more so that she might have something to distract her than for matters of inheritance, for he wished to send her off to the city as soon as she came of apprenticing age. And with each day that passed, the goatherd grew more and more attached to his adopted daughter.

She grew into a curious child, but a serious one as well. She had little interest in the toys Njal's wife had made years ago for the child never borne, nor was she often enthralled by the ancient tales as he spun them. Instead, she spent every day from when she could talk peppering Njal with questions about herding. He answered them truthfully, if reluctantly, for even as he wished for her a loftier apprenticeship than he could offer, he desired far more that she should grow up to be honest.

This ideal was tested one day in the spring of her sixth year while they sat by the hearth after dinner, Njal plucking his lyre and both staring into the flames.

"Father?" Valdis interrupted, so softly that he was unsure at first if she had spoken at all. But she was looking at him now, which seemed to confirm it, so he hummed vaguely in response. "Why don't you have a wife? In all of your stories, the men all have wives."

Njal looked at her long. Then he leaned his instrument against his chair on the floor. "You haven't been listening," he said curtly. "In some they have husbands."

"That's not what I meant."

"I know, child, I know" he sighed. "I do have a wife. She just left this world ahead of me."

Valdis was quiet, evidently considering it as she gazed into the fire once more. "You mean she died."

"Yes."

"How?"

"She was sick with some new illness, one of body and mind both."

"But," asked Valdis, the confusion in her voice painful to hear, "why didn't you send for the Staffkeepers?"

"I did, child," he muttered, voice hard as iron. "And for all the aid they gave us, she would always fall ill again. Time after time we sent for them, and with each visit they offered new treatments, new medicines...new hope." There was an enduring silence broken only by the paltry crackling of their measly fire. "Time and again, that hope was dashed, and all the while I watched my love waste away before me and forget our life together, piece by piece. When she was at last granted release, there was no joy left in her. Only misery. Only pain." Unable to continue, he took a deep, shaky breath. Tears soaked his beard.

"Valdis," Njal eventually concluded, "I don't care one whit if you listen to the old tales of heroes and adventures. But hear me now. If you take one lesson from all my stories, let it be from this one, and let it be this: given the choice between a long life of pain and the mercy of Death, only a Staffkeeper would be naïve enough to choose the former."

He took up his lyre and began plucking once more, slower now. The music, previously so warm, now hung like frosted cobwebs in the air. Valdis said nothing.

***

Some weeks later, Njal was bringing in the flock and closing the barn when he heard a nearby bird's call transform, suddenly, to a pained squawk. Patiently, he finished the task at hand before following his ears to where he thought the sound may have originated. He saw there his daughter, kneeling in the grass and inspecting the bird's remains. She gingerly picked it up by the wing and spread its feathers, turning the body over this way and that way and poking curiously at its joints. Njal coughed loudly to make himself known.

Valdis turned without rising, the cadaver still in hand. She tilted her head slightly, the innocence of the gesture disarming. "Father?" she prompted.

"Valdis, what are you doing?" he asked, otherwise at a loss for words.

"Just looking," she replied easily, and returned her attention to the carcass.

"Did you see what killed it?" said Njal, anxious to hear her answer.

"Yes."

"What was it?"

"A rock. Thrown by me," she said idly.

Njal felt an immense pressure in his chest, a sensation of importance. He knew without knowing that the consequences of his next words could be dire, should he speak without thinking. So think he did, for several moments, as his daughter continued to play with the dead bird.

"Why did you throw the rock?" he said carefully.

"To kill the bird," came her response, factual and unashamed.

"Why did you want to kill the bird?" he asked. He held his breath as Valdis turned back to gaze at him as if confused by the question or waiting for some trick. When no further inquiry came, she shrugged.

"To learn about it," said Valdis, "and so we can have meat tonight."

Njal released a deep sigh of relief. *A perfectly sensible answer,* he thought proudly. "Well if that's all, there's no problem," he said warmly, "as long as it wasn't without reason. Bring it in and I'll get it cleaned for dinner."

Valdis nodded obediently and followed him inside, clutching the bird by its bloody wing.

***

One dark morning, long before the sun rose, Njal and Valdis were seated for a breakfast of porridge and tea. Njal cleared his throat.

"Do you like it here, Valdis?" he asked her. Then he waited, allowing the question time to join them at the table.

Valdis met his gaze but said nothing for a long while. Njal was accustomed to this. He sipped his tea, their sole luxury in an otherwise humble life. Some days the child would not speak at all, and he wondered if today was destined to be among them, but eventually she did answer him.

"Yes," she said quietly. She lifted a spoonful of plain porridge to her mouth and ate.

"But you must be wanting for friends, children your age?" he asked, for their nearest neighbors were a difficult trek eastward, toward the Valley, and they had only two adult sons besides.

Valdis shook her head. "I like it here," she answered.

Njal nodded and resumed eating. The cottage was quiet once more save for the scraping of their wooden spoons and the clunk of cups being set down on the naked table. When they had finished, Valdis took their dishes over to the kitchen and cracked the lid of the snow-melter to allow fresh water into the sink. Njal was glad to see her use it; he had bought the rune-inscribed contraption secondhand in the city at great cost and for it to remain unused should have been a great frustration.

"You're making the right choice, my man," the merchant who sold it had said to Njal. "Most folk ask for the Staffkeepers of Shaefi to make one for them, you know, on account of it being a free service, but I tell you the waitlist is so long you'll be dead decades before they even see your name on it."

Njal had grunted agreement as far as "those useless mendicants" went. After nearly an hour of fierce haggling, they settled on the price of one whole stone-odd and two white-odd on top of it. The goatherd had rolled up his sleeve and unhooked the money from the odd-ring on his arm, then carried the barrel-like contraption all the long way home and set it up atop the roof with some remorse. The leaf-agate used for Melennese stone-odd was a beautiful thing, transparent as spring water save for the plants frozen, timeless, inside the arrow-head-shaped counters. The goatherd had hoped to one day pass his on to Valdis as part of her inheritance; indeed, he had wondered the whole way home if he had made the right choice, but watching his daughter use the snow-melter now reassured him in the investment.

She scrubbed their dishes in silence. Afterwards, they bundled up in their cloaks and scarves, tied their pointed hats round their chins, took up their crooks, and went outside to let out the goats.

When the livestock were set to grazing, Njal cleared his throat once more. "I'll be off to Geluwam tomorrow to sell our wool. Perhaps you might like to come along?" he offered. His face remained impartial, his gaze focused on their flock.

Valdis looked at her father and considered. Njal glanced her way and noted how tall she had grown; already at nine years old she stood higher than the spare crook he had given her, and it seemed she would continue to grow taller still for some time. He worried for his daughter, now of apprenticing age and with no real knowledge of the world outside their plateau.

"What of the flock?" she asked. "Who will feed them?"

"We'll leave them out plenty of feed," he replied, "but besides that I've asked Bjartur to stop by in the mornings and check in on them. Do you want to go or stay?"

Valdis nodded thoughtfully. "He's very dependable," she said. "I would like to go."

"Hmm," Njal hummed his approval. He patted her on the head and walked off to retrieve a wandering ewe.

That evening was Njal's turn to cook, so while he prepared Valdis went outside to enjoy the sunset. In her hand was a rope tied loosely around the neck of her favorite kid, whom she had named simply Snow, though in truth the safety measure was unnecessary; the animal would have stayed by her side regardless. She strolled over to a grassy knoll patched with wild cloudberry bushes, picking a handful and feeding the demure white fruit to Snow. Their land sloped gradually downward, and from here she could see for quite a distance. On summer days, the sun would illuminate the whole plateau in an inviting shade of green, but around this time of year all was grey and dark even during the day. She wondered which she preferred and watched the sun as it sank behind the mountains where she had been found. A light snow was falling.

Sometimes Valdis thought she could remember laying up there in the blizzard, where her father said he found her. She knew this to be impossible, of course, yet a child's mind does not often prefer reason to romance. She stared at those mountains nearly every day, urging the memories to return in earnest. They never did. Still she looked, with an unjustifiable certainty that it would someday work if she only kept trying. Valdis told herself she wanted to see past those mountains, to explore the rest of Naefja and even the other realms of Solabell beyond. Yet these self-assurances never felt completely genuine. In truth, she was content with her goats and her plateau and her small cottage where no one ever came to visit, not anymore. *Not since Mother died,* she reflected. She squeezed false tears from her eyes, trying to mourn the woman she hadn't known, and ultimately realizing that she never would. *I will never be like Father in this way,* she conceded. The thought annoyed her.

Snow noticed her mood and barged onto her lap, unintentionally ramming her in the chest with its tiny, nubbish horns. Despite the pain, Valdis appreciated the kid's distraction. She turned her thoughts toward her impending journey. *Geluwam,* she pondered, *the city. I *wonder how big it must be.* Njal had told her before that Geluwam was roughly the size of their entire land, and then some, and the entire place gouged from the mountain itself. She turned around and envisioned great stone buildings smothering their plateau. *He must be wrong,* she thought, unable to accept that a settlement of such scale stood. *He must be teasing me.* Njal was given to making jokes on rare occasions, though Valdis had never once encouraged it. Still, she appreciated the effort even as she derided the avenue through which it was channeled.

"Geluwam," she whispered to Snow, "doesn't that sound special?" The goat bleated happily before it approached the cloudberry bush and began eating straight from the source. "Yes," Valdis agreed absent-mindedly. She petted Snow and sat in quiet thought until the smells of roasted quail and potatoes beckoned her from her stupor. She stood up, displacing a mound of powder she hadn't noticed accumulating, and tugged at Snow's rope. The goat reluctantly left the berries and followed her back to the cottage.

***

Geluwam exceeded her expectations by far. Even on the approach, Valdis felt the insignificance of her size for the first time in her life. She had grown up alongside the greatest of mountains, of course, those being the Great Peaks; still, a mountain is a distant thing, a concept more than an actual entity. Valdis petted the goats pulling their creaking, splintery cart and spared a glance to her father. She knew that if there were something to be feared in the city, he was sensible enough to fear it, but Njal seemed unimpressed by the colossus so she copied his behavior and walked without worry alongside the goats.

Her apprehensions nonetheless grew as the they walked, and walked, and walked, the distance longer than it seemed, and the city puffing itself up larger and larger with each step. Finally, the rough mountain trail gave way to lustrous cobblestones, the crunch of snow swapped for the clop of hooves. Valdis' feet ached from the two-day journey; she expected the uneven blotches beneath her boots to annoy and exhaust her. Instead, she was surprised to find the texture nearly massaging her soles. The design's simple ingenuity awed her. Her father noticed her interest and spared her a smile, patting her head protectively as they walked on.

If the city's path was jarring, its noise was nearly insufferable. Valdis had lived in the remote plateau amid the mountain's gentle racket, had become accustomed to the cacophony of bird sound and howling wind and the cries of goats and sheep. These noises were comforting. Here the noise was rough and painful. Merchants bellowed at them as they passed, an unnecessary annoyance by her assessment, shouting in languages alternately familiar and foreign. *It must be Flowspeak,* she recognized. Though their home was technically within Naefjan borders, Njal had never valued their tongue, deeming it unnecessary when nearly everyone in the region preferred Woodwhisper. As a result her Flowspeak was rudimentary at best. *I will learn,* she reassured herself.

From above, she heard women call out to her father in voices sweet with innuendo. She looked up and saw an array of ladies in finery leaning from the windows of structures that coalesced at the city's roof, like oversized stalactites. The women were beautiful and dazzling in brightly colored silks, their hair fashionably short and their features as varied as the cobblestones. Valdis understood their proposals even without the language, but if there was any doubt in her mind it was dispelled as they switched back and forth between Woodwhisper and

Flowspeak, casting their nets as wide as possible. Njal ignored their cries.

"Father?" Valdis asked. Her voice was lost even to herself among the city's din. She tried again, louder. He turned to her this time, eyebrows raised questioningly. "Why don't you take one of them to be your wife?" It was clear to the girl that her father was exceptionally popular with women; why else would they all be so desperate for his attentions?

"Those women have no interest in marriage," he laughed, "only making a living, same as you and me."

"What do you mean?"

"They sell company. Some sell sex," he replied casually.

Valdis wrinkled her nose. "How can you sell company?"

"By the hour, usually," Njal said. Valdis felt he was making a joke again. She hated when he made jokes.

"You mean, you pay the woman to spend time with her?" she asked, rolling her eyes.

"Yes, that's the usual way of it," answered her father.

"That sounds stupid," Valdis scoffed.

Njal turned to her, unexpectedly serious. "Don't look down on others who work hard to make ends meet," he reprimanded her. "We're kin in that way. And besides," his features softened slightly as he patted her on the head, "not all are so lucky as we are. Some have no free company at home."

"Like you when Mother died, before you found me," Valdis offered obliviously. "Did you pay for company then?"

"Yes, on occasion."

She thought on this for some time as they walked on, the streets becoming narrower and the noises more varied. To this cacophony of sensations a new element was added: smells filled her nostrils, some pleasant but others foul. Fresh bread, hot mutton skewers, and lavish perfumes were among the former, sour beer and a cocktail of un-pleasantly human odors the latter. It all came together into a curious combination that Valdis would forever after associate with Geluwam. She breathed it deep, savoring the smell of her world opening up.

Eventually Njal stopped the cart before a relatively small building that nevertheless dwarfed their cottage and barn together. It was a neat two stories, and Valdis heard the voices of children echoing in unison from the second floor. She couldn't make out the words.

"Valdis," Njal said abruptly, "you will be tested here. I've already made the arrangements and paid the dues. Go in and tell them your name and take the test. I'll come pick you up after I've offloaded the wool."

"Father?" she asked, confused and hurt. "I don't want to take a test. I want to go sell the wool with you."

"Next time, perhaps," he replied sadly. "But I hope not. Now, in you go." And he urged the goats on before she could protest any further.

Seeing no other option before her in such foreign surroundings, Valdis huffed resentfully and entered the building. Inside, three children were seated before three different desks with three different scholars behind each. They seemed to be in the midst of an interview. The room was tastefully decorated and colorful, with pretentious banners bearing various alphabets running the length of the walls. She squinted at the banners and tried to discern which alphabet was Woodwhisper. The Base Tongue was obvious; all she needed to do was note which of the sets' letters could be found among each of the others. It took her mere moments. *So this is the Base Tongue?* She thought. Valdis had always thought it to carry an air of universal dignity, but these letters were square and formal, lifeless and boring. *How disappointing.*

"Excuse me, young miss?" a composed and steady voice called from the corner closest to the door. Valdis saw now that there were in fact four desks in the room, one at each corner, and the scholar behind the fourth was beckoning her nearer. She obeyed.

"Yes?" she demanded when she was before him.

"Miss Valdis Njalsdottir, if I'm not mistaken?" he said politely.

"I am Valdis, and Njal's daughter," she said, reflexively stubborn.

"Ah, so you're not taking it as a family name then," the man noted, scribbling hastily on a scroll with an extravagant magenta-colored quill pen. Valdis didn't quite take his meaning, so she said nothing. "Well then, are you prepared to begin immediately?" he asked, adjusting the comically small spectacles on his nose.

"Begin the test?" she probed cautiously.

"But of course."

"I'm ready," she said, not knowing herself if she was lying.

The scholar cleared his throat. "Question one: what is the sum of ten and five?"

Valdis blinked at him. He stared expectantly back at her. "Fifteen," she said eventually. Her father had taught her arithmetic so that she might keep track of earnings one day, but she was unsure why this man she had never met in a place she had never been would need to know that.

"Excellent!" the man gushed, and he seemed to mean it. "And you didn't even need to use your fingers! A most promising start!" He scribbled on the scroll again.

This went on for some time, the man asking her questions to test her arithmetic and then moving on to her language skills. Valdis had more trouble with these questions, since she could only speak Woodwhisper and a smattering of Flowspeak, and read and write neither. When those questions were exhausted, the man began probing her with all sorts of queries that seemed to have no rhyme or reason, which she answered with varying degrees of success. He inquired about how certain tools might be used for various constructions, and which materials would be best suited for each. He asked her about her cooking skills, making her describe step-by-step how she might prepare such-and-such ingredients. Then he asked much the same things, only with potions rather than food. Valdis had no answers for these lattermost inquiries.

Finally, he procured a map of Solabell from his desk. She leaned over the desk and examined the document as he made several annotations on his scroll. According to the map, their world was convex, uneven, like an upside-down bowl. She gestured to the rim of the bowl, where charted waters and islands tapered off into nothingness.

"Why does the map end here?" she asked.

"Because it's the edge of the world, so sayeth Sharpaxe" he snorted, in a tone that implied he was making a malicious joke.

Valdis, of course, had no patience for jokes, so she fell quiet once more. The man finished his notetaking and instructed her to point on the map to the place he named.

"We shall start with the easy ones," he said kindly, "point to Naefja." She pointed to the northern-most country. "Good! Now the Melenno Valley." She moved her finger to the right, across the border to the north-eastern land. "And Kichishi?" he asked, more as a formality than anything, for there was only one country remaining. She pointed to the land that stretched to the south like the crooked hilt to the northern countries' cross guard. The man's quill moved, and he paused before continuing.

"Now these may prove slightly more difficult," he said sympathetically. Valdis rolled her eyes; his compassion felt more like condescension.

He continued to quiz her on the locations of many landmarks and settlements across Solabell for some time. Some, like the coastal desert north of the Melenno Valley known as Lesh Fwit and the great Pepen River that carved directly through the Valley itself, were easy to pick out. Others, like the Temple at Enton where the Staffkeepers of Shaefi headquartered or the several Kichishi names whose nature as settlement or geographical feature she could only guess at, proved trickier. Every time Valdis made an error, the scholar pointed out where the place really was, and in this way she learned several useful facts: that Yngmuth was on the north-western point of Naefja, at the cape that resembled a chin, nose, and forehead; that Ehkag, apparently the capitol city of Kichishi, likewise resided on a coastline, though theirs was the southernmost in all Solabell; she even learned the location of that accursed place her father would never speak of, Enton, directly in the heart of Naefja and not as far west of their own home as she had expected.

When the test had been concluded, the scholar scribbled at his scroll for a long time, only pausing every now and then to glance up at her in an approving way that Valdis thought could reasonably be called grating. Finally, he began blowing on the ink, before suddenly jumping as if shocked.

"Ah, I nearly forgot!" he said, opening his desk drawer and exchanging the map for a wooden disk the size of her face. He laid it on the desk and Valdis saw there was a letter carved into it. Unlike the letters on the wall, this one was refreshingly simple and could have been composed in a single stroke, but despite its simplicity, something about the disk caused her to unconsciously lean closer.

"This is called a Disk of Discernment," he said. "The name is a bit ostentatious, if you ask me, but I suppose when you're a Staffkeeper you can name your inventions whatever you wish and no one bats an eye." He began rambling about the double standards of such an allowance while Valdis continued to stare at the disk.

"What is it for?" she asked.

"It ascertains potential," he answered unhelpfully. "The rune inscribed on it, Pert, I believe, has such an effect that..." he trailed off and squinted at her. "Well, quite honestly, I'm not certain how it works. But employing it is an exceedingly simple matter. Please, lay your hand here. Your dominant one, that is."

Valdis did as she was told and reverently laid her left hand on the wooden disk. When she had, the rune inscribed began to glow a faint crimson. "Ah! This is wonderful! It seems you..." the man trailed off once more as the rune continued to glow brighter and hotter. Valdis felt the pattern burning her hand, yet she was enthralled by the pain. She felt seen, recognized...the sensation was intoxicating. She would rather her hand burn to ash than remove it now. The rune grew hotter and brighter still. The red light filled the room, bursting between her fingers and splaying exultantly on the walls and ceilings. Valdis smiled slightly.

And then her wrist was in someone's grip and the feelings, the burning and the light but the satisfaction and comfort too, were gone. Valdis looked at the scholar who had separated them in a daze of fury and loss. His eyes were wide, the glasses on his face wobbling quietly as he shook.

"I had better make a note of this," he said, equally dazed.

And make a note he did, scribbling with shaking hands on the scroll before blowing on the ink with equally shaky breaths and rolling it up in a wax-treated tube. He gave it to her, told her to give it to her father, and excused her, all pleasantness gone from his demeanor. All the while, Valdis stared at the rune pattern now branded on her palm and brooded.

When Njal returned, Valdis handed him the tube with her right hand so he wouldn't see the mark. He skimmed its contents as best he could, which was not very well, and when his eyes fell upon the bottom his features darkened. Valdis felt afraid then, an unfamiliar and infantilizing feeling, but Njal simply sighed heavily, put the scroll back in the tube, and beckoned her to follow to their lodgings. Valdis said nothing and kept her left hand in her sleeve, feeling for all the world like a disappointment.

4

The Flamebud Inn was not especially large, the Staffkeepers being granted three of its four guest rooms in exchange for their services. The rooms were not meant to accommodate more than two, as indicated by the dual single beds on either side of the window, but this was luckily not a problem for the semi-nomadic Shaefini. They were well used to sleeping on hard floors, in those rare cases where they were lucky enough to secure indoor lodgings. In Flamebud it would be no different. The rooms were already set up by the apprentices, bedrolls laid out precisely and deliberately to use every available inch of floor space. There was little else in the way of furniture, merely a modest oak chest at the foot of each bed and an end table between them. Flamebud wasn't an impoverished community, yet it seemed the Kichishi style was far more minimalistic than that of Naefja.

Baggi sat on his bedroll on the floor of the apprentices' room, legs crossed and lost in Contemplation. Never before had he felt so simultaneously exhausted and exhilarated. But then, he had never attuned to Compromise twice in one day. Usually, an apprentice was encouraged to attune no more than once daily, to avoid fatigue or worse; over time, as they acclimated to one another, their body and the magical aura, or "personality", of their staff would merge and the strain would lessen.

The process was a topic of constant interest at the Staffkeepers'
Conclave, that meeting of all Staffkeeping Orders save the Staffkeepers
of Death, which occurred once every decade. Representatives from
each Order fiercely debated, among many other matters, which factors
determined the length of the process, but even with the Shaefini Elder
Sage, the First Disciple of Sawtor, and the Helmsman of Brathus assembled in one place, a definitive answer had never been agreed upon.
Some said it was in the blood, some said it was a matter of rigorous
study, and yet others insisted it hinged entirely on the bond between
staff and keeper. The one point they agreed upon was that the earlier
an apprentice was able to reach this benchmark, the greater potential
they held.

Baggi now pondered these postulations as he Contemplated. *If
younger is better, that means I have potential. Perhaps great potential.*
He focused on the cool air emanating from the staff in his lap, recalling
the ritual which had resulted in this achievement.

***

They were working together, he and Hjordis, bringing the alchemical
tools and ingredients to the proper temperature with the Kenaz rune
when she whispered to him.

"Baggi," she said, eyes darting back to where Amund stood, "what
I'm about to say might make you nervous. It's very important that you
keep a level head. Okay?"

"Okay," he whispered back, already struggling with the instructions, "I promise. What is it?"

"You're going to have to release the sigil."

Ever so slowly, he turned to her with sheer disbelief written on his face. "What? That's nonsense. I'm only an apprentice; you should do it."

Hjordis looked deeply somber, the dusty light of the shop falling across her profile. "This wound should have been treated months ago. Now that it's progressed, the process is going to be much more stressful. Talia is going to be in a lot of pain, so much pain that it will kill her if the anesthetic isn't strong enough. This isn't a matter of technique, it's a matter of quantity. It's going to take just about all I have to keep her stable. In the meantime, you'll use Yngwaz to release the sigil."

"But I've never done this before!" Baggi whispered back fervently. "What if I can't do it?"

"I know you can," she replied with a wan smile, "and I think you know that too. When you go in, just remember who you are. Remember why we're doing this, and that I'm right here supporting you."

Baggi felt his heart pounding in his chest, but not with fear. *Am I…excited?* He took a stabilizing breath and nodded. *Yes, we can do this.* Elof finished with the concoction, and the Staffkeepers took their places as he prepared to feed her the brew. Hjordis attuned to her staff, Satisfaction, without thought and invoked the Algiz rune. Once upon a time, being this close would have made Baggi's body go numb just like Talia's. But now, his aura was resilient, the bond between he and Compromise much stronger. Now, Algiz washed over and around him like a blizzard fruitlessly assaulting a boulder. Hjordis' aura flowed out of her, taking shape over Talia's body as it cloaked the young tailor. *Amund is likely feeling the effects,* the apprentice thought. He turned back toward the door where Amund was watching with alarm and held up a reassuring hand, unsure if it would help. *He'll be fine. Focus on Talia.*

Baggi bowed his head to Compromise and opened himself up to the magic it housed. To his great surprise, it came easily, the energy flowing into him even and patient. *Don't think this time,* he told himself, *just do what you need to. Heal this person.* After a few moments, he raised his head from his staff and approached Talia. Kneeling, he held a hand over the wound, hesitated for a moment, then gently laid his palm on the sigil.

Immediately, Baggi was in a boneyard. He looked about him, at a grey and barren landscape. His friends, the tailor shop, everything else was gone. *I've died. I've failed and died already.* There was no grass, only dirt and bones beneath his boots. There were no birds or animal sounds, only the silence of terrible realization. There was no breeze here, only the sickly stench of still air breathed long ago. Baggi felt something rising in his chest, a nervous energy that was tearing away at the bond between him and his staff. *I know this feeling,* he thought, *this is fear. No,* he amended as the feeling gnawed him, *fear can be overcome. This is the anxiety that accompanies Death. This is terror, and terror is not so easily bested.*

Baggi had felt terror before, exactly twice. The first time, he had been four years old when a boar surprised him at play on the snowy slopes outside Jolk. He had been sure it would kill him, had been so frightened of its long tusks and mean grunts. The boar instead snorted at him curiously, before turning around and shuffling off. His terror had been misplaced then. The second time, unfortunately, was not so gentle. It had been just before he was sent to the Temple at Enton. A procession of dark riders had roared into town, transformed by the skulls and horns on their saddles and garb into something inhuman. The woman leading her grim procession had reared up in front of Baggi where he stood, stupefied, outside their family cottage. He had felt the presence of Death so strongly then. But of course, he wasn't killed that time either.

Baggi gripped Compromise for security, and quickly scanned the bleak and flat landscape. He saw nothing. There were no landmarks, only a flat dark field of dirt topped with bones as far as the eye could see. The gruesome white garnishments stretched cross the land like a field of poppies, some patches densely populated with all shapes and sizes, other spots decorated with an even, almost mathematical distribution. Overhead laid a uniform sheet of dark grey cloud; not a speck of blue could be seen. Baggi fought to channel his rising panic, dropping to the floor and scrabbling amongst the dirt and bones for something, anything. *There must be some clue around here,* Baggi thought, manic, *some indication of where I am.* His efforts yielded naught but scratches from the bones and grave dirt beneath his nails. The sheer lifelessness of this place was still eating away at him and Compromise and now he felt the fear begin to trickle between them, overwhelming both. On his knees, Baggi felt his lips beginning to tremble, threatening to betray him. *Don't cry,* he insisted at first, *start crying and you've given up. Give up, and you're lost here forever. Whatever you do, don't cry!*

But he did cry. Feeling hopeless and infantile, he sobbed and sobbed and keeled over on his knees in the dirt. And then he felt a hand on his shoulder. It squeezed gently, then flicked him on the side of the head in gentle admonishment. Baggi was so startled that he stopped sobbing and turned around in disbelief. There was nobody behind him. *It couldn't be.* He looked down at Compromise, and saw its runes glowing with arcane power. Ice-blue magic pounded forth from the staff in a comforting steady rhythm. *But...my bond isn't that strong,* he thought in puzzlement. Something about the cool energy felt familiar.

He regarded Compromise strangely, an impossible idea forming in his head. *It couldn't be. And yet, how else could I explain it?* He wondered.

"Bjorn?" he asked hesitantly, feeling a bit foolish for even entertaining the notion.

Compromise responded to him, pouring more of its power into Baggi's body. He felt the terror being scrubbed from his being, felt hope rising once more in his chest. He smiled a delirious smile, driving Compromise defiantly into the dirt as he pushed to his feet. Then Baggi began walking, his staff holding him up. *Where I go doesn't matter,* he realized, *only that I go. Only that I stay in motion. Only that I stay alive.*

He marched with confidence in every step, not stopping to question which way he was going or even why he was going at all. The energy spreading throughout his body allowed Baggi to calm down and think clearly, and he realized that this place and this feeling were the antithesis of Shaefi's nature. *Of course it's so draining for us to be here,* he thought, *We're in Death's domain. This must be The Threshold. I've learned about this, I know how this works,* he reassured himself, *Life does not exist here, so to remain alive I must constantly live. I must keep doing.* He continued onward, trusting the bond between him and Compromise to guide the way. *You're much smarter than I am,* he thought as he admired his staff. *Thank you for protecting me.* In response, he felt a reassuring magic pulse. It reminded him of a sunny day by a waterfall, and the taste of cloudberries on his tongue.

After time had passed, perhaps moments or perhaps days or longer, Baggi saw a figure on the ground. His heart skipped loudly as he approached, and as he knelt down he saw it was Talia. *Not exactly Talia,* he corrected, *but some part of her. What remains of her soul has been stuck here, probably since the attack on their village.* He marveled at the girl's hardiness. *This place must have been eating away at her these two years, but Amund said she was still healthy until recently. This is nothing short of a miracle.* Despite his surroundings, Baggi offered brief thanks to Shaefi. Then he turned his attention back to where the girl laid on the bones.

In a place such as this, any presence of life, weak or insubstantial as it may be, stood in stark contrast to its surroundings. That being the case, Baggi had approached with amazement and hope. Now that he more closely examined the girl, however, his confidence wavered. *She looks dead already,* he thought. The apprentice allowed a single wave of respectful sorrow to wash over him as he took in the girl's shriveled, dehydrated skin, the grave dirt smeared across her face, and the bloody, weeping wound on her collarbone. Her heartbeat was slow and irregular, her skin cold to the touch. Even more concerning were the heavy dark iron manacles around her wrists and ankles, the other ends buried beneath the soil. Baggi gingerly tried to pull them up, but it proved impossible. *As if chained to something underground. Poor girl. The recovery will be painful. Assuming we get that far.* He quickly but calmly recited the Shaefini Cleansing Rites in preparation for the procedure.

Having paid the proper respects, Baggi pushed up his sleeves and steeled himself. He held Compromise close and lowered his eyelids, letting the magic enrobe him and focusing as he did so on the goodness and light of the world outside this one. He felt the familiar warmth of his mother's hearth, heard the delicate song of the nightingale, saw a collage of old enemies shaking hands after the Staffkeepers of Shaefi had brokered a peace agreement. He tasted cloudberries, sweet and light and pure, and through it all, he felt his brother's reassuring hand on his shoulder.

Baggi opened his eyes, grinning wildly, and extended a hand towards Talia. Just before touching the wound, he invoked Yngwaz.

In the blink of an eye, he was cloaked in dark steam. It billowed out of the wound, burning his face and neck and arms, but Baggi did not let up. He focused on the girl on the ground, the girl who needed his help. He remembered the terror, and the loneliness, and the grief that the Staffkeepers of Death had gifted him, and then he thought of the countless others that had felt it just as strongly. For the first time, Baggi felt like a Staffkeeper of Shaefi. *I am good,* he exulted, *I am light and health. I am joy and empathy and the bravery of compromise. I am the open hand that reaches into the darkness. I am a Staffkeeper of Shaefi, and you are nothingness.* The dark steam scalding him now, the apprentice heard a faint echo from somewhere beside him. *Hjordis?*

"Now, Baggi," the voice echoed, thousands of miles away, "settle it!"

He spent only a moment trying to make sense of this. Only a moment, and then he did as he was told. He pressed down harder, purging the darkness from this shell of Talia, forcing the pain from her body. The chains were loudly sundered, one last hot burst of smoke swam towards him, and then Baggi was surrounded by *kortas* once more, thoroughly disoriented.

The cool energy inside his chest was gone, replaced by the stuffiness of the tailor shop. Baggi felt his limbs give out all at once, falling back against the wall with Compromise in his lap. Hjordis was shouting something congratulatory, while Kettil and Elof were chuckling nervously, but he paid them little mind, reeling as he was from overexertion. He stared closely at Compromise, only now having the luxury of wondering what had happened. *Was that really you, Bjorn?* He thought. *Where did you go?* Compromise remained still in his lap, seemingly as exhausted as its wielder. He smiled weakly at his staff and pictured his brother's aggressive grin in response.

"I couldn't have done it without you," he whispered.

***

Back in his room, lost in Contemplation, Baggi turned over the events of the ritual and appraised his performance. Unfortunately, this was proving difficult. *The problem with reviewing the ritual,* he thought, *is that I have nothing to compare it to.* He had been taught all about how to use Yngwaz, had been instructed in the motions and how to apply them to release a claimed creature; what the Sages had seemingly forgotten to mention was his journey to the wasteland Baggi had undergone. Recalling Hjordis' advice from just before they began the ritual now cast her words in a new light. *The Threshold. The Land of Lifelessness. A bit more warning would have helped.* He shook off indignance and refocused. *Somehow, by making contact with the sigil, my soul was projected into that place. But how? And why was Talia's soul tethered there, while her body was still here?* Baggi felt a chill down his spine as an uncomfortable realization settled in. *Unless the Staffkeepers of Death severed the bond between the two.* An echo of the despair he had felt earlier resounded in Baggi's mind. *It almost happened to me, too. If I hadn't had Compromise, and Compromise hadn't had a part of my soul bonded to it already, would I have...?* He shivered and shook off such dreadful thoughts.

A gentle knocking on the door drew Baggi out of Contemplation. He arose with stiff legs, stepped carefully between the bedrolls on the floor, and turned the knob to see Elder Sage Hrafn before him. The Elder Sage beamed at Baggi, clapped him on the shoulder, and gently pushed past him into the small room.

"So you've gone and done it, eh Baggi?" he said congenially. "Both Alchemist Elof and Staffkeeper Hjordis tell me you did an outstanding job with the tailor." Had Baggi the energy to pay more attention, he might have noticed the spark in Hrafn's eye as he watched the boy closely, almost worryingly. But Baggi was exhausted, and confused, and didn't notice anything past the Elder Sage's approval. He smiled back, mustering what energy he still possessed, and bowed.

"Thank you, Elder Sage. You honor me," he said, hesitating for a moment before blurting out, "but Elder Sage, I have questions. You see, when I went to touch the sigil carved on Talia, that is, the tailor, she had a skull sigil carved on her collar just like, well, I'm sure you got the details from Hjordis and Elof, or I mean, Alchemist Elof and Staffkeeper Hjordis, but what I really wanted to ask about, well, it's something that nobody really mentioned before and I don't want to worry anybody but if anyone knows it must be you, and so I have to ask, Elder Sage Hrafn: what was that place?"

Hrafn chuckled at Baggi's babbling, but when the boy was finished, the Elder Sage sat down on the creaking wood floor, motioning for Baggi to do the same. He did, sitting directly across from Hrafn. There was silence for some time while Hrafn half-closed his eyes and gathered his thoughts. *I've always admired that,* thought Baggi, *how the Elder Sage takes a moment to think before speaking. Although this is hardly the time.* His nervous energy had turned to restlessness during his Contemplations, and the Elder Sage's patience was proving trying. Finally, Hrafn looked Baggi in the eye and took a deep breath.

"The place you went to was grey and lifeless, and full of bones, if I'm not mistaken?" he asked politely. Baggi nodded. "Yes, the realm you traveled to was Death's domain, the Threshold, as you likely already suspect. But an important distinction must be made here, Baggi. Your body remained here, in Solabell, for the entirety of the ritual."

Baggi nodded again; he had assumed as much. Hjordis had run off to inform Hrafn of the results of the ritual before he had time to gather his thoughts or ask questions, but in spite of this, Baggi reckoned his total disappearance would have at least warranted a mention. *And besides,* he reasoned, *the scratches and dirt on my hands were gone when I found myself back in the korta shop. Which means my body wasn't really there. Or perhaps this body wasn't really there.* He wondered if there was a difference.

"When a Staffkeeper makes tribute to their patron," Hrafn continued, "the offering is taken into that patron's realm. Regardless of what form that tribute may take, be it the fruit of our labor or the blood of a living being, the essence of it makes the journey to their home. Its soul becomes a being distinct from its body. In a way, you underwent the same journey."

Baggi tensed. Although this was not new information, he was beginning to see it in a new light. "Did I...offer myself to Death?"

Hrafn weighed his words carefully. "In a way, you did. With Compromise bridging the gap between, you combined your own aura with Talia's. This essentially branded you as part of the offering, an extension of her. Think of yourself as an extra limb, if it helps," he chuckled lightly. Baggi wasn't sure it did. "It's the only reason you were able to go to her." He paused, allowing the boy to take several calming breaths before continuing. "Luckily, the ritual doesn't end there."

"Had I not been successful," Baggi said slowly, "we both would have been taken." Hrafn's smile faded, taking on a grim sadness.

"Yes," he replied, "that is the risk that we take as Staffkeepers of Shaefi. It's not always as easy as prescribing a potion to cure joint pains." A ghostly smile passed over the Elder Sage's face, a smile that expressed an old, deep pain. "Should your soul, your aura, be consumed by Death, the body is consumed as well. And it is never a graceful offering."

Baggi touched his lips reflexively. "Ove," he breathed in horrible realization. Hrafn nodded.

"Indeed, it is a process you have become unfortunately familiar with," he continued. "Perhaps one day we will find the knowledge to reclaim Ove's soul for Shaefi. But that day has not yet arrived."

"Elder Sage, why did no one warn me? I, well...I could have died. Why is this not taught at Enton?"

"I prefer to have these discussions face to face," Hrafn sighed, "but it seems Staffkeeper Hjordis thought time was of the essence. And furthermore, it seems she trusted in your capability even without preparation. After all, none are ever truly prepared for such a ritual."

The apprentice stewed for several moments as he sorted through his conflicted feelings. *It is nice to be trusted,* he thought, *but even so, my life was at risk. I know Hjordis' judgment can usually be trusted, but with my life? My soul?* Of that he was unsure.

"Baggi," Hrafn interjected, "I know that you must be frightened and worried. But I want you to let those feelings flow through and out of you. Instead, focus on what you felt when you healed Talia. What was that like?"

Baggi did as instructed, relaxing his body and mind and releasing the images of Ove's body, torn asunder, and Talia's corpse, chained to the earth and perpetually dying. He buried instead the fear and hopelessness, then seized Compromise in his hand and in his mind, focusing on the reassuring cool energy from before. *It's still there,* he thought, *just smaller now.* Baggi approached the energy and greeted it with open arms. It enveloped him in the same cacophony of sensations as before: cloudberries, the sun, a bird's song. *How does this feel?* Wondered Baggi. *That's like trying to describe the sky to a blind man. It feels happy,* he tried at first, finding it inadequate. *It feels like home,* he tried again, and that felt a bit closer. *It feels like...*

"My birthday," Baggi realized, aloud, embarrassed by the childishness of his answer. But Elder Sage Hrafn wore a knowing smile, and nodded approvingly.

"Birthdays," he replied carefully, "are among the sweetest days of life. A day repeated once every year, dedicated to the simple joy of living. Few other holidays are so singularly focused on the greatest gift Shaefi has graced us with. From birth, we are gifted life. From life, we offer in return the gift of birth, bringing new life. In this way, the gifting cycle is perpetuated. Shaefi wears these two faces, birth and life, and both are celebrated in the ritual of birthdays. Have no shame, Baggi," he said, and to the boy's great shock, stood and bowed to him. "You have answered most wisely."

Baggi scrambled to his feet and bowed back, making a point of lowering himself deeper than Hrafn had out of respect. When he raised his head, the delighted twinkle was back in Hrafn's eyes.

"Before I go, we should talk business," he said.

"Business?" Baggi's shoulders sagged. "Ah."

"Yes, business," laughed the Elder Sage, the boy's lack of interest not escaping his notice. "Over the course of the next nine days, you will have three Tasks set before you. These Tasks will be presented to you at the sunrise of the first, fourth, and seventh day. You will have the following three days to complete each Task. Should you prove capable, and display devotion to Shaefi in the process, you shall be Marked and gifted a silver brooch as proof of your rank. Do you understand these instructions, Staffkeeper Apprentice Baggi?" Hrafn concluded his description with a mischievous grin.

Baggi's mouth was agape, and he consciously made the effort to close it. *It can't be. Even if I did complete the ritual, even if I did link to Compromise more than once, that doesn't mean I'm ready, does it?* But all at once, Baggi realized that it did. He felt an excited grin grow on his lips, touched them without thinking, then gathered himself and bowed to the Elder Sage once more.

"I understand these instructions, Elder Sage Hrafn. And I pledge to carry out these Tasks to the best of my ability." Unable to contain himself any longer, he looked up and proclaimed, "You won't regret this!"

Elder Sage Hrafn laughed easily. "I know it, my boy, I know it!" Then he turned and left the room, smiling proudly at Baggi one last time as he closed the door.

After he had gone, Baggi sat back down in a euphoric daze. *It's happening,* he thought, *I'm really going to be a full-fledged Staffkeeper! All I must do is carry out my Tasks and in nine days' time, I'll receive my Mark! Even better, my Blessing will manifest!* He began to daydream of the myriad boons Shaefi might see fit to endow him with. *Maybe I'll get sharper senses like Elof! Or perhaps immunity to sickness like Ove has. Had,* he corrected awkwardly. *Who knows? Maybe it will be something to do with plants. I've always wanted to work in the apothecary gardens at Enton!* Baggi chuckled at himself. *Not likely. Look at me, getting carried away already. And I haven't even completed my first Task yet.* He began to consider his more immediate concerns, finding them far less interesting topics. Conveniently, he was distracted from his thoughts by a loud knocking on the door.

"Baggi, I'm coming in!" he heard Kettil shout from the other side, before immediately throwing the door open.

Baggi began laughing at Kettil's impatience, then found himself unable to stop as the laughs grew louder and more manic. He felt the last dregs of Death drain from his body as the tension he had been holding was finally released.

"What? What happened? Are you okay?" Kettil asked, scrunching her features with confusion and a dash of concern.

"Yes, yes, I'm fine, Kettil," Baggi managed after a moment. "In fact, I'm better than fine. I'm to receive my Staffkeeper Tasks starting tomorrow!"

Kettil's jaw dropped. "What, really? And it's about time, right? This is so exciting! What's your first one?" she gushed, "If we get a head start now, maybe you can finish early and have some extra time to explore the village with me!"

"I don't think it's the kind of test you can finish early, Kettil," Baggi yawned, "but I gladly accept your help. Only thing is, I won't receive my first Task until sunrise, and I can hardly stand. So we shall get to it first thing in the morning." Baggi stretched out on his bedroll, suddenly unable to keep his eyes open.

"Alright! Let's do this! We gotta tell the whole village about this! You're gonna be a Staffkeeper of Shaefi! And you're only fourteen!"

"Assuming I complete the Tasks, yes," Baggi replied with as much humility as he could muster.

"The only thing I'm confused about," Kettil mused as she bolted out without bothering to shut the door, "is if the ritual earlier is what did it for you, where's my promotion?"

***

At sunrise, Baggi heard a knock on the door. He had been awake for what felt like hours, nervous energy building inside him, gaining weight and speed like a snowball rolling downhill. *My first Task*, he thought, *should be fairly easy. But I can't make any assumptions. Naturally, it will be representative of one of Shaefi's domains and the corresponding teachings. All I must do is remember those lessons and take them to heart. Now that I think of it, it might be wise to fit some early*

Contemplations in before I receive the Task. So he had, simultaneously awake and dreaming in Contemplation. For as long as he could, he had turned over the teachings in his mind, reexamining them in an almost desperate bid for fresh insight. Ultimately, none came, but as always the Contemplations left Baggi feeling well balanced. Now he arose, fully dressed and perhaps overprepared. The other apprentices were heavy sleepers (how couldn't they be, living in a caravan?) so he stepped carefully over them and turned the opened the door.

Elder Sage Hrafn stood before him, smiling, and silently motioned for Baggi to follow. The apprentice bowed in the Shaefini tradition and followed. Hrafn led him out of the inn, back toward the main road they and the rest of the Shaefini had arrived on. A guard, not the same one from the previous day though just as young, graciously parted the gates enough for the duo to squeeze through. Outside of Flamebud's borders, perhaps a quarter mile of open prairie separated the tree line from the walls. Sunlight crept along the land like a provocateur, slowly, sensually. Hrafn stood in the middle of the road and motioned for Baggi to stand abreast of him.

They remained still for many minutes as the light approached. Hrafn's eyes were closed, and he seemed to be in a state of bliss. Baggi felt a surge of impatience, and immediately chastised himself for it, deciding to take after Hrafn's example and closing his eyes. He listened to the early birdsong, light and sweet, if a bit loud and inconsiderate of its neighbors. The music fell on his ears like a sun shower, tingling and warm; in it he heard quiet dignity, the stubbornly optimistic love of a mother imagining what today may hold in the moment before she wakes her son. He saw his own mother, standing over his bed with such pride and joy but also a touch of loss, on the morning he had departed Jolk for the Temple at Enton. He felt sunlight on his face and heard the Elder Sage speak.

"Staffkeeper Apprentice Baggi, your first Task is to stand beneath the night sky and feel the warmth of the sun on your face. Do this, and you will know the warmth of Shaefi. Do you understand these instructions?" Hrafn was more serious than the apprentice had ever seen him before, excepting the day they had lost Ove, yet the Elder Sage still possessed an air of kindness. Baggi felt a keen desire to impress him and shook the feeling off the moment he noticed its presence. *That's just pride*, he thought. *Are you going to be a Staffkeeper, or aren't you?* He opened his eyes and was surprised to find tears running down his face.

"Elder Sage Hrafn, I understand these instructions. I will carry them out in the name of Shaefi," he recited.

Elder Sage Hrafn smiled proudly at him. The ceremony was over.

"It gladdens me to hear that," he said. "But before you begin, stand with me in the sun awhile."

Baggi smiled back and nodded. They both closed their eyes, faces turned toward the rising sun, and felt warmth.

***

"So what does it mean?" asked Kettil, her mouth full, after Baggi had returned to the Flamebud Inn and described his first Task over a breakfast of wheat porridge and eggs.

"I have no idea," said Baggi as he pushed the porridge idly around his bowl. "Obviously, it seems impossible at first. But that's the whole point, I think. There's some trick to it, some kind of riddle I must unravel."

"You're in luck, 'cause I'm really good at riddles," Kettil boasted, nudging him in the ribs playfully. "Like this one time, at Enton, this kid had everybody with this one: 'it has four hanging, four walking, two pointing, two to fight dogs, and'...wait, was it two for flight from dogs? Or just two for flying?" She frowned and rubbed her temples, struggling to remember. "Hmm...well anyway, the answer was a cow with an unborn litter! Pretty clever, huh?" She concluded, beaming.

Baggi laughed and tussled her hair. "Very wise. Does the riddle master have any insight on my Task? Or are farmyard riddles more your specialty?"

"While I do specialize in animal riddles," she replied seriously, "no puzzle is too great for riddle master Kettil." Baggi was unsure if she was joking. He offered a polite laugh to be safe.

"I thought the night sky might be a mislead," Baggi began, "and the challenge is more about feeling the sun without its physical presence. What do you think of that?"

"Hmm, yes, yes, a mislead, could be..." Kettil mumbled, looking more focused than Baggi had ever seen her before. "Then again, it could be a double mislead. Elder Sage Hrafn is a tricky one, after all. There's a reason his staff is called Mischief." Her eyes went wide with sudden realization. "But wait! What if he figured that we would figure that he would double mislead us, and went for the triple? This goes deeper than I thought, Baggi!"

Baggi was beginning to question the wisdom of collaborating with a ten-year-old on the most important assignment of his life when a different thought occurred to him. *Or maybe it's not that complicated and we're overthinking it.* Kettil was busy talking herself into circles, so Baggi decided to let her work through it as he ate. *Perhaps I should speak to Hjordis. She may not be permitted to solve it for me, but she can at least give me some advice. I'd like to ask some questions about the ritual last night anyway.* Kettil seemed to be sputtering out as Baggi finished his porridge. He explained his plan as they stood up from their stump-table and clasped their cloaks with the simple wooden ring all apprentices used as fastenings. *In nine days time,* he thought, *I'll have a real brooch. My very own Staffkeeper's Mark.*

A quick scan of the inn's common room revealed several apprentices wolfing down breakfast, two Staffkeepers taking notes and assigning chores, and Torny jogging back and forth between kitchen and table with tray after tray of porridge and eggs. His mentor was nowhere to be seen. A sudden mischief occurred to Baggi. He looked about himself, making sure no senior Staffkeepers or alchemists were within earshot, before whispering to Kettil.

"You know, Kettil, finding her would be a lot faster if we had a clear vantage point over the village," he said all-too innocently.

Kettil picked up on his plan right away, her lips twisting into an impertinent smile. "I think you're right, Baggi. But where, oh, where will we find one of those?"

"Well, it occurs to me that a crow's nest has been constructed atop this very building."

"Amund probably doesn't want us up there distracting his watchman."

"Mm, probably not."

Defying wisdom both intellectual and practical, they immediately left via the backdoor and approached the knotty rope ladder dangling down the side of the Flamebud Inn. While Baggi had spent the previous evening recovering, Kettil had been restlessly pacing the grounds of the inn. It hadn't taken her long to spot the ladder, and it had taken even less time for her to loudly proclaim its presence to Baggi over breakfast. It seemed the guard up top preferred to leave the ladder hanging rather than keeping it rolled up atop the platform. No, rather than take that basic precaution, a plank of wood had been nailed to the exterior wall of the inn next to the ladder with the words "Do not climb! Only guard allowed!" engraved in Sparktongue. *Sometimes children can be much smarter than people give them credit for*, thought Baggi, *and other times they do things like this.*

He gestured politely for Kettil to go first. "After you."

She bowed back dramatically. "That's very kind, good sir," she replied in an exaggerated noble caricature. Then she leaped at the rope ladder in the frenzied, energetic manner all children share and all nobles lack. Baggi waited a moment before slinging his staff across his back and following her up.

About halfway to the top, Baggi began to doubt his plan. He had never actually climbed a rope ladder before and was troubled to find it much harder than it looked. Every time he lifted his foot to take another step, the ladder pulled away from him and he was left dangling pathetically until he could wrangle the next one. Baggi made the mistake of glancing down and swallowed hard. The ground looked far less inviting from a height, and he had never been fond of falling. *Come on, Baggi, get ahold of yourself!* He urged. *Are you going to be a Staffkeeper or aren't you? Besides, Kettil is doing simply fine. If she can do it, so can you!*

In fact, Kettil had outpaced him easily and was approaching the top as he passed the halfway point. She looked back down and saw Baggi below her, shooting him a look chockful of impatience and a pinch of confusion. Baggi suddenly stopped feeling afraid and started feeling very silly. He chuckled and began climbing slightly faster.

Kettil pulled herself onto the platform as Baggi caught up, and he followed suit. The crow's nest was not huge, and there was hardly room to stand between Kettil, the open ledge, and the very confused boy sitting on a stool in front of them. The guard looked for a moment like he might scream, then reached a sluggish hand toward a large brass bell hanging on the central post. Baggi noted with intrigue that although the boy appeared to be consumed by panic, his hand was still reaching out at an infuriatingly slow pace. After allowing the boy several seconds, Baggi felt the strange urge to ring the bell himself and get it over with. Instead, he reached out his own hand to cover the bell. It could technically be said that the apprentice moved faster, although in truth he moved without hurry. Still, the boy seemed amazed by his reflexes, shrinking back in fear. *He even cowers slowly,* Baggi thought with equal parts amazement and pity. *Why in Shaefi's name would Amund make him their lookout?* He shot the boy a disarming smile and held up his hands in a universal gesture of peace.

"Easy, friend," he said in Sparktongue, "we mean you no harm. My friend and I simply needed to find someone, and we thought it might be easier from up here. After all, this is without a doubt the highest point in the village. And such fine construction! Nothing to fear from a post this stable!" Baggi knocked on the central post jokingly to illustrate his point, alarmed to hear the wood groan in response. *Ignoring that.*

The boy opened his mouth and, after several awkward moments, began to speak. "Who...are...you..."

"I am Staffkeeper Apprentice Baggi, and this is-"

"Two?" the guard finished.

"Like I said, I am Staffkeeper Apprentice Baggi, and this is Alchemist Apprentice Kettil. Who are you?" Baggi tried again, his smile tightening a bit. The boy's features seized in fright with the speed of a lame goat.

"A...Staff...keeper? D-d-d-d....don't....hurt...me..."

"I won't, my friend, no ne-"

"Please," the guard finished. Baggi's smile once again tightened.

"Perhaps you can just listen, and respond when we're done speaking. How does that sound?" he said, stifling the urge to sigh. The boy stared at him, wide-eyed, before nodding. "We're looking for a girl, nineteen, with black hair and blue eyes. Another Staffkeeper, with a cloak like mine. Have you seen anyone like that around?"

The guard considered this for a long time, giving Baggi a chance to observe him. He wore plain grey trousers, a brick-colored tunic, and a triangular cap with a red hawk's feather sticking out. He had an aquiline nose and a round face that, despite his current mood, seemed well suited to smiles. The boy looked about Baggi's age, though his fidgety behavior and temperament gave him pause. *Hard to say if he's younger than I am, or just more nervous.* He touched his lips and stifled a laugh. *He and Elof would make a memorable team, if they ever worked up the courage to say hello.* The watcher finished thinking and shook his head. Baggi's shoulders slumped.

"Well, if you see her, let us know right away please," he replied, turning away to scan Flamebud himself.

The post offered a privileged view of Flamebud Village, and from the height Baggi saw something that had escaped his notice from ground level. Or rather, he saw many somethings that had no doubt been deliberately hidden away from travelers and other suspicious folk: atop each and every shop and home in Flamebud lay an array of vibrant rooftop gardens. There were wooden planter boxes of all shapes and sizes, as varied as the crops growing within: some houses were topped by tall stalks of grain, like porcupines curled up tightly; others more strongly resembled tortoises, the vines and root vegetables growing low and clinging tightly to their homes as if to protect the roof from danger. Baggi's eyes widened in delight as he took it all in. After mere seconds, the voice of the watcher broke his reverie. He jumped a bit at the unexpected obtrusion.

"There...she's...going...toward...the for...est," the boy drawled, lifting a hand carefully to point toward the edge of the village.

Baggi cast his gaze towards the village border and was pleasantly surprised. Hjordis was, indeed, leaving the village with Elof. Or rather, she was attempting to coax the alchemist into leaving the village with her. Elof was clearly uncomfortable, dragging his feet and turning back constantly. *Ah, now I see,* Baggi thought as he regarded the boy with newfound respect, *He's slow of speech, but quick of sight.*

"Good eye. Where are they going?" wondered Baggi aloud.

"I dunno," replied Kettil, leaning dangerously far over the railing until Baggi gently pulled her back by the cloak, "but we can probably just ask 'em."

"True enough," he agreed. "Let's be on our way then. Thank you, eh...what was your name, friend?" He asked the guard. The boy looked surprised but a friendly smile crept over his face.

"My...name...is...Aghi," he beamed.

"Well met, Aghi. Thank you for your help. If you ever need treatment, don't hesitate to ask," Baggi said.

"I....won't....hes....it...ate," replied Aghi. He gave the duo an undulating salute and yawned.

Baggi and Kettil left Aghi in the crow's nest, descending carefully. It was much easier on the way down, as every step brought nearer familiar and stable ground. *Maybe I could get used to this after all,* Baggi thought, at nearly the same point he had almost given up on the ascent. Kettil, naturally, was already at the bottom. Children were like that, always doing before they had the chance to realize they were scared. *Strange,* he reflected, *how we are at our most fearless when we are also at our weakest. Growing and learning should mean greater safety and confidence. Adults can overpower and outsmart children, after all. And yet, adults are the ones with the greatest fear in their hearts. And soon, I'll be one of them. I wonder what the fear in my heart will feel like.*

Baggi thought sometimes that he could feel the fear growing already. It seemed to be part and parcel of growing up.

Kettil was tapping her foot in exaggerated impatience. "You sure took your time," she said.

"Perhaps I was trying to teach you a lesson in patience," he replied defensively. Kettil huffed.

"Staffkeepers," she said, and left it at that.

Outside the walls of Flamebud Village, both peered into shaded foliage. The path Hjordis and Elof had taken was visible; that boded well. If they weren't attempting to cover their trail, it meant they intended to return shortly. *Still,* Baggi thought uneasily as he held Compromise tight, *this is a foreign wilderness. Kichishi is known to be home to many fearsome beasts. Who knows what monstrous horrors lurk in these woods?* A light brown rabbit hopped unhurriedly along the path, crinkling its nose at them curiously before hopping away once more. *Perhaps I'm being overcautious,* he granted. He took a deep breath and released the tension in his shoulders.

"Shall we then?" he asked.

"You first this time," Kettil replied, "in case you need to defend us."

Baggi frowned. "Defend us? What, from an animal?"

"Yes! Or maybe a bad Staffkeeper or a local that hates our types or something! Anything could happen."

"I'm less concerned with those possibilities" he replied, "than I am with your misconception of my ability. If we did run into danger, what would you expect me to do?"

Kettil rolled her eyes and adopted the tone of a teacher explaining simple logic to a toddler. Given that he was her elder, this was especially irritating. "Perhaps you could use some magic?" Baggi reminded himself that Kettil meant no offense.

"I really do regret being the one to inform you of this," he began with a frown, "but as a Staffkeeper of Shaefi my self-defense options are limited. We don't fight, remember? The best I can do is invoke a rune to help me convince something not to hurt us, and even then-" he said, beginning to slip into lecture mode.

"Yes, perfect, do that!" Kettil interjected, nudging him forward. Baggi released the sigh he had been holding onto since their conversation with Aghi and did as he was told.

Stepping forward into the brush, Baggi was struck once more by how very different Kichishi's wilderness was from the northern lands'. Back home, in Naefja, the mountain grasses and trees were dark and green, the flowers blue and purple. Bird song was common in the morning, especially from the nightingale, and wild boar roamed the passes, free from human predation by virtue of their friendship with Shaefi. Snow-covered cloudberries provided an air of good-natured secrecy, their fruit indistinguishable from the frost to any but the native Naefjan eye. Even on the massive cave roads, where one traveling through might not see sunlight for days at a time, the blue-white glow of cave lichen and fungus lighted the way, hopeful reminders of the comforts that awaited travelers at the other end. The land had its own character, as all land does, and that character was grounded in the joyful and brisk.

The forest Baggi looked upon now was nothing like that. The trees and bushes were green, true, but even there the similarities began to waver. Here, the leaves were lightly colored and ferns plentiful. Their limbs stretched impatiently up towards the light, an endless bounty they were spoiled on by the clear and sunny skies. The animals, too, seemed desperately short on time. He saw squirrels, apparently too busy to bother descending their trees, leaping between branches, then spreading their arms and gliding through the air. They wasted no time in scrambling around the tree the moment their paws touched down. He marveled openly as they leapt overhead. Nearby the apprentices heard bird song, but it was an unfamiliar tune. The singer seemed tightly wound, their call shrill. *Somebirdy is having a bad day,* Baggi thought, and resolved to never speak those words aloud. He was happy to note that the forest floor here was dry and hard, a welcome change from tromping through the snow back home.

Beside him, Kettil was focused on the ground. She hummed thoughtfully.

"What are you doing?" he asked.

"Looking for tracks. They weren't here that long ago, so it should be easy to find."

"But Kettil, there's a trail here."

"We don't know if they stayed on the path!" she replied, looking aghast. "In all the stories, they always check for tracks when they're trying to find someone. Maybe Hjordis went off into the woods on an adventurous impulse."

"That does sound like something she would do," Baggi agreed, "but for now why don't we take the trail? If they're not at the end of it, then all we've lost is some time and not our way."

Kettil reluctantly tore her gaze away from an inscrutable patch of dirt and nodded. Baggi led the way down the footpath, using Compromise as a walking stick. He got the impression that it liked the feeling of the ground beneath. He almost felt like another friend was walking alongside them. It was difficult to explain, but Baggi saw his staff as more or less a faithful companion or pet. Only, that pet also contained a fragment of the owner's soul and housed immense magical power. Whether it be pet or tool, Baggi reckoned it wise to pamper away, though this habit sometimes gave cause for the other apprentices to looked at him strangely when, for example, he stroked

Compromise or arranged the staff in what he assumed would be a comfortable position. Never having been a staff himself, Baggi was unsure if his efforts were in vain, but he still felt it was the right thing to do.

A splash of color caught Baggi's eye as they walked. He held up a hand in front of Kettil. A monkey was climbing its way out of a small clearing nearby, clutching a rich crimson flower. Baggi and Kettil looked at each other curiously, then reached a silent agreement. They began creeping off the path and towards the clearing. As they approached, the air began to feel warmer and drier. Baggi wiped sweat from his forehead and frowned. *I'm going to be drenched by the time we find them. It's unseemly.* He glanced over at Kettil, who was perspiring even more yet seemed not to notice, so fixated was she on their quest. He thought his own worries foolish then and realized, not for the first time, that he could learn a lot from the little girl. She pushed back a leafy branch and gasped loudly. Baggi, alarmed, rushed to peer over her shoulder, but froze in his tracks when he beheld the sight in front of him.

The clearing was on fire. A large, oblong pool of shining red and orange flames licked the air, flashing and twisting like a sword dancer. Baggi felt waves of heat washing over them now, sweat pouring down his face. He raised an arm to shield himself from the heat. *A forest fire!* He thought. *This could be disastrous. Better take care of it before someone or something gets burned.* There was no time to warn Kettil. Fire was a dangerous and unpredictable force, and every second was paramount. Baggi bowed his head and linked to Compromise, focusing intently on the coolness flowing from the runes. He closed his eyes and let the cold fill him up, wrapping him in ice and snow thick as his mother's quilts, until the warmth of the fire was entirely forgotten.

Then he raised his head, filled his lungs to their limit, and invoked a rune.

"Isaz," Baggi blustered, and breathed freezing mist over the clearing.

Kettil shrank back and wrapped her cloak tighter as the cold air settled over the clearing, dousing the flames under a fine dusting of snow. Steam sizzled as the ground settled back into the unassailable stillness of raw earth. He exhaled the rest of the icy storm and began hyperventilating painfully, trying in vain to force the freezing air from his lungs. Isaz was a universally useful rune, adaptable to countless situations. It had even been one of his brother Bjorn's preferred runes, hence its placement near the crown of Compromise's haft, but as to why exactly it had been his favorite Baggi felt he would never understand. *I hate this,* he thought as he desperately tried to force warm air from the surrounding forest into his lungs. *Being cold on the outside is one thing, but this is just insufferable. I feel like I need a hot mug of spiced cream, or perhaps a few mugs.* He was suddenly very cold, the sweat running down his neck now an icy mountain creek. Reeling but relieved, the apprentice collected himself and turned back to Kettil.

"Well, that should suffice," he said, trying to sound casual through chattering teeth.

"Uhh...Baggi? Sorry to soak your socks, but..." she gestured apologetically toward the clearing.

To his immense fascination, the snow was melting at a rapid pace, steam once again billowing up in thick languid clouds. As Baggi and Kettil looked on, the snow made way for a patch of flowers where the fire had been. They were striped red and orange, with six petals and pistils reaching up, claw-like, in the shape of a flame; they seemed, in fact, to be well and truly alight.

Baggi felt the touch of fear and reluctantly began to fill his lungs again.

"Wait a second!" Kettil said as she tugged at his cloak. "Something's not right."

Baggi agreed and released the breath normally, more than happy to take her advice if it meant avoiding another lungful of freezing air. He stifled his unease and focused on their shared curiosity instead. As they watched, the flowers began to slowly slough off the cold dust coating them and stand erect. And then, amazingly, they started to glow. It was soft at first, just a pale marigold light that convinced Baggi for one foolish moment that perhaps fireflies made their homes inside them, but then they began to glow brighter and he felt warmth creep into the clearing once more. Baggi saw now that the circle of fire had been directly atop these flowers. *Did they start a fire? Or perhaps...they were the fire?* He shot Kettil a stupid look and saw the same realization dawning on her.

"Flamebud," he said simply.

"Right," she replied with pursed lips. Then they both laughed at their own foolishness. "And you were gonna freeze them again! I can't believe we thought flowers were a fire!"

"Hey, to be fair," Baggi wheezed between laughs, "they look an awful lot like flames, and we're obviously not the only ones to think so!"

Their laughs died down gradually, awkwardly, as they found themselves transfixed. The warm glow of the Flamebuds washed over them, volcanic waves on an ocean of dust. Baggi felt something stir within him, a comfortable feeling. It reminded him of...*what? What is this feeling?* It was at once foreign and familiar, invigorating and relaxing. He struggled to find its name, found the words eluded him. *Ah well,* he thought, *I suppose there's nothing for it but to look.*

They drank in the heat, feeling the sweltering influence of the Flamebuds as they swayed gently in the breeze. Each time the breeze rolled through the clearing, a whirl of crimson belied the impression of fire, loud and arrogant. Yet beholding the flowers themselves betrayed their true nature. They saw the life, the energy splashing about and above. They saw the sunlight, caught and reflected and enhanced a thousand times in the undulating mass of color, so bright as to shame true fire. In it all, Baggi recognized the sun. For a moment, he was standing on the road with Elder Sage Hrafn once more, eyes closed in rapturous appreciation. And then he was back, looking at the Flamebuds. Baggi tore his gaze from the flowers with great force of will.

"We should probably be on our way then," he said to Kettil, ever so gently.

She turned to him, wearing the face of one betrayed. Then she nodded her head lightly and said, with reluctance, "We probably should."

Baggi and Kettil slowly turned away from the clearing and made their way back to the path. Neither spoke another word for a long time.

5

When walking through the woods, it is near impossible to ignore the mysteries of nature. Many have tried to define the forest in human terms, describing to the best of their ability and arranging the behaviors of plants and animals into neat categories with shared traits and behaviors. Yet this is a gross misrepresentation of nature. As any child strolling through could see, the woods, and to an extent all of nature, is full of wildness and spastic energy. To define nature in human terms is misguided at best, gravely insulting at worst. Elk have no interest in what exactly makes them an elk; they are content to be it. Trees are almost certainly not proponents of such categorization and actively resist intellectualization; after all, the material on which human knowledge is recorded is harvested from their flesh. Their obstinance is only natural.

It is the will of Shaefi that all such life, from tree to elk and everything in between, be savored, no matter how small or insignificant that life may seem when judged by the human scientific standard. So it was that Baggi found himself unable to smash the bright red ants that scrambled up his ankles in relentless assault. The forest surrounding Flamebud seemed to be full of the pests, and what's more, they were aggressive. His ankles itching and inflamed, he forced yet another calming breath and gently swept them off. Beside him, Kettil patted his back. She seemed to pity his situation, being seemingly immune to the ants' advances. *That doesn't even make sense,* Baggi thought, annoyed, *if anything, she should be easier to split into ant-sized pieces since she's smaller. These creatures are stupidly ambitious.*

Disregarding the insects' incursions, he found the walk to be quite pleasant. The woods were good to them, providing equal parts sun and shade, and the songbirds were eager to perform for their visitors. The trail was winding and long, and after half an hour Baggi started to wonder if Hjordis and Elof hadn't left the path some time before. Then Kettil stopped in her tracks and cocked her head to one side.

"D'you hear that?" she asked. Baggi stood still and listened. Nearby, deeper in the tree line, he heard a soft exchange of words. *Sounds like Flowspeak alright. I guess I wasn't too far off.*

"It sounds like we found them," he replied. Kettil motioned for him to go first. He rolled his silver eyes half-jokingly and stepped off the path.

It didn't take long to follow the sounds to the source. As they approached, the duo began to parse out words from the conversation.

"...that I was right?" It sounded like Hjordis.

"...just....the principle of the thing..." Naturally, Elof sounded nervous. But there was also a playfulness to his tone that Baggi had never heard before. Something about it made the apprentice uncomfortable. As they crept closer, more of their elders' conversation became audible.

"...principles..like me...that's my job, remember?" She continued.

"Believe it or not, I remember," he replied, then began to softly laugh; they both did.

Baggi turned to Kettil and frowned. She seemed equally taken aback. *Elof doesn't giggle,* he thought. *In fact, I don't think I've ever heard him laugh even once. He's always too tense for humor.* He raised a finger to his lips, indicating silence. Kettil nodded, and they began creeping closer as quietly as possible.

"Hey, Elof."

Hjordis sounded suddenly melancholy.

"What is it?"

"Do you remember what it was like?"

There was a long pause.

"I do."

"Tell me, please."

An even longer pause this time. It seemed Elof wouldn't answer. Baggi felt his heart beating rapidly and hoped they hadn't been spotted.

"It was ugly and wonderful," he sighed, a strange yearning in his voice. "It was childhood."

Baggi felt the words washing over him, felt the grief that he had never known Elof held. *What was?* He thought. *Are they talking about Elof's upbringing?* Baggi realized that he knew next to nothing about the Shaefini Alchemist, not where he had been born, or when he had discovered alchemy, or even why he had joined the Order. He approached the small clearing, perhaps half the size of where they had found the Flamebuds, and peered through a bush. Baggi felt his insides twist up strangely as he beheld them. Elof was sitting on a small white boulder, seemingly lost in recollection. His face was blank, devoid of the constant twitching he was so prone to, and Hjordis was hugging him from behind, her head on his shoulder, looking for all the world like she was the one who needed comforting. He absentmindedly reached up and laid a hand on hers. Baggi touched his lips by reflex. His fingers were shaking. *We shouldn't be seeing this,* he thought, inexplicably certain of it. He felt his limbs go weak and accidentally rustled the shrub he was hiding behind. *Well, that's it then,* he thought with sudden clarity, *my life is over.*

Elof's head snapped towards the shrub and he leaped to his feet, the sudden upset nearly knocking Hjordis over behind him. He threw one shaky arm out in front of her, his other hand reaching into his cloak and procuring a flask with roiling, stormy contents. He looked ready to cry as it trembled in his hand.

"Who goes there?" he yelped, voice unsteady. Baggi cursed himself internally, pinched the bridge of his nose, and took a deep breath. Then he stood up, hands raised in surrender.

"Oh, hey, Elof, Hjordis. There you are," Baggi said pathetically. Beside him Kettil shot up with less tact.

"Hey, it's me, Kettil! I'm here too, 'cept you wouldn't have even known it if Baggi hadn't given us away!" she beamed proudly.

"Yes, thank you, Kettil," Baggi mumbled, nudging her just a bit too hard in the ribs.

Elof visibly slumped as relief took him. "Oh thank Shaefi," he said, trying to control his breathing as he doubled over weakly. "Just a moment, please. I thought...surrounded by the unknown....well, anyway, I'm glad it's just you two."

Hjordis was being uncharacteristically reserved, Baggi noted, perhaps even embarrassed. Her usually pale face was now vibrant red, though slowly calming to pink, and she was avoiding their gaze. *What's going on?* Baggi wondered. The knot in his stomach wouldn't go away, but he couldn't figure out why. *I don't want to know,* he thought, surprised and confused by his own answer. Baggi was all at once paradoxically aware of how very little he understood. The realization was shameful. He tried to shake the feeling off but found it too tenacious. *What's wrong with me? What's happening?* He cleared his throat to break the uncomfortable silence.

"So, umm…"

"Right, so…" Hjordis trailed off in response. Elof, luckily, had recovered from the fright and, even more luckily, seemed not to notice the strange tension.

"You ought not to be out here," he said with concern, "and really, neither should we." He shot Hjordis a pointed look. She shrugged and sent back an embarrassed grin. Baggi felt discomfort override all sense of decorum.

"Well, it's obviously a bit late for that, but thank you for the warning," he mumbled, and immediately chastised himself. *What are you doing? These are your friends.* Elof looked hurt, then realization seemed to dawn on him and his features softened.

"Baggi," he inquired gingerly, "is everything alright? The ritual must have been, ah…" he momentarily struggled for words. "…difficult. Would you like to talk about it?"

"Oh, right!" Baggi blurted out, seizing on the opportunity. "Yes, the ritual was trying. I apologize for my tone, I must still be on edge. But we came out here to seek my mentor's guidance." Seeing the sympathetic faces turned toward him, Baggi breathed an internal sigh of relief. *It's the truth, after all,* he thought. *Must be. Why else would I feel like this?*

Hjordis smiled a little too wide, attempting to compensate for the momentary discomfort. "Well here I am, and ready to listen! Tell your elder what's bothering you and I'll set you straight." Normally, her teasing tone would have been charming. Right now, Baggi obstinately heard condescension instead.

"Actually," he replied, stiff, "now that I think about it, it's probably more a question for Alchemist Elof. If I may request your audience?" Baggi bowed in the formal manner toward Elof, who for his part looked equally confused, flattered, and amused. He graciously returned the bow.

"Of course, Staffkeeper Apprentice Baggi," he said, also taking the formal tone. "Shall we stroll?"

"Uhh, excuse me? What am I supposed to do while you're off playing in the woods?" Kettil asked, wrinkling her nose.

"Not now, Kettil. I'm sure you and Hjordis can find something to talk about," Baggi replied, and began to walk back into the woods, hoping it looked decisive and mature.

Elof looked at the girls, baffled, then shrugged and followed, glancing here and there at every rustle and trill on the way. After a moment he was gone, and Kettil was left alone with Hjordis. The younger girl sighed and started grumbling inarticulately. Hjordis threw an arm around her shoulder and tousled her hair.

"Don't worry, Kettil, this is a perfect opportunity for us to get to know each other better."

Kettil rolled her eyes, not bothering to hide her distaste. "I can't wait."

Hjordis made the deliberate choice not to take offense. "So, young one, what do you like to do for fun?" she inquired politely.

Kettil turned to her with brazen challenge written on her face. "Know any good riddles?"

"Hmm...how about this one: "I am not alive, but I grow; I don't have lungs, but I need air; I-

"Fire," Kettil said before she finished. She plopped down on the boulder where Elof had been sitting before. "Try a harder one. And if it has farm animals in it, all the better."

"Right," replied Hjordis, wracking her brain and grinding her teeth, "give me a moment..."

***

Elof was quiet as they walked. Baggi wondered what he was thinking, coming up with nothing that could feasibly be called realistic. *It was just a hug. Why do you even care? I mean, you've probably hugged Elof before, too,* he thought, failing to convince even himself. He felt nauseous as the decision to ask about what they had seen turned over and over again like a picky hound laying by the fire, never quite settling on one side. Before he could make up his mind, Elof drew his attention.

"Baggi, come quick!" he hissed.

"What is it?" Baggi asked as he hurried over to where Elof was kneeling. The alchemist pointed to a small patch of grass, ever so slightly discolored compared to its surroundings. He looked at Baggi with astonished excitement, as if waiting for a reaction. "Umm...Elof? What am I looking at?"

Elof looked stricken for a moment, then stuttered "Oh, yes, I forget that you're a Staffkeeper sometimes. Well, I mean, not that you don't seem like a Staffkeeper, it's just, ah, you spend so much time, free time, with Kettil, sometimes I forget you're not an alchemist too." Any other day, Baggi would have taken it as a compliment, but this was not any other day.

"I see. And therefore, you will have to explain it to me, right?" he prodded as gently as he could.

"Of course," Elof responded apologetically. "You see how this grass here is dryer than that surrounding?" He waited for Baggi to observe and nod. "This is a rare subspecies, Creeping Kindling, so called because it spreads slowly through its neighbors, draining the moisture and inviting wildfire. However, if harvested, dried, ground, and properly employed in alchemical formulae, its potent moisture-draining properties can be put to medicinal use. It seems Hjordis was right after all; these woods are full of valuable resources."

Baggi momentarily forgot his frustrations as Elof spoke. He spoke with reverence and enthusiasm, without a trace of his usual skittishness. *I'm seeing a different side of Elof today,* he thought, *though I wonder if it really is him, and not a confident imposter.* His companion unhooked a folding trowel from the belt across his chest and began carefully extracting the patch from the ground, digging much deeper than seemed necessary to Baggi. *But what do I know? I never did get to work in the garden.*

"How did you recognize it? We don't grow it at Enton, do we?" he asked.

"Ah, well, when I was young, that is, younger, around Kettil's age, I spent a lot of time out of doors," Elof stammered. His discomfort with the subject was clear. "Not by choice," he added at Baggi's baffled expression, "but more out of necessity. Or, perhaps, out of fear." He looked embarrassed and rubbed the back of his neck. "But you undoubtedly don't want to hear about all that."

As he switched the trowel for a small, stiff-bristled brush and began separating the blades from the soil, Elof glanced Baggi's way.

"So, ah, Baggi, as I understand, you wish to receive advice? I may not possess a Sage's wisdom, but I am happy to help." He began delicately placing the blades into a glass vial, one at a time.

"That's just what I was hoping to hear," Baggi replied. "For you see," he hesitated a moment, unsure of how to broach the topic without boasting and even less sure if he wanted to do so, "I have received my Tasks."

Elof nearly dropped the vial, his surprise was so great. "Oh my! Oh! Well! I don't know what to say!" he stammered kindly. "Except congratulations, of course! Well done!" Baggi smiled and bowed humbly, feeling sillier by the minute for his misgivings.

"Thank you, Elof, you honor me."

"May I inquire, or, of course, if it's too personal, I understand, naturally, but if that isn't the case, well, I am curious, ah, what your first Task is." In his effort to be polite, the alchemist's nervous speech habits increased in frequency. Baggi made a mental note to Contemplate this later.

"Actually, that's exactly what I needed advice for. My first Task is:" he cleared his throat and paused dramatically before rumbling, in his most wizened Hrafn impression, "Stand beneath the night sky and feel the warmth of the sun on your face."

Elof chuckled softly at the delivery. "That seems a pleasant start. What, ah, seems to be the problem?"

"Well," he replied, certain now that he was overlooking something obvious, "at night, how am I supposed to feel the sun? Isn't that impossible?"

"Ah! I see the confusion now," Elof said. "Um, as you know, I am not, ah, allowed to teach you, exactly, the lessons required for your Tasks' completion. It's not my choice, naturally," he added in haste. "The idea is to test whether you have truly understood and internalized the teachings of Shaefi." Baggi's shoulder's slumped. "Luckily," he continued, "giving hints is a grey area. So I do believe I will be pardoned for saying this: You're right, that is, insofar as feeling the sun. But your Task was to feel it's warmth, isn't that correct?" He painstakingly slid the last blade of Creeping Kindling into the vial and corked it, then tucked it into his cloak and stood up.

"Is there a distinction?" Baggi asked carefully. Elof grinned at him.

"I'm afraid that is all you need, and thus, all I can give you."

Baggi expected frustration, and was instead surprised to find a sense of calm confidence suffusing him. *He's right,* he thought, *I can figure this out. Am I going to be a Staffkeeper, or aren't I?* He bowed earnestly.

"Thank you for your wisdom, Alchemist Elof. I will consider these words," he said.

"You honor me, Staffkeeper Apprentice Baggi," Elof replied, likewise reciting the Shaefini formalities. "Although, soon it will be Staffkeeper Baggi who honors me."

"Yes, soon it will be," Baggi grinned. "Well then, shall we go?"

"Oh, yes, certainly. Those two are no doubt running out of things to talk about by now."

***

" "My tines be long, my tines be short"," Hjordis began.

"Lightning," Kettil cut her off, languishing on the warm boulder with an arm thrown dramatically over her face.

"Alright, how about this: "If a man carried my burden he would break his back. I am not big- "

"Snail," the apprentice drawled.

Hjordis pushed down the urge to sigh, though the urge to scream was not so easily dismissed. It was exceptionally difficult to find a moment alone with any one person when travelling in a caravan, and she had spent far too much time and effort getting Elof away from the village for the apprentices to thwart her now. *Calm down,* she thought, *they didn't know. How could they? Baggi just wanted our help. What kind of loon would get upset over that?* She turned away from Kettil and began pacing, twirling her staff as she did so. Hjordis felt the staff's indignance. *I know,* she thought, *but it can't be helped. We'll just have *to find time later. And we'll have to find a new place later, too.* She felt the annoyance fizzle to amusement in her hand and grinned. *There's a good girl.*

As she paced, Hjordis noticed Kettil was sitting up and watching her. She seemed curious, observing her with intrigue as if expecting something. *So that's the key, is it?* Hjordis continued to pace and twirl her staff, the runes trailing vaporous lavender magic in the air, but said nothing, knowing now that Kettil's impatience was a far more reliable conversation starter. After a few moments, her small measure of tact was rewarded.

"Hey, Hjordis, what are you doing?" Kettil asked.

"Hm? Oh, I'm just twirling my staff. She likes to stay active, you see," she responded, then continued with her pacing as she waited for Kettil to bite the hook.

"What do you mean? It's a staff, right? I mean, I know you Staffkeepers get attached to your tools, but aren't you the one who likes twirling it?" Kettil asked, scratching her head of unkempt hair.

"I do enjoy it, true," Hjordis responded casually, "but so does she." Kettil was quiet for a long moment, lost in deep thought with a hand on her chin.

"What's her name?" she asked after some time.

Hjordis grinned at the girl's quickness. "Satisfaction."

"How come you all give your staffs weird names?"

"We don't choose their names any more than they choose ours."

Kettil absorbed this information greedily. *That's strange,* Hjordis thought, *doesn't she ever talk to Baggi about this?* Hjordis cleared her throat. "Erm, would you like to hold her?" she offered.

Kettil's eyes went wide. "But...is that even allowed? Baggi always gets in a panic when I ask to hold Compromise. Are you sure it's okay?"

Hjordis frowned. "Baggi and Compromise have a special relationship. He..."she paused, unsure of how to phrase what came next. "He...needs some more time to understand. But he will soon. That's what the Tasks are for. Now come here!" She proffered Satisfaction in her outstretched hand. Kettil reverently approached and laid a hand across the haft. Hjordis chuckled and smiled to reassure her. When she was sure her grip was secure, she let go and stepped back.

Kettil held Satisfaction like a baby sister, cradling it delicately in her arms. The staff was taller than the young girl herself, yet this seemed not to bother her. In fact, she seemed not to notice. She gently caressed the runes and waved her hand through the translucent purple mist emanating from them. Hjordis heard a soft gasp as Satisfaction twirled her aura around the girl's fingers, taking the shape of tiny dancers who floated and spun with bewitching grace before returning to formlessness and beginning again. She looked up at the Staffkeeper, a delighted smile on her face. In her expression, the Staffkeeper saw the wonder of first snowfall. *That's better,* Hjordis thought, contented, *now there's a happy child.*

Just then, a rustling in the trees broke the spell. Kettil guiltily forced Satisfaction back into Hjordis' hands as Baggi and Elof returned to the clearing. Elof looked pleased, and Hjordis was happy to note that the self-conscious unease had been lifted from the apprentice's shoulders. *I'm glad Elof could help,* she thought. *To receive his Tasks so young...poor thing.* She briefly thought of her own life at 14 years old, so awkward and unsure. Then she imagined trying to work through her Tasks simultaneously and shuddered. *Poor thing indeed.*

"How did it go?" she inquired politely.

"Alchemist Elof was extremely helpful," Baggi replied, bowing respectfully to the older man. *Always so polite,* thought Hjordis. *That will probably wash away with age.*

"I'm glad to hear it.," she said, glancing subtly at Elof. They exchanged chagrined expressions and turned back to the apprentices. "We should get back to the village. I'm getting hungry," she said.

Kettil and Baggi led the way, talking over each other in the way excited children do when they've learned something interesting. They didn't notice how close Hjordis and Elof walked as they trailed, didn't notice their hands brushing every few steps. *May they never notice,* Hjordis wished, aware of the folly in the thought even as she refused to relinquish it. *May they stay this way forever.*

***

The next day, Baggi stood on the road in the place where Hrafn had given him his Task. The sun was beginning to rise, and Baggi carefully kneeled with Compromise across his lap. Patiently, he watched the sunlight begin to slink toward him. He thought for a moment of Creeping Kindling. Then Baggi closed his eyes and emptied his mind in preparation for Contemplation. Rather than bringing any idea or question into focus, however, he allowed his consciousness to glide through a formless void without slowing, forgetting all else as he prepared to latch onto the singular feeling the sun would bring.

Baggi felt the warmth, ever so slight, on his cloak. He felt how tightly he had wrapped the garment against the early morning chill, then felt the sunlight flow like water into every fold in the cloth. He separated the sensations in his mind, then lightly grasped the warmth. It was toying with him, testing his patience, deciding whether he had the resolve to wait. He accepted its challenge, sitting perfectly still as the rays ever so slowly penetrated the shield of fabric. Baggi was a bit warmer now and allowed the cloak to unwrap itself as he gently straightened his posture. The sunlight covered him like a sheet, complete and reassuring even as it played coy with its warmth. The boy remained patient.

Finally, after what seemed like eons had passed, Baggi felt the sunlight on his face. His heart began to beat ever so slightly faster. He felt a bubble of excitement within and popped it immediately; he couldn't risk the tension. There were times for excitement, times for joy, and times for serenity. This was the lattermost option. His face began to heat up and an image of Hjordis and her wolfish smile flashed through his mind, another time and place where his face had been hot. He diligently swept it out. He sought not warmth from within, but without. The sun was sharing itself with the world, it was smiling on him with bottomless affection, and he had no desire to insult it with the comparison.

At this juncture, Baggi allowed himself a small level of conscious thought. *Now to separate the light and the warmth. Just as before with the sun and the cloak. Both provided warmth, but were beyond compare.* He focused on his own face. His eyelids were twitching slightly in concentration, but his muscles were otherwise relaxed in the gentle heat. The warmth was like sand, he realized, not water. It shifted, funneled, fell and swirled in whatever direction the world saw fit to guide it. And unlike water, it was not a coveted resource. No, it was in abundance, and could help anyone and everyone, if they only knew how to utilize it. *And there's more,* Baggi thought, *there's more buried beneath.*

He took in a deep breath, filling his body with the warmth. It hugged him, sustained him, lifted him. Baggi felt as if he were home in Jolk again, with a fever and his mother for company. She was pulling the covers over him ever so snugly. He felt the love pouring out of her, so much of it he could hardly remember the fever, and he realized what it was, hiding beneath the sands and under the covers. It was a word frequently bandied about and even more frequently misunderstood: intimacy. He felt Bjorn's hand on his shoulder and was content to live the rest of his life kneeling on the road with the sun on his face.

The world, as is its wont, decided a change of plans was in order. Baggi's blissful concentration was shattered in an instant as a toughened voice growled at him in Sparktongue.

"What are you doing?"

Baggi opened his eyes, feeling a deep yet unjustifiable sense of loss. *Don't be ridiculous,* he told himself futilely, *you're still sitting in the sun.* His more immediate concern was the boy soldier standing over him, arms crossed and eyes narrowed. *What does it take for him to relax?* He wondered. *Should I use Ansuz again? No, probably not. That would be rude.*

"Good morning, Amund," he said, standing and stretching his legs. "I was just enjoying the sunrise. You're welcome to join me, if you like."

Amund looked confused. "Join you? What, and sit in the middle of the road all day? Have you no work to do? Or if not, should your caravan not be moving on?"

"Not all day," Baggi yawned. "Also, this is my work. What about you? Don't you have a village to run?"

The chief puffed up his chest. "Of course. I guard the mountain pass every day, just as I did the day your group arrived. I was on my way now when I saw a suspicious person kneeling in the road."

"I don't think that's entirely fair," Baggi said evenly, "considering I personally healed one of your villagers."

"It is not a matter of fairness; it is a matter of safety. To lodge Staffkeepers in Flamebud is to keep wolves in your barn. If they are well-fed, they may not eat your cow on the first night, but to believe they will never do so is a fool's belief," Amund said, gravely serious.

"You and Kettil would have so much to talk about," Baggi chuckled.

"Baggi," Amund reiterated, not a trace of humor present, "I know that you mean well. But in my experience, you are an exception. We are speaking of the lives of my people."

The apprentice flushed with shame. "Of course. I apologize," he said, and began to bow apologetically before remembering the elder boy's discomfort with the display. "Your responsibility for the safety of your people comes first and foremost, and every day we linger increases the risk of drawing darker eyes. I promise to you that we will depart as soon as I finish my Tasks."

Amund's expression softened slightly for the first time since they had met two days ago. "I am glad that you understand. And, Baggi..." he looked unsure of himself for a moment, a thoroughly unsettling sight. "I never thought I would say this to a Staffkeeper, and a foreigner at that...hmm...for your services, you are a Friend of Flamebud Village." He paused, then mumbled "And a friend of the Chief of Flamebud as well."

Baggi smiled, careful not to appear self-satisfied. "You honor me, Chief Amund. Truly." He bowed in the formal Shaefini tradition, not caring this time if it made Amund uneasy. *It's a good leader who chafes at tribute,* he thought.

"I thought I was clear before. Stop with bowing!" Amund snapped at Baggi, but even without Ansuz he could recognize the humor in his tone. "I must continue on to my post," he said before a lull in the conversation had a chance to materialize. "You know where to find me."

With that, Amund spun around and departed, his *korta* dancing languidly in the breeze. *Like shimmering waves of sand,* Baggi mused as he settled back in for further Contemplation.

6

The following day, Baggi rose early as usual. *Today's the day,* he thought, *today I find the answer and complete my first Task.* He felt that the answer was close, had felt it swirling around him since Hrafn had given him the assignment. With each word of wisdom and every Contemplation, it drew ever so slightly nearer. Now it flitted in and around his hand, brushing his palm and daring him to close his fingers. But Baggi knew better. He would only claim his answer when it settled in his grasp willingly.

He spent the day once more in Contemplation, sitting this time in the clearing with the Flamebuds. He arrived in early morning's darkness and found their light and heat was fainter without the sun's refracted rays, but still he felt their presence. All day, Baggi sat, thinking and wondering but mostly feeling. When the sun rose, he thought he could tell the difference between its heat and the Flamebuds'. The sun was soft and enveloping, the Flamebuds ecstatic and excitable. One opened its arms to the world without fear, the others danced and hissed to keep their foes at bay. Their temperament reminded him of Amund. By day's end, they had become fully separated in his mind. Now Baggi could tell the difference between the two merely by the nature of their warmth. To confuse them would be impossible for him, as impossible as mistaking water for milk.

He spent the long, hot hours of the day embracing the sun's warmth, memorizing its touch, receiving its love. When the sun finally set, Baggi didn't immediately notice. So absorbed in the feeling was he that even its absence couldn't take it from him. But then, by some immense stroke of luck, a pinecone fell from above and bopped him on the head. Baggi reluctantly opened his eyes, and immediately began to panic. *Oh no. The day is over. I've missed it.* He scrambled to his feet, heart pounding. After offering Shaefi the quickest prayer of his life, he sprinted back to the path and Flamebud Village.

Baggi burst through the tree line at the village border in a puff of leaves, then froze in place as he beheld Elder Sage Hrafn on the road. He was in the exact same spot they had stood before, and his eyes were closed in blissful rapture. Baggi felt an uncomfortable falling sensation in the pit of his stomach. *Am I too late?* He wondered numbly. *Have I failed my Tasks already, on the first one?* He took a deep breath, made an effort to balance his emotions, and approached Hrafn.

The Elder Sage made no effort to acknowledge his presence. Baggi hesitated, unsure of whether to say something or if it would be better to remain silent and submissive. Then, without opening his eyes or otherwise stirring, Hrafn motioned with one hand for Baggi to stand next to him. He obeyed wordlessly, beginning to understand. *So it's not over yet. This is the end. The evaluation.*

Baggi felt a flash of self-doubt, but then he was surprised to find other emotions and memories quickly showing it out. He recalled the satisfaction that had come with healing Talia, and the reassurance of a firm hand on his shoulder. He thought of Kettil's boundless energy and thirst for life, so strong and palpable that a piece of it had lodged inside him even now. Another feeling that wasn't quite pride accompanied the memories, a satisfying feeling and a hopeful one. *Intimacy. Kinship. The bond we all share,* he decreed, *Even those who forget. Even foreigners and Staffkeepers.* He recalled Elof's words, so carefully crafted, and the concern he had shown toward Baggi. *Not as an apprentice, or a child,* he thought, *as my friend.* He heard Hjordis' nearly melancholy words from the ritual, recognized now the bittersweet acceptance in her voice as she offered him his destiny.

I know you can. And I think you know that too.

He closed his eyes, and thought of his mother brushing the hair from his forehead in that way he had never liked, and felt the warmth of the sun on his face.

"Invoke Sowilo," Hrafn whispered at his side.

Baggi obeyed, bringing Compromise to his forehead and attuning with his eyes closed. Immediately, the warmth intensified beyond anything he could have imagined. He felt as if he were on fire, yet unable to burn. Strangely, rather than pain, Baggi felt serenity. *Perhaps I should be in pain,* he thought, *but what does it matter?* He felt like a blacksmith's mold, poured full of molten iron, yet too small for the flooding magma. It spilled over the edges of him, too much light to be contained.

A gentle voice prompted Baggi to open his eyes. Still, he felt the warmth. *Wasn't it darker before?* He thought. Indeed, they were cloaked in warm yellow light, he and Hrafn, and Baggi was equally astounded and relieved to find the source of the light in his hand. Compromise was glowing brightly, casting sunlight and shadow on the Elder Sage's worn and kindly features. In the past he had been able to cast light with Sowilo, true, but it had been cold, sterile. This light was warm on his skin despite the chill touch of surrounding night. It was very nearly disorienting.

"Staffkeeper Apprentice Baggi," Hrafn declared softly, "you have completed your first Task. Remember well the lessons imparted these three days. May they guide you in your service of Shaefi." Then the Elder Sage bowed slightly.

Baggi returned the bow, savoring the words and feeling an immense pressure lifted. When he looked up, he noticed Elder Sage Hrafn wore a smile and tears in equal measure.

"You honor me, Elder Sage Hrafn," Baggi recited. "Are you well, Elder Sage? You're weeping."

Hrafn drew up to his full height and made no move to wipe the tears from his face. "Yes, Baggi, I am well. You've made me very proud today." He embraced Baggi suddenly, the movement almost knocking Compromise from his hand. For a moment, Baggi was shocked. "And I know Bjorn would have been even prouder." He felt Compromise stir in his hand.

And Baggi wept as well. He wept fully, joyfully, heedlessly. He wept for relief and beauty and celebration. With a shaking hand, Baggi touched his lips and remembered the last time he had cried. Hrafn, too, remembered how the boy had wept the day Ove died, different tears for different emotions. Now the anger and fear were gone. Now, Baggi was one step closer to his Marking. Hrafn wept beautifully as he embraced the child he had come to love like a son. The child who was becoming a young man before his eyes. And despite the years of joy and sadness, celebration and strife, youth and wisdom, the Elder Sage was afraid to let go. He silently laughed at himself, at an old fool who feared departure. Hrafn remained, for as long as Baggi allowed, silent and supportive and full of pride for the boy that he would have to bid goodbye all too soon.

***

The morning sun fell across Baggi's face, stirring him to wake. He rose from his bedroll and surveyed the empty room. The other apprentices were gone, presumably assigned work and lessons, yet Baggi remained. *Why did no one wake me?* He wondered. The notion that he was receiving special treatment due to his ongoing Tasks made him unexpectedly uneasy. *I suppose it's nice to have some time off so I can give them my full focus,* he thought, *but not at the expense of pulling my own weight. Then again...seeing as I apparently have the morning off, I may as well enjoy it.* It occurred to Baggi that he had not had a bath since arriving in Flamebud. He took a leather strap from his pack and tied his hair back in a ponytail, not bothering to braid it today. After searching the room thoroughly for a note or instructions and coming up empty-handed, Baggi gathered a towel and his second set of clothes and tied them around Compromise as a bindle. Feeling quite resourceful and clever, he pushed open the door and stepped into the common room.

The Flamebud Inn was sparsely populated this morning. This didn't surprise Baggi, but it did feel strange to be starting his morning without the surrounding flurry of Shaefini eating breakfast, receiving assignment, and hastily being on their way. He nervously approached the bar and took a stool, careful not to make noise or scrape the floor as he did so. *It feels like I'm back in the archives at Enton,* he thought, *except even the archives were usually full of people.* Torny was in the kitchen, scrubbing at bowls with her sleeves pushed up to the elbows. He wondered if he should say something to get her attention, but the relative silence was oddly cowing. Instead, he leaned slightly to one side, awkwardly trying to shift into her line of sight without being too obvious.

After nearly an entire minute, Torny jerked her head and blew a stray lock of rust-colored hair out of her face. In doing so, she finally noticed Baggi sitting in lame silence. She shouted something unintelligible in Sparktongue, and after a moment she came around the bar, wiping her hands on a rag.

"Baggi, right?" she said. "You'd better get a move on. Everybody else started their day an hour ago."

"Good morning, Torny," Baggi greeted her, "I'll be on my way soon. Unfortunately, I have yet to receive my second Task, so I'm not quite sure-"

"Oh yeah!" Torny interrupted. "About that. Old Man Hrafn left this for you. He mentioned you two worked late last night." She disappeared behind the bar momentarily as she retrieved a letter from a lower shelf before slapping it down on the counter before him.

"I suppose we did," Baggi replied. Unfolding the note, he was greeted with several lines of gorgeously rendered Flowspeak. He recognized the penmanship right away. It read:

Staffkeeper Apprentice Baggi,

Your second Task is to mend a rift in the fabric of this community. Do this and you will know the peace of Shaefi. Do you understand these instructions?

I understand these instructions: (Sign Here)

I do not understand these instructions: (Sign Here)

You did well on your first Task, Baggi. I have high hopes for your next one. Remember your teachings, and you will succeed.

E.S. Hrafn

Baggi squinted at the letter, frowning. To receive a sacred Task through written notice was highly unorthodox at best. He was torn between amusement and genuine worry. *Is this even allowed?* He wondered. *What if I didn't understand the instructions? Will Shaefi be upset that we didn't observe the traditional ritual of assignment?* This last concern seemed unlikely, even by his own reckoning. *But not impossible.* He raised his face to address Torny.

"I don't suppose he mentioned why he couldn't tell me this in person?"

The innkeeper shrugged. "I didn't ask. Maybe he wanted to let you sleep. Why, what's it say?" She leaned over the bar, far too close, as she attempted to read the note. "Huh," she tilted her head in confusion. "Why do your letters look like you spilled ink and didn't bother to clean it up?"

"That's an apt observation," he laughed. "Some Naefjan scholars theorize that Flowspeak was created using just such a method; the fluid, soft linework emulates the natural movements of water, often inspired by real Naefjan creeks and mountain-falls. In fact, we can even go further and find the exact locations that some individual letters are derived from, by comparing-"

Baggi cut himself off as he noticed the blank look on Torny's face. She was nodding politely but paying his words very little attention. *I must have slipped into lecture,* he realized. The expression was familiar to him, having seen it many times before on Kettil. However, there was a marked difference in that Kettil would loudly groan or complain when Baggi started to get carried away, whereas Torny seemed too polite for that, instead resigning herself to an endless stream of seemingly useless information for fear of giving offense. She was not, however, too polite to seize the chance afforded her by the momentary break.

"Wow!" she exclaimed unenthusiastically, "I didn't know that. So, are you needing breakfast, or are you going to be on your way?"

"Breakfast would be lovely," Baggi replied apologetically.

He threw back his cloak and unspun two yellow-odd, his entire meager fortune, from his arm ring. Torny indicated that he should keep it, citing his caravan's expenses being paid for in healing services, and retreated to the kitchen before he could resume his dissertation on Flowspeak. The apprentice was grateful for the gesture; a person without a single odd would be in a tight spot should they ever need a pointed edge or makeshift quill. He turned one over in his fingers, examining the hole bored through the middle on which they hung and thinking with admiration of several other uses they might have, until some time had passed and the mundanity of currency returned.

Baggi sighed and looked about the inn. He couldn't remember the last time he had had such a peaceful morn. Shaefini were almost universally morning people, preferring to complete their assignments or lessons before afternoon rolled in. Baggi had never paid this fact much thought before, but in the wake of his first Task he now realized that it probably was related to the sunrise. There was something promising about the early morning. A new day and its unlimited potential excited and inspired them. The hustle and bustle was comforting, in a way. Starting the day without it felt like he was missing a shoe. *How unnerving. I would rather be helping the other apprentices. Hopefully they're not too upset with my absence.* He laughed, curtly, at his own arrogance. *That'll be the day.*

After some time Torny returned with a bowl containing a hunk of brown bread and what appeared to be some sort of fried leg in one hand, and a teapot and two cups in the other. Baggi was mildly impressed that she could carry it all, but she moved as if completely unencumbered. She set the dishes down in front of Baggi.

"I don't mean to give offense, but, um…what is this?" he asked.

Torny stared at him curiously. "So you northerners have really never had frog before, huh? I thought they were just joking, but you really don't know."

Baggi turned his attention back to the strange leg in the bowl. *Is this…normal, then? I suppose if everyone else was eating it, there's no moral objections. Though even if there were, I wouldn't know it.* He glanced toward Torny, wondering if she was pulling some joke, yet her face showed no signs of deception. He briefly considered using Ansuz to make sure, then immediately dismissed the idea. *What a ridiculous waste that would be. And refusing a meal would be a terrible insult.* Baggi had never thought to cook frogs, but after all, he had an adventurous palate. *I can't offend Torny.*

"Thank you, it looks delicious," he said, then took a bite of the leg.

For a moment, he tensed, expecting a wave of strange flavors. Instead, he was surprised and even a bit disappointed to find the meat itself rather unremarkable. *Seems any meat will pretty much taste the same fried,* he thought with some chagrin. The texture was slightly chewy, but not unpleasantly so. With each bite, he began to pick up on more subtle flavors. There was a humble spiciness that lingered on the tongue, and a delicate, yet earthen, herby note he couldn't quite place offering much needed lightness. As he ate, Baggi realized that he was hungrier than he knew. *Did I eat yesterday at all? No, I think I spent the whole day in Contemplation. It never even occurred to me.* The moment the leg was stripped to its tiny bone, he tore into his bread, eagerly washing it down with the tea. The brew was strong and smoky, and Baggi somehow knew that to ask for milk would be sacrilegious, so he simply sipped the bitter dregs and sighed in contentment. Torny filled the other cup and began drinking from it herself.

"You need more?" she asked. "You didn't eat yesterday, right?"

"No, I didn't," he responded, surprised. "How did you know?"

Torny blushed momentarily. "I didn't see you in here all day."

"My apologies," Baggi said through the pleasant haze of a full stomach. "I was sort of preoccupied with something."

"Your first Task," Torny nodded sagely.

"That's right," he replied, "was someone talking about it?"

"More like everyone," she said, rolling her fiery eyes like Amund. "Your friend's been telling anyone who will listen, and there's pretty much nothing else going on."

Baggi fell silent. He felt the weight of many unseen eyes on him even in the emptiness of the inn. *So everyone is talking about me. They're finally interested. Maybe they'll even want to talk to me about my Tasks. So why am I not happy about it?* Torny was looking at him intently, her gaze unreasonably piercing.

"What are you sad about?" she demanded.

"Umm..." Baggi stuttered, unsure of how to respond and even less sure of how Torny had noticed his distress so quickly. "Well, I suppose I'm just being cautious."

"What?" She all but snapped. "That makes no sense. What are you scared of?"

"It just seems convenient. I've been with the caravan for about two years now, and in that time most of the other apprentices have been...cordial," he sighed. "I'm not sure if it's how I treat Compromise, or maybe that they heard about what happened with Bjorn, but it's been difficult to make friends."

"Ah," the innkeeper replied, "that explains why you only keep company with a little girl. Sort of." He grimaced at her assessment but reluctantly nodded. "Well I don't know about any of that, but I think you're being stupid."

Baggi balked at her. "Excuse me?"

"No problem," she absentmindedly replied, then continued. "Who cares if people didn't talk to you before? They're probably going to now."

Baggi smiled, unable to bring himself to argue. "You're probably right. All that matters is the here and now. Speaking of which," he said, rising from his stool and slinging Bindle-Compromise over his shoulder, "could you point me in the direction of the nearest river or lake? I'd like to go for a bathe."

She took his advice literally, throwing up a finger towards the door. "Go out the door and keep going straight. It's not far."

"Then I believe it's time I was on my way. Thank you for the meal, Torny," he said kindly, "and thank you for the conversation as well. Both were lovely."

"Oh, you're leaving?" Torny said in a too-casual voice. "Okay, well, you better come back for supper tonight. Amund will be really mad if I let someone starve." She gathered up the dishes and hurried back into the kitchen, peeking back over her shoulder briefly and then, after Baggi noticed, pretending she hadn't.

"I will!" he promised, shouting so his voice would reach her in the kitchen. "See you tonight!" A hand poked up through the service window and waved before retreating from sight once more. Baggi grinned and waltzed out into Flamebud Village feeling ready for anything.

Flamebud Village was busy and loud. As he stepped out of the inn, the apprentice found himself immediately surrounded by the sights and smells of a market. *Well this is unexpected,* he thought, gawking at the scene. Stalls had been set up in the town square, built in dizzying concentric circles with the town well at the center. *I didn't even know there were this many people in Flamebud.* Indeed, the shouts of townsfolk fell on his ear from every direction as he submerged himself deeper in the throng of commerce. *So much for a quiet morning.* The stalls were all attended by children, some about his age, others even younger than Kettil. All were busy at work.

Of course, Flamebud is a border village, he realized. *They must be in an advantageous place for export. Though Amund's stance on foreigners may be discouraging to merchants from other lands.* As he surveyed the offerings, Baggi was struck by a strange uneasiness. *Something is different. But what?* Then, all at once, it hit him: there were adults in Flamebud, and not only his fellow Shaefini. It seemed the Flamebud market was large enough to attract folk from neighboring villages. The children still far outnumbered the adults, but even so they stood out, quite literally. And the *kortas*! The specimens in Talia's shop had been breathtaking, but seeing such an array of colors and styles shining in the sun, opals glimmering, was a true privilege. Baggi noted with interest that not every adult wore a *korta*, and even those that did lacked the level of decoration Amund boasted. *Still,* he thought, *what a treat!*

The new arrivals gave Baggi a chance to observe Kichishi customs with a larger and more varied sampling, so he took a moment to watch from under the awning of the inn's porch. He noticed little distinction in who wore what clothing; adults and children alike wore tunics and trousers with sleeves and cuffs that flared outwards like peonies, and unlike in Naefja, where fashion trends were clearly divided along gender lines, here men and women both wore tunics, skirts, trousers, or robes as preferred. Many of the folk had short hooded half-cloaks about their shoulders, Melennese in style and likely imported at great cost, but unlike the heavy insulated cloaks used in his homeland to stave off frost, Baggi reckoned based on their lightness of material that these predominantly served the purpose of expression. There seemed to be no universal agreement on which colors complimented which, and as a result the horde of swirling materials flowed like an undulating rainbow before him. Various symbols adorned the clothes and, in some cases, the skin in the form of tattoos, presumably denoting clans or organizations to which their wearer belonged. The symbol of Flamebud was self-explanatory, but Baggi also noted roam-lizards, bonfires, hounds, and even chickens among them. After his curiosity had been sufficiently whetted, Baggi took a deep breath and waded into the crowd.

He wandered through the streets, taking in the sights and smells, his plans to bathe already forgotten. The roads that had only yesterday been open and clear had become dominated overnight by tent after tent. Some stalls offered exotic wares from the Melennese guild-tribe of Fumvoir or elsewise further south in Kichishi, cheeses, herbs, and spices of such intoxicating aroma that Baggi had difficulty moving on. Others were selling livestock; he saw a chicken or two, and a few ostrich hens, but mostly there were frogs, piled on top of each other in great clay pots. He saw a girl reach into one such pot and pick one out. She handed it to the boy manning the stall, and he immediately killed and cleaned the creature, then rubbed the meat with an aromatic brick colored spice before skewering it and placing the skewer over a flame behind the counter. Baggi watched in fascination as the meat quickly crisped, at which point the boy picked the skewer back up and handed it to the girl. Odd changed hands, and the girl walked off, happily chewing on the snack. Despite having just finished breakfast, Baggi salivated at the smell of spicy cooked meat wafting through the air.

The sounds of a confrontational string duet drew his attention elsewhere. Turning, he saw a boy fiddling madly, his fingers dancing on the strings like a spider in distress while his duet partner sat cross-legged, a dulcimer laid across his lap and a mallet in each hand. After a few moments, the fiddler rested his hands and the dulcimer began to thrum with song, mallets bouncing up and down faster than Baggi could see. He noticed now that it wasn't quite a duet; rather, they were exchanging musical verses, back and forth, challenging and feeding off the other's melody, sometimes interrupting each other but always harmonizing. The display of skill astounded him. He approached and stood at a respectful distance, wondering whose song would win out in the end. The melody was becoming increasingly frenzied, the pauses between verses growing shorter and shorter. Baggi felt a sense of urgency overcome him, accompanied by the strange impulse to run. Around him, a few locals were dancing energetically, shrinking and expanding their bodies in movements both exotic and familiar. They seemed to move in pulses, or waves, never stopping to rest or pausing for even the briefest of moments, the heat of their passionate steps palpable, intoxicating. The dancers whirled and rolled and spun each other about in furious circles, dancing with such freneticism that Baggi began to genuinely worry for their well-being. He was relieved when the music finally died, the last notes resonating in perfect harmony even above the market's din. Noting several onlookers tossing money into a collection plate, he extracted one of his yellow odd and added it to the pile.

"Beautiful, yes?" Amund said from beside him. Baggi flinched slightly but managed not to yelp. Amund had a habit of materializing from thin air, but Baggi was beginning to get used to it. He noticed he was more relaxed than usual, but the spark behind his eyes was volatile as ever and he still wore his weapons.

"Good morning, Chief Amund," he said politely. "Yes, it was. Unfortunately I couldn't tell who won."

"Won?" Amund cocked an eyebrow. "They both won. They all did," he said, gesturing broadly towards the crowd of panting dancers.

"Hm. So just to take part is to win? That sounds almost like something we would say," he grinned, hoping this wasn't prodding too hard.

"Hah," the chief scoffed, "Where would be the meaning in that? No, taking part does not make one victorious. It is dependent upon the effort. Only one who dances their hardest, to exhaustion, can claim victory. But our people are dignified and strong. We have many victors," he explained, crossing his arms proudly.

Baggi thought he understood. "So the steps aren't important either, just the effort?"

"Not so. The steps are only less important. It is still worthwhile to remember them."

"Do you remember them?" Baggi asked, knowing he was testing Amund's patience already yet enjoying himself too much to stop. The elder boy looked at him askance, unsure if he was joking.

"Of course. I am the best warrior in the village," he said, as if that were explanation enough.

"And the best dancer as well?"

"Naturally."

"I don't understand."

"Do you know what your weakness is, Baggi?" Amund asked, suddenly turning to face him head on.

"My biggest one? Well, I'm not great with heights," he replied with impertinence.

"No," said Amund, "you try too hard to understand. Sometimes it is better to simply watch. In fact," he said as he glanced over his friend's shoulder, "watch closely now. I spot a cur."

He marched over to a nearby stall where a young boy was peddling carrots. Rather, the boy was making his best effort, but the older man on the other side of the counter was leaning threateningly towards him and tossing a long knife up in his hand. Baggi followed several steps behind, preparing himself to intervene if need be. Amund closed the gap and tapped the man on the shoulder. He turned around, looming over the boy. Baggi saw that the man wore a thick brown beard decorated with jewelry and a chainmail shirt. *Naefjan,* he noted based on the man's lightness of hair and skin, *or else Einarsfolk.* The sword belt tied around his waist was heavy with steel. He had a bald head and a mean expression that quickly twisted into a sour smile.

"Ah, Chief Amund, how goes it?" Baggi heard the man leer in sloppy Sparktongue.

"Silence," Amund said, putting up a hand in the man's face and turning to the boy. "What is happening here, Kalfr? Are you okay?"

"Amund!" the boy squeaked. "Help! This guy said I hafta give him two bunches of carrots or he's gonna gut me!" The man started to protest but Amund put a hand up once more and turned to him with a withering glare.

"You would kill a six-year-old boy? Over two bunches of carrots? Your honor comes cheap, Geir," he sneered at the man, disgust dripping from his every word.

So he knows this man, Baggi observed nervously, *He must have made trouble in the past as well.*

"You will leave now," Amund continued, "and you will not be welcome in Flamebud again. Goodbye."

The man gaped at him, outrage building, face reddening. For a long time, he seemed unable to articulate a response.

"You think you can talk to me like that?" he finally roared. "I'm a veteran of the Mineral War, and countless battles at sea besides! I've killed five hundred men; be they Naefjan, Melennese, or Kichishi, it makes no difference!" He stepped toward the young man, too close, his face inches away. "One more is nothing to me," he hissed. The threat was obvious, and Baggi noted with unease that his knife was still in hand.

"Am I to understand that you are disregarding my decision on the matter?" Amund replied, apparently unconcerned with the man's approach.

Baggi felt an oppressive silence in the surrounding market, felt many nervous gazes pressing in on the opposing men. Though he dared not look away, he could see in the corners of his eyes that all present were frozen in place, watching. The air was thick with tension and bated breath. The apprentice felt his heartbeat accelerate. *I should intervene, right?* he thought, yet he knew that was not an option. Amund had made a decree, and to intervene now would be in open defiance of that decision. *Legally speaking,* he realized, *I would be in the same position as this man.* He touched his lips nervously and hoped that his friend was as skilled at arms as he seemed.

"That's right," Geir said, his words hanging in the air, "and I suggest you walk away now, *boy.*" He placed emphasis on the last word, abandoning pretexts and making it clear that he intended offense.

Amund sighed, as if disappointed, and so it began.

In a flash, he stepped forward diagonally, his right arm locking into place as he slammed his elbow into the man's gut. A resounding thud echoed in the still air. Geir winced and began to double over, knife dropping from his hand, but to his credit, recovered quickly. Rather than try to push back with brute force, he retreated two steps. In one motion, he drew his sword, a fearsome cutlass of the type popularly borne by sailors and Einarsfolk in particular, and hacked at Amund with a high backhanded slash. Baggi's breath caught in his throat, sure that the unexpected move had been successful, but the Chief of Flamebud was too quick. He leaned smoothly just under the blade and seized the extended arm, snaking around it with his own left. His hands executed a complicated rotation too fast for Baggi to track, and then Amund sharply stepped back with his opponent's sword in hand. The ruffian looked fearful for a moment, but then, unexpectedly, Amund tossed the sword away from them both. It landed in a puff of dirt, and for a moment it seemed that would be the end of it. But his opponent, greedy for blood, launched himself at Amund, wrapping his arms around the smaller fighter and attempting to use his superior weight to throw the boy to the ground.

Once again, Amund outclassed him. The moment he was grappled, he pivoted, twisting his hips and throwing Geir off balance. Then, in a flash, he twisted back the other way and sent his shin smashing into his stupefied enemy's face. As Geir reeled, blood pouring from his nose, Baggi watched Amund trace a graceful half circle with his foot, inches above the ground. There was an effortless poise to the motion. Just before touching down, Amund lifted his other foot and his body exploded upwards as he launched another kick. He rotated extremely, nearly so far as to expose his back, his entire body weight behind the blow. Already reeling, the older man had no time to guard. This time, the kick connected with his throat. A disturbing crack rang out, and Geir crumpled to his knees, clutching his neck and wheezing desperately. Amund approached, looming over the broken man, eyes narrowed with barely checked fury.

"Shameful," he spat. "You will leave Flamebud now, if you are able. If you are not able, you die in the dirt. Either way makes no difference to me. Should you ever return," he continued, leaning close to the man "I will not be so merciful. My blade, too, has gone thirsty."

It was unclear if Geir heard him, or if he was even conscious, now slumped in the dirt and making no effort to move. Slowly, life returned to the market. Nervous laughter turned to cheers and whistles, but Amund gave them no acknowledgement. He turned away derisively and walked back to the booth to reassure Kalfr. Baggi made to approach the wounded man; it was his duty to provide medical attention if possible, or elsewise to perform funerary rites. However, before he reached his patient, another Staffkeeper pushed through the crowd and beat him to it. Baggi noted with relief that it was the First Sage, Runa.

Sage Runa was a middle-aged woman, strict in posture and manner, with a stern face and shoulder-length brown hair that was just beginning to turn silver. She was rather famous as Staffkeepers went. During her youth, back when she was still only Staffkeeper Runa, she had developed several new poultices in conjunction with the most accomplished alchemists of their Order, leading to breakthroughs in magical healing that were still marveled at today. By all accounts, she was a genius with a mind many years ahead of their era. She may have been one of the most popular Staffkeepers in Naefja, if not for her business-like persona. At work, she brooked no foolishness, but it was whispered that she was the life of the party when the work was done. Most found this hard to believe, Baggi included, but it did nothing to tarnish their respect for her and her contributions to their trade.

She stepped toward Geir, then kneeled and began carefully checking his injuries. *Sage Runa can certainly do a better job than I would,* Baggi thought, *but perhaps she could use my assistance.* He made to join her when Amund returned, perspiring ever so slightly.

"Did you watch closely?" he asked, as if the interruption had never occurred in the first place.

"I did," Baggi replied. He watched Runa staunch the blood streaming from the injured man's face with expert hands, struggling to reconcile the beauty of Amund's movements with their results. "It was...impressive."

"And do you understand now?" he asked. "About the dances?"

The apprentice thought hard about what he had seen. There were similarities, undeniably. Both Amund and the dancers had embodied a paradox, by Baggi's reckoning. They moved with elegance and frenzy in equal measure, and the way they spun was remarkably similar to how Amund had twisted and pivoted during his fight.

"I believe so," he said, hesitating. "But one thing stands out to me: you said that in the dance, you win by exerting energy and giving your all. In your fight, you seemed relaxed, only moving when you had to. Is that not dishonorable?"

"Hah!" Amund laughed. "Perhaps so. But there was no honor in fighting such a man to begin with." He clapped his hands together congenially, in better spirits than Baggi had ever seen him. "I must keep moving. There are many such troublemakers about. Enjoy the market." And with that, he strode off on patrol.

Baggi watched him go, conflicted and confused. *It was right to defend the child,* he mused, *but violence and defense are not one and the same. On the other hand, that man would have killed a six-year-old, and still Amund let him keep his life. Could this still be called violence, then?* Baggi touched his lips, staring at his feet as he walked. The market had lost its luster. *Perhaps the bath will help clear my mind.* He set off toward the forest, the crack of the man's windpipe resounding over and over in his mind.

7

Her father was going to die, and Valdis knew it would be soon. His wounds were dire, his body not nearly so resilient as it once was. Snow now dusted his beard even on a sunny day, his features were beginning to sag, and with every passing day he groaned a little louder when he raised himself from bed. But these things would not plague him for long, Valdis knew, because he would die soon.

She poured boiling water over the leaves in their teapot, slowly and deliberately. The only noises in their cottage were Njal's constant wheezing and the perversely gentle slurp of the teapot filling up. It slowly and steadily rose in pitch, higher and higher, until abruptly stopping as Valdis ceased pouring. The teapot was full. She placed the lid on top to keep it warm, three distinct streams overflowing the sides.

"Valdis," she heard her father call softly. She did not respond, instead staring at the teapot and counting in her head the length of its steep. After precisely four minutes, the tea was ready and she could ignore him no longer. She poured their cups and approached her father's cot.

Njal lay blanketed above the waist, but his legs were exposed save for the thick blood-soaked bandages Valdis had sloppily applied. She stared hard at the gashes in her father's thigh, four deep scores from the snow leopard that had opened his skin just like Valdis always slashed their bread before baking, and just as easily. *My father will die,* she thought, *and all for the sake of a goat.*

They had been out with the flock when a loud, frightened bleat alerted them to the predator's presence. *So graceful,* Valdis had thought in the moment it dashed toward their livestock. Her father was more experienced; in the same moment, he rushed forward to fend the creature off with nothing but his crook and knife. The struggle was brief, and by the time she regained her senses it was too late. The results were a goat and a father both covered in blood, and neither with strong odds of survival. Valdis had put the goat down already, drawing her knife across its throat in one smooth motion. *Such a waste,* she thought.

"Do you remember," Njal asked her now after he had sipped his tea, "the day we met the man from Einarsplace? Last year?"

Valdis nodded. It was not a memory easily forgotten.

***

It felt good to be on their way home. Njal and Valdis had spent the last two days haggling hard, in search of new buyers who might be willing to pay for their wool at a fairer rate. Their last merchant, who Njal had been selling to for decades, had grown too comfortable with their arrangement and announced his new (much stingier) rate on arrival, leaving the goatherds in a compromising position: either accept the new rate, and the belt-tightening which would accompany it, or take their chances in the rest of Geluwam. Njal, being a man of principle, hadn't hesitated to choose the latter. Valdis was proud to be his daughter then.

Although the two had succeeded in securing a new buyer, the rate was only marginally better than their old merchant's new price. Still, it was in Valdis' opinion entirely worth the trouble. As they plodded through the summer slush, her crook splattered mud and ice. They were filthy from the legs down, but she knew that her father shared her sense of satisfaction. *Now we know that our buyer is someone we can respect,* she thought. *It wasn't a wasted trip in the slightest.*

A traveler appeared on the pass ahead of them, dipping in and out of sight as the road wound its way through the peaks. Njal pulled the goats gently aside to make room for the man when he came near. Valdis noted his clothes were not well-suited to the Great Pass; he wore a sailor's coat and cloth pants, only a single pair, with stylish boots much too thin. Gold rings glittered in his ears and on his fingers. His features were indistinct, clearly a child of a complicated and varied bloodline. Light brown hair and a pointy goatee accentuated the man's high cheekbones and devilish lips. He removed a seal-skin cap and bowed at Njal in greeting, but his eyes were on Valdis.

"Hallo, good man!" he said jovially. His teeth chattered in the freezing cold. Njal grunted in response and urged the goats on. "Wait, good man!" the stranger yelped, standing in the goats' way.

"Why are you blocking us?" the goatherd asked.

"I was hoping you might help me," the man said. "I seem to be in over my head. They always say 'you don't know cold 'till you know the Peaks', but I never thought anything could be colder than the winter sea. Well, and here I am paying for my arrogance!" He grinned at his own foolishness.

"Then I suggest you start walking faster," replied Njal. "Should warm you right up."

A flash of annoyance betrayed the stranger's mood. "Perhaps. But there are other ways to keep warm as well, aren't there?" he said, then glanced meaningfully at Valdis.

Valdis felt her heart skip, more from indignance than fear. The implication was clear, but still her father considered the man's words.

"Be direct with what you want, then," he said, standing very still with his crook in hand.

The man slipped a gold ring from each of his hands, then held both out to Njal in his palm. "They're yours. All you have to do is go home and tell your wife you lost the girl in the mountains," he grinned conspiratorially. "I'm sure it happens in these parts all the time." Valdis noted with increasing unease the sword in the man's belt.

"The girl is twelve years old," Njal said, his tone neutral.

"Really?" the stranger asked. He seemed genuinely surprised for a moment, but then the grin returned. "Well, she looks old enough, anyway. So, good man, do we have a deal?"

"Valdis," said Njal in a loud voice, "watch closely."

Without warning he brought his crook up hard under the stranger's chin. The crack of wood echoed through the pass, but before it could die out it was joined by two more resounding impacts as Njal struck at the man's face in a frenzy. Before the stranger had time even to fall, the goatherd was upon him, swinging again and again without pause. On his back, the other man tried desperately to guard, but the flurry of blows quickly overwhelmed him. Eventually he stopped trying to defend himself. Still Njal swung his crook, bashing the man in the ribs and chest and then bringing the butt of his tool down on his opponent's face over and over. Blood spattered his clothes with each swing, but still the blows came without end. He grunted harder and louder with every hit until he was screaming and howling, a beast in all but name. Valdis watched in silence.

Finally, her father stopped striking. He panted heavily, his arms gripping his bloody staff as they hung, exhausted, at his sides. He caught his breath before turning to his daughter.

"Were you watching?" he asked, almost in a whisper.

"Yes," Valdis said.

"And do you understand why I did that?"

"Yes."

After a long, long pause, he said, "And do you hate me for it? Do you fear me for it?" His voice was shaking slightly. Whether due to worry or the adrenaline rapidly leaving his body, Valdis wasn't sure.

"No," she said, and meant it. "It's like the bird: as long as there's a reason for it. Right?"

Njal nodded and used a sleeve to wipe blood from his face. It smeared instead. "Let's go home," he said.

Valdis nodded back and followed him. She glanced back at the jewelry adorning the corpse, wondering why her father did not claim the valuables, but her answer came easily. *Tainted spoils,* she decided, *we would never be able to wash the evil from them.* Njal was watching her, she noticed, seeing if she could ignore the temptation; Valdis did, and easily. They walked on in silence.

"You need a new crook," she observed sometime later, "or the blood will scare the goats."

"Yes," Njal chuckled. "Would you make me one?"

Valdis looked at him curiously before nodding. He patted her on the head, leaving blood in her hair.

***

"The crook you carved that night," Njal wheezed. "Bring it here."

Valdis retrieved the staff its place by the door and pressed it gently into her father's arms. He hugged it and smiled slightly. Both were quiet.

"This crook will be yours soon," Njal finally said. He locked eyes with her, his gaze full of authority. "You will take good care of it," he commanded.

"Of course," she replied, a bit surprised. *Doesn't that go without saying?* She wondered.

"Your hand," he said weakly.

She proffered her right, but Njal shook his head and indicated her left. Self-consciously, she gave it to him. He turned her palm upwards, so the runic brand on her skin was visible. *My mark of shame,* she thought, ears burning.

"You know what this mark means," Njal stated.

"No," she answered.

"Valdis," sighed her father wearily, "don't lie. To me or anyone. You know what the brand means."

She remained in stubborn silence for as long as possible. "Yes," she eventually admitted.

"You could be a Staffkeeper," he said reluctantly, "and a damned good one, I'm told."

"I don't want to be a Staffkeeper," she asserted.

"I know," said Njal. He smiled at her. "You want to earn your own living, like a proper hand should. And that makes me happy." The smile melted away. "But I want you to face the choice you have. Even if you decide to stay here, you can't ignore the brand."

"Father, I know already what my choice will be," Valdis insisted. "Why waste time with-"

"Valdis," Njal cut her off, voice sharp with reproach, "I did not raise a coward."

She knew in her heart that he was right; she only avoided considering the life of a Staffkeeper for fear that she might choose it after all, or worse yet, that she might actually enjoy living amongst those who had failed her father so many times before. The comforting pain from the rune on her hand had swirled around in the deep recesses of her mind for these several years, and until now, she had been able to ignore it. *But Father is right,* she thought, *I will consider it.* She nodded once, sharply, and Njal relaxed once more.

"Good," he sighed. "And there is one more thing I must tell you, before I can no longer speak."

"What is it?"

"I love you," Njal said simply.

He stroked her face and pulled her close to kiss her forehead, and all at once Valdis was terrified. The fear burst from her eyes in rivers as she wailed and screamed with all of the noise she hadn't made in childhood. It all came pouring out, painful and exhausting but cleansing too. She sobbed on her father's chest for hours while he patted her head and hugged her close and said nothing.

Then it was time for the end. It wouldn't do to stall Death; they weren't Shaefini. Valdis drew herself up, wiped her face, and went on shaky legs to retrieve her father's knife. *How quickly it all changes,* she thought. She felt as if half of her were still sobbing, the other half looking down on herself for the weakness. Then she knelt on Njal's cot and took his hand. His eyes were open and bright, his lips gently smiling. Valdis looked on him with intense love. She hesitated.

"I love you too," she said. Then she drew the knife across his throat in one smooth motion. *Just like the goat,* she couldn't help thinking. Njal's features seized slightly, as if concentrating, and his eyelids drooped close as he drifted off forevermore.

Valdis sat still, blood pumping from the wound and soaking the already filthy cot. It began to pool on the floor of their cottage. Still she remained motionless. She watched her father's face grow paler and his lips turn blue. His skin was clammy. The blood-flow began to ebb, churning more weakly with each pump. Finally, it was a mere trickle. Valdis stared at her father at rest, wondering if he was with her mother now. Then she scoffed aloud. *Father doesn't believe in an afterlife. He's not a coward. No,* she thought, *he reached the end. And that's all there is to it.* She sat in the quiet pool of her father's life as the sun set behind the mountain where he had found her.

It'll be too cold to bury him, she thought numbly, *I'll have to burn him then. But he won't catch if he's full of blood.* Valdis was loath to move the body, would have preferred to leave it be forever, asleep in its cot where it belonged, but she knew this was folly. So she pried the red-stained crook from her father's cold grip and hauled him onto her back. Lukewarm plasma ran down her back as she struggled to the door with her staff for support. Valdis had always been tall, taller than most girls and some grown women at that, and years of labor had hardened her body. Even so, Njal had been a colossal man; she was panting by the time she reached the barn.

There, she pierced his ankles with a hook and hung him upside down from the rafters to drain with a bucket beneath. *Just like the goats, indeed,* she thought. The ease and familiarity of her actions worried her, yet she forged on. Unable to strip him down, she left him hanging fully clothed, blood trickling pathetically from his slashed throat. On her way out, Valdis glanced toward the goat's pens. They had been strangely quiet, and stood now packed closely together, staring at Njal's body with ignorant curiosity. Valdis found their calm strange and unexpected. She sighed, already fatigued, and went inside to begin the long cleaning process.

She mopped the dark pool from her floor with a rag, moving betwixt it and the door and wringing her father's blood upon the snow over and over again. Hours passed in this way. Valdis focused on the simple labor, the image of the corpse branded on her vision as clearly as the mark on her hand. When the floors were no longer wet, only stained crimson, she scrubbed her arms and face with fresh water from the snow-melter. Her skin, too, was stained. She took up bundles of firewood and went outside to arrange a pyre. Valdis had no knowledge of ceremony, but this did not irk her. She arranged the logs in a large mound, then retrieved more fuel and piled the logs even higher.

When she was finished, she went to the barn and took down Njal's body, now fully drained of its lifeblood, and hauled it on her back once more. She struggled silently with the weight, the day's exhaustions suddenly compounding as she moved step by step toward the logs. Mere feet away, Valdis paused to catch her breath. When she had done so, still she did not move. It occurred to her that she was afraid to release her father. Yet she was too weary for the feeling to last. She shook her head once slowly, marveling at her own weakness, and remembered his words.

I did not raise a coward.

She cried out, a shout full of frustration and anger, and threw Njal's body on the pyre. Then she lit a faggot on the stove a carried it to the pyre, nursing the flames until a mighty bonfire roared in defiance of snowy midnight. The flames ate him slowly, licking and savoring his skin as it gradually fell apart before he began to shrivel. Valdis stood close to the flames, too close, her face burning and hair sizzling, but she did not retreat until the thing that had been her family was reduced to ash.

***

Five mounted travelers rode down the trail. They would be upon her flock in a matter of minutes, by Valdis' estimation. She put out her right hand to stroke Snow's neck comfortingly while her left remained on the crook with rust-colored stains. Her friend was a kid no longer, now a strapping buck with mighty horns that Valdis had been on the receiving end of more than once. She held no ill-will toward her friend, of course. It was an animal; it was in its nature.

"Now," she muttered to her companion, remembering the man from Einarsplace, "what is the nature of these riders?" She stood fast and awaited their approach.

The strangers slowed to a contemplative clop as the distance shrank. Valdis noted the consideration for her flock's nerves. Horses were a rare sight in the Eastern Great Pass, and her goats were digging at the tall summer grass confrontationally. She repositioned herself between the two groups, reprimanding the more aggressive in her flock before they could work themselves into a fighting mood.

"Good afternoon," the lead rider called out when they were close enough. He dismounted to speak with her on even level. The other travelers stopped at a respectful distance.

"Greetings," Valdis called back evenly.

The riders wore strange apparel, to be sure; pure black cloaks flapped in the breeze, they wore riding boots the likes of which Valdis had only seen on the feet of Geluwam's wealthiest citizens—those that could afford horses— and most intriguing of all, their saddles and clothes were adorned with bones of all shapes and sizes. The lead rider wore a cap with two sprawling, twisted antlers. He doffed the cap politely, revealing long black hair tied in a ponytail. His eyes were the color of fire, his skin the blue-black of haunted waters. Despite the procession's grim attire, his face was kind and radiated an effortless empathy. His bearing was affable and his body lean without hardness, clearly a man who lived on his feet yet was spared the hardships of manual labor.

"We seek lodging. Is there any nearby?" he asked.

His Woodwhisper was passable, but his accent very strange; it seemed almost as if something were crackling between his lips as he spoke. It was then that Valdis noticed another feature of the travelers' saddles; affixed to each was a staff carved with many symbols she didn't recognize, and one that she did. She gripped her crook tighter with her branded hand.

"Not for Staffkeepers of Shaefi," she shot back. These folks were dressed differently than the Staffkeepers she had seen during her visits to Geluwam, but this did not register as important to her in her condescension. *What is a uniform?* She thought derisively. *The staffs give it away clear as day.*

But the rider surprised her by smiling. "Then we are in luck. There are no Shaefini here," he said.

Valdis raised an eyebrow. "And those staffs?" she asked, making no attempt to hide her skepticism.

"Oh, we are Staffkeepers, in a way," the man replied, "but we are of a different Order. Have no fear, miss."

Valdis stared at him, dumbstruck. *Different Order?* She wondered. *There are different Orders?* She gazed at the man suspiciously, detecting no signs of deception. She cleared her throat, compelled for the first time in her life to fill the silence. "Then which are you?" she asked.

"We," the man said, "are The Conclusion. They call us Staffkeepers of Death." Then he watched for her response, his gaze intent, his smile ghostly. "Does that frighten you?" he asked.

"No," she replied. "Why should it?"

The man continued to smile at her for several moments, then re-leased a sigh of wonder. "Why indeed," he said, "a complicated question. Perhaps we can discuss it over dinner?" he asked hopefully.

"Can you pay for your dinner?" Valdis demanded.

"Of course," the man replied, shocked by the question. "We have odd, or goods to trade if you prefer."

"Odd will do. Come then, you may stay in the barn."

"You have my thanks," the man called out as he mounted his horse once more. "And what do they call you?"

"Valdis," she replied, "and you?"

The man looked like he might laugh for a moment, but he collected himself and said, "A wonderful name. I am called Birgir."

Valdis made no indication she had heard him, only herded her flock back towards home. They raised a fuss, this being an earlier end to the day than usual, but she grabbed the troublemakers by their ears and set them straight. As they hadn't been far from the cottage, the ensemble reached her croft after mere minutes of travel. Valdis penned in the goats outside, as an apology for cutting their grazing short, then she wiped sweat from her forehead and opened the barn for the riders. They entered cautiously and dismounted. Valdis observed with pleasure that these were quiet folks; only their leader had yet spoken.

"You will be sleeping here," Valdis declared, "but you may come in for tea, if you like." Without awaiting an answer, she went to the cottage door and entered.

"We thank you deeply for your hospitality," Birgir said as he caught the door behind her. He held it open as his followers filed in, bowing their heads deferentially in Valdis' direction as they passed the thresh-old.

"And the odd?" Valdis demanded, unimpressed. "That will be four white odd for all of you."

Birgir raised his eyebrows. "So large a sum, for so small a party?" he asked. His voice was full of cunning, but Valdis had been haggling in the city for years. *I learned from the best,* she thought, proud of her late father's instruction.

"I will need to slaughter a goat to feed so many. You will need to reimburse me," she replied in a voice that brooked no argument. In truth the sum was outrageous, but she knew that the harshness of the Great Peaks offered them no other choice.

Birgir looked about to try his luck anyway, but then he smiled and turned his palms upwards in deference. "Gyda?" he prompted.

An older woman with weathered skin, a grim expression, and a slightly hunched back stepped forward and procured four silver counters from her odd-ring, handing them to Valdis without a word. Their eyes met, and she sensed a probing pressure from the woman's dark gaze, but this was not enough to cow her and she stared Gyda down until her guest retreated. Valdis tossed the odd carelessly on the counter as she cracked the snow-melter to fill the kettle. When the water was boiled and the tea steeping, she passed around cups. Birgir accepted his with closed eyes. He seemed focused on something ethereal.

"The taste of a fearless death lingers here," he said, voice soft. Valdis noticed now he was licking his lips. He opened his eyes and smiled broadly at her. "This is a good place."

"I know," Valdis scoffed. That made him smile even wider.

"That rune on your hand," he said, suddenly and unexpectedly, "were you born with it?"

"No," she answered, wondering when he had seen it to begin with.

"Then it was forced on you?" he prompted.

"No," she said, doggedly reserved.

Birgir squinted and thought for a moment. The expression emphasized his laugh-lines. "Was it a Disk, then?"

Valdis stared at him, unsure if she should answer or not. *They are in my home,* she realized, *the time for caution is past.*

"Yes," she admitted.

Birgir nodded and sighed. "Very crude devices," he said, "and sometimes very painful, as I'm sure you can attest." She nodded reluctantly, though "painful" did not entirely describe the complicated sensation from the day of her testing. "But what else can you expect from the Staffkeepers of Shaefi?" Birgir continued. "They do get so attached to pain."

Valdis didn't know what he meant by that, so she poured the tea and fell back to silence. The Staffkeepers nodded gratefully in turn as she filled their cups. She lit a fire in the hearth and between the bodies and the flames the cottage was soon cozy with warmth. When all were settled, she took up her father's lyre and sat sideways in his chair before the flames, her legs over one plush arm and her fingers plucking randomly. He had never taught her to play, but Valdis was happy to pick and think without concern for melody. The group sat for an hour or so before their host rose and took her knife to the door. Birgir rose as well.

"May I come?" he asked. Valdis raised an eyebrow but, finding no objections, nodded once.

They went to the pen and Valdis began looking among her flock for a young buck she had had in mind for slaughter already. She found him and stroked his neck while she guided him toward the path that led to her tiny, shack-like slaughterhouse behind the barn.

"Valdis?" Birgir said. She turned back to him, annoyed at the interruption. He was stroking Snow's head gently. "This one," he said simply.

Valdis glared at him. *The gall of this man,* she thought, but what she said was "So you are a goatherd and Staffkeeper both? You think that one a better choice?"

"This one," he said, and now she recognized affection in his voice, "should die today." His surety gave her pause. *Perhaps I will entertain the fool,* she thought.

"Why?" she asked.

"Death is here, on the creature already. Can't you taste it?" he responded.

And strangely, terrifyingly, Valdis did taste something. She closed her eyes and focused on the flavor, rich and earthy yet sour and fresh all at once. It tasted like the air had on the night her father died. She couldn't place the flavor, yet her senses recalled it like a long-forgotten dream. It was intangible, but still she tasted it.

Birgir was watching her closely when she opened her eyes. The smile was gone, and he looked on her now with hopeful eyes. Valdis considered the man's suggestion for several moments. Eventually, she released the buck back to the flock and nodded to Birgir.

"His name is Snow," she said. "Bring him here."

Birgir's smile returned. He did as she bade him, then waited patiently among the flock while Valdis took her companion to his end. He petted the goats and whispered comforts to them as he waited, and when Valdis returned and beckoned him over, he went and helped her butcher the goat with practiced precision.

While they were bloodied to the wrist, he asked her bluntly, "Would you like to be a part of The Conclusion?"

She said nothing as they continued to work. Only when the job was finished did she answer. "Perhaps," she said. "That depends on what you do."

"We do what you and I have just done," Birgir answered. "We find those who Death has come for, and we give them peace before the suffering can begin."

Valdis thought of her long-dead mother. She thought how much her father would have liked these people. She thought of how she had already begun practicing their ways, with her goats and her father both. She heaved a deep sigh.

"Perhaps," she said, and left it at that.

Birgir smiled and pressed no further; he knew there was no need.

8

"**M**uch better," Baggi sighed aloud.

He sank beneath the cool water, submerging himself until he ran out of breath. He emerged, gasping, and pushed back his wet hair. The waterfall Torny had sent him to was far from enormous; luckily, it shared Flamebud Village's strength of character. The river feeding the falls was apparently underground, as white water gushed forth directly from the rocks in a great semi-circle, falling a mere dozen feet or so to the basin. Baggi sighed in admiration as he paddled. With everyone else at market, he had the pool to himself, and unlike taking breakfast, he much preferred to bathe this way. This was not due to modesty, of course; the Shaefini and, to a lesser extent, Naefjans in general lacked the discomfort with nakedness that prevailed in the other regions. Pleasure and beauty were among Shaefi's domains, after all. To gaze on the artistry of the human form and respond with embarrassment or disgust would be to insult Shaefi's very essence.

No, Baggi simply disliked being splashed. And as anyone who shared this trait could attest, a distaste for being splashed guaranteed that one would be splashed mercilessly.

No one around to splash. No one trying to rope me into a diving contest. No one shouting. Just me, Compromise, and the sound of rushing water, he exulted, floating easily on his back. The fight from the market hovered over him, the solitary irritant in an otherwise utopian hideout.

He wondered if Geir's cutlass would be returned to him. It seemed unlikely. Baggi stared at the open sky as the gentle rush of water turned him in lazy circles. *Even the sky is different here,* he thought. *Not a cloud in sight. They must not get much snow.* He idly wondered what it would be like to grow up a stranger to blizzards. He found himself thinking of a night during his first week at the Temple at Enton, years ago. *There was a blizzard that night, too.*

He had been staring out the window at the gardens, watching as the dirt was slowly overcome by powder. He was afraid for the plants, worried that they would die from the weight and from overwatering, and then Compromise had been snatched from his hand. Even in reminisce, Baggi felt the touch of fear. The thief had been another new apprentice, a girl whose name had long since been forgotten. Baggi couldn't remember the words she used, but he remembered well their weight. The phrasing was unimportant. Baggi had cried, and begged for his staff back, and the thief had looked down on him with pity, and then anger. And she had shoved him, hard, so hard he had lost his footing and his head had cracked on the stone floor. Then the memory blurred even further as a third apprentice, slightly older with silver eyes and hair, had leapt forward to fight off his assailant. But they were not warriors; they were children. Their movements held no beauty or grace. They had scratched and clawed and bit and pulled, abandoning civilization in favor of that feral instinct called life. Then Sage Ove was in the room, and he invoked a rune that made them both stop. Baggi's defender had wrenched Compromise from the thief's hand, and he returned it before Ove led them both out. He had never seen a Sage look so disappointed.

The apprentices did not return.

Baggi blinked hard and saw the pool once more. *Of course they were cast out. Violence is not tolerated. And yet...without someone else fighting for me, I would have been hurt more.* For the thousandth time, he wondered what the boy who had protected him was doing now. He wondered what his name was, and if he was happy. He wondered if he regretted fighting that night, or if he kept the memory as a trophy, a testament to his honor. Baggi thought of Amund, fighting to protect a little boy just as the apprentice had, and he thought he began to understand the Chief of Flamebud a little bit better.

He suddenly felt a foreign indignation. The unexpected emotion startled him into tensing up, and he sank beneath the water, where he momentarily burbled in confusion before kicking back to the top and treading water. *What was that?* Baggi wondered. He looked around, finding no cause for alarm within sight. There were only his clothes, laid neatly out on a rock, and Compromise, leaning against the same. A strange thought occurred to Baggi. *It may be insane,* he reasoned, *but lately insane ideas seem to be working in my favor.* He swam over to the bank and approached his staff. *Do you...want to swim as well?* He wondered, inexplicably cautious.

Immediately, Compromise pulsed with excitement, ice-blue energy puffing from its runes. Baggi yelped in surprise and tripped over himself, landing back in the water. He scrambled, sputtering, back to his feet as quickly as he could. He knew that staffs had personalities, and even a certain level of preference, but Compromise had never responded to him so directly. Before now, he had occasionally felt vague impressions of feelings, and even then only when attuned. This was completely different. This felt more like conversation.

Well...what kind of Staffkeeper would I be if I said no?

Compromise pulsed again and celebration overwrote Baggi's nervousness. He picked up his staff and waded back into the water. When he was up to his shoulders, he raised his legs and prepared to float on his back once more. After a moment of indecision, he let go of

Compromise and allowed his apple-wood companion to float freely as well.

Baggi felt a brief spike of separation anxiety, the same feeling that jolted through him when Kettil asked to hold Compromise. He took a deep breath and attempted to balance his emotions. It was a difficult undertaking, but he could feel Compromise's reassuring presence in the back of his mind, and after some time the anxiety washed away. In its place came a sense of content. He smiled, nerves calmed. *I suppose there's no use in being alarmed. Though it will take some getting used to.*

Baggi thought that he had been relaxed before, but now, as he and Compromise floated side by side, the feeling was many times stronger. Bliss and coolness filled his mind. He felt the waterfall's waves rock his body, and for a brief moment thought he felt the waves rocking Compromise as well. But the feeling was elusive, so Baggi gave up on trying to sort things out and resolved himself to float. He closed his eyes and allowed time to pass him by.

***

Baggi opened his eyes and was momentarily blinded. The sun had shifted while he floated, now shining down on him from directly overhead. He instinctively raised an arm to shield his face. The movement unbalanced him, and he found himself submerged and disoriented once more. Quickly resurfacing, he gasped and coughed up crisp clean water. *I must have fallen asleep,* he concluded after catching his breath. He glanced around and was reassured to see Compromise still floated nearby. Judging by the position of the sun in the sky, Baggi estimated at least two hours had passed. His skin tingled unpleasantly, and as he reached out to retrieve his staff, he noticed his arm was now an aggressive shade of pink.

"Serves me right," he sighed aloud, "I'll have to see if Kettil has time to mix me an unguent."

He swam back to the bank and began dressing himself. Compromise was subdued, its aura seemingly in hibernation once more. Baggi wondered at the phenomenon as he washed his old clothes. It seemed likely that completing his first Task had granted him fresh insight. It was not a stretch, then, to assume their bond had been strengthened as a direct result of what he had learned. *Could that have caused it to awaken?* He pondered. The relationship between staff and keeper was deeply personal, which meant even the sagest advice could not be applied to every case, and as a result, little information was available regarding what to expect during the bonding process. Baggi concluded that the answers he sought could only be found in his staff. Unfortunately, he was unable to press the query any further until Compromise woke up again. *Assuming Compromise wakes up again at all,* he thought ruefully. Fully clothed, with his hair dripping wet and unrestrained, Baggi picked up his staff and set off towards the village. He carried his spare clothes and towel in hand this time. It seemed rather rude to use Compromise as a bindle again, given the afternoon's events.

The path back was well-maintained. Kichishi was a dry and rocky region, but after such a long soak Baggi found the dusty heat pleasing. Water dripped from his hair, running down his face and soaking his collar, but he didn't mind. He did cringe as his clothes rubbed against him, irritating his sunburns, but even the pain was not unwelcome. It made him feel balanced and human. It reminded him of the fight and illustrated just how much damage Amund's strikes must have inflicted. *If a measly sunburn hurts this much,* he thought somberly,

Geir's pain would have been unbearable. He was unsure if the man had deserved it or not, but he knew for certain that Shaefi would have handled it differently. Baggi raised the hand holding his damp clothes and brushed his lips. They were wet to the touch.

As the trail widened out meet the walls, the market's clamor returned to earshot. Once inside, Baggi observed that although it was only noon, the market was far less busy than it had been in the morning. Some stalls were still going strong, but many others were already packing up and breaking down their equipment. The musicians were absent, either done for the day or taking a much-needed break. Baggi saw the boy named Kalfr hawking carrots relentlessly and smiled. The lad's efforts had paid off, as he was down to his last three bushels. The frog-seller, having sold out already, finished tying a rope about the huge frog-pot and heaved it onto his back. Baggi made to help, worried that the boy would falter under the weight of the clay twice his size, but the child seemed well able. He marched off, pushing a wheelbarrow full of cooking supplies and carrying the pot simultaneously. *Half my size, twice my strength,* Baggi thought.

The apprentice self-consciously examined his own body. He was not unfit himself; after all, life in a caravan meant long days of travel and, more often than not, meager meals. Still, those same factors meant that Staffkeepers very rarely had the opportunity to build muscle. There were exceptions, of course, though mostly among other Orders; to Staffkeepers of Sawtor, for instance, training in the martial arts was as essential to their ideologies as Contemplations were to the Shaefini. Baggi wondered how Amund would react to that information and chuckled. *He's nearly a Staffkeeper of Sawtor already. All he needs is a staff.* The image of Staffkeeper Amund lecturing him on the merits of ambition and justice, staff in hand, turned Baggi's chuckles to guffaws as he walked.

"What's so funny?" shouted a friendly voice from the right.

Baggi turned to see Kettil skipping down the lane toward him. It was not exactly graceful. She skipped the way most others ran, as if the next logical step up from fast walking was not to jog, but to launch herself furiously through the air one foot at a time. She was quicker at it than most, but still it made for a thoroughly entertaining sight. She stopped short in front of him, stared at his vibrant red face, then pointed at his burned skin tactlessly and began to giggle.

"Never mind," she snorted, "I can see well enough."

Baggi pursed his lips in mock distaste, but in truth the relaxation of his soak still covered him head to toe. "Your timing is impeccable as always, Kettil," he laughed along, unable to maintain an air of seriousness. "I hate to impose, but would the best alchemist in town happen to have time for mixing a burn unguent?"

"Easy!" Kettil boasted, hands on her hips. "Actually, I've been working on a little something special!" She looked around cautiously, then tugged Baggi's sleeve and led him back to the inn. "The other apprentices'll be busy with their work for another couple hours, so we've got time. Good thing I'm so talented and finished early," she said without a hint of self-awareness.

They slunk through the door as inconspicuously as possible, though Torny's suspicious glare was unavoidable. *It's her inn, after all,* Baggi thought, *I expect she sees all that happens in here.* In front of the apprentices' room, Kettil fixed Baggi with a gravely serious expression.

"You can't tell anyone about this, okay?" she said. "Nobody can know until I've got it just right. 'Cause if they find out, they're gonna try to tell me how to do it. Promise?" Baggi nodded. She took a deep breath. "Okay, come on. And close the door behind you."

Baggi did as she bade. Inside, the room was unoccupied, just as Kettil had predicted. She scuttled over to one of the two beds and crawled underneath. Baggi heard grunts of exertion, an alarming bumping noise, and an exclamation rather inappropriate for a child of Kettil's age, then she managed to crawl back out, rubbing her head with one hand and pulling her alchemy box with the other. As she fished a key out of her pockets and unlocked the case, Baggi admired the handiwork. Truly, it was a masterpiece. At first glance, it appeared nothing more than a box two feet long and slightly smaller on its other sides. Under closer examination, its charms became more apparent. Clearly an antique, it was decorated with tasteful alchemical symbology and banded with aged, tarnished silver. It struck him as strange, her having this box.

"Kettil?"

"What?" she said, not bothering to look at him as she fiddled surreptitiously with the contents.

"I never did ask; where did you get your alchemy box?"

"Hm?" she turned to him now, suspicion flashing across her face before waving the question off noncommittally. "Elof gave it to me." She set aside several unrecognizable ingredients and closed the case.

"I see," replied Baggi, more confused than before, "and where did Elof find the odd for such a valuable case?"

"I dunno," she said, now digging through her travelling pack for alembic and crucible. The bag was nearly larger than Kettil herself and stuffed to full capacity. "Ask him."

Baggi bit off his further inquiry, knowing it wouldn't do to provoke his friend. *She's about to show me something she's kept secret. I should respect her privacy.* Besides, his Tasks had already provided him plenty of questions; there was no sense in adding another. Her tools assembled, Kettil slipped on a pair of heat-resistant gloves much too large for her hands and turned to him with a dangerous gleam in her eye.

"Alright," she said haughtily, "observe, Baggi. I'm gonna make magic."

He nodded politely and watched as she lit a candle to heat the alembic and poured a flask of indigo oil inside, tapping the container gently so as not to waste a single drop. Baggi respected alchemy, but its methods and devices were outside of his ken. So rather than try to ascertain her intentions, he merely watched as Kettil distilled the liquid and poured it into her crucible, whereupon she used a pestle to muddle it with several foreign substances. She added a blue-burning coal that sizzled as it dissolved in the viscous mixture. The potion bubbled ominously, but Kettil seemed satisfied with the results. She procured a sprig of mistletoe. *Ah, I know that one!* Baggi realized, *Even I recognize mistletoe. And I never even got to work in the gardens.* For one bizarre moment he thought she was going to use it as garnish. Instead, she dropped the sprig into the liquid and started counting under her breath. At the count of twenty, she picked up a small metal hook from her toolbelt, and at precisely thirty, she plunged the hook into the crucible and scooped out the sprig in one smooth motion. Despite the quickness of the movement, not a single drop splashed over the rim.

Her movements were precise and efficient, yet Kettil seemed relaxed throughout the alchemical process. To her, brewing a potion seemed second nature. She had once told Baggi that she could already brew Knit and Bonegrow before she had arrived at the Temple at Enton. He had humored her at the time but written it off as a ridiculous child's boast. After all, those were far from everyday brews, and finding an apprentice who could mix them was a near-impossible task, even after years of teachings. Now, though, as he watched her expertise at work, he began to consider that Kettil's pride was almost deserved. *It's true, after all,* he thought proudly, *she really is a genius.*

"Okay," she declared, grinning and wiping sweat from her forehead, "it needs to cool, but look here."

Baggi drew nearer and saw that the potion was now a translucent sky-blue. There was heat emanating from the crucible, certainly, but it seemed to be cooling at an unnatural rate. Transfixed to the point of stupidity, he reached out a finger to test the temperature. Kettil slapped his hand away before he made contact, staring at him in utter astonishment. He grinned sheepishly. She shook her head, stuck between amusement and pity, then after some moments had passed, she picked up the hot crucible in a gloved hand and transferred the contents to a wide-bottomed potion flask. She handed her creation to Baggi, and he took it with some skepticism.

"Oh, relax!" She assured him on observing his unease. "It's completely safe!"

Curiosity overriding his better judgment, he shrugged and decided to trust her. *When has she ever led me wrong in the past?* He asked himself, countless examples immediately springing to mind. He shook off the doubt. *What am I thinking? I can trust her alchemy skills. This is probably even safer than a potion from a full-fledged alchemist. Kettil would never put me in danger.*

"Right," he repeated, full to the brim with faith in his friend, "completely safe."

He quaffed the shockingly icy potion in one hearty gulp, just in time to hear Kettil cough "Probably."

For a brief moment, Baggi felt an unpleasant mixture of fear and bafflement. Then the potion started to take effect and he found himself unable to focus on anything else. It was torturously cold running down his throat, and the chill began to spread throughout his body. He felt the magic coursing through his veins, pulsing painfully with unrestrained vigor. Baggi felt as if his blood had turned to ice and began to shiver. The sensation was both unpleasant and familiar; it felt as if he had invoked Isaz, albeit amplified many times. His vision clouded over as a breath of frost covered the irises. Fully in the throes of panic, Baggi reached blindly for Compromise, seizing it in a desperate grip. He had hardly the time to regret his decision, when suddenly it was over. He blinked hard, his skin still cold and stiff. Kettil was staring at him in bewilderment, equally caught off guard by the potion's effect. There was a long moment of silence.

"Uh..." Kettil mumbled, "I think it worked." Then she chuckled nervously and started scribbling notes on the scroll she always kept up her sleeve.

Baggi held a tremulous arm before his face and observed the angry pink had reverted to his usual pale white tone. He poked at his face, relieved to no longer feel the burns' irritation. Turning back to Kettil and regarding her with wide eyes, he struggled to collect himself.

With an uneven voice, unable to phrase the query more eloquently, he asked "What was that?"

Kettil looked up from her scroll. "Uh...it's a work in progress," she said evasively, then returned to scribbling her notes.

"Kettil," he pressed, "I think I have a right to know, after you used me as a test subject."

Guilt flashed over Kettil's face. "Okay, okay, I know. Just remember not to tell anyone, okay?" Baggi nodded slowly. She scooted closer to him, pushing her tools aside with a concerning lack of care. "I'm making the Water of Life!" she whispered. "Right now I've got the burns and bruises sorted, but soon it'll take care of cuts too!"

Baggi gawked at her. Between the residual pain and the prickly subject matter, he was well on edge. "The Water of Life? How is that even possible? It can't be made, only received as a gift from Shaefi herself!" Kettil's precociousness was usually inspiring, but this? *This is dangerously close to blasphemy,* he thought. *And the worst part is, she may just be able to pull it off.* His stomach knotted up with worry, prompting him to take several calming breaths.

"You mean it hasn't been made," Kettil corrected. "But that's gonna change. Once I figure this out, everything's gonna change! Just picture it: a world without funerals, or war, or tragedy!" She gushed, oblivious to her friend's tense posture. "No more bruises, or burns, or cuts, or diseases. No more aging, Baggi!" Her eyes shone with a frantic optimism that Baggi wanted badly to match. But he couldn't.

"Kettil," he began, unsure of how to broach his concerns. *If I handle this properly, it will be the end of it. If not, it could sow distrust between us,* he thought. Baggi felt sorry for himself before balancing his emotions once more. *What a terrible position I'm in.* He paused, then sighed. "You know where the Water of Life comes from, don't you?" he asked.

She looked back at him with unease. "Of course. Shaefi gives it to Staffkeepers who prove themselves, for emergencies. Only the most important ones, though," she added. "Not even most Elder Sages have tasted it."

"Not exactly the most important ones, just those who need it most," he corrected. "But you know where it comes from, don't you? How Shaefi..." he hesitated, coughed uncomfortably, "...extracts it?"

She stayed silent. Baggi swallowed, wishing very much not to be having this conversation.

"Well, it's believed that the Water of Life is what runs through Shaefi's veins," he continued. "It's what suffuses her being with life and vitality. In other words..."

"Her blood," Kettil finished for him. She looked to be deep in thought. The expression concerned him.

"Yes," Baggi agreed, looking away. "It is believed that when Pain spilled Shaefi's blood at the birth of the world, the drops fell upon the land and became humanity. Every time the gift is received, Shaefi suffers for it, for us. And, don't get me wrong, Kettil, it would certainly be wondrous to get rid of those things you mentioned. But I can't help but worry about the consequences of unending life. I can't help but think that...perhaps this is a bad idea."

He cringed, bracing for an indignant outburst. There was silence. Baggi slowly turned back to Kettil, and his heart broke. She looked hurt, immeasurably so, as if he had criticized her instead of the potion. *Of course,* he thought helplessly, *just like I would be if she criticized Compromise and our bond.* Tears began to well up in Kettil's eyes. She looked away and roughly rubbed at them with a gloved knuckle. When she turned back, her expression was not sad, or angry, or insulted. Instead, it was composed and formal, and that hurt worst of all.

"Thank you for your concern, Staffkeeper Apprentice Baggi," she said, and began to stiffly pack her tools away.

"Kettil-" he began, but she cut him off.

"It's fine, Baggi," she snapped, "just go worry about your Tasks. You're gonna be a big important Staffkeeper soon." Then her shoulders slumped and her voice softened. "And I'll just be here."

Baggi wanted to offer words of comfort, words of encouragement. He wanted to apologize and tell her to forget about what he had said. But he couldn't, for the same reason that he couldn't have kept it to himself in the first place. *The same reason she said herself,* he knew, *I'm going to be a Staffkeeper. It's my duty to voice my concerns. And this is blasphemy, isn't it?* He opened and closed his mouth, then sighed again, rose to his feet, and left Kettil to her own devices, closing the door gently behind him.

On her own, Kettil allowed herself to feel lost and hopeless, but only for a moment. Then she shook her head, unpacked her tools and opened her alchemy case once more. Along with her supplies, she procured a knife. Kettil stared hard at the blade as she thought about what Baggi had said. Then she drew the blade across her palm and squeezed her hand hard, funneling the blood into a vial. She reached for a flask of Knit and tipped two drops of apricot-colored liquid on the wound. The flesh bound back up immediately.

"Bad idea," she scoffed fiercely. The silence of the room around her was interrupted only by the percolation of her alembic.

***

Amund wiped sweat from his face as he approached the Flamebud Inn. *A long market day, a successful one, and best of all, nearly a peaceful one,* he thought with pleasure. The sun was beginning to descend and by now the market was well and truly over. At times like these, folk were heading home to record sales and take a much-needed rest. Amund didn't spend much time in his family home anymore. He didn't like it there, so open and cold and lonely. Even the sacred flamebud garden on the estate's roof had long since lost its ability to warm him. Since becoming Chief of Flamebud Village, Amund usually spent his evenings at the inn, where he would drink pepper-cider and eat supper and linger for as long as he could justify. It was more home to him now than the place he slept.

Pushing open the door, he was annoyed to find the Staffkeepers occupying most of the stumps and several of the stools. *At least they are few in number,* he consoled himself as took stock of the inn's inhabitants. He didn't recognize most of them, not directly, but he had been taught from a very young age the tell-tale signs of authority. *That one by the north wall, she is a leader. Was it not she who healed Geir Waste-Of-Flesh?* he noted, locking eyes briefly with the middle-aged woman. She held his gaze for several moments before politely lowering her head. Amund found himself responding in kind.

Elsewhere, he saw the old man he had argued with in the pass before Baggi intervened. *He defies convention,* he thought with mild irritation, *displaying no signs of authority. And yet, they all respect him. They all love him.* Hrafn was seated at a stump and seemed to be in the middle of a long and meandering fable about a dog and eggshells. It made no sense to Amund, but the listeners were enraptured. In the middle of a sentence, the old man stopped as something caught his eye. A shy apprentice with long red hair was hovering self-consciously between tables, shifting her weight from foot to foot and attempting to listen without being noticed. Hrafn smiled kindly and motioned for her to join the group. Amund recognized the girl Hjordis as she stood up and offered her seat to the child. The apprentice took it, but Hjordis seemed to be the one who had received a kindness, casually resting her staff on her shoulders and grinning with satisfaction. Amund shook his head in wonder. *They must know how sickening their politeness is,* he thought stubbornly, but despite his best efforts the corner of his mouth twitched upwards.

Crossing to the bar, Amund noticed Baggi sitting at one end, his hair down rather than braided like usual. Despite the apparent lack of seating, there were several empty stools between him and the nearest Staffkeepers. Amund took the spot next to him and nodded gratefully as Torny brought him his customary mug of cider. He took a sip and turned to his Naefjan friend, noting his gloomy expression.

"You look like me, wearing such a troubled face," he said.

Baggi half-turned to him, then sighed. "Good evening, Amund," he replied. "I trust the rest of the market day was a success?" There was an unfamiliar sadness to his tone that made Amund uncomfortable.

"Of course," he replied, "though I have little trust that your day was equally successful."

Baggi sighed again, more deeply this time. *This is not usual for him, is it?* Amund wondered. *It could be. I've only known him for some days.*

"It was successful, yes, though not equally so," Baggi dodged the implicit question, staring into his own half-drained mug. Amund rolled his eyes, quickly losing patience.

"Would you like to explain, or would you prefer to keep sighing?" he asked. The apprentice looked embarrassed momentarily and then shook his head.

"I would like to, but I made a promise," he said dramatically, taking a tiny sip. Amund looked toward Torny and made a questioning gesture, but she only shrugged and threw up her hands.

"Chief Amund," he continued, "I wonder if I might ask a personal question." His eyes remained fixed on the liquid in his mug.

"You may," Amund said after a pause, "although I may not answer." Baggi nodded and took another sip.

"If you could do away with Death forever, would you?" he asked softly. Despite the drop in volume, there was an intensity in his voice. Amund regarded him for a moment before answering.

"I am Chief of Flamebud," he answered. "My duty is to protect my people. Whatever means available to me, whether by combat or decree, I seize on, for I have seen exactly what happens when that duty is neglected. We all have." He saw Torny freeze in his peripherals, abruptly motionless in the middle of polishing a glass. "Let me ask you a question in turn, Baggi," he said, turning to stare him in the eyes.

"What kind of chief would I be if I chose not to free my people from their greatest threat?"

Baggi met his gaze, and in his eyes Amund saw a horrible turmoil. He looked for a moment as if he wanted to agree, but then he bit his lip and sighed. After a moment, he turned back to his mug.

"And what would you do one hundred years from now?" he asked.

Amund tightened his brow. "What do you mean? I would do the same as I do now."

"And your people? Where would they live?" Baggi turned back to him, agitation creeping into his voice. "How will you provide food and shelter for all those in Flamebud now, and all those born for the next hundred years? And the hundred after that? And the thousand after that? What will you do then?" There was a look in his eyes that Amund recognized. *So they can get angry,* he thought. The amusement was bittersweet. *It doesn't suit him.*

"We will grow," Amund answered stubbornly. "We will move into the forest. Eventually, we will move into the mountains. We will find a way."

"And what about when you run out of forests? What about when you run out of mountains?" Baggi all but whispered. His anger had quickly fizzled back to depression.

Amund thought about what such a future would look like, but it didn't take long to find his answer. He was a warrior himself, after all, and many wounds from the Mineral War were still fresh. *When people have nowhere to go,* he thought, *they take the home they need. They take it from ones who they don't call "their people".* The realization made him feel hollow. *No,* he insisted, *there must be another way. There is always a way. And if there is not, then you blaze a new path.* He focused his breathing and fed his inner fire, then released the ashes of his hopelessness and whirled on Baggi.

"Are you not ashamed to be saying these things?" he demanded, aware of the unfairness in his claim yet unable to restrain himself. "Are your people not opposed to Death? Are you not a Staffkeeper of Shaefi?" The words surprised him, but Amund stood by them.

Baggi looked shocked. Then, it seemed something clicked inside him. He turned back to his mug, but this time his expression was intense and deliberate.

"Not yet," he admitted. "Thank you, Amund, you have helped more than you know." He drained the rest of the mug in mere moments, pushed off from his stool and bowed. "And thank you too, Torny!" he shouted down the bar to where the young innkeeper was serving other patrons.

She looked lost for a moment in mid-pour, then called back "You're welcome!" as Baggi rushed out the door.

Amund had hardly the time to process the extreme shift in mood, and then he was gone. The innkeeper finished her pour and made her way over.

"What was that all about?" she asked.

"I do not know," he replied, "but whatever it was, it troubles me."

"He seemed pretty glum," Torny said, concerned. "Hope he's okay."

She stared at the door he had departed from mere moments ago. Amund grinned mischievously as a realization took shape.

"If you wish, I can go after him and tell him how concerned you are for his wellbeing," he offered. Her flustered reaction confirmed his suspicions.

"No! Don't do that! He'll be okay! Or, at least, if you do go check on him, don't mention me!"

"Now, Torny," Amund began seriously, "as Chief of Flamebud it is my duty to provide for the happiness of my people. I can see what needs to be done." He held up his hands in a peaceful gesture. "It is not a bad match, after all. Baggi is a Friend of Flamebud, and only a year your elder. I will catch up with him right away and put forth the prospect of marriage." He made to leave, draining his mug and standing up.

Torny blanched, then slammed a bottle on the counter, stopping him in his tracks. "Do that, and get used to paying double," she threatened.

Amund maintained a dangerous expression for as long as he could, then reluctantly smiled and sat back down. Torny, in turn, smirked triumphantly and retreated to the kitchen to prepare the evening's meal. The Chief of Flamebud looked around at the busy inn, full of apprentices shouting and Staffkeepers laughing easily at the old man's tales. He felt deep nostalgia, a sense of comfort he had not known in years. *For all their silliness,* he admitted to himself and no one else, *Flamebud burns brighter with them here.*

9

The night sky over Flamebud Village was a spectacular sight. As its last traces of warm light faded from orange to purple, and then purple to black, the stars above began to show. One at a time they emerged from the darkness, their shine at once coy and brilliant. Staffkeepers of all Orders shared a special affinity with the stars. As a symbol, their meanings were multitudinous; as pure art, no Staffkeeper was immune to their beauty. For the Staffkeepers of Sawtor, they represented great deeds, the constellations taking the forms of heroic warriors or symbols of glory. For Staffkeepers of Brathus, who held the seas so dear, the night sky was a reminder of the vast ocean of existence, endless depths punctuated by islands of life shining proudly through. For Staffkeepers of Shaefi, they were proof that no matter how all-encompassing the darkness became, there would always be those who held their light against it.

Baggi paced the town square aimlessly and wondered: *What do the stars mean to Staffkeepers of Death?* His conversations with Amund and Kettil had left him more than a little confused and deeply troubled, but what the former had said struck a chord.

Are you not a Staffkeeper of Shaefi?

Baggi felt himself tensing up as he paced. The question had nearly brought something into focus, and he felt the flavor of it on the tip of his tongue, yet it remained tantalizingly out of reach. He knew he was trying too hard to force sense out of his thoughts, but that didn't make it any easier to stop. Baggi ceased his pacing and looked up at the sky once more. After a moment, he resumed pacing, slower this time. *They're both so sure that doing away with Death would be for the best,* he ruminated, *and I should agree. But I don't.* The realization was disconcerting. Baggi sat on the edge of the well as he turned his gaze back to the sky. There were so many stars, too many to count. It was a lucky thing that there was enough sky for all of them. He wondered what would happen if stars could give birth to more stars, like humans could. Would they fill the sky? Would they be forced to fall when there was no more space left to them? It seemed an outrageous idea.

"But humans aren't stars," he sighed aloud.

Baggi wondered again what the Staffkeepers of Death must see in the night above. But try as he might, Baggi was unable to force understanding. He closed his eyes and tried imagining that he was a Staffkeeper of Death. *I serve Death,* he thought, *the end of life. I take the gift of Shaefi and leave nothing where there once was light.* A memory flashed through his mind, of a woman wearing horns and tossing him a skull. Baggi felt his heart pounding, felt fear overwhelm him, and opened his eyes. He held Compromise close to his breast, reminding himself where and who he was. *I can't,* he thought, *I can't imagine it. I can't understand.* But he felt the shame of dishonesty and forced himself to acknowledge the truth. *I don't want to understand them.*

"Beautiful night, isn't it?" Hjordis said, approaching the well and sitting on its edge next to him. He turned and forced a smile.

"Oh, hey, Hjordis," he began, "I-"

"Let me guess," she interrupted, "'I didn't see you there?'" She turned to him and grinned that lupine grin he had grown so fond of.

"Am I so predictable?" Baggi snorted.

He knew his mentor would not have interrupted his solitary reverie if not for good reason; she likely came bearing wisdom that might help him in his Tasks. Yet when his mind drifted back towards his prior thoughts, Hjordis seemed insignificant, and so did he and his Tasks. They both gazed up at the stars and stayed silent.

"You know, when I received my Tasks," Hjordis began after some time had passed, "I felt really alone." Baggi turned to her, surprise evident.

"You? But everyone likes you," he said before he had time to second guess himself. She chuckled, but there was no humor in it.

"Maybe, maybe not. But that's not the kind of lonely I mean." Baggi waited patiently for her to gather her thoughts. He was beginning to sense the importance of what she would say, even if he didn't yet know what it was. "I found a lot of new questions, and it seemed like I was only finding scarce answers. It made me wonder: 'why didn't anyone teach me about this? Has no one else thought of it?' But I knew that couldn't be right."

"Why not?" Baggi asked intensely. She turned to him, an eyebrow raised at the unexpected interruption. After a moment the grin returned to her face.

"Well," she replied, "because I'm really not that wise." Her tone was playful, but beneath it Baggi heard a strange irritation. "So, I found myself where you are now, sitting under the stars, looking up and wondering and feeling like nobody was asking the questions I wanted answers to. But then I realized something: I wasn't the first one to have to earn her Marking, so there's no way the Staffkeepers before me weren't just as lost and confused. And I realized that the questions might be different for each person, but they're always there."

She fell silent. Baggi waited for her to resume the anecdote, but she appeared to have finished. He felt shorted, like a long-winded sentence that ended without punctuation.   A deliberate deep breath dispelled the unjustified feeling. In its place, he felt an unfamiliar sense of validation.

"Thank you for your wisdom, Staffkeeper Hjordis," he intoned, standing up straight and bowing. She scoffed jokingly but returned the gesture.

"It's nothing, Baggi," she replied, waving a dismissive hand. "You probably didn't need it anyway. You finished your first Task no problem, right?" She nudged him with an elbow. "And with your talent, I bet you're already close to finishing the second, too. Makes me proud to be your mentor!" Baggi froze beside her. She nudged him again, a bit harder this time. "Hey, are you okay?"

"Right," he replied slowly, "my second Task. I've been...a bit busy."

"Busy?" Hjordis asked, in a tone implying his sanity may be in question. "With something more important than your Tasks?" Baggi pursed his lips in embarrassment, unable to voice a defense. "Well, hey," she rushed to reassure him, "that's okay! You've still got two days. What are you working on? Maybe I can help."

"Right, yes, I still have two days," he said, taking deep breaths to maintain his composure. He cleared his throat before reciting the instructions given to him by letter.

"Hmm...that's an open-ended one," she mused said after thinking it over. "Have you found a rift yet?"

"Not quite," Baggi mumbled.

"Hey now, don't despair! I heard some locals talking about a town council meeting in the morning. Why don't you ask your friend the chief to let you in? I'm sure they'll have something to argue about. I mean, they're kids." She looked off to the sky thoughtfully. "Really, it's amazing they've lasted this long without completely devolving."

"Amund," Baggi said absentmindedly, "that's his name, and the reason they haven't turned on one another. They trust him, and for good reason. He holds this village together."

Hjordis grinned at the admiration in his voice but decided against teasing him. After all, he was in a precarious position. After watching him sit alone at the bar for far too long and sighing far too frequently, that much was clear to her. She had been on the cusp of approaching him herself when the Chief of Flamebud had arrived and beaten her to it. *Maybe it's just the Tasks,* she thought, *or maybe it's something else, but either way I'm glad Amund talked to him. He's a good influence. Even if he's got a temper.* She rose from her seat on the well and stretched her arms over her head.

"I don't know about you, but I've had a long day," she yawned. "Time for me to get some sleep. And I suggest you do the same. The council gets together just after sunrise."

"Good idea," Baggi replied, catching her yawn. "I'd hate to sleep in again and miss it." He, too, rose, and they made towards the inn. "Oh, Hjordis?" he asked as they went.

"Yeah?"

"Where is the meeting?"

"Right, have you seen the north side of town? With the forum and the big, fenced house that looks like a turtle?" Baggi shook his head. "Well, it's over there."

She pointed down the lane, in the direction of the mountains their caravan had passed through on their way to Flamebud Village. He couldn't see much in the evening's darkness, only a soft black that coated the village and beyond, rising straight up at its walls like a circuitous obsidian monolith. A sudden homesickness overcame him then, a longing for the white snow that glowed in moonlight and made even night familiar, recognizable. He wondered how his mother was faring without him around to tend the sheep. Then he sighed and followed his mentor inside.

***

"Silence!" Amund roared, his voice cutting through the crowd.

The folk of Flamebud fell silent, the clamor of argument that had pervaded the assembly immediately quenched. Their open-air forum consisted of three rows of stone benches carved in a raked arrangement, so that all in attendance could have a clear view. These seats faced a modest stage where Amund stood presently and on which the speakers would be invited to address their neighbors should they have concerns or questions to bring before the council. An arch of richly carved stone curved over the apron, depicting various Kichishi fables and tales of legal justice, and in the center of this arch was a large, round hollow. When the rising sun lay perfectly aligned with the hollow, then the time to convene the council was upon them, and when no trace of it could be seen through the stone ring, then the council had gone long enough and should be dismissed.

Flamebud had in years past been strict about the proceedings during the council meetings, adhering to a system wherein a representative from each household would attend weekly. It need not be the same representative every week, and indeed most households cycled through their members for each session so that all of the family might have their say and stay informed while still advocating for their household's concerns and needs. In truth, the village council more closely resembled an open discussion, loosely organized but rigidly formal.

Of course, now that Flamebud Village was populated by children, rules and formality both tended to fall by the wayside. All that kept the town council meetings from falling into sheer chaos was the steady guiding hand of Chief Amund. He was a fair and compassionate overseer, if a bit impatient, and his stalwart nature was sufficient to keep even scores of children attentive and engaged. He stood now with a hand raised towards the crowd, thumb tucked impractically in his fist, the recognized symbol calling for attention. *This will be a difficult meeting,* he thought, using the brief moment of silence to steel himself and survey the crowd. He saw his people watching him expectantly, waiting to take their cue from his conduct. *I will not let them down,* he resolved, *I will show strength and nobility now, when they most need it.*

As he surveyed his people's anxious faces, he made eye contact with each one. Amund was pleased to see Talia the tailor in attendance today. She was pale and tired, but the fire in her eyes nevertheless burned strong. He suppressed the urge to grin. *She looks alive again,* he noted, *but I must remain stoic.* Many breaths were held in these moments, many faces watched him with the intensity of raptors poised for flight. There was the blacksmith, unevenly muscled arms crossed over a blackened apron, his back straight as an iron rod. There was the hunter, descendant of Melennese immigrants, his forest-green hair tied in a ponytail and gloved fingers twitching impatiently. In the third and highest row, nearly on the end, sat the innkeeper Torny, cross-legged. Next to her, capping the row, sat the foreigner, the Staffkeeper Apprentice Baggi. He leaned forward inquisitively on his staff, glancing sideways at the hushed crowd before returning his gaze to the stage. Amund sighed internally and noted the sun had risen to position in the arch. *No use putting it off.*

"I convene this weekly council meeting in the name of Flamebud Village," he declared. "May whoever wishes to speak indicate it now."

The crowd began murmuring nervously and glancing about. The source of their hesitation was obvious as the more daring villagers turned glares towards the high corner of the forum; who would wish to speak of the village's hardships in the presence of a foreigner, and a Staffkeeper no less? Amund saw the impatient hunter shoot up from his seat and press his hands together in front of his chest, bending his fingers to form the Sign of Flame. *Of course,* Amund thought, exhausted already. He risked a glance toward Baggi and saw him leaning forward shamelessly to observe the gesture. The boy's blue-and-white cloak nearly fell about his shoulders over the head of the girl in the row below him, but he caught the hem just in time to throw it back. *The fool is going to get his teeth knocked out if he is not more careful,* Amund thought in amazement. Then he turned his attention back to the hunter and the uneasy whispers making their way through the crowd.

"I call upon the hunter, Vigi," he announced, returning the Sign of Flame. He stepped back and gestured with his left hand to the center of the stage.

Vigi walked swiftly and proudly to the end of the row and descended the stone steps. Being of mixed ancestry, his skin was lighter than his fellow full-blooded Kichishi, leaning towards the green-grey shades reminiscent of tree bark that the Melennese guild-tribes were famous for. Amund noted he wore his belt quiver, a beautiful family heirloom rimmed with opal and lined with fine leather. He rolled his eyes at the frivolity of wearing such ornamentation to council. *What is he planning on using it for?* He thought. *He left his bow at home, so he knows the pointlessness.* Vigi had always been a thorn in Amund's side, a confrontational young man a mere two months his junior. His fighting skills were better than average, though not close to approaching Amund's mastery, and his archery skills afforded him some lenience of which he took frequent advantage. *He is careful, always pushing but never hard enough to warrant a response,* Amund thought irritably. The hunter stepped lightly onto the stage, his green eyes shining with unspoken challenge as acknowledged his chief.

"My friends," he began, voice crackling like hot oil, "I do not wish to waste our time. We all have places to be, business to conduct, and people to feed." He paused strategically to allow the crowd to relax before continuing. "Yet, it seems to me that we lack the resources to feed the village. It is only just spring, and the harvest is yet months off; our stores are nearly empty, and soon we will also lack the means to afford a share of our neighbors' crops. How is it that our supplies have run so low?" He opened his arms to them, as if it were not a question he placed before them, but a generous offering. With a sinking in his breast, Amund realized that was just so. *He offers them the chance to blame the Staffkeepers,* he realized, *where they hesitated before and trusted my judgment, now he has shown them the possibility of dissent.* He ground his teeth and burned his indignance to ashes. There were times for passion, and times for patience.

"How is that you know these things?" Amund interjected mildly. "Perhaps if you spent more time on the hunt and less in the bank, the issue would resolve itself." He heard laughter here and there, but it was far from pervasive. The lack of response set him on edge. Vigi turned to him with a tight smile.

"As it happens, I was enjoying a meal with my neighbor when she shared this knowledge with me. It seems it would be better for her to explain. If I may call upon the banker, Audr?"

So they are in it together this time, eh? I might have expected it, Amund thought. He stepped forward, restraining the urge to push Vigi aside as he did so.

"I call upon the banker, Audr," he said, indicating with the Sign of Flame a seated girl in the front row.

She was likewise similar in age to Amund, but unlike Vigi, their resemblance stopped there. Audr wore a high-waisted long skirt bearing a striped blue-and-purple pattern, and a delicate short-sleeved tangerine blouse that exposed a narrow line of her midriff. The outfit was impractical for hard labor, and neither was it in the native style, having been imported from Geluwam in the Melenno Valley. However, as the village banker this posed little issue for Audr. She was wealthy enough to import luxuries from foreign lands; in addition, she enjoyed the innate luxury of spending her days out of the hot sun, instead plying her trade indoors and among the company of paper and ink. As a result, she was pale and even a bit frail when compared to her countrymen. She languidly rose to her feet and returned the Sign of Flame, opal earrings reflecting the warm morning light, heels clicking as she approached. They, too, were a Geluwam import, and designed to draw up her height by several inches. She climbed the stairs without breaking stride and took her place in center stage, pausing only to blink inscrutably at Amund on the way up.

"Good people, you know me," she began, smiling winsomely, "and you know of my shrewdness in business and mathematics."

"A little too shrewd, if you ask me," Talia the tailor grumbled, loud enough for the assembly to hear. Several townsfolk emitted resentful laughs, but Audr was undeterred.

"I choose to accept your words as pure compliment," she said loftily, "as matters of business inevitably breed misunderstanding. Fortunately, the matter we bring before you all today is far from difficult to grasp." She cast her gaze downwards, as if reluctant to continue. Then she took a bracing breath and squared her shoulders, apparently filled with renewed resolve. "I know not all among us relish matters of money and deals, so I will state this as plainly as can be said: we have used too many of our reserved provisions and will be unable to feed all come winter."

The assembly burst into chaotic uproar. Some seated began shouting at the stage, others at the folk sitting next to them, but through it all not a single voice could be made out. Amund stepped forward, insulted but not surprised.

"Silence!" he roared once more.

The shouting and argumentation died out, slower this time. Some even dared to cast sour glances towards the stage. *I dislike like the direction this council is heading,* he thought, *but I must let my people have their say.* Audr turned to him and smirked, nodding insincerely in response to his peacekeeping efforts.

"I know this to be troubling news," she continued sympathetically, "but the facts remain. If you have any doubts, do not take my word; ask it of another upstanding business owner, one who has surely noticed this unavoidable truth." She motioned to the far corner and grinned lugubriously. "If I may call upon the innkeeper, Torny?"

Amund saw now the game they were playing. *Torny has been housing and feeding the Shaefini,* he realized, *and she is honest enough to validate Audr's claim. This could be troublesome.* Audr began to form the Sign of Flame, allowing space for deference to Amund's decision, observing the formality just as Vigi had, but another girl's voice interrupted the motion.

"No, you mayn't," Torny called back.

Audr's face tightened, her façade cracking just enough to allow a glimpse of annoyance. She quickly regained her composure and called out, "I must have misheard you. Surely this problem affects your business keenly. Why would you wish to remain indifferent?"

Torny didn't bother standing as she replied, "Because you're slimy and I don't like you."

There was a moment of disbelief and agitation. In the lull, Amund observed that Torny's body language did not match her easy tone. Indeed, her posture was stiff and her expression stiffer. Next to her, Baggi stared at the innkeeper with wide eyes full of admiration and a splash of disbelief. Amund breathed a sigh of relief, thankful that he had the sense not to smile at her blatant insult. Many of the villagers held him in resentment already, and to compound it so would do his caravan no favors. The Chief of Flamebud stepped forward to head off the clamor that would inevitably follow such a disrespectful gesture.

"The innkeeper, Torny, has declined to take the stage," he proclaimed, making the Sign of Flame regardless as a matter of procedure. "The council recognizes her choice."

But the townsfolk did not seem nearly so pacified as he claimed. Here and there they muttered, ribbing one another and looking expectantly to Audr for her response. She forced a smile before offering it to them.

"I understand," she said, her tone stopping just short of mockery, "Torny wishes to protect her new friends. She knows that to testify before us would reveal the true source of our deficit." She again gestured with an open hand towards the high corner, seemingly to the innkeeper, as she continued, "And I tell you, friends, that it is closer than she would care to admit."

As the trap her words had set snapped smoothly into place, it suddenly became clear to all assembled that she pointed not towards the girl who had challenged her, but the foreigner in their midst. Baggi realized it at the same moment, frozen in place with a hand to his lips and his eyes wide with the panic of a snared rabbit. He shrank into himself, turning his face down to avoid their gazes and apparently attempting to disappear behind his staff. Amund tensed and surreptitiously put his hand to the hilt of his sword, ready for the worst.

Audr turned to him with tight, demanding expression. "We have but two options for the continued survival of Flamebud Village. The first is to demand payment from these...Staffkeepers," she said, spitting out the last word as if it were acid. "The second is to force them out of town and pray for an unexpected fortune to fall into our laps. Naturally, I favor the first."

The gaze of the council followed her lead. Amund felt their eyes on him, each carrying an immense pressure he had never known from his people. *I have pushed too far,* he realized much too late, *I have invited the foreigners in without even putting it before council, and in doing so have aroused skepticism. Now these two have seized on that suspicion and fanned the flames. But why, damn it? Can they not see the folly of such demands? The Staffkeepers have no money to give! Could it be so simple as to undermine my authority? Do they wish to overturn my decision to allow them within the walls? But then why insist on receiving payment?* He racked his mind in a fury, but still he was unable to fathom their motives. Just when he was beginning to feel cornered, Amund glanced towards Vigi's gloating face and saw something unexpected over the hunter's shoulder.

Baggi was standing, Compromise slung on his back, and forming the Sign of Flame with his hands. His finger positioning was imperfect, but the intent was clear. Amund felt his heartbeat quickening and realized this was the only option left to him. *It seems I must risk it all on you,* he thought, incredulous at his own decision, *so you had better make your words count.* The council awaited their chief's decision with such intensity that this display went largely unnoticed. The only one among them reacting appropriately was Torny, who had a hand over her eyes and a defeated posture. Amund cleared his throat.

"I call upon the Staffkeeper Apprentice, Baggi," he all but shouted, daring them to oppose with the timbre of his voice. *And please let my voice be enough.*

Slowly, in unison, the assembly turned to behold the foreigner who would dare intercede. Baggi bowed and approached the stage, walking carefully and avoiding eye contact with the astounded villagers.

"B-b-but he's not even a member of this council!" Vigi stuttered, indignant. "He has no right to speak! You have overstepped your authority, Amund!"

The Chief of Flamebud took two steps closer, accentuating their half-head height difference as he loomed over the spindly hunter. "You speak of overstepping authority, when you dare to address me without title?" Vigi reluctantly looked away, desiring argument yet not daring. "It so happens that I have proclaimed Staffkeeper Apprentice Baggi a Friend of Flamebud for his service in healing our very own Talia the tailor. He has every right to speak. Does this suit you, Vigi?" he demanded in a tone that made clear the proper response.

"I apologize, Chief Amund," he grumbled through gritted teeth.

"Good," Amund replied. "Now clear the stage. It is becoming much too crowded."

Vigi stomped off the stage, forcing his way past Baggi with a rough shove. The apprentice, for his part, merely smiled apologetically. This seemed to annoy the hunter yet further; he huffed loudly as he took his seat next to the blacksmith, who had remained motionless throughout the unorthodox proceedings.

As he took center stage, Baggi cleared his throat politely. "Good morning, all," he began in easy Sparktongue.

There was a moment of disbelief. Amund slapped a hand to his forehead. *In such an important moment,* he wondered, *what favors do such niceties do him?* But as he surveyed the council, he was surprised;

the comment had taken them by surprise as well, had even dispelled some of the surface tension. *Dispelled, but not disarmed,* Amund granted, *I hope you have an idea, Baggi.* Then he noticed a faint blue glowing on Baggi's staff. One of the runes was illuminated. As he strained his eyes in the morning sun, Amund could barely discern a vague, misty trail between the rune and Baggi's forehead. The rune felt strangely familiar, although he couldn't place why. Regardless, he turned his attention to the more immediate danger it invoked. *If anyone else notices him using magic, even I will not be able to calm them,* he thought grimly.

"I know you all to be good people," Baggi continued, "or, at least, those of you who I have been lucky enough to meet. I haven't been here long."

His tone was equal parts amusement and apology, a delicate balance, and the risk he took in so directly addressing his own foreignness was not lost on Amund. It seemed to pay off, as a splash of uncomfortable chuckles sounded. But Audr was too wily to allow him to build momentum.

"Yes," she interrupted, "we all know that you are not one of us. We would prefer you to answer for the expenses your caravan has incurred, rather than beguile us with sweet talk."

"Of course," Baggi said, turning and staring at her with a curious intensity. His features softened after a moment. "I am afraid we don't have much money. But I assume that an accomplished banker with a profitable history, such as yourself, has already inferred that. If I may be so bold," he said, bowing slightly as the honeyed words flowed, "please share your idea with myself and the council."

And just like that, the momentum swung back in his favor. The council turned to Audr, curiosity taking precedence over hostility now. "She has an idea?" Amund heard someone mutter. "If she already knew they can't pay, why didn't she start with that?" another grumbled. "Wasting our time like usual," yet another complained. Audr smiled in mock gratitude.

"What a perfect transition," she noted. "If the foreigner is so familiar with my thoughts, perhaps he would share them himself?"

Baggi remained silent, grinning. There was a ruefulness in the grin, but a humility as well. In the simple expression, suddenly he was the good sport and Audr the browbeater. She seemed not to notice the subtle shift in mood.

"No? As I thought," she continued. "Then hear my plan, neighbors and friends of Flamebud Village: these Staffkeepers each bear silver brooches about their cloaks, which they have naturally neglected to mention when arranging for payment with our noble leader."

Amund remained stone-faced, refusing to give her the satisfaction of alarm. The helplessness he felt was beginning to subside, and as it did he called upon his calculating strategic mind. From early childhood, he had been raised and trained in the arts of war and tactics of battle. Even though his father had been a warrior of great renown, a veteran of the Mineral War and many domestic conflicts besides, Amund's potential to surpass his sire had been widely considered a foregone conclusion. Now the lesson his father had always insisted he value above all others echoed in his mind.

Do not struggle against your weaknesses, he heard in the familiar noble baritone, *acknowledge them, and withdraw. Allow others to succeed where you cannot. That is the true nature of leadership.*

It had been a strange lesson, he had always thought, a lesson that could hardly be called tactics, but now Amund thought he was beginning to understand. *This is not my battlefield,* he thought, *this is a duel of speech. Now, I must trust Baggi to succeed where I cannot.* Audr's voice snapped him out of his memories.

"I say to you, let us demand the proper payment these foreigners have withheld! Let them pay with their silver!" She screamed, her words cutting the air like a blade. As she did so, she raised a hand decisively in the air, contracting it into a tight fist. The effect was eerily militaristic. The crowd warmed to their neighbor's words once more, shouting agreement and nodding firmly. She turned to Baggi with a hard expression, no longer bothering to feign politeness. "Well? What say you, Staffkeeper?"

Baggi waited for the crowd to calm down. When he had their eyes and ears once more, he riposted. "I'm afraid you have miscalculated."

Audr narrowed her eyes. "How so?" she hissed, enormous challenge dripping from the few short syllables.

"Firstly," Baggi began, jabbing to size up his opponent with renewed caution, "not all among us carry Staffkeeper's Marks. As you have undoubtedly noticed, I myself have not been granted one." He gestured meekly to the plain leather fastening on his own cloak. "Apprentices don't receive them until they have been earned. But that's neither here nor there," he conceded, "as the fact remains: there are several such silver brooches in our possession; nineteen, to be exact."

"So you concede that you have concealed payment?" Audr demanded, stabbing viciously.

"I do not," Baggi parried, "as we arranged to pay in healing services for our stay in Flamebud Village. However, it is also true that we are now staying longer than intended, and, indeed, longer than originally agreed upon. It is only fair to renegotiate the terms of our deal." He turned to address the council now, carefully studying their faces as he spoke. "Your people are just and honorable; it is with that fact in mind that I must deny offering the Marks of my fellow Staffkeepers as payment." The crowd began to simmer, but Baggi held up a placating hand as a prizefighter raises his guard. "As I said, your people are just and honorable, and I trust you will understand my reasoning. You see, those Marks are not mine to give."

"If you have no authority to speak on these matters," Audr rebuked him, stubbornly maintaining her attack, "then why come to speak before us at all? Do you wish only to distract us and waste our time?"

"Far from it," he said reassuringly, and Amund saw the triumph of a well-timed counterattack on his face. "As I said, those Marks are not mine to give. But what I do with my own Mark is my decision alone, and I hereby pledge to offer it to Flamebud Village in exchange for the kindnesses they have done me and my people."

"What nonsense is this?" Audr snapped as the counter landed. "You said mere moments ago that you have no such Mark!"

"Yes, I have no such Mark," Baggi agreed, finally on the offensive. "But in five days' time, I will have completed my Tasks and earned it." He lowered his voice slightly, pitching it with regret and sorrow. "It is for this very reason that our stay here was extended in the first place," he said, "and it is only fair that I accept responsibility for payment."

Amund smiled triumphantly. *This will work,* he thought, *they will appreciate his acceptance of the blame. He was right to appeal to our sense of honor. Even I feel vindicated.* Indeed, as he surveyed the council, Amund saw that the reactions were markedly positive. Vigi, naturally, was fuming in silence. Most assembled, however, were nodding in appreciation, some of the harsher critics even turning to their neighbors with reluctant approval. Baggi visibly slackened with relief, the duel seemingly resolved in his favor. The moment's relaxation ended in a sarcastic mewl of laughter.

"What a beautiful joke," Audr purred, lashing out with the cruelty of sheer desperation. "Such a noble boy! Such a generous gesture! Yet one silver brooch will not be enough to refill our coffers. I sincerely hope there is more to your plan."

Baggi seemed to stumble for a moment, caught off guard. *Yes, Amund granted, it was a mistake to take your eyes off your opponent, Baggi. You have left yourself exposed. Have no fear now. You fought well. I will deal the death stroke.* He strode forward and raised a hand for silence. His people stared up at him. The aggressive pressure from before was gone, and they sat now enraptured, waiting for his words, the words that would truly decide the battle.

"There is another way," he declared. He paused to allow his people to soak in his words. "We have all sown our crops in our gardens. The rooftops will be bountiful come harvest, and this is enough to sustain us. It has always been this way. Each home has contributed, each home has helped feed our people. All but one," he said.

Out of the corner of his eye, he saw Baggi staring at him with concern and a look like disbelief. It was as if he could sense his intentions. *But that could not be,* he thought, *how could it? He does not know our ways.* By contrast, the council understood very well. An air of anxiety crept through the forum. Amund allowed himself the smallest luxury of a deep, stabilizing breath.

"The solution is obvious!" he proclaimed. "We will plant crops in my ancestral garden!"

The apprentice beside him visibly cringed in anticipation of violent clamor. Instead, the forum remained silent. Amund found this void far more concerning than the sum of all their prior protests. In a moment of reluctant acceptance, the council heaved a collective sigh. Even Vigi, Amund noted, was shaken, the fight fled from his bones. Gone was the defiant expression, the restless energy and fidgeting. He wore now the same mourning expression as his neighbors. The hunter turned his gaze down, defeated, avoiding Amund's eyes as his posture relaxed and resisted all at once.

"Chief Amund," the blacksmith called out evenly. He had ignored protocol, making the Sign of Flame and then speaking without waiting for acknowledgment. Amund nodded to him gently and allowed this minor transgression. "Chief Amund," the blacksmith said, "what of the flamebuds?"

The council turned desperate gazes toward Amund, silently imploring him to reconsider. The question had been in all of them, that much was obvious. Not a one among them would willingly give up the flowers even as practicality demanded it. But they would never dare to openly question his decision. The flamebuds in Amund's ancestral garden were his to tend. And if he so decreed, they were his to displace.

"The flamebuds will be returned to fire," Amund replied, his voice soft with loss yet resonant in the forum. "They will imbue us with their warmth one final time." And before any more questions could be fielded, the Chief of Flamebud held his hands in the Sign of Flame. "I will be speaking with some among you to make arrangements. I dismiss this weekly council meeting in the name of Flamebud Village." Then he turned, his *korta* billowing beautifully as he descended the steps and left the forum behind.

As he walked a short distance home, the heavy silence of grief filled the air. *It must be done,* Amund thought miserably, *for the continued survival of my people.* He walked, footsteps steady, face relaxing just enough to allow a single tear from each eye. Single tears rapidly became multitudinous. *Water for the flames,* he thought, his own meaning escaping him. *How disrespectful.*

10

Baggi approached the wrought iron gate around Amund's home and peeked through the bars. The space between gate and grand entrance was only a few short feet, yet he found his vision unreliable even at such a minor distance. He rubbed his eyes again, as he had been doing near constantly throughout the morning. Invoking Ansuz for the duration of the council meeting had been rewarding, but it had also taken its toll: his eyes were sore and heavy, and he felt the full fatigue and sluggishness of a long day's travel in his bones. *I've never attuned for so long at once before,* he thought, then chuckled. *I'm making great progress in such a short time.* The realization that a mere five days ago his limit for attunement had been under a minute staggered him. *There's something about this place,* he thought, *something about these people.* He followed the thread of thought back to the insights he had gleaned from council.

Much of the discourse had gone over his head. Although he was fluent in Sparktongue, there was a marked difference between conversing with one and keeping pace with the shouts of many. Still, the substance of the words had been clear. With Ansuz, Baggi had been able to ascertain every minute shift in expression and tone from those around him, so that even when the words slipped by, the rune allowed him to respond simply by reading the speaker's intent. Audr, the banker, seemed a well-meaning sort by his estimation. *She's just like Amund,* he had realized upon sizing her up. Without question, there was animosity in her posture and poison in her voice. She fully intended to seize the Staffkeepers, to put them in their place, and their place, according to Audr, was far away from Flamebud Village. In light of the tragedy visited upon them by the Staffkeepers of Death, this seemed to Baggi perfectly reasonable. He had been unable to dislike her, or to even take offense. *It may seem she has ulterior motives, but that's simply her way of defending herself from duplicity,* he thought, *from being taken advantage of. I suppose it must be a necessary part of her work.*

Amund's subsequent declaration had shaken Baggi nearly as strongly as the council. The significance of the ancestral garden was not known to the Naefjan, but with Ansuz he felt the grim resolve, the permanence of his decree. This was not a decision made lightly. *Whatever he's going to do,* the apprentice thought, *it's not going to be easy.* And so, after Torny had ushered him out of the forum and back to the inn, he had decided over breakfast and another cup of her strong, smoky tea to learn exactly what that decision had been. He allowed Amund two hours to gather himself, passing the time in Contemplation before heading down the lane to the house that, in Hjordis' words, looked like a giant turtle.

"Does it?" he muttered to himself, rubbing his eyes. "Hard to make out..."

"Baggi!" he heard shouted from above. "Loitering, is it?" The voice belonged to Amund, and after blinking hard for a moment, Baggi was able to make out his outline standing on the roof of the grand residence, peering down at the gate and the boy squinting through its bars.

"Amund!" he shouted back vaguely, suddenly unsure of what he had come here for. "I wish to...well, may I come in?"

Amund heaved a loud sigh. Baggi heard the sound of leather dropped on stone and then strong, measured footsteps. After a few moments, the main entrance of the home opened, and Amund approached the gate. He unlatched the mechanism and pushed it open, gazing strangely at Baggi as he did so.

"It was not locked," he said.

"Oh, I know," Baggi lied, "but I thought the polite thing to do would be to wait and ask."

Amund shrugged and gestured for him to follow as he closed the gate and returned to the home's front door. The footpath was gently sloped and smooth, likely the result of an artisan's construction, but the yard itself was far less pristine. Weeds sprouted in irregular patches, and Baggi noted several molehills breaking up the pattern of dry grass. He shot Amund an inquisitive look, but the older boy was in too distractable a mood to notice.

"Come, this way," he said as he pushed the main doors open.

Baggi released a soft breath of admiration as he took in the interior's immaculate resplendence. The main hall was tall, with curved outer walls that implied a dome. Each sloped upwards to join a corner of the mansion's great square roof which, in turn, outlined a concave half-sphere several feet in diameter. The chamber these walls housed was uniformly grand. It lacked for much furniture, hosting a long, dark dining table and not much else, but still the place radiated elegance. Everywhere he looked, every surface in sight seemed carved from one mammoth block of marble. He had seen marble before, in sculptures and idols of pure shining white, but this was distinct; veins of coppery swirls ran the length of the walls, pumped through the ceilings and flowed under his feet. Some were thick as two fingers, others were spindly as golden straw, but everywhere they danced and looped over each other in dizzying acrobatic display.

Amund rolled his eyes as Baggi approached the table in the room's center. He leaned against the wall by the stairway he had intended to hurry his visitor up and braced himself for the inevitable questions. He didn't wait long.

"Incredible," Baggi observed with disbelief. "It's petrified wood. Just like the bar at the inn." He turned back to Amund, one eyebrow cocked. "Is this common in Kichishi? Up north, this much petrified wood could buy my whole village. Actually, even that may be under-selling it."

He peered closely at the table, his eyes mere inches away. The spectrum of rich tones was spectacular, warming him with its very appearance. It stood out like a candle in the darkness. *Or perhaps,* Baggi mused, *like a shadow in the light.* The pervasive marble surroundings suddenly felt inappropriate.

"No, is it is not common," Amund replied gloomily, "it is an heirloom. Torny and I have common ancestors who came into such a fortune many generations ago. They were led to it, in fact, by the wild flamebuds. Her ancient-father used his share to establish the inn. My ancient-mother used hers for this table."

"So you're cousins then?" Baggi inquired.

Amund shot him a confused look. "Is that really what interests you?"

"Not really," he admitted, "but I wanted to avoid predictability." At a dismissive wave, he continued, "I suppose I was wondering: why a table? I understand the inn, using it for the bar; that's establishing a business, and a livelihood for your descendants. What does the table offer you?"

"A nice place to put things down," Amund scoffed, pretending to be bored.

Baggi studied him as well as he could through the blurriness.

"I don't believe it's as simple as that," he prodded keenly. A small smile crossed his friend's face.

"No, it is not quite so simple," Amund responded. "The table was intended to be a place for gathering. Flamebud Village is not such a large place; back in those days, it was even far smaller." He slowly approached the table as he spoke, features softening with each word, brushing the polished surface under affectionate fingertips. "This table is so large in order that all in the village may have a seat at it. All may eat together, facing each other as equals, all partaking of the same bounty. So we did, on days of celebration." He stopped pacing, fingertips hovering just over the wood. "And in times of conflict, it was a place for all to strategize. When other villages sought to absorb ours, when our people agreed to sail in opposition of the pirate Einar Sharpaxe, when Kichishi went to war over rocks in the Melenno Valley, then all could stand round it and look into their neighbor's eyes, and decide together how they might die," he said, voice trailing off.

Baggi looked to him to continue and saw that something behind Amund's eyes was claiming his full attention.

"I stood at this table only once," he continued softly, "before the Staffkeepers came."

Baggi remained silent for several long moments as the chief's words resounded in the open chamber. He felt the gravity of this moment, knew that to ask more too soon would disrupt their fragile peace. After a time, he ran a finger through the layer of dust on the table's surface and said,

"It doesn't seem to have been used in some time."

"No," Amund agreed. "Not in some time."

The ensuing silence answered Baggi's remaining questions. In their places, many more appeared. He closed his aching eyes, took a deep breath, and rebalanced his emotions, quelling the tactless curiosity. When he opened them again, Amund was staring at him expectantly.

"Well? Are you satisfied?" the chief demanded, his usual demeanor returned. Baggi nodded and gestured politely for him to lead the way.

Amund led him back to the staircase he had been hovering around moments ago and began to climb. The passage curved gracefully around, hugging the side of the main chamber as it ascended. Shockingly, there was no railing, only the wall on one side and a sheer drop on the other. Baggi felt his heartbeat quicken slightly with each step. *It didn't look so tall from the ground floor,* he thought, *and yet, one could die falling from this height. They trusted their children to live here?* He pressed gently against the wall and hoped with self-conscious desperation that Amund wouldn't notice. The Chief of Flamebud, luckily, was preoccupied with his thoughts.

As the duo came to the top of the staircase, they were greeted by air thick with the odors of mulch and soil. Baggi slowly turned about, taking in the rooftop garden Amund had brought him to. A gazebo had been constructed long ago to cover the passage from interior mansion to roof, with glass panels for insulation, although several of the windows had been slid aside to allow airflow between both. The gazebo was stuffy despite this, but Baggi paid no attention to his discomfort. Instead, he stood gazing out across the garden, spellbound. The rooftop was covered in soil, every inch of it, and from that soil sprang countless Flamebuds, dancing delightfully in the late morning sun. They threw shining rays through the glass house, illuminating the interior in a show of brilliance the likes of which Baggi had never seen. He flinched as one such ray momentarily flashed across his eyes, blinding him completely. After a few heavy blinks, he laughed in embarrassment. Amund rolled his eyes as he approached a homey, wood-paneled door and opened it.

"Follow me closely," he said, picking up two pairs of leather gardening gloves from the stone parapet and handing him a set.

Baggi noted with some interest that they looked remarkably similar to Kettil's alchemy gloves, thick and treated so as to protect the wearer's hands from extreme heat. Then he had no further time to reflect as Amund began to step lightly between the affectionately bundled rows of crimson, barely brushing them as he navigated the path from memory.

Baggi locked his gaze on the ground, pressure mounting and temperature rising as he desperately tried to keep up with Amund's pace. *This is impossible,* he thought, panting among the flowers' thick heat, *I can't keep up. Shaefi forbid they make a garden with footpaths.* He spared a quick glance around, confirming what he had suspected already: the flamebuds were planted in vague rows, but there clearly hadn't been a plan in place for the garden's eventual expansion. At a certain point, it seemed that design concerns had fallen completely by the wayside, replaced by the more organic style of free-growing flamebuds. *And if I step on one, who knows how dire the consequences may be?* He gulped and redoubled his efforts. So focused was he on his feet that he didn't notice Amund had stopped abruptly in front of him. Baggi grunted awkwardly as he nearly bowled over the elder boy. Amund sighed in annoyance but refrained from comment.

The Chief of Flamebud stood silent for some time among the flowers, breathing deeply with eyes closed. Baggi noted this uncharacteristically pensive gesture and, sensing significance, mirrored his friend's actions. As he inhaled the comforting smell of rich soil and the heat emanating from the flamebuds, Baggi felt invigorated. He pulled the air into his lungs, devouring it with his breath just as he would the scent of freshly baked bread. A vision from the woods several days prior came to mind. The flamebuds had been shocking and wild that day, a dangerous piece of magic found in the woods just like in the ancient stories. Baggi smiled gently at the recollection, he and Kettil standing dumbfounded and amused at their misunderstanding. His thoughts turned to their more recent conversation, the hurt on her face. The heavily perspiring apprentice opened his eyes and pushed the thoughts away. That was a problem for another time. Instead, Baggi turned to his present companion and noted that Amund, too, had opened his eyes. He was focused on the flowers as well, caught between wakefulness and dreaming. Baggi wondered if he had forgotten his presence altogether. He cleared his throat politely.

"Amund," he said, "these are beautiful." The words fell short, and he regretted saying them.

"Yes," Amund replied absently, "of course they are." He knelt in the dirt and began picking at the nearest Flamebud. Baggi squatted next to him.

"What are you doing with them?" he asked, curiosity winning over tact.

"I am saving seeds," Amund sighed, "so that someday, perhaps, if our prosperity returns, the flamebuds may return as well." He pinched a shining orange tear-drop shaped pearl at the base of the flower's stamen between two gloved fingers and carefully extracted it, slipping the orb into a cloth pouch at his waist.

Baggi slipped on his own gloves and wiped the perspiration from his forehead with the back of his forearm. "I see," he said. "And in the meantime, you will be planting food crops?" He felt sure Sparktongue possessed a more apt turn of phrase than "food crops", but it eluded him.

"Yes," the chief replied as he continued to extract seeds, "spinach, peas, various beans..." he trailed off half-heartedly.

"But you don't want to," Baggi supplied.

Amund stopped moving, eyes narrowed slightly as he focused on the implied question. "What I want," he said slowly, "is not the concern of Flamebud Village. What is "want", besides?" he continued, glancing sidelong at the other boy. "What meaning is there in wanting? All I want for is a safe home and neighbors, yet life does not often ask my opinion."

The apprentice laughed gently. "Life may not often ask, but I do," he said.

"Yes," Amund replied with a reluctant grin, "you ask too many things. In this way, my life has balance."

"Hmm," hummed Baggi, playfully contemplative. "I'll make arrangements for someone to take over my duties once the caravan leaves. We can't have you losing your balance."

"No need for that," Amund chuckled. "Someone will fill the gap of their own will. My people are headstrong."

For the first time, Baggi detected a faint hint of exhaustion when Amund spoke of his constituents. Usually, his voice was chock-full of pride, nearly boastful, but now there was a resignation, an acceptance of something Amund had previously chosen to ignore. Baggi carefully reached out and peered into the face of a flamebud. Its seed shone like gemstone, cradled affectionately by the sultry curve of flame-shaped stamen.

"They will miss the flowers," he cautiously probed.

"Yes, but they will understand. This was the garden's fate, today or ten years from today."

"You mean you had already been planning for their removal?"

"Baggi," Amund said impatiently, "I am not a fool. As I said before, Flamebud is not a large village. Yet it was smaller still years ago. In truth, it nearly exceeds its boundaries even now." He deposited a seed in his pouch and took respite from his toil to look Baggi in the eyes. "The previous Chief of Flamebud, my father, was preparing to take this very step to address the issue. Back then, there were no flamebuds, but the garden was still full of flowers. While the other homes in Flamebud Village kept us fed, this garden existed solely for the sake of beauty. It was an impractical arrangement." He looked out over his village, its buildings' red and orange paint glowing in the afternoon sun. "But then the Staffkeepers came, and we were not so crowded afterwards." He abruptly raised himself to his feet and rolled his shoulders. "That will be enough seeds," he said. "Wait here if you wish to help."

He danced back through the flowers to the gazebo, walked around to its opposite side, and retrieved two shovels hanging from the paneling. One was full sized while the second appeared to be made for a small child. Amund tossed the latter to Baggi.

"Now, we dig them up," he said.

"All of them?" Baggi asked, daunted by the flowers' density.

"All," Amund confirmed. "Begin at the roof's edge. I will attend to the circle in the center."

Not quite sure what he meant by "the circle in the center," Baggi decided to hold his questions and do as he was told. His shovel was of a vexing length, too short for him to use with both hands but too unwieldy to keep in one. He felt a soreness in his back after mere moments of digging, and as he uprooted his first flamebud, the snow-born Naefjan was already sweating freely. The early afternoon sun was beginning to rest its full weight upon the two of them, and the additional heat radiating from the flamebuds was sweltering. He felt a pang in his chest as he lifted the flower from its resting place in the soil, as if he had committed an incorrigible transgression. As he raised the flower on his shovel, Baggi glanced over at Amund for reassurance.

The Chief of Flamebud was unperturbed, uprooting one flower after another in inscrutable order. His back to the apprentice, Amund lifted his tunic over his head and dabbed his face and neck with the garment before tossing it carelessly to the side. His body had the appearance of stone, rigid and impenetrable; yet when he knelt, or when he reached out to gather up the foliage in his arms, there was a softness in the movement. Amund's was the body of a dancer modified for combat. Baggi wondered at the discipline required to craft it.

"I intended to commend you earlier," Amund called out as he worked, "on a battle beautifully fought."

Baggi furrowed his brow in confusion. "What do you mean? We don't fight. It's our most important rule." He tilted his head, considering. "Or at least among the top three most important rules."

"Then let us hope Audr does not inform your elders of her defeat," his friend chuckled.

"Oh, no," Baggi said, relieved, "that doesn't count. We were only talking."

Amund looked at him as if he had said something incredibly childish. "Yes, you dueled with your words. Lives were on the line. You attacked and defended. What nonsense are you saying?"

"But it's different!" he protested. "I didn't actually hurt her!" *I probably did wound her pride,* he admitted. *She was just trying to help, after all, and now even her own people would rather listen to a foreigner. To a Staffkeeper.* "At least, not physically."

Amund rolled his eyes as he dug. "That is a foolish distinction, Baggi." He had no rebuttal, and they said no more of it.

As he surveyed, the apprentice realized that the Chief of Flamebud was working at an exceptional pace. Already he had cleared away a path of soil and foliage, revealing a strange architectural feature: the roof sloped gently downwards in the center. He continued to move swiftly, uprooting and gathering and shoveling soil as he went, and as he did so Baggi was able to recognize the outline of a great circle. By his reckoning, the full shape would likely have a diameter of a dozen feet or so. He approached and peered down into the recession. *This must be the dip I saw from beneath, in the main chamber,* he thought. It was shallower than he had anticipated, perhaps six inches deep. *It could go deeper,* he entertained, *underneath all the soil.* He turned quizzically toward Amund.

"What's this?" he asked.

Amund glanced pointedly at Baggi's shovel. It lay discarded in the dirt next to the singular flower the apprentice had uprooted before distraction. He rolled his eyes. "It is where we place offerings. Rather, it is where we used to place offerings. It has no special name," he replied.

"Used to?" Baggi inquired. "Why is it not used now?"

"It is used now," Amund retorted stubbornly. "We are using it for the flamebuds' removal!" His tone was testy, even more so than usual, but Baggi was able to recognize it as a deflection.

"Then it hasn't been used since the flamebuds were planted? Are these flowers that old?"

Amund sighed with annoyance. "You not only ask too many questions, you ask them in ways I dislike," he said. "No, not since before the flamebuds were planted; but they live short lives, and several of their generations have already passed since then. They will soon burn themselves, and their children will grow from the ashes. I expect we would have new flowers next week if allowed." Amund paused, drove the shovel deep into the soil, and hauled out a particularly resilient root network. "And I will answer your next question before you ask it," he added. "We used to make offerings of food or luxuries to Sawtor in this place. After she left us to be slaughtered by Staffkeepers, we had little need for it, but we had great need for a symbol of our people, who burned with anger hotter than ever before. So I entered the woods, retrieved the flowers, and planted the flamebud garden here." Amund stopped working and rested on his shovel, panting lightly. The circle had been uncovered in mere minutes.

The gravity of their undertaking was suddenly apparent to Baggi as he reflected on the offering space before them. He thought he could see into the past, just a bit, to the day Amund spoke of. *It was probably hot,* he imagined, *but they would have all been huddled together regardless, for comfort.* He envisioned the children, dirty and scared. He saw their desperate faces turned towards the circle, the yearning for help and safety...*their yearning for a parent.* Baggi stepped back from the circle and faced it as they had. In its center was Amund. Both then and now, there was Amund and the flamebuds. He saw his friend leaning on his shovel, wiping sweat from his face. He saw the Chief of Flamebud Village address his people. They drew new life from his words, basked in the flamebuds, the flowers' heat drinking their tears. *It was a fantastic speech, full of passion and just enough hope.* Baggi knew these things to be true; they were obvious. Yet the words that had been spoken escaped him.

"What did you say then?" he asked suddenly.

"Then? When?"

"When you planted them."

"I said only the truth," Amund replied, now clearing the space surrounding the offering circle, "or what I thought was the truth: that we would never again be taken advantage of by Staffkeepers or outsiders. That we may have lost our favor with the gods, but the flamebuds would protect us." His voice fell, taking on a hollowness. "That I would protect them, that Flamebud Village may have been bled, but our heartbeat was still strong. And the flamebuds were proof of that."

After a long time, Baggi said, "It's my fault. My people put you in this position. We put you all in danger of starvation."

Amund waved a hand dismissively. "No," he said, "as I said, the village was becoming crowded long before you arrived. This was a problem my father struggled to address. The Staffkeepers of Death delayed the issue by reducing the population," Amund chuckled humorlessly and spat before continuing, "but in truth it has been plaguing me for some time. Some of my people will be marrying soon. They will be bringing new villagers to us soon. It is better that we do this now, so the village may be stable when they arrive."

Baggi nodded agreeably, though he was beginning to taste the full bitterness that accompanied their task. "I always wanted to learn to garden, you know," he said, "but I never got the chance. Even back home, at the Temple at Enton, I loved the garden, but they never let me work in it."

"That explains your work ethic," Amund replied without cruelty. His guest grinned wryly. "No matter," he continued, clapping dirt from his gloves, "it seems you will learn now. Bring me that sack, over there – no, the other one – yes, bring that here. We will begin with the beans."

11

Staffkeeper Hjordis and Sage Runa approached the smithy in silence with an apprentice trailing their steps. The sign hanging from the open-air workshop's roof was expressive and colorful, yet as the trio approached, Hjordis found its frivolity stood in bizarre contrast to the smith himself. *Who was it that crafted all these signs?* She wondered. *Certainly not him.* The blacksmith was seated on a wooden stool with his feet planted firm and his arms crossed. His biceps were unevenly muscled, she noted, and very visibly so. Although Amund had claimed to be the eldest among the villagers, Hjordis found that claim difficult to swallow; the Chief of Flamebud was clean shaven and, although muscular, still retained the slightness of youth. The boy before her now wore a thick black beard and carried a mountain of heavy flesh upon his bones, and was by Hjordis' estimation taller than any among the Shaefini caravan.

Sage Runa stopped at the threshold of the forge and bowed in the Shaefini style, bringing her oaken staff Consolation to her forehead. Hjordis mirrored the motion, standing a pace and a half behind her elder. The apprentice, a boy with a shaved head by the name of Guthini, mirrored Hjordis in turn.

"I am Staffkeeper Runa, Sage of Shaefi," the older woman said by way of greeting. Her voice was steady and strong, her expression unreadable. She spoke Sparktongue with a heavy Naefjan accent, but her vocabulary was precise. She gestured without looking back toward Hjordis. "This is Staffkeeper Hjordis. Who are you?"

The blacksmith scratched his jaw with a thick, heavy hand. His brow was furrowed, but Hjordis couldn't say if the expression was in response to the introduction or simply a consequence of his resting features. The Shaefini waited patiently for several long moments as the boy regarded them. Then he stood up with a slight groan usually reserved for the old and weary.

"I am Hallsteinn," he said simply.

"Well met, Hallsteinn," Runa replied. "What do you need?"

"My arm is fractured," he stated matter-of-factly, and held out his smaller left arm. "I was careless in sparring. Chief Amund struck true."

"An easy fix," Runa stated. "Roll up the sleeve."

She bade Guthini draw near so he might observe the procedure. *A perfect fit for the job,* Hjordis thought as the Sage got to work, *No stalling with Runa.* Sage Runa nodded wordlessly toward her. The younger woman approached and raised a hand inoffensively before invoking Algiz. Her lavender aura swirled around the blacksmith's unseen wound, probing, coating the entire arm. Hallsteinn's eyebrows raised as the numbness coated his arm from fingertip to shoulder, but he remained silent.

Sage Runa invoked Ansuz and Pert one after another and began examining the boy's forearm. Guthini watched closely, eyes wide with admiration, as she pressed with her fingertips and methodically scanned the arm for the fracture. Hallsteinn endured this strangeness without question or protest. *Still, he must be curious,* Hjordis thought.

"Sage Runa is looking for the break," she explained unprompted, her Sparktongue clumsy. "The runes she used let her see it, under the skin."

The blacksmith twisted his neck stiffly to face her. "You see beneath my skin?" he asked.

Hjordis grinned. *I knew it.* "Yes. No. She sees your hurt with Ansuz and sees the hidden with Pert. That's enough for a healer as..." She fumbled for the Sparktongue equivalent of 'knowledgeable', couldn't find it. "...good as Sage Runa," she finished.

Hallsteinn nodded, the explanation seemingly to his satisfaction.

"Mm," Runa said, "here."

She invoked Berkanan. Her aura, the grey-blue color of flint, flowed from her staff and measured itself precisely to the dimensions of the fracture before settling into Hallsteinn's body. There was a brief, stony crackle, and then it was over. The treatment, from evaluation to recovery, had taken under five minutes.

"Shall we enchant your tools as well?" she asked, stepping back and looking him in the eye.

Hallsteinn tested the cure, curling and uncurling his arm at different angles. He appeared mildly impressed. "What will it cost me?" he asked the Sage as he did so.

"Your goodwill," she replied seriously.

"Then I accept."

"Staffkeeper Hjordis, if you would?" Runa commanded with the politeness of a request.

"Of course," Hjordis assented with another deferential bow. "Would you like your tools strong," she asked haltingly, "or would you like them to bring you much coin?"

"Strong," he responded immediately.

Hjordis nodded and set to work immediately, invoking Uruz over the blacksmith's hammer, anvil, and, for good measure, just about every other device she came across. She lacked the expertise to differentiate what constituted tool and what was simply material to be shaped or an unfinished product; conveniently, her Blessing filled the gaps in her knowledge. She couldn't have named the tools if pressed, yet with the magical boon her enhanced instincts indicated where to enchant and where to leave well enough alone. *It does come in handy at times,* the Staffkeeper thought begrudgingly, *even if it's not the Blessing I would have chosen.* When she was done, Hjordis had energy to spare, so she enchanted the boundaries of the workshop with Fehu as well, to bring wealth. All the while, Hallsteinn and Sage Runa stood in silence and watched her work.

"That ought to do," she said, more to herself than the others. She wiped sweat from her forehead. The forge's heat was beginning to chafe. "Is there anything else we can help with?" She asked. Hallsteinn shook his head.

"Then we bid you goodbye," Runa declared.

She bowed and withdrew without further warning. Hjordis and Guthini followed her example, the apprentice awed into shy silence by the women's expertise. As they left, Hallsteinn called out to them,

"You have my thanks and my goodwill, Staffkeepers."

Sage Runa smiled slightly as they walked.

"So who's next?" Hjordis asked.

"A boy named Aghi," Runa responded. "It seems he suffered a terrible shock long ago that leaves him slow of tongue."

"Something startled him that badly?"

"No. He was struck by lightning."

"Ah," Hjordis sighed. *Brain damage is always tricky.* "I'll follow your lead."

***

"Are you ready, Kettil?" Elof asked as they stood before the bank.

"Of course," she replied.

"You have all of your materials?"

"Right here in the box."

"Hm. And your parchment?"

"In my sleeve like always. Like you taught me."

"And ink?"

"Yes!"

"And gloves?"

"Obviously!"

"And- "

"I have everything I need!" Kettil snapped. "Can we just get started already?"

Elof flinched at his apprentice's surly outburst then sighed, fiddling nervously with the buckles on his potion belt.

"Yes, ah, I suppose we had better," he said.

He reached out with a shaking hand and rapped on the door. As his knuckles made contact, a plethora of sensory information traveled up his arm and filled his mind unbidden. *Fine oak, seventy years old or so, one and three-quarter inches thick,* he appraised. Several moments passed as he fidgeted and his apprentice tapped her foot. Elof jerked his head sharply to the side as the creaking of a great iron gate sounded from far off. He glanced back toward Kettil, but she seemed not to have noticed. *I suppose it's too distant for ordinary ears,* he thought. He knocked again to distract himself and heard from inside an annoyed sigh coupled with approaching footsteps, light and graceful. He bowed as the door opened, or perhaps a moment too soon, judging by Kettil's curious gaze.

"Ah, you have come after all," the girl who answered greeted them in the Base Tongue.

She wore a skirt and shirt in the Melenno style, and Elof smelled the haughtiness of her perfume. *Mint oil, juniper, almond,* he recognized, *the perfume must also be an import.* Even the perfume, however, could not mask the more brazen odors of wealth wafting from inside: ink and parchment, orichalcum and agate.

"I am Audr. Please, come in."

Elof twitched as the scents momentarily overwhelmed him. Luckily, Kettil did not share her mentor's Blessing.

"Thanks! I'm Kettil," she said, sauntering in as if she were the alchemist and he the apprentice. Elof humbly followed suit.

The bank was composed of a lobby with a surprisingly understated counter to conduct business at. In the corner behind the counter was a doorway with an engraved plaque beside it which read: "Office of Audr, Banker". At the far wall was a staircase and beside it a closed door to Audr's private quarters; Elof had noted the building to be single-storied and surmised the stairs lead to the roof. He felt a pang of longing to visit the impressive rooftop gardens he had spent the past several days admiring but forced his attention to the task at hand. *There will be time for that later,* he thought sadly, *now is the time to work.* The lobby was otherwise sparse, with a few finely crafted chairs for waiting clients and a beautifully woven red and blue rug breaking up the barren wooden floorboards. He examined the rug from the doorway. *Blue dye derived from the Shaeficap fungus back home, red from the native blastbeetle. Weaving in the Fumvoir style. She seems to appreciate the craftsmanship of the guild-tribes. A vestige of sympathy, perhaps, from Kichishi's invasion of the Valley during the Mineral War?* He wondered how much it had cost to import the clothing, perfume, and rug all the way here from Melenno. Fumvoir was situated on the north-eastern edge of the continent; though the trade routes between here and there were reasonably well protected, the journey was long and the costs great. Even as a hypothetical, the figure was daunting.

"In my office, please," Audr said.

The alchemists followed her into a room as luxurious as the lobby was bare. Fine tapestry of similar craftsmanship adorned the room, and shelf after shelf hugged the walls, stuffed tightly with scrolls. Elof smelled fresh ink on some, but most simply carried the musk of age. *Financial records, most like,* he thought. Audr sat behind a grand desk of rich mahogany and gestured for the two to take the seats across from it. They did so, both feeling rather small and beggarly.

"Sir alchemist," she began, "I don't believe you offered your name."

"Oh! Of course, how rude of me. I do, ah, apologize for my, um, insensitivity," he stammered. "I am Elof. It is very well to meet you, or, I suppose, for you to meet me, seeing as I already met you..." he trailed off awkwardly as Audr shot him a weary, withering look. She rubbed her eyes with her writing hand, leaving a faint ink-stain on her dark brown nose. It softened her features strangely, endearingly.

"Yes, well, Elof," she began, "I have requested your presence in order to discuss business. I am told you are a master botanist?"

"You honor me," he responded humbly.

"Far from it," Audr responded with a tired smile. "I simply trade in facts and figures. To this end, and because I have no desire to prolong the conversation unnecessarily, I will speak directly." She handed Elof a long scroll covered in densely packed figures. "These are our agricultural production records, from two years ago to the present." She allowed him several moments to skim the contents, his face growing more and more worried as he read. "I see you understand my dilemma already." She handed him another scroll. "These figures represent the profits reported from each of our businesses in the same amount of time."

Elof glanced momentarily over the second scroll, just long enough to confirm what he had already gathered. "You have, ah, that is, Flame-bud Village, has been operating at a deficit all this time?" he asked, more for Kettil's benefit than for clarity. Audr, understanding, simply nodded. "And the period before this?" he asked.

"Here," she said, handing him yet another scroll. He quickly passed the prior records to Kettil and took it. The older numbers were, in-triguingly, far more favorable. Elof looked up at the banker, confusion evident in his expression.

"Your caravan has been among our people for several days now," Audr said, "and in that time I doubt it has escaped your notice that we lack parentage. For that matter, we lack adults of any kind." Elof nodded politely; Baggi had shared the reason for this phenomenon following their healing of the tailor, he having apparently heard it directly from Chief Amund. "The reason for this is unimportant, but the consequences are clear," she continued, gesturing to the scrolls with acute poise. Despite her deliberateness of manner, Elof observed the telltale signs of discomfort: a tightening of the jaw, an interruption in the rhythm of her blinking, a slight discoloration of the face.

"You wish to consult with us about increasing your production?" Elof provided.

Kettil sighed rudely beside him, evidently bored with the direction their job had taken. He glanced at her with stern disapproval. *She must learn sooner or later that alchemy is not always potions and magic,* he thought, *just as often, it's numbers and logistics. Or perhaps oftener.* His apprentice smiled apologetically, a rare occurrence, and turned her focus back to the records in her hands.

"You are quick to catch on," Audr remarked dryly. She leaned back in her chair and placed her hands on the armrests. "I have heard tales of the great glasshouses in your land and the magically induced growth of the Melenno Valley crops. Surely you will be willing to furnish my people with such knowledge in exchange for our hospitality? We already have one such glasshouse constructed atop our chief's mansion; if you could only teach us to properly utilize and maintain it, that would be sufficient." Her keen gaze met Elof's, and he paused for a moment to admire the intricate golden-flake pattern in her otherwise flame-red eyes.

"Would it not be, well, easier," replied Elof, confused, "to simply purchase the supplies you lack? You don't, ah, seem to be lacking for odd."

The banker grinned cynically. "It is clear you are not a political man, Elof." He blinked, uncomprehending, until she elaborated. "As I said before, we lack adults in Flamebud Village. This means we are quite weak, militaristically, and several other villages have refrained from taking our home for two reasons only: first, out of the respect they had for our ancestors, and second, our alliance with Takkin to the west."

"Ah, yes," he nodded, "the capability of the lizard-masters of Takkin are known even in the northern countries. If Flamebud shares such an alliance, would that not solve your problem? You could purchase crops from them."

"That is the root of the issue," she frowned. "Our arrangement is such that we are the ones who offer food to Takkin in exchange for their riding warriors' support. Between our foot and their drabants, our defenses have always been strong, yet this alliance has also nearly driven us to famine more than once. Now that we cannot provide for even ourselves, there is no hope to uphold our arrangement with Takkin and, therefore, no hope of their coming to our aid when those who covet this land arrive to seize it."

The alchemists brooded over this grim news for several moments. Elof turned the facts over in his head, searching for some loophole or overlooked detail, but in the end he was forced to accept that he simply lacked both the knowledge and context to do so. *She wasn't mistaken,* he admitted, *I'm not much of a political man.*

"Well?" demanded Audr. "Will you help us increase our yield?"

"I'm afraid, ah, that is...well, it is certainly possible...but, ah..." he mumbled, reluctant to deny her. He took a deep breath and collected himself. "Miss Audr," Elof continued, "we can most certainly teach you proper glasshouse maintenance, but such a structure won't be able to reach its full potential without the proper runic foundations. As for imbuing your harvest with fertility, well...that is also a job for a Staffkeeper."

Audr seemed lost in thought. "Is that so?" she reflected softly. "Then we truly have no choice."

She fell to brooding and several moments passed with no indication of whether their business had concluded. Elof was preparing to excuse himself and Kettil when the apprentice piped up beside him.

"What do ya mean?" she asked bluntly. "We've got plenty of Staffkeepers with us. Any one of 'em could do it."

"I'm afraid that is out of the question," Audr replied. Her voice was cold and hard. "Flamebud Village has no need for the works of Staffkeepers. We will find another solution." She stood up, indicating their meeting's abrupt end. "Thank you for your time. I trust you can find the door."

Elof hesitated. Clearly, Audr wished them to leave her to her brooding. *But we can solve their problem, if she would only allow a Staffkeeper to help.* Then an idea occurred to him, an idea that would no doubt be refused by both Audr and the Staffkeepers of Shaefi. *Only if they find out,* Elof thought, his stomach flipping nervously.

He thought of a cold and snowy morning in Yngmuth over a decade ago, and the multiple pains that accompanied it: hunger, frostbite, the bruises and cuts. Little Elof's foraging had been unsuccessful that day; he lacked the energy. He was dying, after all. To go home would be to submit to Death in the form of yet another beating, to stay in the woods would be to submit still in the form of freezing. So he had curled up at the docks, trying to take shelter and remain unseen among the crates and barrels. And that was where Aeskettil had found him, alchemy box in hand, the very same box in his apprentice's hands now. He thought of the misery he had been pulled from, a debt fully owed to the Staffkeepers of Shaefi and their Order. He swayed momentarily on the border between sin and obligation. *If dishonesty is the price to keep children from those pains,* he decided, *I am willing to pay that price.*

"Very well. If you wish for the Staffkeepers to remain out of your business, we will respect that wish," he lied.

Audr nodded and held up a hand as they rose to leave.

"There is one minor matter I wish to discuss further," she said.

Elof began to panic, sure that he had seen through his deceit. After all, she was a woman of commerce, well-practiced at spotting duplicity, and he was far from an experienced liar.

"My ink stores have run low. Might you craft me more?" she asked, distractible and indifferent.

He nearly sighed aloud with relief. "Of course. It would be our pleasure."

"I require five ounces. You will, of course, be paid handsomely."

"Oh, no! We don't take payment," Elof said, his words spilling out a bit too quickly. "That's what separates us, I mean, the Shaefini Alchemists, from the Alchemist Guild. Just the cost of ingredients will suffice. And even then, it's only a suggested donation." Audr regarded him favorably, as if she had initially misjudged. Guilt reared up inside him; he quickly smothered it.

"Yes, the Alchemist Guild," the banker frowned. "Tell me, is it true that they lend money and expect to be repaid a greater sum than initially borrowed?"

"Indeed," Elof replied, grimacing in turn, "they call it 'interest.'"

Audr scoffed. "I call it thievery." She shook her head as if to rid herself of the notion. "Provide me with an itemized list of costs and I will see that you are reimbursed in full, and then some. When may I expect the ink?" she said.

"Well, we are departing, our caravan, in four days' time. Or, ah, perhaps five. You will have it well before we leave," he replied, mind already elsewhere, formulating a plan.

"Excellent. I will draft a contract, and then you may be on your way," she said, procuring a crisp new sheet of parchment and writing furiously. *Considering the speed, her penmanship is remarkable,* Elof thought.

After mere minutes had passed, the contract was ready. Audr signed her name at the bottom before passing the scroll to Elof and indicating two blank spaces at the bottom. He and his apprentice signed, so that the signatures read:

Audr, Banker of Flamebud Village

Elof Shaefison, Shaefini Alchemist

Kettil Shaefisdottir, Shaefini Alchemist Apprentice

Audr read the signatures with approval, then glanced at the duo with surprise. "I did not realize you were siblings," she said as she looked between them.

"We're not," he said, unwilling to explain any further. Conversations of his lineage were generally unpleasant.

Audr shot him a strange look, but as Elof remained silent, she shrugged and escorted them out. Elof gazed longingly at the staircase leading to the rooftop garden one last time as they exited. He and

Kettil meandered as they walked through town, neither in a rush to report the assignment. They were silent for some time, an unspoken query walking like a third companion between them. Eventually, Kettil spoke up.

"I didn't think you would be okay with leaving them to starve," she probed.

"I'm not," Elof sighed.

Kettil nodded. "So, what are we gonna do? Get a Staffkeeper to help anyway?"

"I don't know yet," he replied uneasily.

"'Cause if they find out that lady said 'no Staffkeepers', they won't do it," she said.

"Yes, they will respect her wishes," Elof replied, "even at the expense of these children's well-being." Frustration tinted his voice, a rare and abrasive sound to Kettil's ears.

"Staffkeepers," she said, matching her mentor's tone.

"Staffkeepers," he agreed.

They sighed in unison and left it at that.

***

"And that, young one, is how I learned to sail," Elder Sage Hrafn concluded, sitting at the Flamebud Inn's bar. He took a sip from his mug ever so slowly, savoring the mead's sweetness.

"Huh," said Torny as she polished glasses. "I don't know about all those big words you used, but I think I get it. Those Staffkeepers, the ones who work for...uh..." she trailed off, trying to remember the name from the beginning of the story. It had been quite a while since the beginning of the story.

"Brathus," he supplied patiently.

"Yeah! So, the Staffkeepers of Brathus are sailors?" she asked.

"Exactly so!" he said, beaming with pride. "Although as they see it, they're more akin to fish themselves." His eyes twinkled with humor, and Torny giggled despite herself.

"I might like to sail someday too," she mused. "I'm a really good swimmer, you know."

"Yes, that would come in useful. You have the manner of a strong swimmer," he laughed, "though I couldn't tell you why."

"But if I did get on a boat, and go in the ocean, there might be pirates," she said, "like in your story. And I don't want to kill anyone if I don't have to."

"So long as a Staffkeeper of Brathus is with you, the ocean will keep you from harm," Hrafn reassured her, "just as it kept my vessel. They are exceptionally good at bargaining with the tides."

Torny wrinkled her nose. "But what if the pirates have a Staffkeeper too? I heard that Einarsfolk have lots of 'em. Some people say there's one on every boat!"

"That is true," Hrafn replied. "Einarsfolk are an adventurous people, pioneers who thrive off their voyages into uncharted waters, and Staffkeepers of Brathus value adventurousness and bravery." He took another slow sip and gathered his thoughts. "It's been a long time since I was out to sea. Back when my story occurred, Einarsplace was yet to exist; in fact, it would be another two hundred and fifty years or so before Einar Sharpaxe claimed the land in the aftermath of the Mineral War. It's possible that the dangers have since increased." He smiled at Torny a little sadly. "But life is full of risk. To do the right thing, even when it means facing those risks, is true bravery. And as I said, Brathus values bravery."

The innkeeper looked at Elder Sage Hrafn with wide, skeptical eyes. "Two hundred fifty years?" she asked. "Just how old are you, Hrafn?"

Hrafn laughed deeply. "Very old, young one, very old," he said.

A soft jingling from the bell at the door drew their attention before Torny could ask any more. Elof and Kettil had returned much sooner than expected. The Elder Sage smiled and gestured for them to join him at the bar. As they approached, he noticed the two appeared disconcerted. This was no cause for alarm in Elof's case; Hrafn knew fully well that the young man's Blessing caused him constant stress due to sensory overload. The Elder Sage worried for him, but Blessings were usually exclusive to Staffkeepers, and if Shaefi had seen fit to bestow such a gift upon him he knew she must have had good reason. *Young Kettil, however, is not so easily perturbed,* he thought with concern. They bowed respectfully and sat with Hrafn at the bar. Torny, ever the professional, sensed their need for privacy and made herself busy carrying out mugs and vittles to the sullen Kichishi seated at sparsely populated stump-tables.

"Alchemist Elof, Alchemist Apprentice Kettil," Hrafn greeted warmly, as if they were reunited after eons and not minutes, "how went your meeting with the young woman?"

"Elder Sage," Elof replied cautiously, "I, ah, rather, we may have a problem."

"Then let us solve this problem together," Hrafn replied kindly. Elof avoided his gaze.

"Well, you see, Elder Sage, the banker, ahem, one Miss Audr, requested a magically induced bounty for the village crops," he said, then hesitated.

"That is easily arranged," Hrafn said, noting the younger man's reluctance. "Invoking Jera will guarantee a bountiful harvest."

Elof hesitated for the space of a heartbeat, then perked up with visible effort. "Of course!" he said. "Easily arranged. I was, ah, only hoping for your permission to select a Staffkeeper for the assignment."

His gaze was fixed on something behind the bar. *Such a put-upon man,* Hrafn thought, assuming his skittishness to be a result of their unfamiliar surroundings, *but a good one.* He recalled the first time he had laid eyes on Elof, nearly fifteen years ago, when Alchemist Aeskettil had brought him back to the Temple at Enton covered in balms and unguents. *Aeskettil carried him in his arms while the boy slept, as if he were his own son,* he reminisced. *Ah, Aeskettil, if only you could see what a fine alchemist your child grew into.* A deep longing for his dear departed friend and lover weighed heavily on Hrafn's heart. *Was it really such a short time ago?*

"You have my permission, of course," he replied, laying a comforting hand on Elof's. The alchemist yelped lightly, then chuckled at his own reaction. "Select whoever you deem appropriate. I trust your judgment completely."

"Yes," Elof mumbled, "thank you, Elder Sage Hrafn. I will see it done." He rose from his seat. "If you'll excuse me, I have...ah...ink to craft," he finished vaguely, and scurried off to the alchemists' room.

Hrafn turned to Kettil, who had remained silent. *She's usually a touch more boisterous, I think. But then, adapting to the caravan life is often a slow process, with many ups and downs.* "And how are you, Kettil?" he asked. "Did you learn anything from your assignment today?"

Kettil bit her lip and considered. "Uh-huh," she replied, "I think I learned a whole lot."

Elder Sage Hrafn smiled at her. "It gladdens me to hear that, child." Torny returned to her place behind the bar and poured herself a mug of pepper-cider.

"Got any more stories?" the innkeeper demanded.

"Certainly," he replied, "perhaps too many! Do you know the story of the Alchemist Guild, and how it came to be?" Torny shook her head and leaned forward excitedly. "Well, long ago, our Shaefini Alchemists were the only ones in all Solabell. There were herbalists and healers, of course, but even in Naefja true alchemy was not a widely practiced art. Unfortunately, because we work solely on the basis of charity, the cost of ingredients became difficult to manage. Many wished to begin charging for our services; they argued that no one benefited from the alchemists lacking the resources to do their job. Others maintained that the necessary means would come to us if we only kept true to our ideals. I was of the latter opinion. It was a divisive time for the Order..." As he wove the tale, Hrafn began to relax, but he kept a keen eye full of worry towards Kettil, who sat beside him swinging her legs and thinking hard.

12

The breeze was cold as it tore through Baggi's wet hair. All around him in the rooftop garden, the inhabitants of Flamebud Village stood tightly packed, some with their arms crossed, others hoisting the smaller children on their shoulders or backs. Whether it was for warmth or comfort, he couldn't say. *Just like when they were planted,* the apprentice thought idly. He glanced askance at Torny. She stood like a woman defeated, her shoulders slumped, her eyes dull with resignation. Baggi noted sadly that her disposition was not unique; indeed, it seemed every villager in the garden echoed her. He recognized the mood in the air: the familiar reluctance of a funeral held too soon.

After he and Amund had finished preparing the garden, the chief had sent him off with instructions to return before sunrise. Baggi had left him to his thoughts and returned to the inn to Contemplate. Eventually the other Staffkeepers had returned, bringing with them the loud joviality so typical of Shaefini, but that night their insensitivity had annoyed him. *Can't they show a little empathy?* He had thought. The grieving Kichishi had been forced to depart, throwing resentful glances towards the foreigners who laughed and joked while they themselves prepared for Flamebud's heart to stop beating. Baggi had left with them; he, too, needed space to mourn.

He had returned to the waterfall and sat on the bank and Contemplated in peace. The nights were warm in Kichishi, he found, and with his blue and white woolen cloak the elements posed no threat. He drifted between sleep and Contemplations for hours. Visions of flame and ash, life and death, survival and beauty, these and more swam in and out of his mind. It had become increasingly difficult to separate the dreams from the Contemplations, so Baggi had abandoned convention and made no effort to separate the two. Instead he passed the night half-dreaming, and when the sun was yet hours off he bathed once more in the cool waters. Even on a warm night the waterfall was cold, but Baggi recalled the warmth of the sun and within moments the chill left him. He dressed in soothing quiet and returned to Amund's mansion.

He had expected to be early, to find Amund alone still. Instead, Baggi was surprised to find that he was late. It seemed all of Flamebud Village had assembled for the flamebuds' return to fire. *Of course they did,* he thought. He chided himself now for his surprise, standing among them. *Were you surprised to see all of Jolk at Bjorn's funeral? Certainly not.* He reached out a hand and silently grasped Torny's. She turned to him with a cocked eyebrow, as if ready to make a clever remark, but then sighed, lacking the energy. Instead, she squeezed his hand a bit, holding tight to the comfort it held. They stood this way among the crowd of muted townsfolk for a long time, until the sky gradually began to brighten.

Chief Amund had stood with his back to the crowd before the offering circle. Thanks to his and Baggi's efforts the previous day, the circle was emptied of its soil. It was filled now with a great mass of flamebuds, uprooted and ebbing in the early morning's darkness. All about him, the garden was utterly devoid of life. The crops they had planted would not be visible for quite some time, leaving the garden with a grave, barren appearance. The villagers, equally deadened, reinforced the image. Amund turned to face his people. Torny's hand squeezed a little tighter as the villagers collectively held their breath.

"When I planted these flowers," he began, his voice resonant and gentle at once, "we were a people in pain. We had lost our families, our happiness, our favor with Sawtor. The scars from these pains ache even today." He scanned the crowd, making eye contact with his people, making them seen. "I promised you many things then," he continued, "among them, that the flamebuds would protect us. That they would provide for us. And they have! They have kept our inner fires lit in these most difficult of times. But their time comes to an end. As will ours, eventually."

Silence hung in the air. For a long, horrifying moment, it seemed Amund was at a loss for words. Then he took a deep breath and power returned to him.

"All times end. The time for the flamebud garden ends, true. But our time of pain and difficulty ends as well. For today, we begin a new time! Today, we plant seeds for the revival of Flamebud Village! Today, we show Sawtor our strength, and return to her favor! We return the flowers to flame not with reluctance, not with grief, but with hope! Their time comes to an end; ours is just begun!"

The people had remained silent throughout. They were frozen in the time of pain and grief, and Baggi suddenly understood exactly why the flamebuds were to be offered through fire. *It's the only flame that can thaw them,* he realized, *lest they be frozen in time forever.* He released Torny's hand. Amund stepped forward and gestured for Baggi to come forth. He did so, stomach twisting in knots of unease. They had discussed the apprentice's involvement yesterday, and despite Baggi's initial reluctance, he conceded that Amund knew best how to proceed. *He said this is how they used to do it,* he reminded himself, *back when they had Staffkeepers of their own.* The news had come as a shock to Baggi, though in retrospect it ought not have. Sawtor worship was most common in Kichishi; although their Order had little in the way of formal leadership and no central base of operations like the Temple at Enton, most villages had a Staffkeeper or two among them. Flamebud Village was an exception.

Baggi approached the offering circle and suppressed the deeply ingrained Shaefini impulse to bow. *That's not how to approach Sawtor,* he thought, summoning up Amund's words, *he said they keep their heads held high. She respects self-respect.* So he did as he had been instructed and approached the offering circle with what he hoped was confidence, pausing only to show courtesy to Chief Amund by making the Sign of Flame. He turned to the crowd and saw a multitude of reactions: some were baffled, some outraged, some curious, some bittersweet. None such feelings were strong enough to pierce the melancholy. The apprentice cleared his throat.

"On behalf of Flamebud Village," he pronounced, "I offer these: the heart of its people, the heat of their passion, the flamebuds that have protected them. May you, Sawtor, find them worthy offerings."

He recited the words Amund had taught him, feeling a familiarity in the ritual. *It may be different than how we make offerings,* he thought, *but the nature of it is the same.* Decisively, he turned to the offering circle and the mound of flowers within. For a moment, he hesitated, looking to Amund for approval. With a sharp nod, it was given. Baggi closed his eyes, took a deep breath, and visualized a fire inside his chest, just as the chief had instructed. After his first Task and his newfound familiarity with the sun, the gesture was straightforward, simple even. When he felt his inner fire warming him from the inside out, Baggi opened his eyes.

"Kenaz," he proclaimed, his voice commanding.

He used Compromise to draw the rune in the air over the offering, the ice-blue trail of magic bizarre and out of place. Still, Baggi felt the flame pulled from his chest, through his staff, and into the circle. In the blink of an eye, the flowers were consumed by an almighty blaze. He formed the Sign of Flame towards the circle and then towards Amund before returning to his place in the crowd beside Torny.

It was she who grasped his hand this time, and tightly. He squeezed back, willing comfort to flow between their grasp. The flames were climbing higher and higher, brilliant and dazzling in the sunrise. He and Torny stood closest to the offerings, and Baggi worried for a moment that they might be dangerously close. But Amund stood directly adjacent to the circle, unmoving, stoic. Baggi took after his example and forced himself to endure the heat. He felt his hair rapidly drying and risked a quick look at the villagers. They seemed to be warming to the flames, stirring vaguely, biting their lips or rubbing the backs of their necks as if embarrassed by their previous behavior. And then they began to smile. Not all, of course; some were harder pressed than others to accept the flamebuds' passing. Some cried without shame, and the flamebuds drank their tears as they had those two years ago. Yet all seemed at least to have thawed.

He remembered the first funeral he had been to, his brother Bjorn's. The people of Jolk had been likewise frozen; he had been likewise frozen. Bjorn had been the pride of their village, a loving son, a patient brother, a loyal friend, and an upstanding Staffkeeper. When the Staffkeepers of Death had arrived to deliver Compromise and his skull, they had abstained from killing the villagers, but even so they had delivered a community its death. The Staffkeepers of Shaefi had shattered that layer of frost coating them. Through their ritual, life had returned to the people of Jolk. Life had returned to him. *No,* Baggi corrected himself, *the people of Jolk had returned to life. I returned to life.* It seemed an important distinction.

Now the Staffkeeper Apprentice saw a crowd of people finding their way back to life once more. Torny wept beside him, sniffling loudly. Baggi cried too. He squeezed her hand tighter, and felt the fire wipe the tears from his face. *Welcome back,* he thought, *folk of Flamebud Village.*

***

Baggi stood by the offering space, lost in thought as he stared at the embers. The flamebuds had taken a long time to succumb to the fire; it was in their nature, after all, but even a fish may expire in freshwater if pulled from the ocean. He leaned heavily on his staff, one hand touching his lips, silent, Contemplating. The sun was past its zenith by the time the last of Flamebud's villagers left the garden. Amund had taken the time to speak with his people, comfort them, reassure them on an individual basis as they slowly filtered out. Now he stood on the roof, surveying the town and watching his people march through the streets just as blood pumps through the veins.

"The clot has cleared," he whispered aloud. "The lifeblood of our village flows once more."

The words brought him immense relief. Finally, the Chief of Flamebud allowed himself to acknowledge his weariness. Turning back to the garden, he slumped to the ground with a sigh, his back against the parapet. *We must scatter the ashes elsewhere, tonight, before the flamebuds grow back,* he reminded himself.

"You did well, Baggi," he half-shouted across the garden. The apprentice raised his head and turned to him, surprise evident even without the eyebrows that had been neatly singed off.

"Truly?" he asked.

Amund nodded. "It was just like when I was a boy. You had the same expression as my mother."

There was a pregnant pause in which he reckoned he could actually hear his friend restraining himself from outburst. Then, "Your mother was a Staffkeeper?"

He nodded again. "A Staffkeeper of Sawtor."

"Hm," said Baggi.

"Is that all?" he asked, amused. "No more questions for such a confession?"

"No," he replied slowly, "it makes sense, once you know it. So that's how you knew how to conduct the ritual?"

"Exactly so," said Amund, warming to the topic. He thought of his mother then, truly tried to recall her face. It was slightly lacking for detail, but he managed it. It felt like much longer than two years since he had seen her. "She taught me much about Sawtor, about our will and our strength as Kichishi. She taught me about our history, how we sprang from the obsidian with fire in our blood." He paused, lost in the recollections of childhood.

"You were being trained," said the Naefjan, voice soft in realization. "You were going to be a Staffkeeper too."

"Yes, for a time. But I had not the intellect for it," he replied, then grinned. "It suits you better."

With a sigh, Baggi plopped down in the dirt beside him. "Maybe," he said, "but I'm not a Staffkeeper yet. I still need to finish my Tasks."

"And today, you have finished Task number two," Amund replied good-naturedly, "It was to mend a tear in our village, is that not so?"

Baggi nodded, unsurprised; word traveled fast in Flamebud Village. "Come, Baggi, up!"

He stood and gestured impatiently for his friend to rise as well. He did so, groaning dramatically. Amund rolled his eyes even as he snorted in good humor. "Look at my people," he commanded. The younger boy obeyed, watching them just as the chief had moments before. "You see how they are alive, where before they were asleep?" Baggi chuckled at the imperfect comparison but nodded. "Does that not settle the matter?"

"I suppose it does," Baggi replied, oddly subdued.

"And yet, you do not appear excited."

"I'm not. But I am hopeful."

After a questioning look to obtain consent, Amund put his arm around Baggi's shoulder. "As am I," he said.

They stood together in silence. With a start, the apprentice realized his companion was crying. *He hadn't the chance during the ritual,* Baggi realized. *He had to be strong. That's what they always say.* He nearly scoffed aloud. *How stupid.* It seemed to him that the Amund was much stronger for weeping, much braver for accepting and facing the grief in his heart. He thought then of his mother, and how she had spoken to the villagers after Bjorn's burial. *She saved her tears for later as well. Or perhaps she was obligated to. Such folly,* he thought, and the epiphany was full of helplessness, *such injustice.*

"I miss her very much," Amund said suddenly, his voice small, as if they were sharing thoughts, "and my father too. I miss the times before I knew grief."

"Yes," agreed Baggi, "me too." He smiled, the expression bitter-sweet, and allowed his friend to weep for as long as he wished.

"Now," Amund eventually said, releasing him from the embrace and smiling wanly, "go report your victory. Receive your final Task. And if possible, obtain a new cloak."

"What's wrong with my cloak?" Baggi asked, before glancing down and finding the answer to his own question before his eyes.

The beautiful sky-blue to white gradient had been badly scorched by the ritual fire. Now, it bore an uneven pattern, striped and blotched, made up of silver, grey, and black. He regarded the garment for a long time. Then he glanced toward the offering circle and the pile of ashes, the remains of the flamebuds.

"I think I'll keep this one," he said. "It fits better now, somehow."

Amund shrugged. "So be it. If you desire any patching or decoration, Talia will be overjoyed to repay her debt to you."

"Perhaps I will pay her a visit then," Baggi said. He bid his friend goodbye and, sparing one last glance at the circle, descended through the gazebo and out.

The Chief of Flamebud was now left truly alone. He took a deep breath; the smell of smoke still lingered in the air, but the scent was comforting. He turned to the village once more, gazing with unfocused eyes until they came to rest on the mountain pass the Staffkeepers of Shaefi had arrived through six days prior. Amund knew it was still his duty to guard the road. Though Flamebud Village had been full of excitement lately, its leader could not afford to enjoy the distraction for a moment longer than necessary. Ignoring the ache in his muscles from the previous day's labor and the morning's martial training, he pushed off from the parapet and made to gather the ashes, preparing to depart.

***

Baggi meandered through the streets of Flamebud Village. As he took in the blacksmith pounding away, the baker kneading relentlessly, and many villagers tending their own rooftop gardens, he was amazed at how calm they all were. *This morning, they woke with hearts full of grief,* he reflected, *and now, merely hours later, they're all back to feeling fine.* But as he surveyed the expressions thrown his way, Baggi admitted that wasn't quite right. The villagers were passionate before, but now they held warmth in their eyes as well. Some even waved or smiled to him as he passed.

Since the ritual, Baggi had been grappling with his Task and the lesson it represented. The inner fire he had fed per Amund's instructions still burned within him, albeit gently and meekly. *Is this the peace of Shaefi?* He wondered. Baggi looked down at his singed cloak. *A final gift from the flamebuds. Consumed by fire, and now only the ashes remain.* He remembered then the all-important final step of the meditative exercise the Chief of Flamebud taught him and visualized the flame inside dying out, becoming ash. He exhaled in steady measure and felt a bit better afterwards.

Talia's tailor shop came into view on his right, and Baggi considered taking Amund's advice. Yet the ruined cloak had endeared itself to him already, and he was in no hurry to see it restored. *I'll see to it later,* he told himself, *first I must speak with Elder Sage Hrafn. There's been plenty of mending for one day.*

Back at the Flamebud Inn, Baggi found many eyes on him. He ignored them and strode to the bar without hesitation.

"Be right there, Baggi!" Torny called from two stump-tables away where she stood serving three shy Shaefini apprentices.

Though the age gap was virtually nonexistent, the Naefjan youths appeared intimidated. Baggi reckoned it must be the way Torny cut to the quick of things, both in conversation and work. *She really is wonderful,* he thought as she bustled, watching her curls bob around her face and noticing for the first time how striking were the features upon that face. He waved a hand at her as if to say *take your time, I don't have anywhere to be.* After a few minutes she came around the counter.

"Sorry about that," she said, dabbing at her forehead with a rag. "Let me get you something to sip. You know your cloak's all burned up, don't you?"

"I do," Baggi smiled, "but I like it this way. It's a sort of souvenir."

Torny poured him a mug and set it in front of him.

"So," she began, haltingly, "so, it was pretty amazing, how you did that offering earlier." She looked at him as if searching for her next words in his expression. "It would be nice if we still had someone to do that around here. Once you leave, I mean. Since there's no Staffkeepers here."

She was avoiding his gaze now, polishing a glass with great intensity. Baggi wondered why she bothered, since the drinks always seemed to be served in mugs.

"Well, Amund tells me you had Staffkeepers here once," he offered. "Why not have them again?"

Torny looked at him confused. "Who would teach them?"

"You could send for one from a neighboring town," he suggested. "They might be willing, if only to spread the knowledge."

"Or," she said idly, "maybe one of the Staffkeepers in town could just...stay here. At least for a while." She eyed him surreptitiously as he considered it.

"Yes," he agreed, "maybe someone could." The innkeeper perked up momentarily before he continued, "I might suggest Staffkeeper Ulf or Sage Runa. They're both excellent teachers." He smiled at her, apparently proud of his contribution.

"Right," Torny sighed, "I'll remember them."

"Oh, that reminds me," Baggi continued obliviously, "have you seen Kettil come in yet? I need to speak with her."

"Yeah, she's in the back."

"Thank you," Baggi said, then drained his mug and, with a polite nod, adjourned to find his friend.

"Uh-huh," Torny said glumly to the empty seat before her. "See you around."

Baggi knocked politely at the door of the apprentice's room. He could just as easily have entered without warning, since they shared the quarters and were equally entitled to the space, but that seemed to him a poor start to a reconciliation. He heard scuffling and then the door opened a crack. Kettil peered through the gap at him. Guilt appeared briefly on her face, but she said nothing. Baggi coughed, already uncomfortable.

"Hello, Kettil," he said lamely.

"Hi Baggi," she replied.

"May I, um...can we talk? I'd like to apologize," he said, unsure of what exactly he intended to say.

"Sure," Kettil shrugged and opened the door.

As before, she had apparently finished her work early in the day and retreated to the room for some time alone. Baggi saw no sign of her alchemy box or tools. They sat down on the floor, cross-legged. The silence was beginning to turn awkward when at last he allowed words to spill from his mouth.

"Kettil, I'm sorry," he said all at once, "I shouldn't have told you what to do, or said your idea was a bad one." He hesitated. "It's just..."

"I know, Baggi," she replied, "and I'm sorry too." She appeared embarrassed. "You were right. I thought about it a lot and decided to give up on the Water of Life."

"Really?" Baggi balked.

"Well you don't have to act so surprised!" Kettil snapped, but there was humor and sincerity in her tone. "I guess I just wanted people to live, but I didn't really think about what would happen after." She looked up at him with wet eyes. "And I don't wanna be by myself all the time. It's been awful! The other apprentices all hate me 'cause I'm way more talented than them!"

"Oh, Kettil, come here," Baggi said comfortingly, and pulled her into a hug. "The others can be clannish, can't they?" he laughed.

Kettil jerked her head up to look at him. "Yeah! That's not what Shaefi teaches at all! Even I know that, and I'm not even a Staffkeeper!" She pulled away, wiping roughly at her eyes with the palm of her hand. "And anyway, why wouldn't they want us in their clans? We're great!"

"Probably why they're still apprentices," Baggi agreed in a conciliatory tone.

"Heh," Kettil giggled, "probably."

"Do you want to go out into the commons and have some supper?" Baggi asked.

"Yeah! I'll be there in just a second," she replied. She waited until Baggi left, smiling apologetically once more to be safe, before finally relaxing. Kettil carefully pulled her alchemy box out from under the bed and tidied the mess it had caused when she had hurriedly shoved it out of sight. As she reorganized the spilled contents, she mumbled to herself, "A little lie's okay. It's for the best." Even in her own ears, the words sounded unconvincing.

***

Baggi sat at a stump-table with Compromise across his lap, patiently waiting for Kettil to finish whatever business she had in the room. He felt relief coursing through him, relaxing and pure. *I should have given her more credit,* he scolded himself, *Kettil is the smartest person I know. Of course she saw the issue once she gave it some thought.* The door to the inn swung open gently, and he turned to see the Elder Sage enter with Sage Runa. She spoke seriously, but Hrafn laughed as if she had shared a deeply hilarious joke before setting his sights on the apprentice. He touched Runa on the shoulder gently and excused himself before approaching the stump.

Baggi stood and bowed as the Elder Sage approached. Hrafn returned the bow and slowly took a seat, groaning slightly with the weariness of age. He nodded gratefully as Torny placed a mug in front of him unprompted, then drank and gathered his thoughts. Baggi watched him in silence. *I should be nervous. I should be wondering if I completed the second Task,* he thought. Yet he wasn't. Instead, only a mild puzzlement resided in him as he struggled in vain to decide why his Tasks seemed so arbitrary.

"I hear you have made a strong impression on the people here," Hrafn began conversationally.

Baggi grinned. "Yes. Whether that impression is good or bad..." he trailed off and shrugged.

"From what I am told, you have assisted them in a long-abandoned ritual. They say they will have enough to eat, thanks to you," Hrafn countered gently. It was the closest he ever got to chastising.

"I suppose I played a part," Baggi said.

He fidgeted with his scorched cloak, absentmindedly rubbing ash between his fingers. He had been fiddling with it for an hour or more now, yet there seemed no end to the grey powder falling from the fabric. Hrafn said nothing for some time, but eventually he leaned forward conspiratorially.

"What is it that troubles you, my boy?" he asked.

Baggi flinched at the concern in his voice. *Of course he noticed. He's the Elder Sage.* The boy stared intently at wood grain in the table, concentric rings growing and growing, expanding as the tree had aged. *And then,* he thought, *it died. Cut down. Its life as a tree ended, and its life as a table began.* He wondered which of the two the wood preferred. He wondered which of the two he would prefer.

"Elder Sage Hrafn," he began, speaking slowly, "I burned the flamebuds in Amund's garden today, so that there may be room for food to grow. Isn't that strange? I had to kill something so magnificent so that more humans could live." He looked up at Hrafn, their silver eyes meeting. "It just seems unfair."

"Baggi," Hrafn replied tenderly and laid a comforting hand on his shoulder, "you have done no wrong. Except, perhaps, for ruining a perfectly good cloak," he jested. His eyes twinkled like snowflakes as he smiled warmly at the boy, forcing him to return the smile before continuing. "There was a rift in this community. Not the lack of food, my boy, but the loss of their magic. You have reminded them of what they had once. Now they remember our sister Order, the Staffkeepers of Sawtor." He stood with some effort and bid Baggi do the same. "Staffkeeper Apprentice Baggi," he declared, gravely serious, "you have completed your second Task. Remember well the lessons imparted these three days. May they guide you in your service of Shaefi."

Baggi bowed in deference of the Elder Sage's judgment. *I suppose Hrafn would know best.* Still, he doubted himself. *It's not exactly what I expected. Hardly feels like the peace of Shaefi.* In truth, he felt more conflicted than ever. The pile of ashes flashed before his eyes, and Amund's congratulations for a well-fought battle rang in his ears.

That is a foolish distinction, Baggi, he heard.

The apprentice took a deep breath to rebalance his emotions, resolving to unravel them through Contemplation before bed. Then he recited his acceptance.

"You honor me, Elder Sage Hrafn."

"Baggi," Hrafn said as they took their seats once more, "I suspect you are faced with many new feelings and ideas stemming from this place and these Tasks." A guilty expression appeared on the boy's face, but Hrafn hurriedly reassured him, "This is perfectly normal. I wish for you to feel these things and think these thoughts. That is why we undergo these rites, after all. Remain open to the wisdom of many sources, and I know you will find answers to all of your questions." He beamed at Baggi once more. "Tomorrow you will receive your third and final Task. In the meantime, sleep well tonight knowing that you have rightfully earned the gratitude of Flamebud Village, and that I am immensely proud of you," he concluded.

"Thank you, Elder Sage," Baggi replied.

He sounded still unsure, yet hopeful, and Hrafn was wise enough to know that the concepts Baggi grappled with would not be subdued by reassurances alone. He excused himself and left the apprentice to sort out his thoughts on his own.

Kettil, having watched the proceedings with a shocking degree of tact from the bar, now bounded over to her newly reconciled friend. "So you did it, huh?" she gushed, "You finished your second Task! What was it? How did you do it? Tell me everything!"

Baggi laughed, extremely grateful in that moment that he and Kettil had made up. "It was to mend a rift in the community, so that I may know the peace of Shaefi," he replied, "but all I did was make the villagers burn Amund's flamebud garden and plant food there." He sighed. "It doesn't much feel like I helped."

"Hmm," Kettil pondered, "did the locals seem happy about it?"

Baggi considered how to answer such a question, eventually snorting at the absurdity of transmuting what he had felt during the ritual into words. "Not exactly, but they seemed grateful. And Amund says they were asleep before, but they're alive now."

"Well there you go!" Kettil proclaimed decisively. "What's there to wonder about? If he says you did it, and the Elder Sage says you did it too, then you did it! That's just logic!" She leaned back and crossed her arms in satisfaction. "Besides, if anyone knows logic, it's riddle master Kettil."

The simplicity of her claim baffled Baggi, but then he found himself agreeing. *There's no sense in overthinking it,* he thought. *After all, I completed my second Task. Kettil's talking to me again. The locals are warming up to us. All is well.* He smiled at Kettil.

"You're right, I'm being foolish," he said.

"Of course I am, and of course you are," she snorted. "So what's your last one? Maybe I can help you with it."

"Maybe," he agreed, "but I won't know until tomorrow. Come find me when you finish your assignment and we'll get started on it."

Kettil's dark blue eyes sparked for just a moment. Baggi recognized that look; it was the expression Kettil wore when what she considered a spectacular idea occurred to her, the same one that landed her in trouble more often than not.

"Actually," she said innocently, "you should come with me tomorrow. Elof and I are on a special assignment, working on some lady's garden."

Baggi perked up instantly. "Really? I would get to work in a garden?" Kettil nodded. "I actually just learned quite a bit about gardening from Amund these past two days. I would be thrilled to put it into practice!" He looked at her quizzically. "Are you sure Elof wouldn't mind?"

"Of course not!" Kettil scoffed. "He loves you! Plus, you both love plants. It's a perfect fit for the job!"

"Once more I can't fault your logic," Baggi agreed. "Alright, I would be thrilled to join you! Then we'll get to my Task afterwards."

"Great," Kettil yawned. "Oh, and go to sleep early. We gotta get going before sunrise."

Despite this last instruction, he and Kettil continued to talk and laugh for several hours, only stopping to relocate to the bar when the tables started filling up. They chatted with Torny and told stories of their hometowns in Naefja; she absorbed them as if it were her only chance at committing the tales to memory. Kettil spoke of the great harbor in Yngmuth, and the imposing tower of the Alchemist Guild that loomed over the city, and the orphanage where she had put her talents to use brewing potent seafood stews before discovering alchemy; Baggi spoke of the mountainous woods and the ever-snowy crest just up the path from Jolk, of the fungus-lit cavern highways they took to visit neighboring towns, and sweet spiced buns and braised goat and the snug cottage with an eternally smoky chimney where they three had lived, his mother, his brother, and he. Then Amund arrived and told his own stories of how Flamebud Village had been when there were adults, how the children had all been taught by his parents how to fight, practicing every day, even holidays. He told them of the *kortas* that had been a common sight, at least one for every household, so that not a day went by without color filling the streets. He described with great pride and excessive detail the lineage of every family in Flamebud, which consequently necessitated describing much of the lineage of their neighbor village of Takkin. And all the while, they drank pepper-cider and laughed when Torny occasionally butted in to correct him or offer her own differing viewpoint.

It was a warm night. Eventually they peeled off, Kettil first, then Amund, and at last, after talking and smiling with Torny for far longer than he intended, Baggi bid her goodnight as well. The innkeeper looked around and sighed contentedly. She thought of the ritual that morning, of her neighbors and her cousin, and the foreigner who had helped make it possible. She felt a sudden desperate desire for the night to stretch on forever, for the next three days to never come, for the Staffkeepers of Shaefi to stay in Flamebud. Or at least, for one of them to stay. She recalled the joke Amund had made before, about marriage. Then she smiled at her own frivolity and thought about the Staffkeepers they had once had, and even in the lonely, drafty inn, she felt the warmth of the flamebuds flowing through her veins.

Amund, too, felt its warmth as he walked home. Even when he arrived at the empty place where his family had once been, the Chief of Flamebud did not ignore its barrenness. Instead, he set a chair at the head of the grand table and sat down. He tried to imagine his parents and their neighbors sitting around it, feasting as they had every holiday on spicy roasted roam-lizard and sweet, juicy melons. He tried to picture his family. Instead, he heard the laughs and voices of his Naefjan friends in their place. He imagined Kettil shouting at the other kids and stumping them with riddles, saw Baggi lecturing Torny and the innkeeper pretending she wanted him to stop. Amund smiled dreamily.

"I am feeling sentimental because of the flamebuds," he sighed to the empty chamber, voice reverberating grandly. "Or else I drank too much pepper-cider." He didn't bother considering it any further. Amund let his eyelids fall and drifted off to sleep.

13

The Alchemist Guild Tower was a behemoth structure, rising from the bay higher than even the mountains outside the borders of Yngmuth proper. Its beacon fifty stories up had once been the top floor, and it cast brilliant light in a sweeping continuous circle every few seconds to guide ships in even in darkness; without this crucial feature, Yngmuth could never have evolved into the bustling port town it had become. But the Guild had not stopped there, for as their wealth and influence grew, so did their conceit, and so too did their tower. The alchemists felt their headquarters inadequate in conveying the nobility and grandeur of their trade and had begun building the tower ever higher, stacking a new floor atop it nearly every year since its establishment. Now it stood well over one hundred stories and the structure's growth showed no signs of slowing. Such a feat would never have been possible without each and every brick being inscribed by artisan runologists for stability, an enormous expense only the Alchemist Guild could ever dream of affording.

Nowadays, the constant expansion had evolved into an industry in of itself, with a significant portion of Yngmuth's population finding employment and even residence on the floors above the beacon. It was impractical to have common folk entering and exiting the building every day, the alchemists reasoned, and besides, the lower floors were home and workshop to the Guild members themselves, who mistrusted their own laborers. To this end several floors had been designated barracks for their builders and other servants, not only for the purpose of saving time and money, but to entertain their paranoia and keep the vagabonds under close supervision and out of their workspace.

Valdis gazed skyward to the place where cloud and tower met, the taste of Death heavy on her tongue. *So many inside,* she thought, *so many who need us.* Yet the Tower was famously well-guarded, and she saw no entrance lacking for armed and armored men and women. Its main gate was open during the day, and they might have been allowed to call upon the Guild as customers, if their garb had been less conspicuous. As it stood, the five guards on either side of the ten-foot opening would seize and likely kill them before they ever set foot on the ground floor. The stone wall around the tower was nearly two stories tall itself; they could never surmount it and reach the rear entrance without drawing attention. Valdis entertained the idea of using disguises to enter incognito, but the logistics of navigating through floor after floor of unknown territory, locating those they sought, taking their lives, and leaving the Tower once more, all without being discovered, struck her as an impossible task. She retreated into the alley where The Conclusion waited and looked wordlessly to Birgir, wondering how he planned to proceed. He caught her stare and smiled reassuringly.

"There is no need to enter," he said, as if she had spoken her worries aloud.

"They will not leave," Valdis argued softly, "they have no need. Most stay on the upper floors for years at a time."

Birgir chuckled. "Yes, and who was it that taught you that?" he asked.

She lowered her head. "You. I apologize," she said.

"Your palette is keen, nearly as keen as mine already," he said kindly. "But you have far to go before it has fully developed. The taste of death is strong here, yes; you probably think it must come from many within." He turned to address the other four Staffkeepers in the party. "Who else agrees with that?" he asked. They remained silent, all but one.

"Aye," said Fritjof, curt and impudent, "it must be. We should go in and get to it."

Valdis glared hard at him. Even as he agreed with her, she wished he hadn't. Fritjof was the newest addition to the party, and at twenty he was a mere year younger than she herself. His features were manic, and he often surrendered to his passions when killing. She hated him for this weakness, despised his stupidity and cruelty and lack of understanding. *He still thinks we kill for pleasure,* she thought derisively, *Were it my decision, he would be banished today.* Yet Birgir, for all his wisdom, took pity on the young man and hoped – futilely, in Valdis' opinion – that he would come around if only given time and proper instruction.

"Patience, young ones," Birgir said coyly. "He will come to us. For it is only one 'he' that we seek today."

Valdis took his claim as fact without question. She knew and respected Birgir, and to entertain doubt was a wasted endeavor. Instead, the young woman marveled at his precise assessment.

"Just one tastes so strongly?" she asked, more an exclamation of wonder than a real question.

"That cannot be," Fritjof insisted.

With wicked delight, Valdis knew that this was one step too far. Birgir turned to him, his natural smile fading. The other Staffkeepers instinctively took a step back.

"Fritjof," he said with great deliberation, "I have decided on your role in this plan. Prepare yourself; the flavor grows stronger. He is approaching." And with that he turned back to watch the street once more.

Valdis was disappointed, but only for a moment. *His punishment will come,* she knew, *Birgir will show him discipline.* With great effort, she quelled her excitement, knowing that to take further delight in Fritjof's suffering would be a great hypocrisy. She drew her knife from her sheath, the soft hiss of leather echoing around her as the other Staffkeepers mirrored the action. Then she reached across her chest and opened a cut on her right bicep, sheathed her blade once more, and placed her left hand over the wound. Valdis squeezed blood from the cut until her fingers were painted red, then gently smeared the blood over the runes she had carved on her crook. They began to glow more intensely with the same crimson light the Disk had once cast, so long ago now. *Wake up, Relief,* she thought, the link between them now all but tangible, *prepare yourself.* She felt Relief pulse with solemn approval.

"Valdis, come," Birgir waved her over as he likewise blooded his own staff, Solace. "I want for you to know the taste, so that next time you can differentiate between many and one. You will kill this man," he commanded.

"Of course," she said immediately. "I relish the opportunity."

Birgir grinned warmly at her. Suddenly, a crier's voice pierced the gloomy morning fog.

"Make way for Grand Alchemist Bui!" the voice cried.

Birgir peered around the corner, towards the call's source. "I believe he has arrived," he said, though he needn't have; the taste of death filled Valdis' mouth and nose now, nearly so powerful as to be choking.

She nodded and focused on the task at hand, as she had always done. Birgir donned his cap, hoisting it atop his head by the antlers.

"Ready?" their leader asked. "Then let's get to it. Fritjof, he is accompanied by two bodyguards; see that they are not in our way." As a grin formed on the young man's face, Birgir added, "Without killing them."

Fritjof looked as if he had been slapped, but he seemed to sense the folly in openly questioning Birgir a second time. He gulped and stepped out of the alley, directly into the path of the three men who had come around the corner.

"Move it!" barked one of the hired thugs.

Valdis couldn't resist leaning out of the alley to observe. The Guild Alchemist was dressed in extravagant finery fit more for a feast than a laboratory, making him easy to pick out. He pinched the hem of his robes in each hand, holding them up so that they didn't drag in the filthy streets and soil their exquisite materials. His gaze was unfocused, and seemingly incapable of seeing the poor laborers, merchants, and sailors that populated the street. *That is the gaze of one who has never seen danger,* she recognized, *only comfort and wellness.*

His bodyguards were just the opposite, huge hulking men wearing roughened boiled leather and rougher glares. Each carried a sword on one hip and a spiked iron cudgel on the other, presumably for when a greater level of restraint was required. Valdis wondered which weapon would actually be less lethal, and which would be used on Fritjof. Either was acceptable to her, so long as he didn't die. He wasn't supposed to die yet; the taste wasn't on him.

Fritjof mockingly bowed and backpedaled several steps without moving from their path, perhaps twenty feet away. Still bent over, he scooped a rock from the ground and hurled it without warning directly into the closer bodyguard's face. It took him by surprise, thwacking loudly from his brow and drawing blood straight away. The man stood dazed for a moment, then he unhooked his cudgel.

"You're gonna regret that!" he roared, charging Fritjof.

Even as he did so, the Staffkeeper threw a second rock at the other bodyguard. His surprise was evident, but after a moment he ignored his employer's panicked protests and likewise charged forward with weapon in hand. Valdis watched Fritjof block the first swing with his staff before the second man caught him directly under the arm. A wet crack rang out and was swiftly joined by the young man's painful cry.

"Now," Birgir commanded.

Valdis tore her attention from the violence. Birger motioned for the other three Staffkeepers to rescue Fritjof while he and Valdis strode toward the man called Bui.

"Bui," she said gently as they approached, "it's time. You can stop struggling now."

But as soon as he laid eyes on them, the alchemist fell back on his rump, all concern for his immaculate clothing forgotten, and scrabbled for a small flask from an inner pocket. He uncorked the concoction and quaffed it in a single gulp before Valdis had even the time to note its color. Bui then dared to glare at them, gloating from his pathetic position on the ground.

"Ha!" he shouted, trying to mask his fear with volume. "Good luck hurting me now! Not even a guillotine could best my own personal batch of Stoneskin!"

"Good man," said Birgir compassionately, "don't you see you've only made this more painful than it needs to be?" The alchemist simply stared up at him in wide-eyed disbelief. "Ah well," he sighed to Valdis, "what else can you expect, with the Staffkeepers of Shaefi leading them astray at every turn?"

She nodded in agreement as her companion invoked Algiz over their target. The alchemist began waving his arms frantically, nonsensically.

"It's only numbness," she consoled him. "We are trying to make this painless for you. You aren't making it easy."

Bui made no answer, only kept on waving his arms and trying in vain to regain his feet, so Valdis shrugged and invoked Ansuz-Jera. Power rushed betwixt her and Relief, and with it a sobering reminder of her responsibility. It comforted Valdis, this sense of purpose and duty, and she channeled her acceptance of the role into her magic. Her crimson aura flowed from the crook and entered Bui's body. He began convulsing, blood pouring from his orifices, and gasped like a fish out of water. His whole body seized up for a half-second, his back arched, then he slumped to the ground, his soul released from life. The process had taken roughly half a minute. *Fool,* Valdis thought, *the knife would have been much gentler.*

Immediately, Valdis drew her blade and set to carving Death's sigil on the alchemist's forehead. She took great care and poured her aura into the markings, ensuring that the part she played here would not be overlooked or forgotten. Her mouth was full of the fresh flavor of Bui's passing, but the man's cowardice and resistance tainted the profile with an unmistakable bitterness. Still, she felt glad Birgir had given her the chance to experience such a concentrated flavor. She felt sure she wouldn't mistake it for many smaller ones again.

"Well done," Birgir complimented her. "And do you taste the difference?"

"Yes," she answered, "it seems obvious now."

"I thought you might say something like that," he chuckled. "Well, we had better see what to do about the other two."

They turned to their companions and saw that they had managed to best the guards. The Conclusion were no strangers to fighting, naturally; everywhere they went, their intentions were misunderstood, and they were frequently forced to defend themselves. Still, they were not warriors, not Staffkeepers of Sawtor, and Valdis suspected the bodyguards would have soundly beaten them had they not held the advantage of surprise. Fritjof was hanging weakly from the shoulders of Staffkeeper Gyda, blood pouring from his face and only half-conscious. The two men at arms laid in the street, squirming weakly, having been bludgeoned to near-death themselves.

"Well done, Fritjof," Birgir commended him. "You have more than atoned for your insolence." The young man smiled painfully back at him.

"I don't taste Death on them," Gyda said to the duo. "I think we should leave them as is."

"Agreed," said Birgir. "Valdis?"

She wondered for a moment at their leader asking for her opinion before answering, "Agreed."

"Then let's do as you say, Gyda," replied Birgir, gracious as always. "Would you mind retrieving the alchemist's valuables?"

She nodded and began searching the corpse, taking several gem-studded rings and a pure gold odd-ring from his right arm. It was heavy with stone-odd, but not of leaf-agate like Valdis had seen in the Melenno Valley; in Naefja, shell-agate was used instead. She admired the wavy stripes of white on them as Gyda handed the money over and dove into Bui's pockets. The elder Staffkeeper found therein three potions of uncertain content. She left the man's Guild belt out of respect. At that moment, they heard shouting and the stamping of many feet from the direction of the Guild Tower just around the corner. Silently, the Staffkeepers slipped back down the alleyway and off, not looking back until the sounds of pursuit had faded.

***

Hours later, the Staffkeepers huddled close around a meager campfire. The sun had long since descended and they had stolen out of Yngmuth in the ensuing darkness, cloaks flapping as they swam through the shadows like the manta rays in the harbor at their heels. After putting several miles between them and any potential pursuers, they hunkered down in a rocky overhang to shelter from the cold and hail. Valdis missed the horses sorely, not only for convenience but for companionship as well. *But we had to eat,* she knew.

Bui had been their first target in weeks. They had followed Birgir's tongue for days and days of travel, growing ever more perplexed and ever hungrier all the while, for weeks without a kill meant weeks without a payout. It was a lucky break for the man to be a Guild Alchemist; the wealth on his person would feed the Staffkeepers for a long time to come. Perhaps they could even replace their steeds, if only they could escape pursuit and survive until the nearest village.

Fritjof had managed to tear a large hunk of yak from a butcher's hook during the initial pursuit, Valdis tossing its owner a random handful of odd from Bui's bounty as compensation. *I probably overpaid,* thought Valdis stubbornly, but as the meat slowly crisped over their paltry flame, even she was grateful for Fritjof's shenanigans. She glanced over at him, bandaged heavily with his right arm in a sling, and her expression softened slightly. He had suffered enough for his misbehavior already without her compounding the pain.

She thought instead of Bui and his desperation to escape them. It was not without precedent. Nearly all of those they approached tried to best them, either through combat or flight. None had yet done so, though some had gotten close. Still, not all hope was lost; on exactly two occasions, the Staffkeepers had tasted of fearless deaths. The first was a woman, about the same age as Valdis was now. She had closed her eyes, kneeling as if in supplication, and it had been clear to the Staffkeepers that she did not shut her eyes in fear, but in blissful rest. It was a beautiful death. The second was a little boy, perhaps too young to understand or perhaps too young to misunderstand. He had been curious, excited even. He died with a smile on his face and not a shred of fear in him. Valdis brushed her fingers along the woman's shinbones stitched into her trousers, then the boy's jawbone slung around her neck. The serenity and fearlessness of their owners echoed through the mementos even now.

"Birgir," she asked softly, "why do so many misunderstand?"

"Because it's what they are taught," he sighed, "by the Staffkeepers of Shaefi. Nearly all in Naefja call themselves Shaefini; is it really so surprising?"

"Why do they want to be Shaefini?" she insisted. "Why do they want to be afraid of Death?"

"Now that, I do not know." He turned the meat over. "But I suspect that they're not so much afraid of Death as they are afraid of grief."

Valdis was ready to point out, needlessly, that pretending Death and grief don't exist didn't make it so, but at that moment Gyda half-rose and raised a finger to her lips for silence.

"We've been followed," she whispered.

Arrows suddenly filled the entrance to their little cave, three slamming into Birgir and piercing his chest. Another sank into Valdis' thigh, yet another grazed her brow. She had no time to see where the remaining missiles fell; Birgir looked over at her and grinned, shrugged, then fell forward onto the cold stone. If there was any doubt in Valdis' mind whether he would survive the wounds, the resounding crack of his skull as it landed dispelled them. A pure deliciousness filled her mouth, but it was tainted by the prematurity of the death, like an underbaked loaf of bread: crusty and firm on the outside yet soggy and raw beneath. Valdis struggled to her feet, using Relief as a crutch in place of her wounded leg. Her own free-flowing blood painted the runes and woke her staff. Valdis wished he hadn't come to, wished her partner could have slept through the whole ugly ordeal, but now that he had, she was grateful for his support. He pulsed seriously, urging her onward. Gyda and the others scrabbled to the cave entrance and ran out into the night without looking back.

Valdis made to follow, yet her footing was uneven. She fell hard to the ground and grit her teeth as the impact jarred the arrow in her thigh. Then, as if by miracle, someone seized her arm around their shoulders and hauled her to her feet. She looked to her savior and was baffled to see Fritjof, his staff slung on his back to free up his arms for rescue. He struggled immensely to walk on his own, wounded as he was, yet he grunted and nearly screamed with exertion to carry her away from danger. Valdis snapped to and eased his burden with her functioning leg and Relief. He grinned at her for a moment, thankful, as if it were she saving him and not the other way around. Valdis saw his slinged arm doggedly gripping the yak skewer. She wondered at his audacity before turning her focus purely towards escape.

They limped out of the cave and then dragged each other through the woods, as quickly as they could manage and for as long as they could stand. With every step Valdis imagined she heard pursuit. It bolstered her stamina, pushing her ever forward despite the howling pain in her thigh and on her face. Blood flowed from her brow and into her eye, blinding and stinging; she ignored it. Eventually, neither she nor Fritjof could continue. They collapsed, panting, and crawled under a cage-like root network, covering their entrance with sticks and puce leaves that cracked distressingly. There they stayed, catching their breath in their utmost quiet, for a long time. Valdis noted that Fritjof had escaped the arrows, but with his broken arm and scourged face his condition was still no more favorable than her own. She saw blood beginning to soak through his shirt and realized his ribs must have suffered the spiked cudgels as well. He hid the pain masterfully.

When they had recovered somewhat, Fritjof tore into the yak meat, then handed the skewer to Valdis.

"At least we didn't lose the meat," he said weakly.

Valdis scoffed but ate, ripping a mouthful of fatty meat from the stick. Warm, but not hot, fat dribbled down her chin. She wiped it away half-heartedly, then wiped the blood from her brow as well. Drawing her knife, she winced as she extended the laceration so the blood would pour around her eye rather than into it. They continued to pass the skewer between them with each bite.

"We lost Birgir," she eventually said.

"Then someone else will find our targets," he replied, nonplussed.

"I will," she declared out of the blue. Relief pulsed in agreement.

Fritjof looked at her curiously. "Fine by me," he said after a pause. "Gyda might want to, though."

"My palette is strongest. I will lead," she responded.

Fritjof shrugged inscrutably with his healthy shoulder. They finished off the skewer in silence, then used what little energy the meat restored to invoke Algiz over each other and dull the pain. The numbness wasn't complete, at least not for Valdis, but it helped. Then, after hours had passed and the sun risen, they got to their feet and limped forward once more in search of their companions. They walked without direction, save for that of Yngmuth and the rotten taste of early deaths at their backs, and hoped that The Conclusion would find them before those that hunted.

As the sun approached its zenith, a figure in a black cloak and humble bone adornment on her sleeves stepped into their path. She appeared uninjured, but she was filthy and alone. It seemed the other two had not been so lucky.

"Gyda," said Fritjof, then collapsed without warning under the weight of their deliverance.

Valdis fell with him, the arrow digging painfully in the meat of her thigh even through the anesthetic of Algiz. She grunted, half in pain and half in sheer resentment. Gyda rapidly approached and looked them over with concern in her eyes. After sizing up their wounds, she withdrew one of Bui's potions from her cloak and handed it to Valdis. The liquid inside was a gentle orange, like apricot.

"This should close your wounds," Gyda said, but her voice was uncertain. "When I pull out the arrow, pour a bit on there right away. Are you able?"

"Yes," said Valdis. She uncorked the vial and steeled herself.

Without warning her, Gyda planted her feet and yanked the arrow through the back of her thigh. Valdis screamed and tried to follow the older woman's instructions. Her hands shook violently, and she splashed more than intended, but she had at least not missed the mark and the wound closed up within seconds. Gathering her composure, she dabbed the liquid on her finger and applied it to the entry site, on the front of her leg, much more carefully. Afterwards, she held up the vial and noted regretfully that only a third of its contents remained.

"I will tend Fritjof," she said as Gyda made to take the vial back. "He helped me live. Now the debt will be paid."

Gyda looked ready to argue but withdrew. Valdis lifted Fritjof's shirt to reveal a row of painful punctures layered atop deep purple bruises. She dabbed the potion as before on each of the punctures, sealing them up one after another. Then she removed the bandages on his face and used the last few drops to close those wounds too.

"Valdis," said Gyda, "your face."

The wound on her brow had been completely forgotten, but she remembered now that it was still only just clotted. She rubbed the residual alchemical liquid from her fingers on the gash. It closed, but not completely. It was enough for Valdis. She struggled to her feet. The skin may have been knit, but the muscle underneath was still rent; it would be some time before she could walk freely once more.

"I will guide us now," she asserted. "Do you disagree?"

Gyda looked her in the eye. She was the elder Staffkeeper, and had a wealth of experience that Valdis lacked, but she could not deny the younger woman's taste for Death was far superior. She shook her head.

"Good," said Valdis. "Because I will rely on you the most."

Relief pulsed with irritation. *Yes, but on you more than the most,* she told it, *that goes without saying.* Her crook began to drift back to sleep, the blood dried and its insecurity appeased.

"Of course you will," replied Gyda dryly. "There's only us three now."

Valdis didn't respond. Instead, she made to depart. *We are still not safe,* she reluctantly acknowledged. She looked on their unconscious companion and considered his past indiscretions, his rampant violence inflicted on unclaimed lives. Then she thought of his disregard for his own life as he had hauled her out of the cave, barely able to support his broken body. *Perhaps Birgir wasn't mistaken after all,* she thought begrudgingly, *perhaps he can still learn.* Besides, Gyda was right; they were only three now.

"Carry Fritjof," she commanded, forcing herself forward with Relief for support. Gyda took the still unconscious young man on her back and followed without question.

"It is a shame we can't recover Solace," Gyda said after some time. Birgir's staff had no doubt been claimed as a trophy by their assailants, or else sundered on superstitious grounds.

"Yes," agreed Valdis.

They said no more. There was no more to be said.

***

Valdis dismounted before her quarry, four Staffkeepers remaining in their saddles behind her. The sour stench of premature death filled her mouth and nostrils as she gripped Relief in a gloved hand stitched with bones. The fingers moved with her own, as if displaying the Staffkeeper's skeleton and not that of a long-dead villager. Her cloak, too, was adorned with bones from shoulder to waist, human mostly, but some animal as well. She bit her lip, hard enough to draw blood, dabbing the tear with her thumb then smearing it on Relief to wake him. Her staff ascertained the situation in a heartbeat, readying itself for a clash. Then she addressed the man standing over the corpses.

"Fritjof," she said evenly, "do you know who killed these men?"

"Yes," he replied, "it was me." He stood grinning deliriously at them, apparently proud of his accomplishment.

"Why?"

"Because that's what we do."

"They were not ready."

He straightened his back proudly, his own bone adornments knocking like chimes. "I am a Staffkeeper of Death. I kill all- " he began, before Valdis interrupted.

"Not anymore," she said. "You are banished. Leave us now. You know that to return would invite Death upon yourself, and I will have no such qualms then."

Fritjof looked her up and down, slowly, analyzing. "I saved your life once," he said.

"And I yours, several times," she replied quickly. "It means little to me. My patience has run out. If a decade is not enough long for you to understand, you never will. Go."

Fritjof frowned at this uncharacteristically verbose rebuke, and Valdis saw him consider clashing, yet even Fritjof was not so deluded as to think he could best her. He bowed, shook his head as if in wonder, then put a foot in his saddle stitched with bones and mounted, riding off on his horse with filed teeth. Gyda and the other three Staffkeepers came closer.

"It was necessary," the venerable woman said.

"I know," Valdis replied.

She mounted her horse once more, never taking her eyes from the direction Fritjof had left. *Towards Geluwam,* she predicted, *he is their worry now.* The sun was beginning to set.

"Come," she commanded, and led them back to the familiar mountain trail.

After another hour of quiet travel, they arrived. Her cottage was just as she had remembered it, excepting the disrepair caused by nearly twenty years' erosion. She dismounted and led her horse by the reins, into the barn with a great hole in its roof. Her Staffkeepers followed her example. Wild goats had made the structure their home, most likely descended from the very herd she had set free when she left to begin her new life among The Conclusion. The goats challenged her, but she expertly wrangled them with her crook and dragged them outside by the ears. It was more difficult than she remembered. Valdis smiled a bit, the labor nostalgic.

"I remember this place," said Gyda as they unloaded the horses.

"I expect so," replied Valdis.

"Elder Sage Valdis?" asked a gentle voice. "Where are we?"

Valdis turned to the Naefjan boy she had taken on as apprentice weeks ago. "Do not call me Elder Sage," she reprimanded him. "Rank and titles are Shaefini nonsense."

The boy, Hakon, did not shy away. There was a confidence in his sculpted features, a brazenness in the brow that offered challenge to all Solabell. Of course, this challenge did not extend to Valdis. At her rebuke, he averted his silver eyes, long metallic-blonde hair tossing slightly with the motion.

"As you say, Valdis."

"This was my home," she granted him, "before I was a Staffkeeper."

He raised his eyebrows and looked around curiously without response. When they had finished unsaddling, Valdis went to the house, Hakon following close behind. His constant focus was both an asset and an annoyance, but Valdis had become patient in her maturity; she allowed him to stay close without admonishment.

She was forced to bow her head slightly in order to enter now, just like her father had in days past. When they crossed the threshold, Valdis' senses were flooded with long-forgotten sights and smells: the woodsmoke in the fireplace, the snow-melter over the sink, even her father's lyre still stood exactly where she had left it, leaning against the chair that had first been his and then had become hers. Remarkably, the taste of Njal's death, strong and intense, still lingered after so many years. It brought tears to her eyes, tears she didn't dishonor by wiping away.

Valdis entered the kitchen and picked up the kettle, then cracked the snow-melter and filled the jug with water. When she placed it on the stove, her hand came away covered in dust. The imprint of her fingers lingered in the grime on the handle. It occurred to Valdis that her hands were so much bigger now; she could heft the kettle with only a few fingers, rather than her whole fist.

A gentle plucking interrupted her reminisce. She turned to see Hakon with lyre in hand. He adjusted the pegs as he plucked, bringing the harsh notes slowly in tune. The other Staffkeepers looked to Valdis questioningly. She approached him with slow footsteps.

"You can play," she observed.

He nodded. "They taught me at Enton. Of course, I can't make proper Naefjan music alone."

"What do you feel?" she asked.

Hakon considered the question, stroking the lyre. "From the lyre, I feel...care. Love, maybe. From the cottage..." he knelt and stroked the clay-colored floorboards then looked up, his silver eyes meeting her green. "I feel a good death. It's soft and warm, like cashmere."

Gyda chuckled from the other side of the room. The other two wore curious expressions, but she offered no explanation. Valdis smiled and patted Hakon on the head.

"Very good," she said.

Valdis commanded their second-newest companion, Arni, to start a fire. He retrieved a bundle of firewood from the barn and piled it atop the ashes on the hearth, then invoked Kenaz. The logs ignited, filling the room with warm orange light. He and the others sat close to it on the floor as Valdis set the tea from her pack to steeping. As she counted precisely four minutes, she rinsed the dust from the cups in the cabinet, then poured and distributed the tea before sinking into the worn, moldy armchair by the fire. Gyda sat in the other chair, the one Valdis had first used as a child. The Staffkeepers sipped their tea and enjoyed the warmth in silence.

"I would like to die here," Gyda requested apropos of nothing.

Valdis nodded. "Before we leave?" she asked.

"Yes."

The others gaped at Valdis. Hakon laid his hand on Gyda's, features scrunched in confusion.

"But I don't feel Death on you," he said.

"You are still a child. Your senses are still developing, and easily confused. This place is masking it, but my time is here," Gyda explained gently.

Valdis nodded agreement; she had noticed the taste yesterday, holding her tongue out of trust in Gyda. She knew the old woman would not flee her conclusion, knew she was only waiting for the perfect moment to arrive. And arrive it had, along with them, at the cottage that had once been Valdis'.

"After dinner, perhaps," she said.

"Thank you," replied Gyda, and those were her last words.

Hakon cooked their dinner on the antique stove and they ate quietly, savoring each bite. Valdis herself drew the knife across the old woman's throat, just as she had in the very same spot so long ago, and just as before, Death was greeted with bravery and serenity. Valdis tasted it anew, Njal's acceptance renewed in Gyda's.

"Oh," said Hakon afterwards, grinning ruefully at his mistake, "I feel the difference now."

As they bundled up on the floor preparing for sleep, Arni asked uncertainly where they were headed next. Valdis stared into the flames and contemplated her answer. *So beautiful,* she thought, full of admiration for the simple force. The smoke filled her mouth, and with it a tantalizing fragment of their next charge. It was far from here, very far, but even so the flavor was intense. *We will need to bolster our ranks,* she realized, *Many will need us where we go.* Valdis remembered the day in Yngmuth, and the alchemist named Bui. She felt sure her assessment was correct.

"South," she eventually announced, "to Kichishi."

14

Baggi woke in the darkness to small hands shaking him awake.

"Baggi," Kettil whispered, "come on, get up."

Rubbing sleep from his eyes, he groped blindly for his rucksack and fumbled inside for his vial of Toothsave. He dipped a finger in the minty alchemical paste and rubbed it on his teeth, front and back, working it in with his tongue. Then he picked up Compromise in one hand and his leather hairband in the other. Kettil led the way as they tip-toed to the door, he half-heartedly combing his fingers through his hair in a vain attempt to break up the tangles and abandoning the idea almost immediately. She turned the knob and pulled, revealing Elof alone in the hall, more alert than ever and dimly illuminated by the glow of the potions on his sash.

"Ready?" Kettil whispered. Baggi quickly tied back his hair and nodded. "Good. Let's go!"

Elof nodded politely in greeting and they departed in silence. It was a cool morning, full of that peculiar impatience summer nights bring. Baggi looked to the east, where the slightest hint of purple-grey colored the sky. *About an hour till sunrise,* he estimated, *perhaps two. Strange that we must begin so early.*

"Elof?" he said softly, mindful of the slumbering village. The young man flinched, then shivered before turning to Baggi. "It's quite early to be out. Must this work be done in the dark?"

"Yes," Elof replied hesitantly, "ah, that is accurate. Or, ah, perhaps, that is greatly preferred." He avoided Baggi's gaze and offered no further explanation.

They arrived shortly at a building Baggi had not seen before. Over the door a sign was affixed. *A bit too dark to make out,* he thought, *an easy fix.* He invoked Sowilo, tempering the spell so that it cast little more light than a candle. He held it up and observed a colorful design of a woman reclining on a pile of coins, hands full and outstretched as if offering them to the viewer. *The bank,* he realized, *so this is where Audr lives. She wanted help from us?* It struck him as odd, the girl who had so vehemently opposed him in council requesting the help of their caravan. *But then again, if her intentions were to provide for the village, it's not so far-fetched to expect she might swallow her pride.*

"Baggi," Elof whispered urgently, "please, put that out!"

"Sorry," he whispered back and dissolved the attunement, "that was stupid. We don't want to disturb Audr."

"Ah, yes, exactly so," Elof mumbled as the dark returned. "Which is why we must, well, take a somewhat, ah...inconvenient route to the garden."

Baggi looked at him quizzically. Elof gestured for he and Kettil to follow as they crept around to the rear wall of the bank.

"Are you ready, Kettil?" the alchemist whispered.

"I'm ready!" she whispered back, fiercely excited, then backpedaled several feet.

Elof bent his legs slightly, back to the wall, and formed a net with his hands. *No,* thought Baggi in disbelief, *they can't seriously mean to...*

But they did. Before the apprentice could protest, Kettil ran towards Elof and stepped into his hands as he launched her upwards with all his might. Unfortunately, his aim was imprecise, and she didn't quite reach the rooftop. Instead, Kettil scrabbled manically for a moment before her face slammed into the wall and she fell painfully onto Elof's head. He collapsed in a mangled heap of limbs. The duo lolled in the dirt miserably for several moments while Baggi regarded them with the indifference of pure shock. Then he snapped out of the lull and rushed to check on his friends.

Elof gathered himself as quickly as possible and hurried to examine Kettil. She sat up in a daze and her companions both drew sharp, nervous breaths as they saw blood streaming from her mouth.

"Heh. Guess we needed a practice run," she said through a woozy grin.

One of her front teeth was missing and her lip was visibly swollen. Baggi winced and touched his lips while Elof quickly retrieved a flask of Knit, bade Kettil open wide, and dabbed it gingerly on the spot the tooth had been. She yelped in pain despite his efforts. Then he quickly swapped out the Knit for a lime-green unguent and applied it to her lip. The swelling was reduced, if not eliminated, within seconds.

"I sincerely think this is a ridiculous idea!" Baggi urged, marveling at the fact it had to be said in the first place. "And I think Audr would agree, if she knew we were doing it on her account! Besides, we probably woke her in all of this commotion anyway."

Elof shook his head. "No, no, she yet snores."

I forgot Elof can hear so well, Baggi thought, *although just now I wish he couldn't.*

"Yeah!" Kettil agreed. "And anyway, now we know how to do it!"

"You mean now you know how not to do it, right?" he asked, though the question came off as rhetorical. He shook his head disapprovingly as they squared up for a second attempt. "Kettil I understand, but you, Elof? You're wiser than this!" The older man shrugged helplessly at him but gave no explanation. "I can't watch," Baggi sighed and turned away.

He heard short, quick footsteps, followed by Elof's grunt of exertion and a small squeal from Kettil. Wincing preemptively, the Baggi turned around and sighed in relief as Kettil peered down at them and waved, energetic and triumphant, the injury from moments before already forgotten. It seemed extremely unfair to him that a ten-year-old should have such a high tolerance for pain, much higher than his own.

"Good!" Elof said. "Now, your turn Baggi."

"Again, I sincerely think this is a ridiculous idea!" Baggi whispered back fervently.

"Oh, come on!" Kettil scoffed from above. "If I can do it, so can you!"

"But I'm heavier than you!" He glanced toward Elof and his spindly frame. "No offense intended."

"Naturally," replied Elof. "However, I needn't ah, toss you, necessarily. Just a boost should be enough. That is, for you to reach and pull yourself up. With Kettil's assistance." He shot Baggi a chagrined smile, apologetic and imploring at once.

"Fine," Baggi sighed, slinging Compromise on his back, "let's get this over with."

After several long moments of uncoordinated flailing between them, the alchemists managed to hoist Baggi onto the roof. Then Kettil and Baggi each reached down an arm and Elof jumped up to grab them, nearly pulling them right back down in the process. Still, they managed to lift him and took a moment to survey the garden as they caught their breath. Baggi invoked Sowilo once more, keeping it carefully smothered in his cloak so as to allow only a controlled portion of light. Neatly inscribed placards denoted the crop assigned to each waist-high planter box, their names written in clean, professional Sparktongue script. *Spinach, carrots, onions, beets, eggplant, turnips,* he translated as he walked. *She has quite the variety.* His stomach grumbled petulantly as he entertained the myriad delicacies the crops might one day become.

"Ah, Baggi," Elof mumbled beside him, "I really have no wish to rush you, since, after all, you are helping us voluntarily, but, well, ah...we don't have a surplus of time with which to, ah, complete the assignment."

"Right," replied Baggi, "sorry. What do you need me to do?"

"I trust you are familiar with the Jera rune?"

"Of course. We aren't assigned to a caravan until we pass all of our runic exams. Jera is the second one I learned," the apprentice replied, aware that Elof's question hadn't required an answer but unable to resist elaborating. "Actually, it's a thrilling story. I had just learned Ansuz, but I was really nervous because Ansuz applied to myself and Jera would be the first time I enchanted something else. On the day I showed up for the exam, a-"

"Baggi!" Kettil snapped a little too loudly. "He just said we don't have a lot of time!"

"Forgive me. I'll get right to it."

Baggi touched Compromise to his forehead and invoked Jera, then carefully traced the boundaries of the nearest planter box. His aura left a visible trail as he pulled it along the borders, and when he connected it to the corner in which he had begun, the magic slowly filled the empty space. It settled like fog, descending into the soil and misting the carrot-tops icy blue. Baggi wiped a light sweat from his forehead. Compared to when he had taken the exam, he had already enchanted a greater area and his level of fatigue was inconsequential. He smiled, proud of himself, and continued to the next two boxes in much the same way.

He was beginning to feel the exhaustion of his invocations when Baggi suddenly found he was looking not at a dark rooftop garden, but a brightly lit glasshouse surrounded outside by the glare of white snow. He saw his hands waving Compromise, forming Jera and enchanting the crops just as he had been moments before. It felt as a dream. Then he heard the door swing open and turned to see a little boy with short auburn hair and silver eyes waddle in. He was bundled tightly and seemed as a result to lack full range of motion. Snow coated him from head to toe, his eyelashes and brows frosted.

Little Baggi, he recognized in two voices. The boy saw the magic pouring over the crops and gasped.

"What...Bjorn! You said you would wait!" He rushed over and pouted as he swished an irritated hand through the magical fog. Baggi heard himself chuckle and patiently pull the fog to mend the tear in the enchantment.

"Well, I did wait," he said in a voice deeper than his own. "Let this be a lesson: sometimes you have a choice between playing in the snow and watching magic at work. So you have to choose between two wonders, and you did."

"Pft," scoffed the child as Baggi put out a hand and ruffled snow from his hair. "Maybe I was trying to teach *you* a lesson! Be patient and keep your promises! How about that?"

"Oh, relax. I've just started anyhow. There's still plenty of magic to be done." He saw his hand reach out and slap his younger self's own as it cut mindlessly through the blue fog. It was a dizzying experience. "Just stop messing with my aura so I can get on with it!"

Baggi saw himself pull a hand back from the enchanted cloud and put it behind his back, nodding eagerly. Bjorn's arms began drawing Jera in the air with one hand, the other resting on the boy's shoulder.

And then he was in the dark once more, his head spinning and his sense of self thoroughly muddled. Without warning, he doubled over and retched. As Elof rushed over and placed a concerned hand on his back, Baggi waved him off.

"Just need a moment," he mumbled, unsure of what else to say.

"Don't push yourself too far," Elof whispered back. "We can always come back later, if this is too much."

"No, no," insisted Baggi, "I can do it. I just...felt something unexpected, is all." He righted himself, pushing back up to height with Compromise, and regarded his staff with bewilderment. *It's awake again. And apparently, it wanted to reminisce.* The runes pulsed happily, as if at peace. Baggi shrugged and, finding no more surprises as he continued to enchant, focused on the task at hand.

After another half hour, Baggi was panting and his entire body was one uniform ache, but he was finished. The eastern sky was lighter now, much closer to sunrise than Baggi had anticipated.

"There," he gasped. "Now, I wouldn't mind a break. We can just wait here for Audr to wake and report our success."

"No!" his companions urged in unison. Baggi narrowed his eyes.

"Why not? There's no sense in jumping off the roof."

"Ah, well, of course we will report our success," Elof stammered, "but, ah...oh! We should be getting back to the inn! The Elder Sage will be making assignments for us soon."

That's bizarre, thought Baggi, *wasn't this their assignment for today? Waking before sunrise is reasonable, trying not to disturb Audr's sleep is plausible, but this? This is suspicious.* Slowly, ignoring his fatigue, Baggi raised Compromise to his forehead and attuned once more. This time, however, he invoked Ansuz. Elof opened his mouth as if to object, but then decided to bite his tongue. He looked away. As the magic settled into his eyes, the apprentice looked upon his companions with fresh insight, and as he did so, two things became immediately clear:

First, that they were lying to him. Second, that he had been rather naïve not to notice it sooner.

"Elof, Kettil," he began, his voice quiet with hurt, "tell me the truth."

Kettil was grinding her toe into the floor. *She's too stubborn*, he knew, *even now she won't say it*. Elof, on the other hand, nodded reluctantly.

"I will. But first we must go," he said.

Baggi said nothing for several long moments. He observed the alchemist's nervous fidgeting, ultimately deeming the agreement honest. He knew Elof's mannerisms well, even without Ansuz, but with the runic magic at work there was no chance of mistaking the man's sincerity. He nodded back once, curtly, then released his attunement and, without another word, dropped lightly off the roof. He landed harder than he anticipated, stumbling to his hands and knees. Baggi remained there for several moments, anxious and confused. Then he set Compromise in the ground and forced himself to his feet. He began walking back to the Flamebud Inn without sparing a glance behind.

***

"So?" Baggi demanded when they were all three seated at a stump-table.

The sun was still not risen, but even so Torny had entered the kitchen and begun cooking a large breakfast. They could hear the clang of metal, the rattling of spices being shaken out, and an occasional half-asleep curse even from where they sat across the room.

Elsewise, the only noises were vague stirring sounds coming from the rooms.

"Ah, well, Baggi, I would rather not discuss this where others might, ah, overhear," Elof mumbled.

He glanced towards the back hall from which the Shaefini would emerge at any moment.

"Then speak quickly," said Baggi impatiently.

"Alright, fine!" Kettil cut in. "We weren't supposed to have a Staffkeeper do it. That lady wanted us to do it with alchemy, but that wasn't gonna work, and if we told anyone then they wouldn't do it, and then people would starve!" She leaned back in her chair as if exhausted by the explanation.

Baggi stared at her in bafflement. "So the most reasonable response, to you, was lying to me and Audr both?"

He put particular emphasis on the word "lying". Elof rubbed the back of his neck.

"It's not exactly lying," he mumbled, "as you are not yet a Staffkeeper."

"That's...what...you decided this was acceptable based on technicality?" the apprentice stammered.

His stomach began tying itself in intricate knots. Knowing it hadn't been his fault, that he had been deliberately misled, did nothing to loosen the binds.

"'Honesty is naught but a series of technicalities,'" Elof quoted meekly.

Baggi recognized the proverb: Aeskettil the Generous, from his tome "*The Legal Conduct and Judicial Processes of Various Staffkeeping Orders*". He knew, too, that Elof had studied under Aeskettil during his own education at the Temple at Enton, though the exact nature and extent of their relationship was unclear.

"And were you aware," he sighed, "that I and Chief Amund were addressing the food scarcity already?"

"Not at the time," Elof replied apologetically.

Baggi sighed again, angry at his friends yet unable to fault them. *Our goal was the same,* he thought. *But that doesn't change the fact that they lied to me.* Then an even more worrying thought occurred to him.

"Does the Elder Sage know?" he asked.

"Yeah! Of course!" Kettil reassured him. "I mean, kind of. He knows the important parts."

Baggi's head was beginning to spin. Trying to unravel the morality of his friends' actions was proving far more difficult than he expected. *I need to Contemplate,* he thought. Along with the urge came all of the exhaustion he had been ignoring since working his magic. *I really need to Contemplate.* He stood up wordlessly and turned to leave.

"Ah, Baggi," Elof stammered, "I, ah...well..."

"I won't tell anyone," Baggi said to the floor. "At least, not until I'm completely sure it's the right thing to do."

Their fellow Shaefini finally began to filter into the commons. He said no more and pushed through the crowd to his room. There he sat on the floor as his fellow apprentices gathered their things and, ignoring a curious glance from Staffkeeper Apprentice Guthini, began to Contemplate. Guthini lingered after the others for a moment, opened his mouth to speak, then second-guessed himself and scampered away in meek silence.

Meanwhile, Elof and Kettil sat quietly. They looked at each other and sighed.

"Well that coulda gone worse," Kettil offered.

Despite himself, Elof chuckled. "That may be true," he said.

Then the caravan began to fill the room, and they spoke no more of it.

***

Honesty. Survival. Opposites and enemies, Baggi Contemplated.

The Staffkeepers of Shaefi valued life, and the preservation thereof, above all else. But that didn't mean they allowed the justification of immoral behavior on its behalf. The crucial concept that each Staffkeeper grappled with essentially boiled down to this: which of these behaviors were acceptable in the pursuit of life, and which were unjustifiable? Which behaviors incurred a greater loss of spirit than could be justified by the saving of body and mind? When at last a Staffkeeper of Shaefi answered those questions, they were often faced with one further dilemma: could such mathematical assessments of life and death be considered immoral in and of themselves?

For every Shaefini, and nearly every Naefjan, agreed that life was a priceless gift. They were taught it from birth; but more importantly, they experienced it from birth. Naefjan culture cast Death as the greatest enemy of humanity, a foe to be battled, a force to be desperately held back for as long as one managed. To concede to Death's advance was considered the greatest shame of all, and Baggi was not exempt from these influences. He was Naefjan born, as were his parents and their parents, and it was assumed – safely so, based on the unbroken chain of silver eyes and red or blonde hair – that it had been that way for a long time, perhaps even since the Water of Life had spilled from Shaefi's veins upon the snow and birthed the first Naefjans.

Since arriving in Kichishi, however, Baggi had begun to entertain thoughts he had never before entertained. These thoughts would no doubt be considered misguided or worse by the common Naefjan, and acknowledging this offered him no relief. Chief among these thoughts was a radical idea, a blasphemous idea, one that churned his stomach and burned his face whenever it came to him. It returned even now as he sat in intense concentration.

The Staffkeepers of Shaefi are wrong, he thought.

Quickly, he swept the thought away, but it was too late; his focus was broken. He opened his eyes with a sigh and gazed blankly at the wall.

"Maybe not wrong, exactly," he sighed to no one.

Still, no words would come that seemed a better fit, so he gave up. Instead, he thought of the strange memory from the garden. There was no longer doubt in Baggi's mind; part of Bjorn lived on in Compromise. What remained to be seen was just how large a part, and how. He knew, of course, that a Staffkeeper's soul and that of the staff itself gradually merged over time. It was an ongoing process that he and Compromise underwent even now. *Just as it must have with Bjorn,* he thought. *But Bjorn is dead, there's nothing left for Compromise to cling to. So how does it retain Bjorn's memories?* Baggi decided to defer his questions and instead focus on what he did know. *First, that something of Bjorn remains in Compromise, some remnant or echo perhaps. Second, the memory Compromise showed me was of Bjorn using the Jera rune, just like I was. That seems to imply that it has some awareness of the situation. Third...*but he couldn't come up with a third. In fact, even the second fact seemed a bit of a stretch. Baggi ran his hand over Compromise in his lap. *I don't suppose you could just explain it to me?* He thought, chagrined. Immediately, another memory flashed through his mind.

He saw a Melennese family of four huddled beneath a lush canopy. Heavy rains poured relentlessly from above, dripping through the dense leaves, coming together in heavy globes that fell loudly onto those below. The water ran off their round canaled caps in serpentine rivulets. Baggi felt his heart pounding, but underneath was a calming sense of resolve. He heard himself speak in his brother's voice.

"My life for theirs," he said evenly. "Doesn't that suit you better?"

Then he turned and paradoxically felt a deep-seated terror in his own mind even as the one he visited remained serene. *It's her,* he thought from far away, *from the Staffkeepers of Death.*

"You are kind," the woman in bones said gently. She paused for a long time, evidently evaluating the offer. "It is an acceptable exchange."

"Will you return my staff to my family in Jolk?" he asked, far kinder in tone than Baggi felt the woman deserved. "Compromise knows the way."

The woman nodded.

"As you wish," she granted.

He saw himself look down at Compromise and heard Bjorn's voice whisper "I suppose this is it, then. Take care of Baggi, won't you?" The staff pulsed in his hand, anxiously, wildly. For just a moment, both of his minds filled with the same desperate protest. *No, no, don't leave,* Baggi and Compromise thought together, *I'm nothing alone.*

"You won't be," Bjorn assured them. "We'll do it together."

Then his brother whispered a complex runic sentence that Baggi couldn't decipher, a sentence with complicated nuance and unpredictable syntax.

"I'm ready," he said to the woman in bones. She nodded and slowly approached.

And just as suddenly as he had left, Baggi was returned to the apprentice's room. His breath was fast and full of fear as he looked about with wide eyes. Compromise's runes released slow, mournful mist. Baggi pulled his staff to his chest and hugged it tight. Inexplicably, he felt Compromise clinging to him for comfort just as desperately. The apprentice rocked back and forth, holding on to his staff like a rope tossed to a man overboard, until his breathing finally slowed and he felt safe again. Then he wiped away the tears he hadn't noticed shedding and cradled Compromise in his lap once more.

"Heh," he sniffed, feeling oddly validated, "you could warn me next time."

Compromise exhaled its ice-blue aura in a reassuring gesture halfway between a laugh and a sob. The magic passed over him, and it felt like a comforting hand on his shoulder.

A hesitant rapping at the door kept him from further consideration. Baggi shook his head as he gathered his wits. He took a deep breath and tried without much success to balance his emotions before forcing himself to his feet and answering the knock. Before him stood an apprentice with a shaved head, holding tight to a staff of coral-pink wood. Unlike Baggi, the other apprentice wore his Shaefini cloak over a pristine set of temple garb. The robes were of the same blue-white coloration as the cloak, but this set seemed just a bit too long in the arms for a child of his stature. Keeping his hands on the staff, he bowed too enthusiastically and smacked his forehead on the crown. He shook the stars from his eyes and tried again, slower this time, and with greater caution.

"Staffkeeper Apprentice Baggi," said the child, his Flowspeak slow as he tried his utmost to impart the words with the solemnity he felt they deserved, "the Elder Sage Hrafn has asked me to retrieve you. If you would, please follow me." He bowed again and stayed in the position.

"Guthini, isn't it?" Baggi smiled wearily. He slung Compromise on his back as the boy nodded. "I thought so. Lead the way."

Guthini was younger than Baggi by roughly a year, but one would be forgiven for assuming the gap to be larger. His manner was shy, mousey, and he preferred to listen rather than speak. For these and other reasons, Baggi could not recall the last time they had spoken. *Actually, have we ever spoken?* Baggi wondered. *After so many months, we must have.* If so, the memory did not deign to return. So instead, he reviewed what sparse knowledge he could recall.

He knew Guthini had been born and raised in Enton, and upon turning ten years old had joined the Staffkeepers as a matter of course. *That's the usual way, after all,* he reflected, nodding to himself, *for those who grow up in the embrace of the Temple, it must be difficult to imagine a life led elsewhere.* He wondered what it must have been like, seeing Staffkeepers every day. Even the villagers of Jolk were only blessed with a visit every other week, and they were luckier than most.

Baggi remembered the thrill of those mysterious, sporadic visits. Their great boars would pull down the narrow path between fortress-like walls of snow and ice into Jolk, squealing and joyfully licking up the handfuls of grain or cloudberries offered them by affectionate hands. The Staffkeepers of Shaefi were understanding and kind, and so Bjorn was usually among those that made the insignificant journey to Jolk. Little Baggi had always found an excuse to ask for their help, just for the chance to see real magic at work. Sometimes it would be their sheep, Fleecy, who he swore up and down had been limping all week. Other times he would invent a long-lasting headache or sore throat, and if all else failed, he could always ask for a renewal of Jera on their glasshouse.

Yes, things were easier then, Baggi thought. Nostalgia filled his heart, full and staggering. He shook his head and tried to focus on the present. Guthini had led him outside the walls, down the path to the waterfall, and at this time of day Baggi could hear congenial shouting and laughter even before they arrived. Shaefini and Kichishi alike populated the area, though there was a clear divide in purpose. While the foreigners splashed about, playful and naked, the smaller group of Kichishi pointedly averted their eyes and scrubbed at their clothing. Baggi couldn't help chuckling at their squeamishness. *Southerners. Don't they realize how lucky they are? If I lived somewhere as warm as here, I would be naked all the time.* Guthini tugged at his sleeve and led him to the water's edge, where the Elder Sage was wading.

"Elder Sage Hrafn," Guthini squeaked, "I present Staffkeeper Apprentice Baggi, as requested." He bowed inhumanly low.

"Thank you, Guthini. You have been most helpful," replied the Elder Sage and smiled kindly at the younger boy.

He trudged back to shore and groaned amiably as he settled onto a nearby rock. Several villagers likewise groaned upon witnessing the old man, dripping wet, naked, and shameless before them. Their reaction apparently escaped his notice.

"I hope you don't mind if I sit," he said as the apprentices stood before him.

"Of course not, Elder Sage," Baggi replied. "I am only eager to start my third Task."

He realized the noise around them had died down. *They're all probably watching,* he thought. *Like Torny said, there's not much else going on.*

"I'm sure you are, my boy!" Hrafn laughed. "So why don't we get right to it?" He laid his oaken staff, Mischief, across his lap and drew up his posture with his hands on his bare thighs. For a moment, the pose's dignity reminded Baggi of Amund. "Staffkeeper Apprentice Baggi, your third Task is to sound the bells of laughter throughout the village. Do this, and you will know the mirth of Shaefi. Do you understand these instructions?"

Baggi bowed back, mind already gnawing at the riddle's edges. "Elder Sage Hrafn, I understand these instructions. I will carry them out in the name of Shaefi."

Conversation began already to return to the clearing. It seemed his business had not attracted much attention after all. *Perhaps they thought a ritual assignment would be more exciting,* he thought. He felt an unreasonable sense of guilt for not having matched their expectations.

"Good," Hrafn replied, posture loosening to a relaxed slouch, "and, Baggi, there is one more facet to this Task."

"Another facet?"

"Yes. I will be assigning you a partner."

"Ah," Baggi breathed in relief. *That's not unheard of,* he acknowledged, *nothing to fear here. Perhaps I'll have the chance to learn from one of the other Sages.* "I see. And who will I be working with?" he asked, already considering what wisdom he might plumb from the depths of a genius mind such as Sage Runa's.

Hrafn smiled mischievously. "Your partner is the Staffkeeper Apprentice, Guthini," he said.

Both boys were mute. Hrafn raised a hand and gestured to Guthini in a futile effort to break the ice. Baggi slowly turned to the younger boy and shot him a strained yet polite smile. For his part, Guthini appeared equally dumbfounded.

"Elder Sage Hrafn," Baggi said, "far be it from me to question your judgment, but....I always thought partners were assigned in order to fill a gap in the apprentice's knowledge. And, well, Guthini is beneath me." He turned to the other boy and winced at his own lack of tact. "No offense intended, of course."

"Not at all," Guthini agreed with wide eyes and trembling lips.

"Baggi," the Elder Sage chided gently, "remember humility. Learning from your juniors is a deeply rewarding undertaking – and I can personally assure you of that fact. I've been doing it for centuries!"

He guffawed loudly. Baggi couldn't help but grin along with him. He turned to his new partner.

"Seems we're in it together then. Any ideas on where to start?"

Guthini looked around desperately, as if expecting to find his answer hiding in the tree line. He glanced at the Elder Sage and made a vague thinking noise. Baggi waited patiently for several long moments. Then he waited several more. The late morning sun was hot and he thought he could feel his skin crisping with each passing moment. *He's waiting for me to say something,* Baggi realized with dismay, *too afraid to even have an idea. What do I do now?* He turned helplessly to Hrafn, but the Elder Sage was already wading back into the water.

Baggi sighed and began undressing. "Well, while we're here, I may as well go for a swim," he said.

The scorched cloak fell silkily to the ground in a heap, the rest of his clothes quickly following.

"Good idea!" he heard Guthini gush at his side, slightly too relieved. The younger boy began to follow suit.

Too exhausted and confused to consider his new Task just yet, Baggi dove in and allowed the waters to envelop him. The Tasks, the garden, the lying, the partner, the memories – he forced his eyes open and told himself he could see them wash away.

15

Hjordis was not in a good mood.

Since arriving in Flamebud Village, she had spent most of her time at work and what little remained in conversation with the other Staffkeepers. At nineteen she was the youngest Staffkeeper in the caravan, and this peculiar position meant that, paradoxically, she was obligated to exude a certain air of maturity in order to set a good example. The youths looked up to her, she was told. They would take after her behavior, she was told. Many were relying on her to represent the next generation of Shaefini, she was told, and that was saying nothing of her familial expectations.

As if there weren't enough pressure already, she thought. Her parents' faces came to mind as she remembered them best, their expressions vaguely disappointed even as they attempted to hide the fact. She scoffed indiscriminately.

Her lineage was storied, her clan's accomplishments renowned. When the first Naefjans had learned crumbs of Shaefi's language and echoed her nature in the runes, Hjordis' ancestors had been chief among them. They mastered the Shaefini runes, and when the Kichishi came exploring from the south with their own Staffkeepers and runes the Naefjans had never heard of, Hjordis' clan had been the first to insist on sheltering them and exchanging magical knowledge. They ultimately shared more than information; her signature black hair, so uncommon in Naefja, proudly proclaimed the influence of her Kichishi blood even today. For hundreds upon hundreds of years since then, the descendants of those Staffkeepers had remained in Shaefi's service, their tales and deeds stacking higher and higher until they towered over even the Great Pass.

So it may be understood why Hjordis was in desperate need of escape one day years past, back when she had still been an apprentice. She hadn't been progressing as quickly as expected; that much was clear from the parade of chagrined expressions and sympathetic reassurances that trampled her daily. Although an apt learner, she always seemed to plateau at a middling skill level. It was frustrating, to say the least, and Hjordis had decided she couldn't take any more. So she had snuck ashore, leaving behind the hooded open-air sloop that served as their lodging among the Goesoir river-tribe in order to seek solace in the Melenno Valley's thick, wet forests.

***

Hjordis pushed through fuzzy-panicled grasses twice her height and marched. The Valley was much wetter than home, and far less rocky. She hadn't anticipated this land being harder to traverse than deep snow, and now she was paying for her thoughtlessness in filth and discomfort. *At least the trees are pretty,* she thought, looking up at the verdant canopy that hung over her like a tent, blotting out the sky in every direction farther than she could see. Naefja was home to green trees as well, but those of her homeland were hard and needly, not curving and graceful and bushy like the plants in Melenno. She jumped up and swung from a low-hanging branch over a mud pit of indiscernible depth, loosening a shower of wet leaves that stuck in her hair and hood. Hjordis rubbed the dirt from her hands, then found there was a stickiness upon them that wouldn't let go. Pink sap clung to her palms. She smelled the substance; it had a pleasant, sweet fragrance. She stuck out her tongue and gingerly licked at the sap, then spat upon finding its flavor far more bitter.

A bubbling noise drew her attention downward, and she yelped in exasperation as a dark shrimp the size of her head burst forth from the mud underfoot. Its groping feelers, long as her forearms, lashed blindly around. After a moment, a brood of smaller shrimp followed. They scuttled off, following their guardian, and submerged themselves once more. The mud released a repulsive groan as it slowly filled back in. Hjordis grimaced and tread more lightly as she pressed on. The mud sucked at her too-big boots, scraping painfully as it aggravated the blisters on her heels. Her cloak was thoroughly soiled at the hem; Hjordis briefly considered holding it up, out of the mud, before realizing the chance to protect her garments was long gone. The obvious counter to the mud would be to use her staff in the traditional sense, as a trekking tool, yet that seemed disrespectful, and so her yet-nameless partner remained in its sling on her back.

She was just beginning to chalk up the whole journey as a loss when she noticed boot-tracks leading in the same direction the shrimp had gone. Hjordis tilted her head in puzzlement and began to follow them.

She tromped as cautiously as she was able, but mud accumulated with every step so that finally it was all Hjordis could do to lift her feet. Suddenly she thought of the danger she might be in. *I didn't tell anyone I was going,* she realized, *and this isn't Naefja. This place is dangerous. What was I thinking?* And yet she felt no regret, not a shred of hesitation. She continued onward, following the tracks that were rapidly becoming more pronounced. Then she heard a voice before her, closer than she was expecting. Hjordis ducked behind a tree, sinking inches deep in the mud with a loud *glomp* and held her breath. Luckily, the valley's heavy rainfall seemed to sufficiently muffle her error. Ever so slowly, she peeked around the trunk.

A boy covered in mud was crawling along a tree branch perhaps fifteen feet high. His arms and legs were wrapped tightly around the bough and grime smeared across his chest with every inching movement, but he apparently cared even less for the state of his attire than Hjordis. She glanced further down the branch curiously and saw a cluster of discolored leaves. She wrinkled her nose and stepped out from behind the tree.

"Excuse me!" she called.

Immediately, the boy shouted – *or maybe squealed is a better word*, considered Hjordis as his grip failed – and flailed wildly for a hold before slipping from the branch and landing on his back in the mud with a doughy smack. Hjordis cursed under her breath and rushed to the boy's side.

"Hey, are you okay? Sorry, I didn't intend to- " she stopped suddenly as the boy, in a daze, wiped mud from his face. "Elof?" she recognized. His Shaefini attire was nearly indiscernible beneath patchy layers of filth.

"Hello, Staffkeeper Apprentice Hjordis," he managed as he peeled himself out of the mud.

"Are you alone? What are you doing out here?" she asked as she helped him to his feet.

The encounter felt somewhat surreal. *Elof? Of all people? He's afraid of his own shadow. And that's not an exaggeration, I've seen it.* He was an alchemist in their Order, recently graduated from apprentice. They had worked together on many occasions, usually to great effect, but that synergy had never lingered after the work was done, and by Hjordis' reckoning they were only acquaintances still.

Elof's face lit up as he answered. "Do you see those flowers up there?" he asked, pointing to the cluster of leaves.

"They look like leaves to me," she offered cautiously.

"It's a common mistake," Elof grinned, "which is why they are exceptionally rare. They're called Meekleaves. At least, that's what we call them. I'm not sure of its proper name, in Woodwhisper."

Hjordis squinted, still unable to make out any distinguishing features besides a faint brownish note absent in its neighboring clusters. "Just those ones?" she asked, pointing.

"Right. The rest are common leaves."

Hjordis turned to him and didn't bother hiding her confusion. "How can that be? They're growing from the same tree."

Elof smiled patiently, an expression she had never seen before. Even with mud on his teeth, she thought it a handsome smile.

"Nobody knows," he answered, "except maybe the natives, of course, but you know how secretive the guild-tribes are." He gazed at the flowers as if in a dream. "Meekleaf serves a ceremonial purpose among the Melennese, to say nothing of its more unique attributes. Or, perhaps, because of its unique attributes. Regardless, I hope to be the first Naefjan to unravel its secrets. Unfortunately..." the smile fell from his face. He probed at his lower back and winced. "...obtaining a sample is proving far more difficult than I expected."

Hjordis listened patiently. As he spoke, she heard passion in his voice, strong and energetic. *This isn't Elof,* she thought. *Or maybe that wasn't Elof,* she amended as memories of his skittishness presented themselves. Hjordis admired passion and expertise, even craved it. When people spoke of their callings or their interests with genuine excitement, she inevitably found herself getting excited along with them. She liked to imagine they were peers, that they shared the passion and that Hjordis was equally invested in whatever ordinary detail her conversational partner found so engrossing. It made her feel like she had a special talent, too. Now as Elof spoke of the flowers and the grand plans he had made for them, Hjordis felt something new rising in her. It was not quite familiar, but not unpleasant either. She didn't know what the feeling was, but she did know that she wanted very much to know Elof better.

"Well then, why don't we collaborate?" she grinned. "I'm not a bad climber, you know." Elof looked surprised, but before he could respond she ran toward the tree and jumped for a branch with both hands like before, nearly losing her balance and face-planting in the mud in the process. She played it off as intentional, grinning at Elof over her shoulder.

He took a deep breath, shook his head as if in wonder, then followed suit. His balance was weaker than Hjordis' and he nearly couldn't cling to the branch, but she somehow caught his slippery hand in hers and helped him up. They caught their balance, straddling the bough and facing each other. Sitting so close together, Hjordis felt exposed, as if under inspection. She shook the feeling away and stood up quickly on the bough, nearly losing her balance in the process. Elof clung to the branch like before. He stared up at her in disbelief.

"Are...that is, I have no wish to question your ability, Staffkeeper Apprentice Hjordis, but, ah...are you sure you don't wish to crawl?" He asked.

There's the bundle of nerves I know, thought Hjordis. She puffed herself up and scoffed.

"I think I can manage it."

Without giving herself the chance to be afraid, she turned and began walking with her arms out wide toward the Meekleaves. The tree was thick with soaked moss and dirt, and Hjordis nearly lost her footing too many times to count. With each step the branch became narrower and narrower, until at last it was no wider than her hand. She kneeled slowly, ever so slowly, and reached out to grasp the cluster of leaves. It was just beyond her fingertips. She heard Elof clear his throat pointedly behind her. She turned and saw him hugging the branch and shooting her a meaningful look. She rolled her eyes and followed suit. With the extra few inches of reach, she carefully plucked the bundle and slowly turned on the branch to face Elof. They sat up on the branch with the Meekleaves in Hjordis' grasp between them. Elof beamed, caught between excitement and awe. He leaned close, breath soft with wonder, examining the leaves' every fiber. Then he looked up at her with those silver eyes of passion and Hjordis' heart skipped.

The wind carried a soft whisper through the forest, and in it they heard the words "You are lost," in forbidding Melennese.

The duo froze as there arose a great rustling in the canopies nearby. They looked up, and at the same time, a lithe figure descended. The fright was enough for both Naefjans to lose their grip this time. Hjordis landed awkwardly on one leg. She cried out, more in fear and surprise than pain. Elof landed next to her, his foot catching her in the stomach and knocking the breath from her lungs. Lying on her back, she saw the figure take their place on the bough, perched with a single foot on a spongy patch of purple moss.

Hjordis scrambled to her feet as she struggled to breathe. More figures appeared in the surrounding canopy. She pulled Elof to his feet and they stood close together. *Don't be afraid,* she told herself through the haze of pain and fear, *we're Naefjan. We're Shaefini, damn it! They wouldn't hurt us.* Slowly, her breath returned to her, and with it her calm. She observed their ambushers as they descended.

They wore wide, circular hats with canals carved into the tops for keeping the near-constant rainfall of the valley off their faces. This was unsurprising, as a Melennese with such a hat was as common as a Naefjan in furs. But these people, unlike the Goesoir the Staffkeepers of Shaefi were lodging with, were dressed in layers of lumpy vegetation that somehow remained silent even as they brushed against each other in sly undulations. They hopped gracefully from branch to branch as they approached. Hjordis expected at least one to lose balance, if only for a moment, but of course they did not. Her jaw dropped in amazement as she watched. The Melennese continued to approach, slowly, dancing between boughs and displacing not a single leaf.

"Bough-Bouncers," Elof whispered with dread.

Hjordis hushed him and shot him a glare. *Don't call them that to their faces,* she thought in terrified amazement. Their exploits during the Mineral War were either inspiring or diabolical, depending on who you asked, but all agreed that to utter such a demeaning title within hearing of the legendary mixed-tribe commandos was tantamount to a death-wish. The figures stopped moving; she and Elof were surrounded.

"You know not what you hold," the voice from before said.

Even with the troop of Bough-Bouncers so close, Hjordis found it impossible to discern who had spoken. *That's the point, isn't it?* she thought. *That's why we call it Woodwhisper.* She examined the Melennese more closely now, saw that under the thick vegetative garb were exposed portions of skin. Pools of deep leaf green set into faces of brown or grey-green indicated that their features were not concealed; there was no need for it. It was said the Melennese were born of tree bark, after all, and their natural camouflage proved it. Their exposed legs, cuffed high above the ankle, reinforced the image as they perched motionless on the branches, seemingly connected to their ancestors at the soles.

"Let go," the voice continued.

In the blink of an eye, with a silent rush of cold air, one of the Bough-Bouncers stood before her in the mud. There was an unmistakable air of authority about him. He held out his hand to Hjordis and said no more. She was beginning to feel afraid once more; it was one thing to believe in diplomatic immunity when the danger is near, and another thing entirely when it is just before you.

"I don't understand," she said, her Melennese thick and exhausted. "We found it. Why let go?"

She tried to filter every last drop of reticence from the protest. *Don't give them the chance to lose temper.* The Bough-Bouncer smiled inscrutably.

"You found it. You did not earn it." He took a small step closer; he was smiling still, but there was something eerie in the expression.

"Ah, of course! Here, it is, well, they are, yours!" Elof babbled nonsensically as he snatched the Meekleaves from Hjordis and presented them to the man. Hjordis shot him an annoyed look, but Elof returned the expression without giving ground.

The Bough-Bouncer took the Meekleaves gently, even reverently. He looked the foreigners up and down for several moments. "Naefjan?" he asked.

Hjordis nodded. "Shaefini," she added.

The man took this into consideration. "You are friends," he said, his voice a gentle hiss on the wind, "not family."

Then he jumped to the very branch Hjordis and Elof had struggled with and swung himself over it with one hand, cradling the Meekleaves in the other. He whistled, low and slow, and in complete silence the Bough-Bouncers melted back into the canopy.

Hjordis and Elof stood in the mud for several moments, unsure of how to proceed. Then, awkwardly, she said,

"I'm sorry about your flowers. Thought I might have been able to keep them for us..."

"No, no, that's okay," he chuckled. A note of mania colored the laugh. "Our lives are more important."

"They wouldn't have hurt us," Hjordis said dismissively as they began walking back to the river, "we're Shaefini. And you heard him, we're friends!"

"Not family," Elof pointed out, "yes, I heard him. What do you suppose that means?"

Hjordis thought about her family and friends. *What is the difference, really?* She wondered. *Other than what they expect of you?*

"I don't know," she said absent-mindedly, "but I'll Contemplate it later and get back to you."

Elof chuckled again at that. Hjordis hopped onto a fallen log, half-sunken beneath the mud, and watched him from the corner of her eye. She looked away quickly as he turned to her with a curious expression.

"I never did ask: What was it you were out here for, Hjordis?"

"I don't know that either," she admitted. "Maybe sometimes I just need to get away and be alone." She fell silent, unsure of what else to say.

"I understand that," Elof sighed, "and, you know, if, ah, I mean, in the future, not here, of course, but later on, if you feel that way again, ah, maybe we could, well...get away and be alone...together?"

His voice cracked noticeably on the last word and he gazed intently at the mud beneath his feet. Hjordis felt a smile growing.

"That could be fun," she said, hoping she sounded more in control than she felt.

Elof lifted his face, amazement evident. Then he smiled as his blush slowly drained.

***

Since then, Hjordis and Elof had found time to slip away at nearly every stop the caravan made. Usually it was under pretext of searching for alchemical ingredients, but in truth this was a ruse crafted by Hjordis in order to prod Elof into his comfort zone. She learned much about him in the following months: that he had been born and raised in Yngmuth ("Though perhaps 'raised' is being generous," he said) by a violent, drunken cutpurse who would leave without explanation for weeks at a time, that he had used nature and plants as an escape for both body and mind, that he had been discovered shivering and nearly dead on the docks by Aeskettil the Generous and never looked back. He seemed not to like talking about these things, and Hjordis had no wish to push him, but she was a careful listener and over time came to know much of his past.

Elof, too, learned all about Hjordis and her life in Enton. He listened patiently as she told him stories of her famous ancestors, pretending he hadn't already read them, gasping and raising his eyebrows in all the right spots as if hearing the tales for the first time. He learned how she had no siblings, and hardly even a cousin ("He's only three, so that doesn't count," she insisted). He learned about her insecurity, her desire to be special and her fear that she wasn't. She seemed to like talking about these things, so Elof would push her to do so. He watched her closely and thought she always seemed happier afterwards.

Then, a year later, during their second day on the Northern Highway, they had slipped away from the camp in the cave and found an offshoot path. It was dark on the Highways inside the mountains, so they had held hands in order not to become separated. At the end of the path, they had found a great wall of softly glowing Shaeficap mushrooms. In the dim light, face half-obscured by shadow, Hjordis had felt her heart pounding wildly. They stood so close now. She saw the fear and excitement in Elof's eyes too, noted the nervousness. He looked away at the glowing fungus. Hjordis giggled quietly.

"Coward," she teased.

Elof looked back to her, surprised, and then before another moment could pass, he kissed her. They were hesitant at first, afraid to shatter the illusion of love, but then they kissed more and realized it was no illusion. His arms circled her waist, and hers his neck, and then she felt a dampness on her face. She pulled back, alarmed to see tears running down Elof's cheeks.

"What's wrong?" she asked softly, wiping the tears away. "I can stop."

"No, nothing is wrong," he whispered back, voice wobbly and weak. He pressed his forehead gently to hers. "It's only...after how I grew up, and all of it...I thought this was impossible." Fresh tears emerged even as he smiled at her. "I thought I would never be happy."

Hjordis' heart broke for him even as it swelled with the love she could finally name. She pulled him close and stroked his hair, and they kissed again. And after an eternity, far too quickly, they pulled away and began walking back to camp, hand in hand.

***

Nearly two years ago, as the caravan made its way home from the tragic visit to Geluwam that cost them Sage Ove, Hjordis and Elof had peeled away as usual and lain down on the grassy hills connecting the mighty mountains of Naefja and the lush river valley of Melenno.

Clouds swirled listlessly overhead, but the exposed pockets of black sky allowed brilliant starlight to pierce the veil. They were quiet. Much of the caravan had been, since Ove died. *And he didn't even have any children,* Hjordis thought, *no one to carry on his legacy. No one to remember him. No one but the people he worked with.*

"Hey, Elof?" she said softly.

"Yes?" he whispered back.

She hesitated. "Do you want to have children?" she asked.

There was a long pause. "Hjordis..." he sighed.

"Because I was just thinking," she continued, "Ove never had children. His bloodline ends with him."

"Sometimes that is the best option," Elof said strangely.

Hjordis looked at him askance, confused. *That doesn't sound like him.*

"How can that be?" she asked gently, giving him the benefit of the doubt.

"Perhaps some bloodlines are not worth keeping," he sighed.

"And you think Ove's was one of them?"

"Of course not!"

"Then what are you talking about?" she asked in frustration.

Elof looked left and met her gaze. His silver eyes were full of tears and worry. His lip trembled and he looked away, swallowing hard.

"Oh," she said stupidly, the pieces sliding into place. Then, more comfortingly, "Oh, Elof." She hugged him tight. "You can't mean that."

"You know who I come from. You know what sort of blood flows in my veins. I couldn't inflict that on you, Hjordis," he whispered. "I couldn't taint your lineage."

Hjordis wanted to scream in his face, to tell him how ridiculous he was being and how little she cared for the reputation of her clan compared to him. She felt dizzy and guilty and all at once she wanted to pound the grass and dirt and cry and curse her family and their hopes and even their ancient progenitor who had damned her with greatness. Instead, she ground her teeth for a moment and rebalanced her emotions the way she had been taught. Then she rolled over and laid across Elof's chest. He was pleasantly warm.

"Coward," she whispered. She felt his chest heave as he laughed and sobbed all at once, and then she joined him and they clung to each other and reveled in their comfort.

That was the first night they made love.

***

Hjordis smiled at the memory despite her mood. *You're right,* she thought as Satisfaction pulsed happily, *that was a good night. What do I even have to be miffed about? Sure, we have to wait for another chance to get away, but that will come in time.* She lightly slapped herself on the face and exhaled the moodiness in one sharp breath. Sage Runa looked at her, inscrutable as always, but refrained from acknowledging her as they walked. When they arrived at the Flamebud Inn, the sun was beginning to set. *And so ends the first day of Baggi's final Task,* Hjordis thought, the words sounding melodramatic even in her head. *I wonder how he's doing. Probably just fine; he must realize by now how talented he truly is.* She noticed Sage Runa watching her expectantly in her peripherals.

"I'm sorry, Sage Runa?" she said politely.

"You did well today," Runa repeated. "Your work is genuine and your bedside manner impeccable, but I urge you to review your

Kichishi texts. Your fluency leaves something to be desired." The Sage spoke evenly and fairly, with praise and criticism given equal emphasis.

"Of course, Sage Runa," Hjordis replied, bowing deeply.

Kichishi texts? Do I own those? She wondered. Since receiving her Blessing, Hjordis no longer studied; in fact, she had never studied Sparktongue in the first place, merely picked up on fragments when their southern relatives visited. It had been enough to clear the exams at the Temple at Enton. Now that the arcane boon bestowed upon her by Shaefi supplied the appropriate intuition, Hjordis considered herself fairly able in the language. Clearly, however, her Blessing was not infallible.

They entered the inn and reported the day's assignments to Elder Sage Hrafn as he meticulously recorded the services provided in his immaculate Naefjan script. Elof seemed not to be back yet, but she spotted Baggi sitting at the bar with Staffkeeper Apprentice Guthini on one side and Chief Amund on the other. Concerningly, Baggi was holding a blood-soaked cloth to his nose, but the way he was talking and carrying on with his friends told her it was nothing to fret over. The innkeeper went between them and the tables, filling mugs and smiling as they energetically argued and occasionally laughed.

Hjordis thought to sit with Hrafn's group as usual for one of his customary dinner fables, but a nostalgic yearning to be alone filled her heart and she quietly took her leave of the Flamebud Inn. Instead, she strolled through town, looking over the buildings and exaggerated signage with unfocused eyes. The rest of the Shaefini were filtering back to the inn, hair wet and smelling of freshness. She swam against the current, shrugging or grinning non-committedly whenever someone called out to ask where she was going. As the sun dipped ever lower in the sky, she weaved without aim, becoming dizzier and dizzier.

Villagers she and Runa had treated called out thanks to her as she passed. She graciously held her hands up in a gesture that conveyed "no thanks necessary", as she always did. The baker handed her a loaf of dark, crusty bread with the same hand that had been painfully crushed only that morning. The blacksmith silently hailed her and, without a word, forced a box of miscellaneous iron wagon parts into her hands before returning to his work. An arrow lodged itself in a wall mere inches in front of her, a flying squirrel hanging from it via impalement. She turned in the direction it had come from to see the hunter whose bow she had enchanted yesterday. He waved at her with the hand holding his weapon, apparently pleased with the results. After her heartrate slowed, Hjordis took the arrow and waved back.

Eventually she found herself in front of Amund's house, gazing up at the foreign architecture. The gifts were stacked atop the box of parts beside her on the ground, and she tore a chunk of the dark bread off to amuse her mouth. The main building was large and round, its walls curving gradually inward and upward like a great, flat-topped shell. Spaced evenly along the perimeter were four smaller buildings reminiscent of limbs, each attached to the main house only by a short hallway. The footpath was straight, extending neck-like from door to gate. Hjordis stepped back, willing the larger picture to appear. And appear it did, the iron filigree before her transforming into the visage of a smiling gentle giant. *Yep,* thought Hjordis, *like a huge turtle.*

"There you are," she heard Elof pant behind her.

Finally, she thought. As soon as she turned to face him, Hjordis detected a disturbance. She knew Elof's anxieties and fears backwards and forwards, and that included the expressions that accompanied each. *Uh oh,* she thought, *he's feeling guilty.* She smiled at him as they briefly embraced.

"So what's bothering you?" she said by way of greeting.

Elof looked surprised, but only for a moment. Then the guilt returned. He nervously rubbed the back of his neck. "There is something I must confess," he mumbled.

16

Baggi had never thought himself a special talent, and that was perfectly fine by him. His home village of Jolk was a tight-knit community, and all he had ever wished for was to be of use to them and to Shaefi. He had been six when Bjorn went off to apprentice at the Temple at Enton. He didn't remember the day well; he had been too young to realize its importance. But he couldn't forget the day of his brother's first visit home if he tried.

Bjorn had been afforded space on a wagon headed their way, but their path had not passed through Jolk, so he tromped into town on foot, waving his arms and his new staff overhead. The whole village gathered in their cottage to force on him his favorite foods and shout excited questions about his studies such that even he, usually so outgoing and loud, had been a bit overwhelmed. That didn't last, of course, because Baggi's older brother was not the type to be cowed. Instead, he stood up on his chair, lifted his staff dramatically, and as a hush swept through the cottage, spoke a single strange syllable.

In the air before them, the image of a boar appeared, scaled down so that it might fit the room. The creature appeared wispy, translucent, as if undecided about its own existence. Then, with sweat pouring down Bjorn's face, the boar squealed and happily ran in three small circles before dissipating. The villagers shouted praise and amazement, pressing in on the hapless child and hoisting him over their heads like a victorious athlete. In that moment, Baggi knew how he could serve his village and Shaefi all at once: he was going to be like his big brother. He was going to be a Staffkeeper.

It wasn't a rune he invoked, he knew now, *just a piece of one. A fragment of Wunjo, to be specific. He had only just started, after all. It's beginner magic.* He released a frustrated breath and nearly threw Compromise to the floor as helplessness overcame him. *So why can't I do it?*

"That's weird," Guthini muttered uneasily at his side. "Maybe you just mispronounced?"

"I did not," Baggi sourly replied. "Show me again, please."

They stood in the town square, by the well, where Baggi had for nearly an hour now been attempting to replicate the trick. Guthini nodded energetically and made the same wispy, whooshing sound as Bjorn had on the day of his visit. The younger apprentice looked around, seemingly confused, before turning to Baggi and shrugging.

"I guess I messed up too..." he said. Then, he perked up and gazed intently at Baggi. "Unless...is that...I think it is!"

He leaned close, squinting, then reached behind Baggi's ear. When the hand returned it held a tiny fairy in a gilded bathtub, sighing in relaxation. The fairy languidly opened its eyes, saw the giants towering over them, and released a squeaky scream before jumping from the tub and flitting around the elder boy's head in quick circles. Trails of Guthini's pale pink aura dazzled him in its wake, and when he regained his bearings the pixie was gone. His partner looked up at him expectantly, grinning ear to ear. Baggi found himself grinning in kind.

"A bit much, but thank you," he said.

Sure enough, his pronunciation was not at fault, nor did there seem to be any previously overlooked technical aspects. *Could it be a mental block? Am I not feeling it like I'm supposed to, like with the sunlight and Sowilo?*

"Guthini," he asked, "what do you think of when you invoke this...spell?"

A subconscious pretention about dignifying this trick as a "spell" nagged him momentarily, but he remembered Hrafn's admonishment from earlier and quelled the feeling.

"I dunno. Mostly just how cute the pixie's going to be," he replied.

Baggi stared at him hard. "And what about when you're not making it look like a pixie?" he asked patiently.

Guthini cocked his head and considered this for apparently the first time. "Hm," he said, "let me check."

He took a step back and repeated the syllable, this time procuring a bowl of yellow butter.

"I thought of how tasty butter is, and then the butter showed up," he shrugged. "Why? What have you been thinking about?

"My brother," he sighed.

Guthini clammed up, shifting in place from one foot to the other.

"Oh. Sorry about that," he offered meekly.

Baggi laughed then. "Don't apologize," he said, "you had nothing to do with it. As far as I know," he joked, gazing at Guthini with mock-suspicion. His partner half-smiled, amusement and pity waging war across his face. *I know it's well meaning, but I really wish he wouldn't look at me like that.* "Besides, it's been years," he continued, "I've made my peace," he said.

Yet he wondered if that were true. *It seems dependent on perception,* he analyzed. *If I've made my peace, then I should have no problem conjuring an image of Bjorn when I think about him. But for that matter, I can't produce an image of anything else either.* He tried in vain to copy the butter method. *So what am I missing?* Compromise stirred in his hand, and this time Baggi was just able to brace himself before being thrown into a memory.

Strangely, Compromise showed him the same memory he had already been reviewing, but this time, Baggi saw it through Bjorn's eyes. He saw the people urging him on, heard them immediately quiet down as he stood up on the chair. He felt Bjorn's nervousness and was baffled. Then he looked at his younger self, tiny arms wrapped around their mother's legs and eyes wide with excitement. He felt the pressure lift in that moment, and Bjorn's face smiled as he summoned the image of his little brother's favorite animal.

Baggi blinked hard, back in the town square. His head pounded painfully as he weathered a wave of nausea and focused on the sensation of the ground beneath his feet. The dizziness quickly passed. *I see you remember it differently,* he thought to Compromise. His staff emanated patience.

"Are you...well?" Guthini asked.

"Yes," Baggi waved him off, "just...remembering something, I suppose."

"Ah. Hm. So...should we keep trying?" his partner queried, beginning and halting several times in the process.

Baggi thought of his fellow apprentice's method from earlier and compared it to the vision supplied to him by Compromise. *Perhaps I should try visualizing something else. Something with strong, personal, and pleasant associations.* The flamebuds presented themselves in his mind, but he had the wisdom to discard the idea immediately. *Too many emotions attached to that,* he thought, *many of them painful. No, not the flamebuds. There's Kettil, but she lied to me just yesterday. Same with Elof. Maybe the Elder Sage? No, probably not a person. Think simple, Baggi, simple!* And suddenly, as Guthini procured another bowl of butter unprompted, Baggi decided.

He took a deep breath and balanced his emotions. Then he closed his eyes and visualized a viola cake with cloudberry syrup, his usual birthday treat, focusing intently on the sensory recollection. *Floral sweetness in my nose, tartness on my tongue, and moist crumb filling my mouth in bites too big,* he reminisced, smiling dreamily. Guthini gasped in excitement, prompting Baggi to open his eyes. In his hand was the round, layered confection as he had pictured, albeit washed out and vaguely-defined. Syrup ran down the sides of the cake but, rather than pool in his hand, the stream disappeared into nothingness. His image was, on the whole, far uglier than Guthini's.

Still, it's a start! he thought in relief. The image faded along with his focus as Guthini bounced up and down on the spot, gushing praise.

"You did it! That was great! It even had syrup on there!" he yelled happily.

"You honor me," Baggi chuckled. "It's nowhere near as detailed as yours. Not yet."

"But you know how to do it now," Guthini replied, "so you'll probably surpass me before we've even left town."

"Ha!" Baggi chortled. "I doubt it. But at least now we can get started on the Task, right?"

Guthini stared at him, dumbfounded. "What do you mean?" he said.

"Wasn't that the point," Baggi said, furrowing his brow, "that this was how we could accomplish the Task?"

"Uhh...no," Guthini admitted. "I just wanted...uhh...it's stupid..."

"Guthini," Baggi sighed, "we only have three days. Two and a half, now. Please be direct."

"Well, since you're such a prodigy, I wanted you to think I was good at magic too," his partner answered guiltily, "but really, this is about all I can do."

"I have several questions," replied Baggi after a confused pause, "First, who in their right mind would call me a prodigy? Second, what do you mean "all you can do?" We aren't even allowed on caravans until we can invoke all the Shaefini runes."

Guthini shrugged unevenly. "I can do the runes, just not well. Even Hallr is better than me, and he's not very bright." He snapped his gaze toward Baggi. "Please don't tell him I said that."

Baggi laughed again. "The chances of my talking to Hallr are slim, and the chances of his talking to me even slimmer."

The younger apprentice was quiet for several moments.

"I always wanted to ask," he eventually said, "why don't you like us?"

Baggi stared back at his partner, dumbfounded. *Did he just say...?*

"I must have misheard you. What was that?"

"Well, when I joined the caravan, and Staffkeeper Hjordis showed me around, that was actually the only time you ever talked to me," Guthini elaborated. "Until today. And I asked Hallr and Dagrun about why you don't ever sit with us, but they said you don't talk to them either, so they didn't know."

Baggi's mouth was agape. *Could I have misunderstood so completely? Could I really have been this stupid? But it wasn't all my doing, surely!*

"I don't recall any of you seeking out my company either!" he snapped, flustered. He regretted the harsh tone immediately, seeing Guthini shrink back and clasp his hands nervously in front of him. "Forgive me, Guthini," he sighed, "I'm only surprised and confused."

"We wanted to get you to sit with us for meals, but you were always with Alchemist Apprentice Kettil," Guthini said, oddly apologetic, "and she..." he swallowed hard, "...scares me."

Baggi snorted, allowing Guthini to relax somewhat. *That part, at least, is sensible,* the elder boy thought.

"To be truthful, we all thought we wouldn't have anything to say," continued Guthini, "You're a boar among pigs, and we're just normal apprentices. It would be embarrassing."

"This isn't the first time you've overstated my abilities, Guthini," Baggi replied, brow wrinkled in concern. "Where did this idea come from?"

"Uhh, from you, I suppose," he answered vaguely, counting off the points on his hand as he spoke. "You're friends with Staffkeeper Hjordis and Alchemist Elof, so you must be pretty mature; you already know your staff's name, even though you haven't gotten your Blessing yet; and the important people always want you around, like Elder Sage Hrafn and even the Chief of Flamebud. And us?" he grinned wryly. "I can barely attune at all. Hallr is worse than me. Even Dagrun can't do the things you can, not even close, and her runology's way better than me and Hallr's."

Baggi's face burned as Guthini sang his praises. He was conflicted; it was nice to be spoken so highly of, yet as he reexamined experiences with the other apprentices his shame rose higher and higher. *It was me all along,* he thought miserably, *a self-imposed exile.* He remembered in quick succession the days he had been partnered with his peers in past villages: tending to the boars and making conversation with the animals rather than Hallr; proudly assisting a Staffkeeper in a healing procedure by procuring the necessary tools and providing the necessary information as quickly as possible, much too fast for Guthini to get a word in edgewise; and most embarrassing of all, back when he had been slightly infatuated with her, the three hours of sheer, sickly silence in which he and Dagrun had washed the caravan's laundry, he intimidated by her beautiful tangerine-colored mane and affability, she by his solemnity and unfathomable disdain. Baggi cringed as these memories and more, the results of two years' misunderstandings, made themselves known again.

"Lady Shaefi," he cursed and shook his head, amazement at his own social ineptitude rendering him otherwise speechless.

"What?" asked Guthini. "Is that wrong? It's just how we see it, anyway."

"No, nothing you said is wrong," Baggi managed, still cringing. "That actually explains much." He sank into mortified silence. "Although I do have one amendment," he forced out after a moment. "The only reason I know Compromise's name is because he was my brother's before me."

Speaking of Bjorn reminded him that he had work to do if he meant to complete his rites and earn his Staffkeeper's Mark. He bundled the distressing memories and used them as fuel for his inner fire, as Amund had taught him. The shame burned away, its ashes blowing out of him and leaving in their place a manic desire to move on.

"I never thought of that," he mumbled. "I know he's not around anymore, but...what happened to your brother?"

Baggi regarded him suspiciously. "You really haven't heard this story?" he asked. Guthini shook his head, no trace of maliciousness present in his eyes. "Well, suffice it to say he passed Compromise on to me," he answered, "and I'll tell you about it some other time. For now, let's focus on the Task."

Guthini graciously snuffed the curiosity in his eyes and nodded. The boys sat in the dirt, heads heavy with their respective revelations, thinking hard. Then Guthini's ears perked up like an excited rabbit and he turned to Baggi with an idea.

***

Amund reached the end of the hidden trail from the mountain pass to his village's borders as the sun was beginning to set. His heart was light today, remarkably so. There had been no trouble at the checkpoint, only two traveling parties, and both were Kichishi returning from the northern lands. He had welcomed them home warmly and sent them through without issue. The Chief of Flamebud had otherwise spent his day attempting to master a skill that had been eluding him for years: for as long as he could remember, Amund had been struggling to learn how to whistle.

He blew slow air between his lips and tried modifying their position for the thousandth time. The results were predictable. Amund took solace in his consistency, even in failure. So focused was he on this task that he took little notice of his surroundings entering the village. Without warning, a squat man with grotesquely stretched features and an outrageous, terrifying grin stepped around the corner of the butcher's shop dressed in a ragged grey cloak. The monstrosity honked, a mad, inhuman sound, as it reached toward him with one hand. Amund reacted without thinking, slipping left of the thing's grasp and snapping his right fist into its face. It wailed pathetically and fell flat on its back. Only then did Amund have time to appraise his assailant.

"Baggi?" he asked, peering over his friend whose nose now freely poured blood. "What happened to your face?"

Baggi sat up slowly. "What do you mean? You just punched it," he replied woozily.

Amund rolled his eyes even as he proffered a hand and helped his friend to his feet.

"And before that? I would not have struck you if you had not been wearing such a garish mask."

Yet as he glanced about, Amund saw no such mask lying in the dirt where it ought to have been. A squeaky voice began babbling incoherently in Flowspeak as an apprentice with a shaved head rushed to Baggi's side. *I recognize him,* Amund realized, *he was making frivolity in the square when they first arrived.* Baggi said something to him in their language and made a pacifying gesture with one hand while the other gingerly prodded his nose. He winced.

"Yes, I suppose that was a fairly predictable outcome," Baggi managed, switching now to the Base Tongue. "It's difficult to justify in retrospect," he continued, "but we thought this might accomplish my last Task, 'sounding the bells of laughter'. In Naefja, some find harlequins highly entertaining."

Amund gaped at him. Then, unable to contain himself any longer, he loudly guffawed at the Shafini's ridiculous plan.

"And I suppose it worked, in a way," Baggi said with chagrin.

"Come, Baggi, let us get you treated," said the chief after he had collected himself.

"No, no, I deserve this," he insisted, "I should live with the consequences of a natural healing. Otherwise I'll never learn."

"Then let us at least get you cleaned up, and find a cloth to staunch the bleeding," Amund compromised, still chuckling.

Baggi nodded and allowed him to lead on. As they walked, he spoke through the sleeve of his tunic pressed to his nostrils.

"This is Staffkeeper Apprentice Guthini," he said in a nasal voice. "We've been partnered for my final Task. Guthini, I'm sure you know of Chief Amund."

"Well met, Chief Amund," the boy squeaked, bowing even as they walked.

"Likewise," he replied.

When they arrived at the Flamebud Inn, Amund ushered in the apprentices and guided Baggi to a seat at the bar.

"Torny!" he shouted to the kitchen. "Bring a cloth right away!"

Torny peeked around the doorway, clearly annoyed by the demand. When she noted Baggi's bloody face, however, she gasped.

"What the...Amund! What happened?" she demanded.

"Torny, the cloth please!" he insisted.

She shook her head and rolled her eyes but did as ordered. When she brought the rag forth, she attended to Baggi directly.

"Here," she said, replacing his sleeve with the cloth and placing his hand on it. "Keep pressure on that," she said.

Her voice was uncharacteristically affectionate. Amund rolled his eyes, grinning. *As if he needs instructions,* he thought. *They are healers by trade.*

"Thank you, Torny," Baggi said as he followed her instructions.

"So?" she demanded, the moment of tenderness gone as quickly as it had appeared. "Were you fighting?" The question was aimed at Amund, but Baggi was the first to reply.

"Oh no, nothing like that. Shaefini don't..." he trailed off. "Well, anyway, it wasn't that."

Amund noted his hesitation to claim pacifism with great interest. *It seems he really does listen to me,* he thought, pleased.

"Baggi and his friend Guthini attempted to surprise me, as a joke. I reacted on reflex," he said unapologetically.

Torny raised an eyebrow. "You mean overreacted on reflex," she asserted.

He waved a hand to dismiss the correction. "A meaningless difference."

Baggi and Guthini began to laugh as Torny and Amund started arguing in earnest over the altogether minor distinction. After they had made their cases, Baggi chimed in with his opinion, which Amund suspected had less to do with his principles and more to do with argument for its own sake. The debate became a three-way brawl, half angry and half amused, until even Guthini worked up the courage to offer his opinion and it became closer to three-quarters amused.

"Fine!" Amund eventually conceded. "I overreacted! Of course, if it had been a real threat this conversation would have gone a very different way," he insisted.

His friends dropped the issue, having exhausted its relevance. The inn had filled up during their discourse, and Torny now went between the bar and tables as was her duty.

"I was thinking," Baggi said after a comfortable break in the conversation, "it would be helpful to understand the Kichishi sense of humor if I'm to accomplish this Task. For example, Naefjans tend to enjoy wordplay and puns." Amund caught Guthini glancing at Baggi dubiously when he said this, but the younger apprentice remained silent. "What do your people find funny?"

That resulted in another argument, much more intense than the first, but also much more fun. Amund and Torny both claimed to represent local sensibilities, yet their answers seemed not to align on even a single issue. In the end, the only point they could agree upon was that humor required bleakness in order to be effective; after all, how could one tell apart joy and sadness if one had never felt both for comparison?

"Hmm," Guthini ruminated, "I think in Naefja we call that 'gallows humor'. Most folk don't like it."

Torny shrugged. "Whatever you call it, that's what you should try," she said.

"Agreed," said Amund, "and for proof, look no further than this afternoon. Did I not laugh at my own mistake after striking you?"

"You laughed, yes," Baggi retorted, one eyebrow cocked skeptically, "although it seemed to me more at my expense."

The Chief of Flamebud chuckled again in recollection. "Perhaps so," he granted. Baggi snorted too, wincing suddenly as the motion agitated his nose.

"You know, there's a lot of people in Flamebud," said Torny. "How do you expect to make everyone laugh in two days?"

"What do you mean?" replied Baggi. "We just need to think of something clever and bleak, right?"

"No, she has a point," Guthini agreed. "Even if our joke is hilarious, not everyone has the same sense of humor. Even these two don't, and I'm fairly sure they're close friends."

"Cousins," Amund explained. Guthini nodded as if he had expected as much.

"And even besides that," continued Torny, "how do you expect to make it to every person in town in two days? It's not practical."

Baggi sat stumped, thinking hard for several long moments. Amund likewise found himself without an answer, so he stayed silent, trusting his friend to find a solution.

"Amund," he asked, "do you ever have performances in the forum?"

The Chief of Flamebud grinned, nostalgic. "We did, once," he answered.

"Before," Torny added, the implication obvious.

"And what sort of performances were they?" Baggi pressed.

Amund shrugged. "Sometimes music, sometimes poetry. Often tales were told of victories in battle, with warriors acting out the account. And on holidays, we would have puppets."

Baggi balked at him. "Are you serious?" he asked, a grin that made Amund feel self-conscious creeping across his face.

"Of course," he huffed, defensive for a reason he couldn't describe. "The young children enjoyed the puppets very much. And for that matter, so did the adults."

"But Amund most of all," Torny butted in, smiling wickedly. "Our chief just loves his puppets."

A glare from her cousin convinced her to fall silent, but an irritating smile remained on her face.

"I think I may have a plan after all," Baggi sighed, voice full of self-satisfaction.

"What, do you think to put on a puppet show?" asked Amund as mildly as he could manage.

Say yes, he thought desperately in the same moment, *do not disappoint me now, Baggi!*

Baggi chuckled, but then he said "Well, seeing as you personally insist, who am I to refuse the Chief of Flamebud?" Before Amund could muster a denial, Baggi rose from his seat. "Do you suppose Talia the tailor is at home?" he asked.

Amund glanced around the inn. "Since she is not here...most likely," he said.

"Good. I believe it's time I paid her a visit. Come, Guthini," he said. His partner scampered out of his seat, quaffing the remainder of his mug with inhuman speed before trotting off behind his fellow apprentice. They didn't bother bidding him goodbye.

"Farewell," Amund waved, indignant and vaguely slighted by the whole exchange.

Still, he found himself unable to hold on to his feelings of disparagement, for the Chief of Flamebud was far too excited about the prospect of a puppet show. *We have not had such a show in years,* he realized. *It will be good for the village to have entertainment.* Then a horrible, sickening thought struck him. *Do they know how to puppeteer?*

Amund squared his shoulders in resolution. *It seems I must lend the outsiders my expertise once more,* he thought nobly.

"Torny!" he shouted across the inn. "I am going to instruct Baggi in our performance style!"

"You know can just say you want to be in the puppet show, don't you?" she shouted back, much too loud for his comfort. "You're the chief, no one's gonna stop you."

Amund sighed and narrowed his eyes. He strode out of the inn with as much dignity as he could muster, ignoring the amused and curious eyes of Shaefini and Kichishi alike. Then he set out for Talia's shop, to teach Baggi and his friend the time-honored tradition of Kichishi puppeteering.

***

"Are we really putting on a puppet show?" asked Guthini as the two apprentices weaved through the village.

"We really are," Baggi replied.

"But where will we get the puppets? And who will make the set? And who will do the advertising? And who will actually work the puppets?"

Guthini voiced his concerns like a regretful deckhand, asea for the first time: full of innocence at first, then increasingly agitated as the reality of their situation sinks in.

"Guthini," said Baggi reassuringly, before the younger boy could whip himself into full-blown panic, "we'll face those challenges as they arrive. As to your first question, I happen to be owed a favor by the local tailor. It's my hope that she has the necessary skills."

"Your hope?"

"Yes, my hope."

Guthini swallowed hard but said nothing for a while until they approached the tailor's shop, at which point he tugged at Baggi's sleeve and pointed up the road toward Amund's mansion.

"Is that Staffkeeper Hjordis? And Alchemist Elof?" he squinted, whispering unnecessarily.

Baggi looked down the road and confirmed the younger boy's assessment, though at first he thought it couldn't have been them; for their elders were talking intently and both making frustrated hand gestures.

"Seems like they're excited about something," Guthini remarked.

"No," Baggi corrected him, reluctant to do so, "they're fighting."

But what about? He wondered. *Those two are Shaefini through and through. They don't fight.* Yet his own eyes told a different story. They were engaged in a verbal battle, the same as he and Audr had been just days earlier. *Could it have something to do with his and Kettil's deception? Did Elof confess? But why to Hjordis, of all people? Why not the Elder Sage?* Then he remembered how he and Kettil had found the couple in the woods, embracing and speaking in soft voices, and admitted to himself that he knew exactly why it had been her. Baggi was sorely tempted to intercede and attempt to make peace, but he forced himself to focus on his own matters.

"Huh," Guthini said simply. "I'm sure they can figure it out, whatever it is."

"As am I," Baggi agreed, not entirely honestly.

He knocked on the door exactly five times, just as Amund had when they had last visited. It seemed unlikely that the number of knocks was an important cultural custom, but then one could never be sure in foreign lands. *And when in doubt,* thought Baggi, *exercise caution. Even if it means observing a fictional custom.* After some time, Talia answered the door wearing a confused expression. It brightened upon laying eyes on her mender.

"You are Baggi, correct? I was beginning to wonder if you forgot where I live. Come in!" she gushed. "It was not locked. This is a shop, after all."

"Oh, I know," Baggi lied, "but I figured the polite thing to do was to knock and wait."

The words were embarrassingly familiar. Talia, luckily, seemed pleased with his manners.

"Oh, wow!" Guthini exclaimed in Flowspeak as he entered, then switched to a mish-mash of Kichishi and the Base Tongue. "These are gorgeous!"

He stared slack-jawed at the *kortas* covering the walls, spinning around and around as he struggled to see all at once. The boy reached out a hand to feel the fabric of a blue garment that caught his eye, and for a moment Baggi thought to stop him from spoiling the pristine garb. Talia though, seemed flattered at his interest and nodded encouragingly. Guthini sighed in delight as his fingers stroked the material.

"Your interest pleases me," the tailor beamed. "I crafted each of these garments myself! All except those two," she said, gesturing to the twin *kortas* on display over the counter. Baggi found their scarlet silk and shining threads just as mesmerizing on second viewing. "Those, my mother and father made for each other."

"They were both tailors?" Baggi asked, distracted from his objective by the artistry surrounding them.

Talia nodded. "Exactly so. My father was from Ehkag down south, but when he stopped here on his way north and met my mother, they could not endure parting and joined their businesses. He had to have his whole shop shipped here, one crate at a time! These were their wedding *kortas*."

"There aren't any opals on them," Guthini observed, "like there are on Chief Amund's."

"Of course not," Talia giggled. "I just said they're wedding *kortas*." Guthini's subsequent blush rivaled the very garments before them. "So, what brings you in today?" she asked congenially. "Is it your cloak that needs mending? Damaged as it is, you may be better off simply replacing it."

"We were hoping you could help us with something else, actually," Baggi began. "You see..."

At that moment the door swung violently open to reveal Amund standing at the entryway.

"Baggi and friend!" he loudly declared. "I have decided to teach you the Kichishi style of puppeteering. No doubt you will require my knowledge and experience."

"You two are performing a puppet show?" Talia gasped. "How can I help?"

Baggi grinned at the absurdity of Amund's declaration and his extremely timely arrival. *This was a good idea,* he thought.

17

"Okay, let's take a break," said Baggi, wiping sweat from his forehead.

The hot Kichishi sun bore down on the forum and the three boys on its stage. It was just past noon by Baggi's reckoning, and the set was nearly constructed; another hour or two would be enough to finish. *But even so, we could use some respite,* the elder apprentice thought. His ashen cloak lay on the steps, long ago discarded along with Compromise as he and Guthini labored under Amund's management. Baggi may have been annoyed at the arrangement, if not for the fact that the young man was somehow able to direct them and work as fast as both Naefjans put together all at once. Guthini slumped down on the edge of the stage next to Baggi, grateful for rest.

"A break? Now?" asked Amund. "We are all but finished."

His assessment was not inaccurate; the frame that would span the length of the small stage was nearly done, and all that remained was to form a half-wall to shield the performers from sight during the performance. After that, they would paint the frame black and assemble the smaller set pieces, environmental backgrounds like trees, hills, and whatever else their story demanded. *But we can't do that until we decide on the tale,* Baggi thought. It had been in the back of his mind all day, but he decided not to fixate on that aspect of their project until at least the stage was readied, instead throwing himself headlong into the labor of construction.

"You forget, esteemed chief," Baggi panted, grinning, "that we aren't warriors like you. Our bodies need rest."

Amund scoffed as he joined them on the stage's apron. "For travelers, you tire easily."

"We don't usually lift heavy things and walk both," Guthini snapped, short-tempered in his exhaustion.

His eyes widened at his own affront and he began to apologize, but Amund laughed at the meek lad's change in attitude and waved it off.

"So long as you two are resting, you might begin working on a script," said Amund.

"Yes," Baggi agreed, "there's no putting it off any longer. With Talia already making the puppets, we're restricted to Kichishi fables, but that shouldn't pose a problem. Guthini? Any ideas?"

"Not really. Um, I did have a head concept, but it's probably stupid," his partner replied.

Baggi restrained his wince and tried not to let Guthini's clumsy Sparktongue embarrass him. *Probably meant 'an idea in mind.' You can't just translate that sort of turn-of-phrase directly,* he thought dolefully, *the syntax is completely different. I'll need to help him out with it later.*

"An idea for a comedy, you mean?" demanded Amund, far too seriously.

"I meant...it's a bad idea."

"I will be the judge of quality. Speak!"

Guthini gulped and began to clam up, but he was saved by another arrival in the forum. Torny entered by the far stairs and waved at them with her left hand, a tall woven basket covered with cloth in her right.

The boys waved back in greeting. She joined them on stage and forced the basket into Baggi's hands.

"I thought you might be getting hungry about now," she said.

Baggi lifted the cloth covering and peered down at the basket's contents. A wave of aromatic spice and fresh sweet bread reared up at him, as forceful as the innkeeper herself. His eyes began watering from the bouquet alone. He pulled back and blinked fast.

"Oh, yeah, that might be spicier than you northerners are used to," she offered belatedly.

Amund reached an undiscerning hand into the basket and pulled out a dark brown roll, then a leg of quail. It was an intense shade of red, darker than the frog legs had been, and with minced black and green chilis crusting the skin. He bit into it without hesitation. Guthini followed his example, albeit with greater caution, nibbling at his own fowl then sucking air rapidly into his mouth. Torny and Amund laughed at his discomfort, though not unkindly. The innkeeper withdrew a flask of water from a sling on her shoulder and handed it to him. Possessed by great desperation, he gulped down half its contents before sighing in relief.

Baggi emptied the bag of its remaining provisions: several more rolls, the quail's breast meat, and a bowl full of charred okra. He set the bowl down where everyone could reach it and claimed the meat for himself, but just before partaking, an important consideration occurred to him.

"Torny, there's not another piece of meat for you," he observed.

"Don't worry about me, I can make myself something when I get back," she replied.

"Nonsense," said Baggi. He pulled the meat apart with his hands and handed her half. "We can share."

She blushed slightly and sat beside him. "Well, alright. Since you insist."

Already the spices were beginning to make his hands tingle, but the smell was too tantalizing for Baggi not to eat, never mind the insult it would pose Torny. He took a deep breath and decided to go all in, biting with nearly as much zeal as Amund. The flavor poured into his mouth, coating his tongue and cheeks with a painful tingling. Yet even the immense spiciness was overshadowed by the meat's rich fat and the saltiness of the spice paste, elevated to still greater deliciousness by the minced chilis' playful tang. It tasted like the musician's duel from the market, dizzying and full of vitality, captured and ground to seasoning then infused in the meat. Baggi even recognized a note of black pepper, the familiar bite at once nostalgic and entirely new in a foreign context. He chewed quickly, wanting to clear the intense heat from his mouth as soon as possible, yet the moment he had swallowed Baggi found himself taking another bite. He sighed in satisfaction.

"Ha!" yelled Amund proudly. "It seems he enjoys Kichishi cooking, Torny. Or perhaps it is only your cooking he enjoys."

"Good," she replied, "but I'm worried about this one."

She gestured to Guthini, who was faring far worse. Upon witnessing Baggi's gastronomic bravery, he had steeled himself and faced his fear, chomping down with a vengeance. Unfortunately, his willpower was unable to conquer his own tastebuds, and he now alternated between gulping water, stuffing his mouth with bread, and hyperventilating.

"He will be fine," Amund said dismissively.

"If you say so," replied Torny, clearly skeptical of her cousin's assessment. "How's the show coming?"

"Very well," answered Baggi. "We've nearly finished the set; Talia said she expects to finish the puppets tonight; all we need now is a story to tell. And with Guthini on our side that should be no problem. He never missed an evening tale in his life."

They turned hopeful faces toward the young apprentice, his face and shaved head bright red and bearing an uncanny resemblance to a rowan berry. He seemed in a trance, uncomprehending of his surroundings and the conversation taking place therein.

"Perhaps he can join the discussion when he has recovered," frowned Amund. The others nodded in uneasy agreement.

The trio continued to chat as they munched on the grilled okra. It, too, was spicy, though far less so than the meat, and evened out with a refreshing splash of lemon juice that brought out the vegetables' mild sweetness nicely. The slimy membrane inside was deeply pleasant to the dehydrated youths, and after he had regained his senses Guthini eagerly partook of them as well.

"A fable, huh?" Torny reflected. "You should do 'The Tailor and the Florist.'"

Amund snorted derisively. "That one will bore the entire village. We need a more exciting tale, like 'The Man Who Sought Strength!'"

"I happen to find romantic stories very exciting!" huffed the innkeeper. "Besides, there's a great big fire in that one! How is that not exciting?"

"But there is no honorable combat!" insisted Amund. "We need a tale to remind the villagers of our strength!"

"We need a tale to remind us of fire and tragedy bringing people together!"

The duo growled at each other and nearly butted heads as they argued. *Like when Fleecy and his friend Woolhoof used to fight,* thought Baggi, the resemblance to the sheep of Jolk providing him deep amusement. *But these two are perhaps even stubborner.* He cleared his throat pointedly and waited for his chance to intervene.

"I'm not as familiar with your folklore as I would like to be," offered Baggi, "but isn't there a story that has romance and excitement both?"

"Yeah, and it's called 'The Tailor and the Florist,'" mumbled Torny petulantly, but she dropped the issue and crossed her arms as she considered. Amund, too, fell silent as he thought.

"What about 'The Stolen Treasure?'" he suggested after some time.

"Hmm...I guess it does have a little romance," admitted Torny.

"And some honorable combat," agreed the chief, "although there could be more."

"What tale is this?" asked Baggi, glad they agreed yet wary of a tale he had not heard before.

"Oh, I know it!" Guthini interrupted. His skin had cooled to a warm pink and he seemed to have regained his senses. "It's about a hunter, Arnbjorg, and all the animal friends she makes while tracking down dastardly kidnappers!"

"That is more or less the tale," agreed Amund, clearly surprised by the Naefjan's knowledge.

"My father is a skald," explained Guthini, "so I know lots of stories and poems, even Kichishi and Melennese ones."

"Really?" said Baggi with surprise. "That must have been great fun."

"Yes," beamed his partner, "it was! I learned a lot; there's some really smart lessons in stories, you know."

"This is wonderful news!" Amund declared. "Since you know the story so well, you can write the script, and Baggi can provide editing and fine-tune the linguistics."

Guthini stared blankly, unsure of several words he had used. Baggi laid a hand on his shoulder to reassure him.

"He means you tell me the story, and I translate to Sparktongue."

"I can do that," the younger lad consented.

"And while you do, I shall finish the set on my own," decided Amund. "It should not take any longer than if you two were helping." Baggi bit off a retort as he noticed the spark of humor in his friend's eyes.

"Probably true," he grinned. "And there is humor in this tale as well, yes?"

"Oh yes," Amund assured him, "there is much physical comedy in the villains being dealt their deaths by Arnbjorg's animal friends."

Baggi looked to Torny for confirmation, finding this an odd response. She nodded as if her cousin had made perfect sense.

"By the way, don't you think you should have an actual Kichishi working on the script too?" she suggested. "I'm sure your father knew his stuff, but stories can change when they travel."

"That's an excellent idea," Baggi nodded. "And who would know the local tales better than the innkeeper?"

"Probably no one," she agreed without a trace of humility, "so I'll help you."

"Do you not need to attend the inn?" shouted Amund from across the stage, where he had already returned to construction.

"I left Aghi in charge," Torny replied nonchalantly, "and since the Staffkeepers fixed him he's almost as fast as a normal person, just a little shakier. He can run the place for one day."

"Then it's settled," Baggi declared. "We have our playwrights, we have our editor, and soon we'll have our puppets and set." He procured the journal he had brought along expressly for this purpose, as well as the everquill that had been his ninth birthday present and, naturally, required no external inkpot even to this day. Baggi looked up at the duo expectantly.

"You tell it, and I'll correct you when you get it wrong," said Torny.

Guthini nodded excitedly, every trace of his usual shyness gone as he entered his comfort zone. He cleared his throat and began.

"The Jarl and his wife were the richest people Kichishi had ever known."

"'Richest people' doesn't sound like something we would call the Jarl and their family," frowned Torny.

"Let's try 'wealthiest nobles,'" suggested Baggi.

Guthini nodded and started again. "The Jarl and his wife were the wealthiest nobles Kichishi had ever known."

Torny nodded approvingly and Baggi smiled as he took down the first line in ecstatic Kichishi script.

***

Audr the banker sighed and rubbed her eyes. It had been a long afternoon, and a hot one, but the sun was beginning to show through her western window and that meant her workday was finally over. She stood up from her desk and stretched stiffly, then went out to the lobby to lock the front door. As she approached, she noticed a sheet of parchment had been slipped underneath. A cartoon of a woman holding a bow adorned the page with clean text above and beneath. The banker picked it up and read aloud, more to fill the silence and wake herself up than out of necessity.

"'The Stolen Treasure, A Classic Kichishi Fable Performed Through the Noble Art of Puppetry,'", she said, curiosity mounting with each word.

She turned the poster over; the reverse side was blank. Audr went to the stairs and opened the door to her newly flourishing garden, squinting as the sunlight met her eyes painfully. She strolled the rows between planter boxes, pleased with the unexpected growth spurt she had been blessed with. Indeed, her crops had never shown such fertility. Already the beanstalks stood nearly at harvest height, and her chilis weren't far behind. *Perhaps we have returned to Sawtor's favor after all,* she thought proudly. *Our chief was right to burn the flamebuds in the end.*

"Audr!" shouted a familiar voice from below. She peered over the roof and saw Vigi waving up at her with his own poster in hand. "Did you see? A puppet show, tomorrow! Come watch it with me!"

The banker rolled her eyes at his childishness, inadvertently turning them back into the scalding sunlight and embarrassing herself with a squeal. It occurred to her that her eyes would not have hurt so badly had she not spent the entire day indoors. Then it occurred to her that she had not left her home and her garden, except to attend the weekly council meetings, in many months. She even paid handsomely to have all of her home goods delivered, rather than go to market herself and lose precious work time.

"I suppose I could use a night off," she admitted.

***

Elder Sage Hrafn eased into a seat at the stump-table that had quickly become his favorite and sighed happily. The Shaefini had completed their work before even the morning had passed, and that meant the villagers were no longer in need of healing. This was good. For the rest of the day, his caravan had milled about the village, making conversation and forging friendships with the local Kichishi. *Their Spark-tongue will improve from this,* the Elder Sage thought with pleasure, *some may even approach Baggi's fluency.*

Thoughts of the apprentice brought forth another swell of pride. His Tasks were nearly completed, and then Hrafn himself would see to the boy's Marking. Usually, the Elder Sage would trust the ritual to a Sage, while he himself oversaw the proceedings as a formality, but Baggi's potential was vast and his progress during the Tasks had exceeded even Hrafn's expectations. He could feel it in the boy's aura, an intense concentration of power without precedent. Hrafn knew that, should the exponential rate of growth continue, he would need guidance from the most knowledgeable and consummate sources available. And while he trusted in the wisdom of Sages Runa, Ingrid, and Folke, Hrafn harbored no delusions; he knew the difference in experience would prove crucial.

"Hey, wow!" came an excited voice from behind the bar. "This looks great!"

The speaker, a boy in a triangular cap running the inn in Torny's absence, beamed at the girl before him. He held in his hands a parchment, but from his table Hrafn couldn't make out its content. He made to rise from his seat when the girl turned his way with a stack of sheets in hand and approached before dividing the pile into halves and offering one to him.

"You are Elder Sage Hrafn, correct?" she asked in excited Sparktongue. "I am Talia. Baggi wished for me to ensure you received posters and distributed them among your caravan."

Hrafn took the proffered stack and read, recognizing Baggi's handwriting even in a foreign script. *A puppet show,* he thought with great delight, *how charming! And tomorrow evening, just enough time for pleasant anticipation to build. So this is what you came up with, eh Baggi?*

"Thank you, child," he replied with a benignant smile. "If it's what Baggi wishes, I will see that it is done."

"Wonderful!" she said. "And arrive early if you desire a good view. We take the puppet shows very seriously." With that, she skipped off, handing out flyers here and there to excited villagers.

Hrafn marveled at her vitality. After all, she had been infirm and near-death only a week past. But Baggi had cleansed the sigil with great competence, and children were so full of life that no further treatment had been required for her full recovery. Besides, her life force was particularly strong. Otherwise, she never would have fought for as long as she had against Death's claim.

After a few further moments of simple joy, Hrafn used Mischief to hoist himself up. His staff was equally pleased at the prospect of the coming show, but in their old age the two could no longer hope to match the exuberant excitement of the Kichishi children surrounding them.

"Shall we spread the excitement to our own young ones?" he asked Mischief. Hrafn's bones creaked as he rose, and so did his staff, mellow and affirmative, as they set out to distribute the flyers.

***

"Uhh...apologies for the interruption," a girl's voice butted in.

Hjordis whipped toward her, immensely straining her will so as not to glare at the unwelcome third party in her and Elof's conversation. Her frustration melted away as she recognized the tailor from their first evening in Flamebud.

"Staffkeeper Hjordis and Alchemist Elof, correct?" the girl continued. "You may not recognize me in the daylight. I am Talia, the tailor. I wished to thank you for your part in healing me. I wished to give you this as well." She handed Hjordis a decorative poster with Kichishi text she couldn't decipher at a glance. "We are hosting a puppet show."

Elof leaned over her shoulder, the friction between them momentarily forgotten. "'Noble Art of Kichishi Puppetry?'" he read aloud, haltingly, his voice equal parts amusement and interest.

"That is correct," affirmed Talia.

"This looks very fun. We will definitely see you there," said Hjordis.

Talia nodded and skipped off towards the smithy. Elof looked at her askance, eyes shining with unspoken appeal.

"Alright," Hjordis said, "we can call a truce. But only on the condition that you confess after the show!"

Elof gulped. He was shaking heavily, had been for the duration of their fight, but he made a visible effort to steady himself. "Very well," he granted, "but I insist Kettil's name remain clean. I can't allow her to suffer for my stubbornness."

Hjordis sighed, torn between love of his protective nature and frustration at his transgression and lack of remorse. *At least he acknowledges he's being stubborn,* she thought.

"I really think you should be completely honest," she insisted. "You know that half-honesty is dishonesty by a different name." Elof looked ready to resume their argument, but she held up her hands in surrender. "But if that's the compromise, then so be it. I don't want to keep arguing either."

Silence hung over them for some time, the silence of a fight resolved but not yet expiated. Elof stared at her, the ghost of a smile clinging to his face and irritating her. But Hjordis found herself, as always, unable to maintain her anger when it came to her beloved. She took his hand and his smile as well as they returned to the inn.

*****

"Good afternoon, Hallsteinn!" Talia shouted, loudly so she could be heard over the metallic din of the smithy.

The blacksmith turned to her, expression inscrutable beneath the bushy eyebrows and thick beard, and nodded without dropping his tools.

"It's good that you are well," he said, then resumed pounding the wedge of iron that would mature into a door hinge.

"Thank you!" she shouted again. "I came to give you this!" Talia held out the flyer in her hand from a safe distance and made no move to come closer.

Hallsteinn made no indication he had heard her until his hammer work was done. Then he laid down the tool and approached. He rubbed his hands with a cloth hanging from his waistband before taking the poster. He read it silently, then went to a thick wooden post supporting the forge's roof and nailed the flyer to it, in plain view from his workspace. He nodded at her and made to resume his labor.

"So will you be coming?" the tailor cut in before he could get to it.

"Of course," he replied, his voice remarkably dour for a man assenting to a puppet show.

"Wonderful!" Talia shouted, the smithy already filled with clamorous iron echoes, "I will save you a seat in front!"

"Where I sit makes no difference to me," he shouted back, "I'll see just the same."

Talia giggled. She knew Hallsteinn well enough to recognize his understated brand of humor. She marveled at his stature, bigger in the shoulders than any man she had ever known, and only still a teen.

"I suppose so!" she laughed.

She skipped off to hand out the few remaining posters in her arms. Hallsteinn paused to watch her go. Ever since she had painted his sign, the blacksmith had been strangely fond of the tailor, though he struggled to show it. He chewed on his beard as he glanced at the poster with the tailor's hand-drawn illustration, clearly displayed where all visitors to the forge might see. Then he huffed his approval and got back to work.

***

Kettil took the flyer from Hrafn and walked off wordlessly, scrunching her face as she read. She opened the back door of the inn and sat in the dry grass against the wall.

"Sounds real fun," she said to herself. No one was around to answer. "Sure woulda liked to be in that."

She wondered why Baggi hadn't asked for her help. But then, Kettil was a bright child, and the answer was obvious. *He doesn't like me anymore,* she thought, *since we argued. I thought we were okay after, but then with the garden...* she was beginning to regret lying to him, but still she had no regret for breaching the banker's trust. It made her wonder what the difference was. *Is it just 'cause Baggi's my friend, and the kids here aren't? Does that make it okay?* Then an even scarier question occurred to her. *Is Baggi still my friend?* It made her nervous, thinking about it, so she pushed the thoughts away and didn't think anymore.

"Guess not even he wants me around anymore," she said aloud to drown out the thoughts. She did not cry, or sigh, or otherwise feel sorry for herself. She believed it to be the truth, plain and simple.

Kettil went into her room to retrieve her rucksack.

"Hey, where are you going with your bag?" asked another apprentice. Kettil had never bothered to learn his name. She had no use for it.

She ignored him and departed.

***

Baggi laid down his quill and stretched his hand as he blew the ink dry on the last page of their script. It had taken the better part of the day, but they were finally finished.

"This is gonna be a really great show," declared Torny. The apprentices nodded their agreement.

"You have finished?" asked Amund.

He was perched, bird-like, on the stone bench in the front row, squatting with his feet flat rather than sitting. Baggi found this a strange pose, and doubted it could possibly be comfortable, but then he was not nearly so flexible as his friend.

"We have," replied the apprentice. "Now all that's left is to rehearse. Who will be playing who?"

The return of Talia the tailor interrupted their discussion.

"I spread the news and requested your leader do the same, as you wanted," she said to Baggi, beaming.

"Perfect," he smiled back. "Did the villagers seem interested?"

The three Kichishi stared at him as if he had asked whether he should continue breathing. "Well, yes," Talia eventually said. "It is a puppet show."

Guthini guffawed at their earnestness. Baggi couldn't help chuckling himself, but all he said was, "Good."

Amund stood up and stretched his limbs. "We should all rest," he said.

"Yes," agreed Guthini, "we have much rehearsing tomorrow. I hope one day is enough time..." he trailed off nervously. Baggi laid his hand on the lad's shoulder.

"It will be," he said, "so long as we give it our full effort."

"And so long as we secure an early start," added Amund.

"Yes, yes, we heard you," yawned Torny. "Let's get going then."

And there the group fractured, Amund and Talia returning directly home while the apprentices went back with the innkeeper for a late supper and a night of well-deserved sleep.

18

Baggi's stomach was churning. He had never been in a play before, or really performed at all. Back in Jolk, he had played the flute for the goats and his mother, and occasionally a neighbor would stop by to listen and flatter him as adults often do, but that was the extent of his experience. Now, kneeling behind the chest-high barrier with the combined jabber of the entire village and caravan filling the forum, Baggi was beginning to feel truly nervous. *I'm going to look like an absolute fool,* he thought, *What if I forget my lines? Or miss my cue? Or just plain flub it?* He began the mental review which had occupied his mind for the last hour or so and compulsively double-checked the script.

The space they waited in was narrow and dim; the set was made up of a long, high wooden wall spanning the arms of the stage, with a rectangle cut from the core and a luxurious white muslin curtain that parted from the middle. Compromise lay propped against the barrier next to him; it was slightly impractical for his staff to remain in the already limited space, but Baggi needed its presence for comfort and would not hear of handing it off even for the duration of the show. He stood stage right, as did Torny, while Guthini waited on the left. In order to perform, they would stand just out of sight and hold their arms straight out, above the cut-out, and operate the strings from there. They were all dressed in black, so that when their characters crossed the stage and the performers were forced to step into view, the audience's immersion in the tale would be maintained. This technique was obviously Kichishi; when Torny and Amund's dark complexions complimented their equally black garb, the puppeteers would melt into the shadows almost completely. Not so for the snow-pale Naefjans. When they were forced to appear, their faces would stand out as clearly as a candle in the dark. Baggi tried not to focus on this. *Just look at Guthini,* he told himself, *he's not worried about being seen.*

Guthini appeared more relaxed than ever. He, too, kneeled behind the set, but he possessed the skill that Baggi lacked in puppetry and his hands were occupied with idle dances the characters would not even be performing in the tale itself. He was shockingly dexterous, the puppets moving in intricate and complex gestures. Baggi envied the younger boy's hand skills, but he envied his state of mind even more. Guthini noticed him watching and had the puppet wave jovially. Baggi smiled through his nausea.

Amund returned backstage, having made sure all were seated, or at least as many as the forum would allow. Some were forced to stand, the arena not having been designed for quite so large an audience, but as the chief reported, this seemed not to bother anyone. He took up his puppets himself, as well as his place next to Guthini, and grinned at them, then jerked an excited thumb towards the packed rows as if the size of their audience might have somehow escaped their notice. Baggi nodded in nervous acknowledgment.

The apprentice struggled to balance his emotions, focusing on the delightful smells emanating from outside. Several stalls had been set up to dispense refreshments: one sold popcorn by the scoop, the locals having apparently been prepared as they presented bowls or even buckets brought from home; at another the boy carrot-farmer Kalfr chopped his produce into long, thin strips before coating them in a honey mixture and caramelizing them in hot oil, the sweet shells crackling delightfully. There were more substantial savories as well, meat skewers and sandwiches and bowls of unrecognizable spicy pastes that the villagers scooped up with flatbread. Baggi breathed deeply and let the aromas intermingle, filling his mind and, in doing so, temporarily evicting his anxieties.

All too soon, Torny tugged at his sleeve. "Ready?" she asked.

Baggi nodded and turned to his friends one last time. They too gestured in the affirmative. He took one side of the curtain atop the barrier, Amund the other, and they drew it open as Torny began the narration.

"The Jarl and his wife were the wealthiest nobles Kichishi had ever known," she began.

The forum that had been so full of noise before now fell silent save for the gentle sizzling of hot oil and the scrabbling of hungry hands. Baggi closed his eyes and continued his relaxation exercises. His part was small, and he only came in at the end of the tale, so rather than spend that time worrying and waiting he thought it could be put to better use Contemplating. *This is my third Task,* he realized. It felt at once overwhelming and insubstantial. *It's only a puppet show. Is this truly sufficient to prove my worth to Shaefi? But then, if it's 'only' a puppet show, why am I so afraid?*

He thought back to Jolk, where his audience had been far smaller. It seemed strange to him that such a thing as the number of listeners could induce this much greater anxiety. *If I really think about it, all the goats in the village would sing along sometimes. And there were nearly as many goats there as people here.* This was not mathematically true, but believing it helped. *So if the numbers aren't the problem, what is?*

He remembered Fleecy, the sheep that had been his best friend before Kettil, and how she had bleated appreciatively at the flute. *She always seemed to milk better after a good song,* he reminisced. *And it was nice knowing that she wouldn't criticize my playing. But then, the other villagers never criticized my playing either. And it's not that there was nothing to criticize, that's certain; they were simply happy to hear music.* Baggi wondered if the villagers of Flamebud would criticize his performance today. After all, it was clear they took the puppet shows very seriously.

Guthini raised the giraffe-neck puppet with one hand as he guided the tale's hero, Arnbjorg the hunter, with the other. She climbed the tree and began conversing with the animal, Torny providing the woman's voice and Guthini the giraffe's.

"'I can help you'", said Torny, voicing both the tale's hero and its narrator, "'if only you swear to tell me truthfully which direction the man went afterwards,' for she was canny and knew a giraffe will often lie if not sworn to truth."

A chorus of approving grunts from the audience signaled their agreement of the narrator's assessment.

Baggi thought of the pure exhilaration on Talia's face, the joy gushing from her voice when she had learned of their plans to put on the show. He thought of the full house just beyond the flimsy wall of wood. He thought of how even the ever-serious Chief Amund had reverted to childhood, the childhood he should never have been forced to leave, when presented with his beloved puppetry. *Perhaps it's not that they take it seriously, exactly,* he thought, *Perhaps it's more that they've been so starved of frivolity, so devoid of hope for so long, that this show is their relief. Even after their awakening in the heat of the flamebuds, they were offered no relaxation, no release of tension. It was mourning. Beautiful mourning, healing mourning, yet mourning all the same.*

Suddenly Baggi had no doubt about the importance of this 'only a puppet show'. It was not entertainment. No, it was the final stroke of a calligrapher's quill, capable of finalizing a heartfelt poem of forgiveness and acceptance if proper care was maintained till the end. Yet should the quill waver even a fraction of an inch, should it lose balance for a single blink so close to completion, the whole piece would be for naught. *And even if I start over from the beginning,* he realized, *even if it's perfect on the second try, it won't be the same poem, not quite. The first draft will be gone forever.* Baggi opened his eyes and took a deep breath, well and truly dispelling his nerves. He waited attentively for his cue.

It wasn't far off now. The tale was reaching its climax, as Arnbjorg approached the bandits' cave and the titular treasure therein. Amund puffed up his chest, as if readying to take the stage with his whole body rather than hands and voice alone. Guthini had played every animal Arnbjorg encountered, yet now he took on even more characters: the bandits of the tale with words lugubrious and cruel, as they boasted of their criminal accomplishments. Baggi remembered, a moment too late, that his puppet was supposed to be in this scene, too, even though he didn't speak yet. He hoped none would notice his late arrival. He cautiously snaked his puppet, a bound man in finery, into sight near the cave's mouth. Amund laughed, his puppet's hands on its belly as the motion shook his entire being.

"You all may have claimed great treasures," he boasted in the bandit leader's voice, "yet none approaches the value of my prize! Stolen from the Jarl's home and carried so far without leaving a good trail for tracking, mine is truly the greatest heist!"

He laughed again, a confident belly-laugh. *He's obviously having fun with this,* Baggi thought. It relaxed him somewhat.

Torny and Guthini carried out a conversation between Arnbjorg and the bandit leader's yak, wherein the hunter healed the abused yak's swollen joints and the Jarl's stolen treasure was revealed as none other than his own son, the bound man in the cave. Baggi's stomach flipped, but he steadied his hand. *Besides,* he reasoned, *if I shake, it can be dismissed as a character choice. He must be scared, after all, as hostage to bandits.*

As Arnbjorg urged his character to flee with her, Baggi nodded his puppet's head in what he hoped was enthusiastic relief but feared was simply clumsy puppeteering. Torny and he were standing close together, a logistical necessity of the set. She grinned at him reassuringly, nearly as exhilarated by performance as her cousin. Baggi's face was hot, though whether from embarrassment at his lack of skill, or the girl's proximity, or perhaps both, he was unsure. The fictional duo took off from the cave, and then the bandits took note, and the chase was on. Just before the scene change, Guthini's yak gored one of the pursuing bandits, operating both characters one-handed. Chuckles greeted the display.

"Run swiftly!" yak-Guthini called after the fleeing pair. "I have killed one, but three remain!"

So it continued, Baggi and Torny operating the fleeing couple for two additional scenes during which the pangolin and giraffe Arnbjorg had helped on her journey each claimed a bandit's life and evened the odds. A chorus of laughs greeted each of these deaths as well, just as Amund had predicted. Finally, only the bandit leader remained. He surrendered, begging for mercy as he had done no violence. The heroic Arnbjorg deemed this a half-truth, as the villain had inflicted pain on each of her new animal friends on route to his hideout, so she hobbled the man with an arrow and Baggi's puppet hauled him along. This was the trickiest part for him to learn, but he had practiced it desperately and, by some miracle, the strings now remained untwisted. *And the rest should be easy,* he told himself as he cleared his throat.

"You have my thanks," he projected towards the forum in the most genteel and honorable voice he could muster. Baggi had never met any person of nobility or great renown, excepting Hrafn and the Sages, but he reasoned that it was of little import so long as the voice represented the idea of high birth. "And the Jarl will surely reward you for my return, as I am his only son."

With that, the final scene change was upon them. The curtain closed briefly, then parted to reveal the Jarl on his throne in Ehkag and the trio before him, the bandit leader bound by tiny ropes hastily tied during the transition.

"You have my gratitude," the Jarl said through Amund, "and my promise holds true: you may claim my son as your husband if you wish, and with it the right of succession."

"With respect, my Jarl," replied Torny-Arnbjorg, "I will marry your son only if he will have me. To claim another life as my own property would be shameful to my ancestors."

And then his part was all but over, Baggi needing only to bow the son's head in acceptance as Torny narrated the resolution and eventual success of the heroic hunter Arnbjorg's Jarlship. The curtain fell on the finale and the forum was filled with shouts and applause. The puppeteers walked on stage into the light of early evening and presented themselves to the assembly, making the Sign of Flame as they offered the show and the labor put into it to the villagers and to Sawtor.

Amund beamed, happier than Baggi had ever seen him. It was refreshing to see his heart so light. A thought seemed to occur to him, and he pushed Guthini, who had been half-concealed behind the others out of shyness, directly in front of the rest of his peers. Amund began clapping enthusiastically and shouted:

"Good people, I present the one who worked the hardest, played the most characters, and made this show possible!"

Baggi applauded as earnestly as the rest of them. *He's right,* he thought, *I never could have made this happen without Guthini.* He thought of his initial reluctance to work with the younger lad, his pretentions and his delusions of victimhood. Baggi chuckled at his own ignorance. *It's incredible how much you can learn in three days.* Then he thought of the first day they had arrived in Flamebud Village, how drained he had felt from his brief attunement in the pass, and his fear and unease and complete self-conscious discomfort. *And even more incredible how much you can learn in nine,* he added.

After much longer than Baggi expected, the applause died out and the performers began packing away the puppets, carefully and deliberately like Talia and Guthini had demonstrated so as not to tangle their strings. His puppet, the Jarl's son, laid in the felt-lined box next to Arnbjorg. *They make a sweet couple,* he thought as he examined the precise, if rushed, painted expressions.

"You did pretty good for a first performance," said Torny, leaning over his shoulder.

Baggi started slightly. He turned to her and looked for signs of teasing, finding none in her expression. Her red curls half-obscured her face, catching the sinking sun majestically. He apparently spent a bit too long studying her, a fact made obvious by her eventual blushing and turning away.

"What are you looking at?" she demanded, brushing back her hair and quickly tying it into a rambunctious knot.

"Nothing, sorry," Baggi replied. "I just couldn't tell if you were joking. But thank you."

"I wouldn't joke about the puppet shows," she replied, and once again Baggi found himself unsure of her intention. He decided to take her words at face value for simplicity's sake.

"You were impressive too," he offered. "Between the main character and the narration, I'm not sure how you managed it." She perked up proudly. "You and Guthini both did a great job."

Torny cocked an eyebrow, and now Baggi recognized her expression: the exhaustion of one who had not the energy to explain some seemingly simple concept, knowing that once begun, it would rapidly convolute.

"Yeah, that's true," she said instead. She picked up the boxes. "I'm going to drop these off at Talia's house. See you back at the inn?"

He nodded and she went off without another word. Baggi watched her go, knowing intuitively that he had made a misstep yet puzzled as to its identity. The sound of splintering wood and a frustrated sigh drew his attention. Amund was using a bearded hand-axe to split the set into parts that could be reused, pocketing the nails and separating the scraps. He shot Baggi an amused, but somehow still disapproving, look.

"What?" demanded Baggi, feeling more and more foolish by the moment and still unsure why.

"Baggi," Amund began thoughtfully, "you are not stupid. In fact, you are very intelligent. Yet sometimes I do not understand the things you say and the choices you make."

"Such as?"

"You know that Torny has love for you."

Baggi sputtered defensively. "I think that's an assumption, and she hasn't said anything like that, and besides, 'love' seems a bit extreme, since we've only just met..." he trailed off as he realized he was wasting both of their time. "I suppose I suspected," he admitted.

Amund laid down his hatchet and sat on the floor next to him. "It is true you have only met nine days ago," he said, "and it is also true that we have only met nine days ago. Yet we are friends, is it not so? We are lifelong friends, I think."

The apprentice grinned. "I think so."

Amund grinned back at him, though there was some chagrin in his. "Then what difference does such a number make? You have love for Torny too, do you not?"

"Well," replied Baggi uncomfortably, "I think highly of her. And I think she is beautiful. And I like how she takes care of the villagers, and how she speaks directly with me even when I'm acting a fool." His face burned hotter and redder than the sunburn days before.

"So why do you insist on pretending not to know these things?" the chief interrogated.

He sighed. "Even if I do feel that way, I'm not going to be here forever. I'm probably leaving tomorrow or the day after. What use would it be? At best I would see her once a year, if the caravan happens to come through this way, and at worst it would be never again. You see? When I stop to think about it-"

"Baggi," Amund cut him off, "allow me to share a piece of my father's wisdom. This piece comes from the tale of he and my mother's courtship. We have had a long night, and already a long tale, so I will not add another, but the lesson is this: love is not a thing to think about; love is a thing to be felt."

Baggi stared at his friend. "That sounds like Shaefini wisdom," he said eventually.

Amund scoffed humorously. "You believe that only Shaefini know love? Now I am not surprised at your clumsiness."

A polite cough behind him interrupted the conversation. It was the Elder Sage. He held his staff, Mischief, in one hand, and a bowl of caramelized carrots in the other. *Oh, yes,* Baggi remembered all at once, *my final evaluation. He's here to tell me if I'm going to be a Staffkeeper. It slipped my mind.* This last fact was itself deeply strange to him. Amund stood and nodded to acknowledge Hrafn. He withdrew with a meaningful look towards Baggi, but not a single word.

The Elder Sage approached slowly, glancing around at the set and the confined space the performers had worked in. Then he spotted Compromise, leaning against the wall beside its owner.

"May I?" asked Hrafn, gesturing toward it. Baggi hesitated briefly, then nodded. The Elder Sage picked up the staff and examined it, gazing at the runes inscribed.

"Elder Sage Hrafn?" Baggi asked, too weary to beat around the bush. "Did I complete my final Task?"

Hrafn smiled gently and handed Compromise to him without a word. He stood silent for some time.

"How does it feel?" he asked.

"Good," replied Baggi. "Of course, I'm tired, but that's to be expected."

Hrafn chuckled. "I meant Compromise. How does it feel in your hand?"

Baggi closed his eyes and focused on his staff. The aura flowing between them was not thick, but it was constant. In truth, he had felt no desire to examine Compromise lately. He could feel its presence now without effort. *I wonder if I could invoke a rune spontaneously,* he thought. The idea sent excited chills down his spine.

Staffkeepers usually focused their aura through attunement before invoking runes, and the process for attunement took as many forms as the Orders themselves. Staffkeepers of Shaefi attuned through mental focus and symbolically bowing, forehead to staff, to remind themselves of the connection between magic and mind; Staffkeepers of

Brathus dipped their fingers into the salt-water bowls at their hips and flicked the drops into the air to land where they may, representing the winds of chance; Staffkeepers of Death offered blood, the grim exchange compelling their runes to great power. These processes amplified a Staffkeeper's abilities, definitively, and in a dire situation not a one alive would skip this simple yet crucial step, regardless of their Order.

Be that as it may, attunement was not strictly necessary; some smaller degree of runic magic was possible on the fly, if the one invoking the rune was skilled enough and the bond with their staff stalwart. *Shall we try it?* Baggi asked Compromise now. He felt it, too, shiver with their shared excitement. Baggi stood up and mentally invoked Ansuz, focusing on the rune's image without speaking.

His aura swirled vaguely about his eyes and Baggi felt the magical insight filter into them. It was a weak effect; he had used Ansuz plenty enough before to discern the difference. He looked to Elder Sage Hrafn and noted great interest, but also a touch of inexplicit worry. That surprised Baggi enough to dispel his magic's already nebulous effect.

"Elder Sage Hrafn?" he asked, his evaluation completely forgotten. "Is there something wrong?"

"Baggi, my boy," Hrafn replied reluctantly, "you have a keen eye for insight."

He looked away and considered his words for a while. Baggi began to drum his fingers impatiently on Compromise. He felt nervousness building in his companion. *I know,* he commiserated, *but we must remain patient.* Baggi scoffed along with Compromise at his own advice, but managed to follow it.

"Have you spoken with Alchemist Apprentice Kettil today?" Hrafn eventually asked.

With a start, Baggi realized he had not; in fact, he had not spoken to Kettil in several days, or even seen her since the garden incident. His heart sank, weighted down with guilt and paranoia.

"No," he answered, "not today."

Hrafn nodded. "Then I am afraid trouble is upon us. She was seen leaving Flamebud Village wearing her rucksack by Alchemist Apprentice Bror yesterday. None have seen her since. I had hoped she was only in need of solitude and would return for the performance, yet she has not shown. I therefore reasoned that if anyone knew her whereabouts, it would be you."

Baggi's eyes widened. *Oh, Kettil, no,* he thought desperately, *what were you thinking?*

"I'll go look for her," he decided immediately. He made to depart when Hrafn stopped him.

"You must not go alone," he said, gravely serious. "We mustn't have two missing from our caravan."

"But, Elder Sage, she could be in danger!" Baggi protested.

"Yes," agreed Hrafn, "so I will be sending groups to scour the woods, each with a Staffkeeper for protection. You will, of course, be among them. Report to Flamebud Inn and I will be along presently to organize the search."

Baggi felt impatience and worry tear at his insides, but he forced himself to bow. *Even now,* he acknowledged, *we must trust the Elder Sage's leadership. Especially now.* Compromise, who had been pulsing frantically since receiving the distressing news, now begrudgingly forced calm. *I'm worried too,* Baggi agreed. He took a deep breath, balancing his emotions, then set off at a sprint for the inn.

He ran past Amund without stopping, the elder boy afforded not a moment to call out before he was gone. Villagers shouted praise and thanks for the show as he ran, but they fell on deaf ears. Baggi could think only of his own behavior, the choices he had made that he suspected had caused his friend's departure. *If I had only tried to understand her and Elof, rather than take insult, then...then what?* He couldn't put together a coherent thought, so worried was he. Compromise pulsed, offering its own anxiety but its consolation too. Baggi held it tight as he ran.

He burst through the door of Flamebud Inn, the inhabitants all turning towards him with surprise. When they saw it was only he, they returned to their affairs. The Sages Runa and Ingrid were speaking together, quickly and decisively, while the newest Sage, Folke, scribbled on a parchment. Baggi drew nearer and saw they were splitting the names of the Shaefini into groups, three or four strong each. Sage Ingrid saw him approach and her expression darkened. Yet she offered him a comforting smile even as she raised a hand barring his approach. Baggi sighed in frustration but obeyed, taking a seat at the bar.

"Hey, it's you! Baggi!" said an enthusiastic boy's voice behind the bar. It was the boy from the crow's nest, Aghi. He wore his dandy triangular cap even indoors.

"Hello, Aghi. I see Torny hasn't yet returned," replied Baggi, granting him only half of his attention until the boy's speedy speech sank in. He cast a curious glance toward the formerly slow lad. "You seem well," he said diplomatically.

Aghi beamed. "I feel great! Ever since Hjordis and Runa helped me, I can talk like normal again! I can even move like normal again!" He made to pour Baggi a mug of mead, spilling a splash or two onto the bar as his hands shook. He grinned, embarrassed. "Almost normal, at least."

"I'm glad to hear it. Sage Runa is the best healer in the realms," replied Baggi.

At that moment the inn's true proprietor returned, wiping her forehead with the curved hem of her shirt as she entered. Baggi blushed at the flash of stomach revealed in the casual action. Then he chastised himself for having such a thought in the midst of crisis. Torny approached the bar and came around to face him.

"Thanks for running the place, Aghi," she said. "You can head back up if you want."

Aghi saluted over-formally and made for the back door.

"And if you see Kettil – you know, the girl I was with when we met – let someone know right away!" Baggi added as he went. Aghi saluted him as well.

"What do you need her for this time?" asked Torny.

"She's gone off on her own, into the woods. We're about to go out in groups to search."

Torny stiffened. "That's bad news," she said. "I hope you find her quick."

"Yes, me too," sighed Baggi, "If I hadn't been so focused on my own affairs, perhaps this wouldn't have happened."

"Come on, Baggi," said Torny, "even if that's true, it's not fair to you. You're not her father; you're allowed to have your own business. And you were working on your Tasks. That's what you should have been focused on anyway."

Despite himself, Baggi smiled a little. "I suppose you're right. As usual." Then he thought of his last conversation with Amund. "That's what I like so much about you," he added, cringing at his own maladroit diction. "Not just that, but it's one of the things." This amendment did not appease his discomfort. He touched his lips and stared at the petrified wood beneath his mug.

Torny snorted. As the silence grew, so too did Baggi's nervousness. Eventually he worked up the courage to look at her and found that, ridiculously, she was avoiding his gaze as well. She made noncommittal noises several times.

"Thanks," she finally said.

"Mmhmm," hummed Baggi, too mortified to summon another word. Again, the silence stretched.

"Uh, I'm going to…" she said, gesturing to the tables with a pitcher in hand.

"Right, yes. I'll be here. Obviously," Baggi replied. Torny hurried off, her face red and her gaze fixed deliberately away toward the common room.

Baggi felt Compromise laughing at him, the exchange having apparently provided it deep amusement. He managed a weak smile, shaking his head in mock offense. *I'm glad you enjoyed that,* he told his staff. *At least it took our minds off of Kettil, if only for a moment.* At that, the humor left Compromise and him both, and they gathered their resolve once more for the imminent mission.

Guthini arrived after some minutes and took a seat next to Baggi. When he learned of Kettil's disappearance, he attempted to lighten Baggi's mood with jokes and riddles. Unfortunately, these efforts flopped completely; all Baggi could think of was how much greater Kettil's appreciation would have been for the wordplay. Still, he appreciated Guthini's effort. Eventually the boys fell silent, each holding to their staffs for comfort.

After what seemed hours, Elder Sage Hrafn entered. He scanned the assembled Shaefini, counting to make sure all were present and accounted for. *All but one,* thought Baggi dourly as Hrafn approached the Sages. Sage Folke handed him the list and the Elder Sage skimmed it before nodding. He turned to his people.

"If I may have your attention, please," he began. His voice was polite yet resonant, somehow gentle and commanding at once. "One of our own has gone missing. You all know Alchemist Apprentice Kettil. She is a valued member of our caravan, and she may be in danger even now." Those assembled began to stir with worry. Hrafn used his voice to still them. "We will need to remain calm and work together to ensure she is found swiftly and without incident. I will call your names to assign groups. Please follow the directions of the senior-most Staffkeeper or alchemist in your group."

He began to list off names, assigning them a direction in which to travel so that all possible routes might be covered. Baggi waited impatiently for his name to be called.

"Group seven: Staffkeeper Apprentice Guthini, Alchemist Apprentice Frodi, and Staffkeeper Baggi. Please search westward."

Baggi nodded seriously and all but dragged Guthini behind him by the sleeve. He quickly glanced around, located Frodi, and beckoned him to follow without stopping. They were already out the door and entering the tree line before Guthini had a chance to sputter:

"Wait, so, you're a Staffkeeper now? You passed? But you haven't had your Marking yet. Is that okay?"

Baggi shrugged. "That's not important. It's probably just so we have enough people to cover every direction. Keep your eyes open."

But he was not nearly so unmoved as he claimed. Actually he felt slightly cheated by the whole thing; cheated out of his Marking, out of his Blessing, cheated out of his day of celebration and even cheated out of his Mark. *I promised it to the village,* he thought irritably, *I need that Mark.* But even so, these worries were mere trifles compared to finding Kettil. That much held true.

19

Kettil huffed loudly and allowed her rucksack to fall heavily to the ground. The warm sunlight filtering through the canopy was waning, the grass beneath her feet far too enticing. This was as good a place as any to stop for the day. As she plopped down with her legs outstretched, the runaway unlatched her bag and dug around inside for food. She scrounged up a handful of dried berries and mushrooms, examining her paltry provisions and wishing she had had the foresight to stock up on vittles before departure. She could likely find edible flowers or roots if she looked long and hard enough, but after a full day's hike she desired more substantial subsistence. Kettil shrugged helplessly and began eating her rations slowly, one miniscule piece at a time, chewing for much longer than necessary in order to convince her stomach it was full. This survival technique she had developed on her own during her orphan days in Yngmuth, and it remained equally effective here.

"Guess I need to find somethin' to eat," she said thoughtfully between nibbles. Talking aloud helped her stay calm; just as she ate to trick her stomach, likewise she talked to trick her mind into believing it had company.

Still cupping her meager meal in one hand, she tugged at her alchemy box with the other. It was jammed tightly in her rucksack, so that she was forced to lean with her entire body weight until it suddenly and violently slipped free. The unexpected force sent her sprawling on her back, provisions scattered in the grass about her. Kettil yelped, half in alarm and half in frustration. She combed through the grass for several minutes, grunting with irritation, and when she was done she had only reclaimed two-thirds of her already sparse supplies. To make matters even worse, grass and dirt clung stubbornly to what she had found.

Kettil nearly cried then; she was, after all, lost in the woods, hungry, and worst of all alone. But instead of weeping, she bit her lip, hard, until it hurt enough to draw her attention away from her misery. Then she took a deep breath and opened her alchemy box. The latches had luckily remained fastened during the tumble, and its contents were more or less still in order. She tasted blood and realized she had bitten a touch too hard, so Kettil dabbed a drop of Knit on the raw spot. Then she stared at her ingredients and her potions, waiting for an idea to announce itself.

"Maybe I can make a trap or snare somethin'", she said vaguely. "But I probably don't have anything the animals 'round here want for bait. Looks like I've got a real-life riddle on my hands."

Shifting her perception thusly made the whole operation much more exciting. She crossed her arms and thought hard. A rustling overhead drew her attention and she saw a flying squirrel flitting through the treetops, just like the day she and Baggi had gone into the woods a week prior. Kettil wondered where it was headed.

"It might be goin' toward water," she mused, "and where there's water there's fish."

This did not seem particularly likely, and she had no wish to abandon her campsite. But the squirrel reminded her of Baggi, and that in turn reminded her of her project and what he had said about it.

I can't help thinking that perhaps this is a bad idea.

Her face burned with indignance. Then she thought of the solution to her problem, so obvious, and the burning became embarrassment at her own oversight.

"Hah!" she shouted triumphantly. "If I can't catch meat, I'll just make my own!"

She unlatched the secret compartment in her box. On the inside flap was an inscription that read:

Property of Aeskettil the Generous.

It had been a wondrous surprise, finding the compartment and the secret history of the box's ownership. But when she had, it had deepened her admiration of her mentor significantly.

"Who knew Elof learned from the best?" she chuckled, amazed even now. "Guess that's why they let him teach the best."

On proud impulse, Kettil used the tip of her knife to tack on another two lines. It now read:

Property of Aeskettil the Generous
Given to Elof the Timid
Given to Kettil the Precocious

She felt guilty for leaving Elof without warning, but then she focused on the pride and grandeur of her new self-given title and swept the guilt away. She seized the potion inside the compartment and held it up to examine its contents. The mixture glowed and swirled, stripes of faint blue and rich crimson languidly interweaving. It had taken several batches and more than one unpleasant round of self-testing, but her Water of Life was close to completion. When she had granted Baggi the privilege of testing her first batch, it had only functioned as a combination of Knit and Quickchill, treating burns and lacerations, but she had developed it even further since then and succeeded in additionally bundling the effects of Bonegrow and Reconstruct. She touched her left earlobe, reassuring herself of her work's efficacy.

"If it can grow my ear back when I put it on my wound," she hypothesized, "it should grow some meat if I pour it on the cut off part. Right?"

The woods did not answer. Kettil retrieved her knife and spent half an hour sharpening the blade. She knew now, from experience, that this would go much easier with a razor-sharp blade. But the young alchemist had an immense tolerance for pain, and truthfully, she could have grit her teeth and borne it even without the sharpening. No, she mostly went through the motions in order to steel herself for the unknown. She knew not what might arise from the severed tissue, but she did know that the chance of failure was high. She knew that no Shaefini Alchemist, past, present, or future, would ever approve of her work. She knew it was for good reason.

But for all of her talent, all of her intelligence, and all of these many things she knew, Kettil was still a child.

She set a wooden bowl in the grass before her, took three deep breaths, and knelt, eyes closed and the blade resting lightly against her earlobe. When she had run this trial before, she had wedged a stick between her teeth and bit down hard to suppress her cries. It had been a necessary precaution, to keep her project secret. But here, alone in the forest in the dying light of day, none were around to hear her. None were around to stop her.

In one hard, jerking motion, she cut off her earlobe and screamed without concern for secrecy. Through a thick haze of pain she dropped the wet chunk of flesh in the bowl. The hurt was shocking, deep, stealing her breath and her confidence as she fumbled through infantile tears with her potion. Somehow, she managed to uncork the bottle and clumsily splashed far more than intended on her openly bleeding ear before resealing the flask. She sobbed while the potion did its work, the regeneration that took only moments feeling like an eternity of suffering.

Finally, the pain subsided. Kettil cradled her legs and rocked back and forth, still weeping and struggling to collect herself. By the time she had calmed down, the sun was gone. She felt carefully for the bowl and carried it to her bag, setting it atop her clothes and fastening it shut so pests wouldn't get at the meat while she built a campfire. She groped blindly for sticks, cursing her short-sightedness that now made her task far more difficult. Eventually, she had a pile assembled and arranged the sticks in a cone. She knew she ought to have used her flint and steel for sparks, but Kettil was exhausted and had not the patience to nurse an infant flame for what could be hours. Rifling through her alchemy box once more, she procured a tin labeled 'Spark'. The greenish metal was specially treated to house the potion without activating it, just like alchemical glass. Liquid inside sloshed weakly, nearly empty; this fire would be the last it produced. She thought again of Baggi and wished for a moment that he were there to invoke Kenaz to solve the issue for her. But she shook the thought away, anger and betrayal amplified in her weariness. She poured the last few drops of Spark on the kindling and a fire puffed up on contact.

Finally, Kettil dragged her rucksack closer to the fire and sat near it before the evening's chill had a chance to settle upon her. She took the bowl in her left hand, the open container with the Water of Life in her right. One last pang of fear and nervousness echoed in her stomach, reverberating in her bones all the way to the tips of her toes and the crown of her skull.

"No point stopping now," she mumbled. Then she splashed a bit of the potion on the lump of flesh in the bowl and sat back.

The flesh soaked up the liquid like a sponge, drawing in every last drop before it began to grow. Kettil leaned close and observed with fascination, and some disappointment, as the flesh formed an ear.

"Well that's not gonna be much good to eat," she sighed.

The ear, however, continued to grow. It slowly formed new tendons, new muscles, reaching up like a plant toward the sun with its tentacular threads. They slowly weaved together, shaping a jaw, and then bones formed to support the expansion. Kettil's heart began pounding as she watched, yet she could not look away as the flesh continued to grow. It did not move quickly, but the growth was constant. It formed the outline of a head, and a neck as well, blood seeping from the mass as it exceeded the bowl's inadequate boundaries. Skin formed over the developed areas. Kettil felt a horrible fear then, a fear that compelled her to push the thing into the fire before it could become real. But she did not. She only watched in horror.

After some time, the flesh stopped expanding. Kettil hyperventilated as she beheld the grotesque thing. It had stopped growing at only one shoulder below the neck, but the head was nearly complete. It had no eyes, no brain, and lacked bones and skin on the one side, but the mass of gore was clearly human in its anatomy. And worst of all, it was not of adult proportions; no, it seemed about her size. The chunk laid in the grass near the fire, squelching as blood left its unfinished body.

Kettil looked away and vomited.

Her stomach was nearly empty, and there was not much to lose, yet she continued to dry-retch painfully for several moments, blinking away tears. Finally, she went on hands and knees toward the thing she had made. Still averting her eyes, she kicked it into the fire. Then she sat by her pack, turned away from the blaze as she wiped her face and hugged herself close. Blood from the monstrosity stained the toe of her boot. She found herself unable to look away from it.

"What was that?" asked a boy's voice, curious and innocent, from the dark forest at her left.

He spoke Sparktongue, but she recognized the accent as Naefjan. Kettil whipped toward him and fumbled for her knife. She jumped to her feet and brandished her blade toward the darkness.

"Who's there?" she demanded in Flowspeak.

A bright white light issued forth from the brush, momentarily blinding her. She held up a hand in front of her eyes and squinted painfully.

"Sorry, that was thoughtless," he replied, shifting to their native language to suit her, "I'm just curious. I saw you performing alchemy, then you kicked what you made into the fire. What was it?"

The boy stepped into the firelight and the white brilliance evaporated. Kettil retreated, keeping the fire between her and the stranger. He wore black and carried a staff. His blonde hair fell freely over his shoulders and his eyes were silver. He was similar in age to Baggi, but Kettil did not recognize this boy from their caravan. He wore a necklace woven with cord and irregular white stones about his neck. In the firelight Kettil saw the metallic shine of scar tissue beneath, reaching all the way up his throat to his left cheek. She narrowed her eyes, muscles tense and suspicions raised.

"I said, who are you?" she demanded again.

The boy nodded and raised his free hand in a gesture of peace. "My name is Hakon." He gestured to his staff. "This is Selection. We're not trying to hurt you. Just curious."

"You're an apprentice?" she asked, ignoring his own inquiries. "Where's your caravan? And where's your cloak?"

"They're nearby," he replied, "but we don't really use titles like 'apprentice.' And that's all I'm going to say until you answer my question."

Kettil regarded him warily. She had no knack for reading intent and had learned to offset this shortcoming by erring on the side of caution. The situation at hand warranted this treatment, yet the boy's appearance gave her pause. Clearly he wasn't a local, and if he were a Naefjan Staffkeeper that meant he must be Shaefini. She wondered if she had traveled farther than she thought, far enough to encounter another caravan's route. Unfortunately, Kettil did not know how many Shaefini caravans existed, or how varied their paths might be. In that moment, she wished she had paid more attention to Baggi's unprompted dissertations. But she hadn't, and Hakon was looking to her for an answer.

"It was a mistake," she answered, dodgy, "an experiment I didn't think through. But I'll get it right next time."

She wondered if that were true, wondered if there would be a next time at all, after what she had seen. Yet she was too stubborn to admit this to herself, much less a stranger.

"Fair enough," said Hakon. He looked at her curiously. "Are you alone out here?"

"No!" Kettil shot back immediately. She knew it was an overcorrection, and Hakon seemed to pick up on it.

"Well if you were," said he, "I would invite you back to my campsite. We have plenty of food, if you're hungry. If you're not, then at least you wouldn't be lonely."

Kettil remembered then that the entire reason she had run the experiment was to feed herself after a long day of hiking. After witnessing the results, her stomach was emptier than when she started. She had barely the reserves to remain standing after such a day, and debating the safety of the offer was a simply overwhelming concept, so she resolved to accept her fate either way, as long as she didn't end the day hungry and alone.

"I'm actually by myself," she admitted, unnecessarily, "so I guess I'll go with you. Just let me get my things."

She packed away her alchemical supplies in her box. When she opened the secret compartment to stow her Water of Life, the inscription and her hubristic title stared her in the face, mocking her. She clenched her jaw and slammed the compartment shut hard. Then she approached her rucksack to pack it out of sight.

"Allow me," Hakon said graciously.

Kettil acquiesced and stepped back. When he took the box, his features tightened a bit, as if perplexed. He packed it away and hoisted the rucksack, watching her. He looked suddenly unsure of his decision to invite her along.

"What?" she sneered, "Too heavy?"

"No," he answered, "it's nothing. This way."

He lit his staff once more and led the way into the woods. Kettil allowed herself one look back toward the fire. Logic and her common sense insisted she stay, that following a complete stranger dressed in black into unfamiliar woods at night was sheer folly. Yet to stay would be to remain near her creation, to sleep where it had been. The lump of burning meat was unrecognizable now. Still, she wanted, on a primal level she didn't quite understand, for the thing to keep roasting until it was reduced to ash.

"This is so stupid," she muttered, then followed the stranger into the woods.

***

In a clearing not far from Kettil's own campsite, Valdis and her Staffkeepers sat round a fire. While they ate a supper of stewed lentils and wild squirrel, the only noise was that of Arni humming with appreciation as he devoured his meal. The Melennese Staffkeeper had taken nearly as strong a liking to Kichishi cuisine as Valdis had. It made her proud to see her people happy even without the luxuries they had left behind in Ehkag.

They had spent far too long in the Kichishi capitol, nearly an entire year. Every day had brought them new targets, fresh flavors of death that filled Valdis' mouth and nose even despite the musky incense from the multitudinous tea lounges that operated from early morning till the elder hours of the night. Ehkag was a towering metropolis, buildings ten stories or higher packed so tightly together one could reach out their window and touch that of their neighbors across the street, and populated just as densely inside. The bricks were colorful, the streets sandy and unpaved, and the styles of their garb more flamboyant than even Geluwam, though in most cases the quality was not as fine. Public theatres were popular fixtures in every district, where one could gain admittance to their ever-popular puppet shows for a mere three yellow-odd in most places, and even cheaper in others. Yet what had proven most exciting for her, what Valdis herself had come to love, was the local fare. Kichishi was full of beasts and edible flowers of great variety, and this expansive assortment of ingredients was reflected in the myriad options presented to them every mealtime. It was a welcome break from the limited cuisine of the northern lands where, even despite their famous glasshouses, practicality demanded only the hardiest of ingredients were cultivated.

The southern people were well taken care of by their Jarl, that was clear, much healthier and wealthier than the northern folks her Staffkeepers were accustomed to claiming. Valdis had worried about her party, worried they might come to love the comforts and entertainment afforded by their location and grow complacent, yet she could not have led them away earlier. *There was much work to be done,* she thought. *And it seems my fears were misplaced besides.*

Their stay had not been solely successful, of course. The Kichishi were better fighters across the board than Melennese, and certainly more skillful than the average Naefjan. They were energetic and alert, especially in bustling Ehkag, and The Conclusion had needed to employ the utmost caution in approaching targets. One such target, a woman who fought skillfully with two staves, had sensed their attack and claimed the life of two Staffkeepers before she could be subdued. Valdis had replenished her ranks with another local woman of nearly twenty named Myrgjol, whom she had discovered training in one of the city's many fighting academies; her expertise and knowledge had proved invaluable in navigating the realm and preventing further losses.

Valdis pulled herself away from reminisce. She tasted a strange flavor in the air, growing stronger by the moment. That was good. It meant that Hakon had found the source, as she had commanded, and was returning. *Unless he was the found one, and now it closes in on us,* reflected Valdis. She pricked her thumb with her knife and squeezed until the blood could easily flow, out of caution, but yet refrained from waking Relief.

An emanating white light indicated Hakon's safety. He put it out as he drew near the campfire, and in the orange light Valdis saw he carried a bulging rucksack on his back. He stopped in the clearing and turned back, beckoning. A girl stepped cautiously forth. She had short hair the same color of Hakon's, dark eyes, and a finely honed knife in hand. She was small and young, but she carried in her posture a lifetime of lessons painfully learned. Draped about her shoulders was the distinctive blue-and-white cloak Valdis immediately recognized as

Shaefini uniform. Valdis tasted the girl's aura from her seat by the fire; it tasted of Death, undoubtedly, yet it was and was not her own dying.

"Who have you brought?" asked Valdis when Hakon had set the rucksack down near the fire.

"She wouldn't tell me her name," he replied. He took up his lyre and began plucking a mellow melody.

The girl remained on the edge of their clearing, pointing the knife indecisively between them.

"Who are you?" Valdis said to her, a little louder. There was no answer but a fearful and cautious glare. "You have met Hakon," she continued, gesturing to each Staffkeeper as she spoke, "I am Valdis. These are Arni, Myrgjol."

"Kettil," the girl finally answered. She slowly lowered the knife and approached the fire, keeping several feet between them. "Hakon said you have food I can eat."

Valdis looked to Hakon, who verified the claim with a nod. He handed her the remainders of his dinner. Valdis, in turn, passed the bowl to Kettil. She took it and began devouring the scraps, unabashed.

"Kettil?" confirmed Arni through a mouthful. "Isn't that a boy name?"

Kettil shrugged noncommittally. "Doesn't Arni mean 'eagle'? I don't see any wings on your back," she quipped.

"Hah!" Arni laughed, choking on his lentils. "You have me there! So what brings you into the woods at this time of night, alone?"

"I never said I was alone."

"Yes you did," interjected Hakon mildly, "you told me so." She glared at him, but he took no notice, eyes closed as he played.

"Do not lie, child," said Valdis. "I have no patience for dishonesty."

Her voice was chilling and authoritative; it drank the good humor from the clearing. Arni turned his gaze downward, collaterally cowed to silence.

Kettil nodded slowly. "Fine," she said.

"Answer Arni's question."

"I ran away."

"What else did you do?"

Kettil scrunched her features in apparent confusion. "Nothing. I've just been walkin' and then I made a fire when Hakon found me."

The boy stopped playing, though his eyes remained closed. The campfire's crackle was loud in the night.

"You will not have another chance," said Valdis. "Already you have had more than most. The repulsive flavor of undeath was in the air tonight. It led Hakon to you."

"That and the screaming," the boy added.

Valdis ignored the interruption. "Tell me," she commanded.

Kettil's eyes widened and she looked to Hakon as if betrayed. He did not acknowledge her, sitting in blissful silence like one asleep. Her rucksack was on the ground before him, and he had one foot through the straps. Finding her odds of escape none too favorable, she took a calming breath.

"I was hungry" she answered in a shaky voice, "so I tried to make meat. But it didn't work, at least not the way I wanted."

"How?" Valdis asked.

"I made a potion," Kettil answered. She slumped visibly, all fight seemingly gone from her. "It's supposed to be the Water of Life. But it's not done yet, and I used it wrong."

Ah, here is the truth at last, thought Valdis, *and it is as simple as Shaefini hubris. Just as expected.* The Conclusion froze at Kettil's words; Valdis tempered her outrage. The Water of Life was a well-known relic, a gift boasted of by the higher-ranking Staffkeepers of Shaefi. Its very nature was in direct opposition to her own Staffkeepers and their philosophy. *The child wants to undo Death,* Valdis thought. If she were the type of woman to laugh, she would have. *Such shortsightedness. Such gall.*

"Did you learn your lesson?" she asked after calming.

"I learned a lot of lessons," Kettil answered, and then before the interrogation could continue, she pointed to the adornments on Valdis' black garb and said, "Are those bones?"

"Yes," she replied.

"Why are you wearing them?"

"To remind myself of my purpose."

"What's your purpose?"

"To prevent suffering."

Kettil nodded. "Yeah, that sounds like a Staffkeeper alright."

Valdis looked at her curiously. "You are Shaefini," she stated.

"Yeah, I'm one of you. Well, maybe not anymore," Kettil answered. She tugged at her cloak uncertainly.

"We are not Staffkeepers of Shaefi," snorted Arni, having regained his courage.

Kettil looked at him curiously. "But you are Staffkeepers," she asserted.

"We are," he agreed.

"We are The Conclusion," Valdis clarified. "Called Staffkeepers of Death, by the ignorant. Does that frighten you, child?"

Kettil stared at Valdis with wide eyes, then examined the rest of her companions with similar shock.

"Yes," she said.

Valdis smiled a little then. "An honest answer. You're learning."

"Are you going to kill me?" Kettil asked in a small voice.

"No," said Valdis.

"Why not?"

"It's not your time," said Hakon. "We can tell when it is."

"But how?"

"I can feel it," the boy explained, "and so can Myrgjol. But Arni sees it. And Valdis tastes it."

"Have you ever sensed Death, child?" Valdis asked.

Kettil took a long time to answer, scooting closer to the fire and holding her hands near the base of the flames. "Maybe," she said, "I don't know."

"Then join us," offered Valdis, "until you know."

Kettil said nothing. Then she nodded.

20

"Baggi," panted Guthini, "I don't think I can keep going."

The light thrown by his staff began to peter out as he slowed, then stopped walking altogether.

"Yeah, me either," agreed Frodi.

Baggi shot him a glare. *You haven't even been using magic,* he thought disdainfully, *what do you have to be tired over?* But he stopped and took several calming breaths to rebalance his emotions. *It's not fair to take out my worry on Frodi. He's searching just as hard as we are.*

"It's okay, Guthini. I'll take over," he said after they had rested a moment.

He touched Compromise to his forehead, invoking Sowilo, and toasty orange light illuminated the woods as far as they could see. Frodi whistled lightly in admiration, but Guthini threw a nervous glance toward Baggi.

"Are you sure?" the apprentice asked. "We've been out here for a long time. And you've been casting most of the light. Aren't you getting tired?"

"Not at all," said Baggi brusquely.

This was a lie. His feet ached, and Guthini wasn't exaggerating; he had kept up Sowilo for the better part of the past three hours, his junior relieving him only in what short bursts he could manage.

Baggi's limbs were shaky, like after a long day of trekking without a meal, and his head was spinning.

"I can keep going," he insisted. "We need to find her."

"Baggi," his partner said gently, "even if we do, we won't be able to make it back tonight unless we turn around now. We can keep looking on the way back. Or maybe someone else already found her, maybe we'll get back and find out we've been worried over nothing!"

The newly appointed Staffkeeper sighed helplessly. He looked around in a slow, sweeping circle, as if he still might find Kettil at the last moment if only he kept searching, but of course she was not there. He listened hard for her demanding voice, her laugh that was somehow friendly and derisive at once. But the only noises that fell upon his ears were the buzzing of nocturnal insects and his companions' ragged breaths.

"Perhaps," he granted, not believing even himself. He turned to lead them back toward Flamebud Village, motioning with an arm to follow.

***

The Flamebud Inn was sadly subdued. As Baggi pushed open the door, hopeful eyes greeted him, then many shoulders slumped as their gazes returned to their tables or mugs.

Not quite the reception I was hoping for, he thought. Torny attended to tables in respectful silence, refilling mugs and clearing plates without a word. Baggi made for his regular place at the bar with a heavy heart.

"Baggi!" called Hjordis from a table across the room. She motioned him over.

"Yes?" he said wearily as he approached.

Hjordis indicated he should sit; he did so. On his left sat Sage Runa, on his right Sage Ingrid. They had never spoken before, never had the occasion to, but the boy felt immediately at ease in her presence. She nodded towards him with a polite smile on her round face, running a distractible hand through the light brown hair cropped above her ears as she did so.

"Congratulations, Staffkeeper Baggi," said Ingrid by way of introduction. "Although I wish the circumstances of your accomplishment were not so worrisome."

"You honor me," Baggi replied automatically. "I assume there has been no news?"

"You were the last group back," said Hjordis. She sighed. "We were all holding out hope you boys would find her."

He chuckled humorlessly. "My apologies."

"I am afraid your Marking has been delayed until the search is resolved," said Runa, "Did your party prove acceptable?"

Baggi was tired, fighting to keep his eyes open; he had no energy for subtext. "What do you mean?" he asked.

"Would you like to change your group's composition, Staffkeeper Baggi?"

"Oh," he replied, "no, Guthini was fine. So was Frodi."

"Then I suggest you sleep now. The caravan will be doing likewise, now that your group has returned. Rest well, for we will resume the search come morning. You may, of course, relocate to the Staffkeepers' room if you wish."

Baggi shook his head. "It doesn't matter where I sleep. The sooner I rest, the sooner I can get back out there."

He stood, bowed half-heartedly to his elders and left them. The apprentices looked at him curiously when he entered the room, but they said nothing. No one seemed in a talking mood. Baggi crossed his legs and laid Compromise on his lap to Contemplate and devise a search plan. Yet try as he might, all he could think of was the great danger Kettil might be in. *Just like she said when we went in after Elof and Hjordis. There could be dangerous animals, or locals who hate our types.* A chill ran through him and Compromise both. *That's just paranoia,* he reassured himself, *We must stay optimistic.* Compromise pulsed uncomfortably, clearly unconvinced, but it didn't press.

Baggi sighed and uncrossed his legs, then laid on his back with his ashen cloak under his head. "Tomorrow," he promised in a whisper. "I'll find you tomorrow."

***

Amund ducked right and retaliated with a low hook. Vigi managed to backstep in time, but the chief's fist grazed his body, and even such a graze was enough to inflict great pain. The hunter couldn't fight the urge to double over slightly, and Amund took full advantage of the split-second opening, unfolding his arm into his opponent's face as his leg swept the hunter off his feet. Vigi landed on his back in the dirt and groaned. Amund grinned and offered him a hand.

"That was better," he said.

The younger lad snorted in irritation as he took the proffered hand and regained his feet.

"Not better enough," he said.

"Yes," Amund agreed.

He sent the winded boy back in line to recover and waved on his next sparring partner. Kalfr stepped timidly forward. He had no fighting uniform yet, only pants rolled up past his knees and a washed-out orange shirt.

"Have you been practicing your stance?" Amund asked.

"Yes," the boy gulped, "but I'm still scared."

"Relax, Kalfr," he commanded. "You cannot move quickly if you are tense. And besides, we will not be sparring. You are still too young; only footwork for you. Try to stomp my foot without letting me stomp yours. Are you ready?"

And without waiting for an answer, Amund surged forward. Kalfr yelped but somehow managed to keep the fighting stance the chief had taught him. *He is stiff,* noted Amund, *but experience will take that from him.* He stomped at nearly half-speed, raising his foot higher than necessary in order to accommodate the child's yet unrefined reflexes. Still, he barely managed to draw his foot back in time. To Amund's pleasant surprise, the young lad retaliated with his own stomp immediately, though he leaned too far back as he probed.

"Closer," Amund commanded as he easily dodged, "You do not have my range, so you must get closer."

Kalfr obeyed, rushing in and stomping in a mad frenzy as if trying to squash his own fear. Amund maintained his footwork and smoothly danced around stomp after stomp, finally catching his pupil's foot with his own only when the younger boy's attacks began to slow.

"You have bravery," he said in closing, "now you must learn grace. Stay relaxed. Keep practicing."

He released the trapped foot and ruffled the boy's hair. Kalfr beamed and skipped back in line. *Very promising,* thought the Chief of Flamebud. Ever since Amund's confrontation with Geir at the market, the adolescent carrot farmer had been attending the morning training sessions every day. *It is good that he wishes to defend himself, rather than be defended.* Amund waved on the last fighter. Torny stepped up, wearing a short, sleeveless tunic and loose-fitting pants cuffed at the ankle, hair tightly restrained. The innkeeper held a wooden sparring knife in each hand. She tossed him one, and he twirled it in his hand as he caught it.

"You have not worn fighting garb in some time," Amund grinned. "Shall I go easy on you?"

Torny snorted and took her stance without comment. Amund shrugged and did likewise. His cousin held her knife in the earth grip, blade protruding from her fist on the side opposite her thumb, while he held his in the more orthodox sky grip. Both fighters stepped lightly, rolling their bodies to mask intentions and feinting as they dipped in and out of range. When he felt comfortable with her movements, Amund lunged with a lightning quick thrust. Torny hooked his arm with the back of her blade and turned it aside, stepping in and striking back directly upwards at his chin. He pivoted away then sent an angled knee toward her chest. She caught it with both forearms and forced it back to ground, using the momentum to push back out of range. They both grinned with exhilaration.

"I have missed this," said Amund.

"Me too," Torny admitted.

She stepped in again, swiping rapidly at his face and neck. Amund parried each blow and waited. When she at last feinted high and sunk low to swipe at his leg, he was prepared. He lifted his leg defensively, catching her arm before the strike could land, then opened his shoulders like an archer as he snapped a backhanded punch at her jaw. She managed to block with her left arm, but now the momentum was his. In desperation to make distance, Torny shot up and overextended with a high downward slash. Amund snared her right arm with his left, spun to disrupt her footing, and as she instinctively flailed her left arm for balance, struck her neck with his wooden weapon, tempering the force expertly.

He released Torny and stepped back, maintaining his guard out of habit. Torny gasped a bit, rubbing at her neck. It would bruise, but Amund had masterful control and the damage was not serious.

"I'm just a little out of practice," she said defiantly.

"You are," agreed Amund, "though I am impressed with how much you have retained." He formed the Sign of Flame towards his students, a gesture they returned in kind. "The sun has fully risen. Go begin your work," he dismissed them.

Already the day was hot. Torny sat on the edge of the well to catch her breath while Amund hauled a bucket from its depths.

"Kalfr's fighting now? I didn't expect that," panted the innkeeper.

"Yes, I inspired him at the market," boasted Amund.

"Good for you."

Amund sloshed water on his bare chest and face, then shook his hair to dry. "How long have you been absent?" he asked, pulling his shirt back on over his still-wet body. "Months, it seems."

"Yeah," she replied, "a few months." She took the bucket and dumped its remaining contents over her head, sighing as the cool liquid soaked her head to toe.

"You would have stood a better chance had you been practicing during those months. Your assistance in instruction would also be appreciated."

Torny rolled her eyes good-naturedly. "Thanks, chief. Some of us have businesses to run. I should be making breakfast for our guests right now."

"A poor excuse," Amund complained. "If I have time to train and fulfill my duties as Chief of Flamebud Village, then you must also have time." He fastened his *korta* about his shoulders and his sword belt around his waist.

"Ha!" laughed Torny. "Right, 'your duties'. Like sitting up in the pass all day and intimidating people. Which you haven't even been doing lately."

"Those are not my only duties," argued Amund. "I, too, am responsible for making our guests welcome and representing the hospitality of Flamebud Village."

"And yet, I'm the one who ends up doing all the work."

Amund was ready to make a retort concerning his hard labors on the puppet show and the flamebud garden besides, but then the Shaefini began filing out of the inn in groups of three.

"Oh, no," sighed Torny. "Speaking of hospitality, they're heading out without breakfast. That's never wise."

"Heading out?" repeated Amund incredulously. "They are leaving?"

"What? No," said Torny, "they're looking for Kettil. Didn't you hear she's missing?"

"Of course not!" Amund all but roared. "We should be searching with them!"

"Amund, calm down," Torny said, not unkindly. "There's only so many directions, and they've got a system down that covers all of them already. I think the best thing we can do is be here. If she finds her way back, she'll want to see a familiar face."

Amund seethed at his own helplessness. *Such a crisis in my own village,* he lamented, *and I did not even know. I have failed today.* He focused on his inner flame and fed the shame to it. It burned away and left him energized despite the intensive training session. *I must atone.* He marched and Torny followed, back to the inn, dripping the whole way. Amund scanned the uniforms while his cousin scurried into the kitchen, and when he spotted a single scorched grey cloak among the remaining Shaefini, he was glad that Baggi had never taken Talia up on her offers to repair the garment.

The northern boy was tapping his foot impatiently as another child, slightly younger, hastily struggled with an overflowing alchemy box. The younger child mumbled something apologetic in Flowspeak. Guthini, who Amund had not at first noticed standing behind Baggi, offered a soothing remark. Baggi said something else; he sounded terse.

"Baggi!" Amund hailed after he had stepped lightly behind him. "You are going to search for Kettil?" He spoke the Base Tongue for the apprentices' benefit.

Baggi greeted him with mild surprise. "Good morning, Amund," he said, matching the language. "Yes, we're leaving as soon as Frodi has his alchemy box packed."

"There!" said the lad, presumably Frodi, as the container finally snapped shut. "We can go now!"

"Good," said Baggi. "I'll see you when I return, Amund."

"Wait," urged the chief. "What if you should find danger? I shall send fighters with your groups."

"Amund," Baggi sighed, "we really don't have time. Frodi has delayed us long enough already." Frodi looked at the floor, stricken. "Through no fault of his own," Baggi added hastily.

"Then I will join you," Amund declared. "As I am already here, there will be no delay."

"Okay," he relented immediately, "thank you. We go west."

Torny materialized among them with two baskets. She handed one to Baggi and one to Amund. "Breakfast for the road," she said. Unlike her cousin, she spoke in her native language with no consideration for the others. "That should be enough for all four of you."

"Torny," Baggi smiled wearily, yet again switching tongues to match her speech, "I can't thank you enough."

"Just find her and be back in time for dinner," she grinned. "I'll make something special to celebrate your success."

Ignoring Frodi's questioning glances after the brief exchange, Amund allowed Baggi to lead the way. His Naefjan friend seemed needful of some measure of control. He reached into a basket and passed around fried frog legs as they entered the woods.

"Searching west was a wise impulse," he offered between bites. "Our allies of Takkin can be found in in this direction, and slightly south. They are the nearest village from Flamebud."

"The next village?" Baggi gaped. He slipped back into Flowspeak momentarily in his excitement, before catching himself and reverting to the Base Tongue. "Perfect! If she wandered into it, she would still be there now! Let's go!" He adjusted their direction and doubled the pace.

Amund grinned and trailed just behind. *It is a welcome change, being the follower,* he thought.

***

"So, uh.... where are we goin'?" Kettil asked as they rode.

She shared a saddle with Hakon, and although they had only begun riding less than an hour ago, her legs already ached. Their steed maintained the rear position in their miniature caravan. Its gait was listless and heavy, sending unpleasant shocks through the saddle and riders with each step. It annoyed her that Hakon seemed perfectly comfortable.

"We're following Valdis," he answered.

"Okay," huffed Kettil impatiently, "but where is she goin'?"

"I don't think she really knows," Hakon said thoughtfully, "but her palette is incredible; she can taste Death from halfway across Solabell. Maybe even farther. So, she follows it, and we follow her, and eventually we find the next person who needs our help."

"And by 'help', you mean..." she trailed off, uncomfortable with the implication.

"We kill them, so they don't suffer."

Kettil snorted sarcastically. "Yeah, that makes sense."

"It will," Hakon assured her, unperturbed, "once you see it. Some people are in a lot of pain, but no one will just let them die, even if they want to. Especially back home."

"In Naefja?" Kettil asked. "You're Naefjan too, right?"

"Yes, I'm Naefjan too."

They rode in silence for a while. Whereas Kettil had tromped through the woods, intending to obfuscate her location from any searchers, The Conclusion followed an established road traveling east. Their boldness surprised her.

"Aren't you worried someone will see you? People don't like Staffkeepers of Death, you know."

"I know," Hakon smiled. "But it's much nicer being on the road."

"Well," said Kettil, "it probably won't be so nice if someone comes along and kills you."

He shrugged. "Nothing to do but accept it then."

Kettil shook her head incredulously. "So you don't care if you die?" she asked.

"Obviously I don't want to," replied Hakon, "not before it's my proper time. That's the important part, you see, and Valdis made sure I remembered it." He twisted in the saddle and pointed to the scar on his neck and face. "But if someone kills me, it doesn't really matter whether I want to keep living or not, does it? I'm already dead."

"Isn't that somethin'," mumbled Kettil. Hakon seemed not to hear her. "Why'd she have to clobber you to teach you that?" she continued. "I like the old-fashioned way where you just tell someone the lesson and then they know it."

"I made a mistake," he answered, "a bad one, in a village near here, actually. I was new, and my sense for Death was still unreliable, so I got confused and started to claim a girl who wasn't ready. Well, we got chased off before I was done, but that's not the point, you know. She had to make sure I understood how much pain I had caused. It was my fault, and I deserved what I got."

The sun cleared the treetops on either side of the road and began to shine down on them in earnest. Kettil closed her eyes and let its warmth relax her. It had been a confusing and frightening evening, and when she awoke in the morning to find its events truth, rather than nightmare, her heart had begun accelerating and her mind filled with an addling guilt. Kettil had thought these symptoms would leave her once she relaxed, but among her new companions, who wore mementos of their kills and spoke of Death as others spoke of the weather, this was easier said than done. The bumpy ride certainly didn't help alleviate her pain either. Yet she saw no other choice before her than to remain among them until an opportunity to part presented itself, preferably without their notice.

"So if you're from Naefja," she said, trying to distract herself from the discomfort but also straining to understand her new caravan, "why didn't you just join up with the Staffkeepers of Shaefi?"

Hakon glanced toward the front of the column. He seemed nervous. After a moment, the other riders offered no reaction, and he responded:

"I tried, at first. When I turned ten, I went off to the Temple at Enton to be taught. But I was cast out."

"Why?" asked Kettil.

"Because I got in a fight," Hakon replied. There was a touch of pride in his voice.

"That was dumb," said Kettil.

"Maybe," agreed Hakon, "but I don't regret it. And if I hadn't been cast out, Valdis wouldn't have found me, and I never would have known what a talent I have. It was a blessing, really."

"A blessing from Death?" queried Kettil, then snorted. "You're strange."

"Not a Blessing, not in the way Shaefini think of it," said Hakon. "Valdis says what they call Blessings are really just talents, but they can't understand anything unless Shaefi's involved."

Kettil wondered if Baggi had received his Blessing yet. She wondered if he had even completed his third Task. It seemed more likely than not.

A far-off voice echoed through the woods. The young alchemist perked up her ears at the sound, and she was not the only one to hear it. Arni pulled gently at his reins, stopping his mount.

"Did anyone else hear that?" he asked.

The others likewise halted and strained their ears. After several moments, Kettil thought she had heard the voice again, but then, she couldn't be sure it wasn't merely birdsong. Valdis' face was inscrutable. The scar above her eye shone silver, and her bone adornments jangled slightly in the gentle breeze. Though Valdis did not look at her, Kettil felt somehow as if she were being examined, rather than the noise.

"Myrgjol," Valdis said, "what lies in that direction?"

"Several miles of woodland," replied the Kichishi Staffkeeper. It was the first time Kettil had heard her speak, and her voice was strangely soothing in its spiritedness. "Eventually it leads to a waterfall just south of Flamebud Village." After a moment's hesitation, she added, "I could not be sure, but that noise did not resemble any animal I am familiar with. It could have been a voice."

Valdis considered her counsel in silence.

"Arni, Hakon, investigate. We must not be ambushed," she finally said.

"Of course," Arni replied.

He urged his horse off the path, down the slight incline toward the noise. Hakon followed without a word.

"Hey!" yelped Kettil. "What if I wanted to stay back there?"

"Shh!" Hakon entreated her. "When Valdis makes a command, what we want is not important."

Kettil huffed loudly, but then she wondered why she was arguing in the first place. The leader of The Conclusion frightened her nearly as much as her horrifying creation from the previous night, and Hakon and even Arni were much friendlier and easier to talk to. Besides, as they approached, it became evident that the noise was, in fact, a voice or even several voices. Perhaps she could slip away from her captors with the new arrivals. She glanced at her alchemy box, secured to the saddle, and made a mental note of the quickest way to unfasten it, should the need arise.

After they had ridden some ways, Hakon dismounted quietly and helped her down. He and Arni tied their reins to branches and the older Staffkeeper held a hand to his lips for silence. Kettil nodded dishonestly. They crept through the brush in the direction of the increasingly loud voices.

"Keeeettiiiiiill!" shouted a boy from somewhere out of sight.

Her heart leapt in her chest; it seemed, despite her best efforts to be lost, that someone had found her after all. Never in her life had Kettil been so happy to fail. Unfortunately, Hakon and Arni were just as close to the sound and had no more problem deciphering its content than she. Arni motioned for them to retreat, and Hakon grabbed her by the wrist to pull her away. Kettil knew that this was her best chance to escape; she wasn't going to waste it. Feeling a sick sense of nostalgia for her orphan days, she pulled Hakon's wrist to her mouth and bit down hard, breaking the skin right away. He cried out, and she bolted in the direction of the voice.

"Help! Over here! I'm over here, help!" she screamed frantically.

The sounds of pursuit followed close behind. She heard Hakon urging her, trying to win her over with reason, but she had no intention of listening. Arni shouted less friendly but equally frantic words at her back. She ignored them too, running as quickly as possible and ducking under brush and leaping over logs with the natural athleticism of childhood. Then an obstacle emerged from the brush without warning and she crashed painfully to the ground.

"Oof," grunted her rescuer in a brilliant scarlet *korta*. He rubbed his elbow as if annoyed. Then he spotted her on the ground and grinned.

"There you are," said Amund.

***

"Kettil!" Baggi shouted, pushing through the shrubs in the direction of the distressed cry. "Amund!"

Finally he caught up, panting, just in time to see the Chief of Flamebud pull Kettil to her feet. Baggi's heart melted with relief, but before he could even cry out, two more figures entered the clearing on the opposite side. There was a man and a boy, both dressed in familiar black and adorned with bones. They carried staffs, and Baggi almost laughed. *I should have given fate more credit,* he thought. *It's crueler than I realized.* Compromise pulsed, unamused.

The boy's eyes locked on Baggi's. He looked familiar, somehow. *Naefjan,* thought Baggi, *there are many that look like him in Naefja.* Yet it seemed more than that. The other lad glanced at Baggi's staff, and in the same moment, recognition flashed in both boys' gazes.

"Baggi, right?" the lad asked. "We were just speaking of you, or close enough."

"It's you," Baggi marveled, incredulous.

"You don't remember my name?" the boy seemed half insulted, half amused.

"I never learned it. They wouldn't talk about you after you were cast out."

"It's Hakon," he smiled.

"So you were only the bait, is that it, girl?" sighed Arni. "Well we've been snared before, and I can tell you I have no interest in repeating the experience."

"I don't know what you're talking about," Kettil yelled from behind Amund's legs. "Just let me go back to my caravan!"

"Can't do that," said Arni. He sounded regretful. "Or you'll tell others, and others will come for us."

The Chief of Flamebud drew his sword as the older Staffkeeper stepped slowly forward.

"Do not approach," he hissed. "I am not so merciful as the Staffkeepers of Shaefi."

"Neither am I," chuckled the man. "Shame. I can see it's not your time. Either of you."

"Baggi, can you handle the other?" Amund demanded.

Baggi gulped, grinning to hide his nerves. "Well, I've never clashed before," he replied, "but there's a first time for everything."

Hakon smiled, a smile full of pity. "You never were a fighter, eh? Sorry about this. It's not how we usually like to do things."

He bit his thumb and smeared blood on his staff, the runes glowing a hostile crimson. Baggi bowed his head and attuned to Compromise. *We can do this,* he thought, *we can.* Compromise pulsed with nervous energy as his icy-blue aura flooded forth to meet Hakon's.

21

Baggi shivered atop a snowy mountain. The space was flat and even, the sky endless and somehow oppressive, like a miasma that pressed in on him from every conceivable angle. He looked out and saw the world; it was blurry, ill-defined. He did not think the world looked like this, yet he knew it was the world he saw. The horizon stretched forever, yet there was no sun or star light in it and he wondered how it was he could see at all. All was grey and lumpy Baggi tried to discern the features of the ground beneath him, but he could not. Wherever he focused his gaze, only a melding grey and white pattern presented itself. It was like a dream, wherein his peripheral sight was clear as day, yet the moment he turned to look more closely, the nature of what he saw began to fade and he suddenly forgot what he was looking at in the first place.

The painful crack of wood on his face brought momentary lucidity. Baggi fell to his hands and knees in the snow. His fingers were cold, or perhaps they were the idea of cold. He touched his lips and saw his blood on them, or perhaps his life or perhaps his soul. He pushed to his feet with Compromise, his staff's texture constant and grounding, and looked behind him. Hakon stood there, his own staff in hand, not quite facing his opponent. The wood in his hand bore Baggi's blood, just a bit. He felt indignance at the theft, and the pain on his face intensified.

"You don't understand," said Hakon as if disappointed.

A new type of pain flowed from his words and settled in Baggi's skull. Compromise pulsed steadily, urging its partner to stay calm.

"You're right," said Baggi, taking a deep breath and rebalancing his emotions through force of habit. He didn't know whether he responded to Compromise or Hakon, but it seemed to be the right choice. The pain subsided. "I have never clashed," he continued. His words felt heavy and slow like cold syrup. "Will you teach me?"

Hakon recoiled as if slapped. He growled quietly, still not looking directly at him.

"Why? You will be dead soon, and then it won't matter," he replied. "But I will help you, so it doesn't hurt so long."

As he spoke Baggi's head began to ache. *Perhaps it would be nice to let him win,* he entertained. *It does hurt, after all.* Compromise pulsed with concern. *That sounds foolish, doesn't it?* He thought. *It's a good thing you're here. Elsewise I might forget who I am entirely.*

"I don't need your help," he replied. "I'll die on my own sooner or later."

Hakon frowned as the piece of Baggi he had snatched left the staff in his hand and returned to its owner. With it came a piece of Hakon, dark and roiling. When it joined him, Baggi felt an impatience that wasn't his own.

"So this is you?" he asked with great fascination. "You seem frustrated."

Hakon was panting. Baggi found this, too, fascinating. *Is he tiring? Does that mean Hakon's body is here? Or just that a version of Hakon's body is here?* He remembered the last time he had been spirited away, during the cleansing of the sigil. It was difficult to recall, like digging a hole through sand that keeps filling itself in, but Compromise provided his focus. *It must be like then,* he concluded, *our bodies are still back in the woods. Probably just standing there. It must look funny.*

"Imagine a horse breaks a leg," said Hakon. "You know it needs to be killed, else it will only suffer for the rest of its life. But holding it down and doing the job is still tiring. It makes you mad that you have to be the one. But someone must."

He strode casually around Baggi as he spoke. When he was finishing, Hakon punctuated the last sentence with a blow of his staff to Baggi's knee. Baggi crumpled and winced, hurting in his leg and his skull even knowing neither were here. Again, his blood left him, but it was not so much as to alarm.

"It sounds hard," he agreed. "Much easier to try to heal the horse, isn't it? You could have spent the time holding it down applying medicine, or at least sending for someone else who can do it for you."

He tried to rise as the skull pain departed but found his knee had not recovered. *Was that not enough, then?* He wondered. *Or am I missing something?*

Hakon sighed. "You are persistent. I haven't clashed much myself, but those I have met started to lose focus right away. Seems like you're too sharp for that. But that doesn't matter; you're still going to lose. You know why?" he asked. His words began to echo painfully in Baggi's mind once more.

"No. Please tell me," he replied. It mitigated the harm, but only slightly.

"Because you don't fight, and that's what a clash is," Hakon said.

He raised his staff overhead and brought it down hard on Baggi's skull, driving him to the ground once more. As his face met the frozen stone beneath, lifeblood poured from Baggi's nose and mouth. *That hurts,* he thought, all other words abandoning him in his time of need, *it hurts so much.* Compromise pulsed in alarm. *What?* Baggi managed through a haze. *I know he's killing me, but you'll be okay. Calm down.* His staff bellowed at him to stand and prove Hakon wrong, to rise to his feet and fight with whatever blood he had left. *We don't fight, remember? I should have thought of that. This was foolish.* He thought of Amund dancing in the market, beautiful and gentle as he struck out at his opponent. He remembered his triumph over Audr in the council meeting, and how the chief had commended him for his performance. He wondered why he was remembering these things now, felt the answer just out of reach with the pain and the bizarre grey place between them. And then Compromise pulled those memories together and force-fed them to Baggi as one.

Oh, he thought, or perhaps said, *I see now. They're the same. Debate and combat. It's all fighting, in the end. Just different styles.*

"'That is a foolish distinction,'" Baggi quoted as he struggled painfully to his feet, "Isn't that what he said?"

Without warning, he pivoted on his good leg and swung Compromise hard into Hakon's throat. He used the Chief of Flamebud's grace, an elegance that wasn't his, plucked directly from his memory and wielded as a weapon in this place where mind and body were one. A crack rang out, the same sickly crack of a windpipe breaking that had lingered in his mind since the market day.

"I hope that doesn't kill you," said Baggi. He meant it. "But there's no sense in holding back, is there? A friend of mine says you must use your full effort in order to win. Otherwise, it's disrespectful. He didn't take his own advice with Geir," he granted, "but apparently he didn't deserve respect in the first place, and you do."

Hakon grasped at his throat as the blood flowed between the duelists once more. Baggi felt his own life replenished in the exchange, and a surplus from Hakon filling him as well. His opponent was baffled, at a complete loss.

"You're Shaefini," he gasped. "You can't do this."

"I did do this," replied Baggi, perplexed by the assumption.

"Then," snarled Hakon as he rose, "you have abandoned Shaefi." His words were short, but heavy. They seized Baggi's mind in a cold, terrifying grip and squeezed hard.

Have I? he wondered.

"I don't think so," he said pensively. "We've always fought. I think I'm just the first one to admit it."

And just like that, Hakon's footing melted away. He fell to the floor once more, the very ground under his feet fading to nothingness and denying him the chance to stand. Eventually, he stopped trying, falling motionless to the ground in a great crater that had formed beneath him. Only then did the mountain stabilize. His life filtered out of him and took refuge inside Compromise. When it was nearly depleted and Hakon lay shivering in the snow, Baggi shut the gate and forced the last dregs of his opponent's soul to stay in his body.

"I suppose I won," he said. It didn't feel real, but then nothing in this realm felt quite real. He glanced down at his fallen foe, still as a stone and already accumulating rime. "You look cold," he said, "but I'm afraid you're going to get much colder."

***

Amund panted heavily, his ribs where his opponent had struck throbbing with each inhalation. The Staffkeeper of Death had been skillful, much more skillful than he ought to have been and far more capable than expected. Yet as the blood dripping from Amund's sword attested, he had not been skillful enough. Arni coughed weakly and said something in Flowspeak.

Amund delivered the finishing blow tastefully, as cleanly as possible, kneeling as he plunged his sword into the man's chest. He removed the weapon and wiped the blade clean with an oiled cloth, allowing blood to pump freely, painting the brown grass red. The light in Arni's eyes was extinguished in moments.

"What did he say?" asked the Chief of Flamebud after a moment of respectful silence.

"'The End'," Kettil answered seriously.

"Did…did you kill him?" asked Guthini in a weak voice.

She rolled her eyes. "No, he just needs some patching up. Go ahead," she said.

Her sarcasm was not lost on Guthini. He gulped loudly. He and Frodi had caught up during the battle; their arrival had caused the distraction that led to Amund taking a staff-blow in the first place. *I should not have lost focus,* the chief reprimanded himself. *The wound would have been far more dire, had he wielded a blade of his own.*

"It's just that I've never seen someone die before," the apprentice whispered to no one in particular.

Kettil looked away. Amund thought he saw an emotion close to jealousy flash across her face, an emotion that echoed in him as well. Guthini's gaze remained transfixed by the corpse for several moments before he shook his head and turned to observe the second battle, yet unresolved. Baggi and Hakon both stood perfectly still, eyes closed and minds far away. Amund had never witnessed a clash before, but even to the untrained eye the advance of Hakon's crimson aura was deeply frightening. Baggi's own aura was shrinking, giving ground and occasionally retaliating. He seemed not to be keeping pace with his opponent.

"Should we, y'know…" Guthini said vaguely, motioning toward Hakon.

Amund glared at him. "Are you asking me to kill Baggi's opponent while he cannot defend himself?"

"Um...yes?" squeaked Guthini.

Amund felt fury explode inside him and forced himself to contain it. *He is a foreigner, and does not know what he says,* he told himself.

"Do not dare to insult my honor again," he snapped, "or the honor of Baggi." He turned to watch the clash with arms crossed and jaw set. "He will win."

"But we don't fight," mumbled the apprentice meekly.

The chief rolled his eyes but said nothing.

Suddenly, Baggi's aura roared back in a great wave of magic. It washed away the crimson in one thundering expansion, leaving only the smallest flecks of red as it encircled Hakon's body. Baggi gasped loudly and sank to one knee, panting, as Hakon simultaneously fell to the floor without grace, unconscious. Baggi struggled over to the other boy and held Compromise over his body. *He will not kill him,* Amund thought, *of that I am sure. Yet what is he doing?*

Baggi filled his lungs with a mighty inhalation. "Algiz-Isaz," he invoked.

He slowly breathed a snowy mist over Hakon. It swirled around him, settled onto his body, then disappeared. Baggi knelt and held his wrist against Hakon's skin. He nodded, apparently satisfied, and collapsed himself.

The apprentices rushed to him and began jabbering over each other, all rushing to provide support. Kettil roughly shoved the others away, claiming precedence due to their history. Baggi laughed, and when the laugh ceased, they sat in silence. The others waited uncertainly for someone to speak. Without warning, Baggi reached out and hugged Kettil.

"I was worried," he said.

Kettil sniffled. "Are you alright?" she asked.

"Me?" he chuckled, "I'm fine." He looked at the corpse in the clearing and touched his lips thoughtfully before turning to Amund. "I see you were victorious as well," he said. "Can't say I'm surprised."

"Yes," agreed Amund, "but he did land a strike." He began to lean to one side, stretching, before a sudden shooting pain caused him to stop. He winced.

"Hey, we can fix that!" said Kettil, alarmed. "We just gotta grab my alchemy box. It's back with the horses. Not you," she scoffed as Baggi made to rise, then turned to Amund, "and not you either. You two aren't in a good way. We can get it."

She motioned impatiently towards Guthini and Frodi. The intimidated lads bowed in acquiescence and scurried over. Amund frowned.

"Is that wise?" he asked. "We have only just found you. To lose you, any of you, would be unacceptable."

"Oh, relax," huffed Kettil, "we'll be gone two minutes. If we're not back then, come after."

Before either Amund or Baggi could further protest, she jogged off past Arni's corpse, not sparing it a second glance. Guthini and Frodi followed, though the grisly monument to Amund's victory pulled their attention as they went. Both remaining boys sighed and looked at each other with tired eyes. Then Amund grinned.

"Well fought," he said.

"And you as well," Baggi smiled back. "I don't suppose he's had his funeral rites yet?"

Amund shook his head, and Baggi limped over to the dead man. He began chanting in Flowspeak, then abruptly stopped. He started up again after a moment, but he was no longer chanting. Amund couldn't make out what he was saying, but the tone was different; it sounded more conversational. Eventually he stopped and began fidgeting with his cloak. A sudden thought seemed to occur to him. Baggi scraped a pinch of ash from his cloak and tossed it lightly over Arni's body. The Staffkeeper wore an expression of mourning, yet it carried satisfaction as well. He managed to rise to his feet and strolled back toward Hakon, his thoughts clearly elsewhere.

"What did you do to him?" Amund inquired as he, too, approached. He stooped to examine the boy's motionless body.

"I froze him," explained Baggi, shaking himself to attention, "with Isaz, the ice rune, and Algiz as well. It's sort of a new application. I wasn't sure it would work."

Amund laid a hand on Hakon's forehead. It was still warm.

"Yet he is not frozen," he observed.

"It's difficult to explain," said Baggi, nonetheless giving it his best effort. "While I was clashing, I learned a great deal. I went somewhere else, a place where the physical and the mental and the spiritual were not distinct things. They all simply...were. It was bizarre." He stopped talking, a far-off look in his eyes. Amund cleared his throat and Baggi snapped to. "Well, while I was there it became clear to me that things are not as literal as I thought."

"Which things do you mean?" asked Amund. His friend's words were vague and nonsensical in his ears.

"All things," Baggi answered. He thought hard, searching for a clearer explanation. Eventually he gave up and shrugged. "Like I said, it's difficult to explain. But the important thing is that Hakon is frozen in place. It won't last forever, of course, but I should be able to keep it up until we return to the village."

Amund glanced at Baggi with a raised eyebrow. "You want to take him back with us?"

"Well, yes," said Baggi uneasily. "Is that okay? I don't know what else to do with him, but the Elder Sage will have a solution, no doubt."

"I could kill him," suggested Amund with obvious reluctance, "if you release him and allow him to fight."

Baggi looked off and gave the suggestion serious thought. *That is good. He is thinking it through,* thought Amund. Eventually Baggi shook his head.

"No, I don't think we should kill him," he said. "We can learn a lot from Hakon. And even if that weren't the case, I wouldn't want him dead."

Amund snorted. "He wanted you dead."

"Perhaps he did."

The Chief of Flamebud sighed as the young ones returned, leading two dark horses by the reins. "As it is your request, we shall take him with us," he consented.

"Thank you," Baggi said.

"We should probably get out of here," said Guthini, glancing around nervously. "There might be more of them."

"Only two, and they're waiting way up the hill," said Kettil dismissively.

"I doubt they have stayed in place after such a long time," frowned Amund. "Still, merely two is welcome news. Come."

They loaded Hakon onto a saddle and secured him in place with spare ropes found in the saddlebags. It turned out to be an exceptionally difficult procedure, as Baggi's spell had not only rendered the boy immobile, but also paralyzed him in the exact position he had collapsed in. Luckily, Amund was an experienced rider and knew several tricks for efficiently loading the saddle. Hakon balanced like a beam on a scale, wobbling back and forth the whole way. Flamebud Village was an hour or so on foot, yet the party remained largely silent throughout the journey.

Finally, their destination appeared. Amund turned to his friend.

"Are you certain this is your wish?" he asked.

Baggi nodded.

"Very well," said Amund, "then let us consult with your Elder Sage."

***

Elof kicked a rock in a rare spat of rage. He immediately regretted the act, as the stone ricocheted and clonked hard against his shin. He made a loud, indistinct noise, half pain and half frustration.

"Elof!" cried Sage Ingrid as she rushed to his side. "Are you well?"

The alchemist motioned with a stiff arm toward the sheer wall of stone blocking their path.

"Another dead end," Ingrid acknowledged. She sighed with restraint; the gesture of impatience was irritatingly polite. "Seems we'll need to double back for a bit and go around."

"And how long will, all, of that, well, take?" mumbled Elof. "We'll, ah, we'll never, never find her at the rate we're going."

The alchemist's anxieties about Kettil produced a stutter in addition to his usual nervous speech habits. This happened infrequently, on occasions when he was under incredible duress. Elof struggled to contain his emotions, tears rising in his eyes. He began to feel sorry for himself, which only turned his mood ever bleaker.

"We may not," agreed Ingrid, "but someone will." She gave Elof a sympathetic hug.

"I, ah, wish I could, um, well, share your calm," Elof sighed.

Ingrid pulled away and looked at him incredulously. "You could, you know. It's just a matter of practice and faith."

Elof focused on a patch of wild tulips. "I, ah, don't believe it could be that easy."

The flowers swayed lightly in the breeze, their cup-shaped petals and elegant stems far more reassuring to Elof than Ingrid's words could ever be. He knelt and reached out a hand, gently stroking the red-and-white flowers' swirling patterns. As he did so, he felt their youth on his fingertips, their stems so fragile in his hands, so strong in their own will. He smelled the wild allure of their pollen, sugary and bright, yet lighter than the finest sweets humans could produce. He saw the exact measurements of their patterns, but these he closed his eyes and ignored; it would not do to subject the plants to mathematics. Elof allowed the flowers to overwhelm his senses, cradling them gently in his hands, and after some time had passed, he found his serenity.

He stood up and turned back to Ingrid. The Sage had watched him without interrupting. Elof was glad she was a tactful woman.

"You look better," she said, smiling joyfully.

"Let's keep searching," he replied.

As they doubled back to find another path, Elof thought of the day he had found Kettil. *Yngmuth was a hard place,* he told himself, *much harder than here. If she could survive there, she must be well now.* His thoughts drifted away as Ingrid led.

***

It had been a rainy day, but the port of Yngmuth was well prepared for inclement weather. The market stalls boasted water-proof tarps to keep goods and proprietors protected from the elements. Even on a sunny day, spray from the ocean could be a hazard for those closest the docks. There was a common saying in Yngmuth: 'If you plan on doing business, your first investment should be in a tarp.'

Alchemist Elof huddled under a large market tent with an awning, alchemy box in hand. He generally avoided marketplaces; the bustling businesses caused his sharp senses to turn on him, transforming a gift for perception into a clamorous curse. But he was in Yngmuth, not Enton, and restocking his alchemical supplies was not so easy as simply walking downstairs to the storeroom. Elof adjusted his waxen earplugs, an invention of his own design, and wished there existed spectacles that dampened the wearer's sight rather than enhancing it. *There would be no demand for it,* he thought miserably, *but perhaps I could craft a pair for myself.* He knew much about medicine; it was his trade, after all. Still, he was not a lens-crafter, and the project would be more than a casual commitment.

He leaned down the lane and scanned the crowd for a stall that might fit his needs. As he did so, his keen gaze couldn't miss a forlorn wooden cart standing in the rain without a tarp. In truth, it was closer to a box than even a mercantile cart. Elof couldn't see the owner from this angle, but he saw the glowing of a potion in a tiny hand. *Perhaps a potion stall?* He thought. *But without a tarp? How irresponsible. It must be a charlatan.* But if it weren't a charlatan, merely an ignorant alchemist, it was his duty to educate them on the dangers of improper potion storage. *I could be rushing to conclusions,* he thought without much optimism. He sighed, then looked around nervously before plunging into the stream of foot-traffic.

As he approached, the voice from the cart began to make itself heard amongst the shouts of many. It sounded like a girl, and a rather young one at that. Elof deduced it must be an apprentice from the Guild. *That would explain the carelessness,* he thought. *The Guild standards are slipping to let an apprentice with so little knowledge go to market.* As sailors' shoulders buffeted him in their wake, Elof squeezed out of the main crowd before the cart.

"POTIONS!" a little girl screamed from behind the counter. "GET YOUR POTIONS! I GOT BONEGROW! I GOT KNIT! YOU NEED IT, I GOT IT!"

Elof clamped his hands over his ears and winced in pain.

"Please," he whimpered, "if you, ah, wouldn't, well, wouldn't mind, that is, lowering your voice?"

He glanced at the child. She was tiny, even smaller and younger than Elof had expected. Her hair was silver-blond, like many Naefjans, and it fell past her waist in knots and clumps. She was dirty, bruised all over, and dressed from countless scraps of cloths stitched roughly together, yet she stood up straight as the haughtiest merchant. She cocked an eyebrow at him.

"Uh, sorry, I guess," she said, not sounding sorry in the slightest. "Just tryin' to bring in business. You wanna buy a potion?" She pushed a plank of wood into his hands with Naefjan script carved into it listing the names of potions and, beside them, a price in odd.

The moment the plank touched his hands, Elof knew it to be driftwood. He knew it to be weak and worthless. Yet he also knew it to be waterproof, at least more so than parchment, and certainly more so than the potions themselves. He examined the cart with its barren countertop.

"You, ah, sell these?" he asked.

"Uh huh."

"I don't, well, I don't wish to insult you, but, ah, where...?" he trailed off awkwardly.

"Hey!" she snarled. "Are you tryin' to rob me? Lemme tell you, you wouldn't be the first! And I bite!"

The girl bared her teeth at him and hissed like a snow leopard. By all rights it ought to have been a ridiculous display, yet he unconsciously took a step backward.

"No, no, no!" he insisted. "I, um, I'm looking for supplies. For my own potions." He held up his alchemy box for her to see. "See? I'm an alchemist, same as you."

She snorted derisively. "We're not the same. Just look at you!" She gestured vaguely to his clothing. Elof pulled his Shaefini cloak tighter, suddenly self-conscious. "Guilders," she scoffed.

"Ah, no, well, I'm not in the Guild," he rushed to say. *And we are the same. Those bruises on your face are all too familiar,* he thought. But he kept that to himself.

"Well fine!" she huffed. "Look, do you wanna buy something or not? You're holdin' up the line!" She gestured behind him, where no such line existed.

"You sell Knit?" he asked, perusing the makeshift menu.

"Yep!"

"May I see it before I buy?"

She glared at him suspiciously until he procured double the asking price from his arm ring. Then she unlatched a door on the cart and reached inside. She held up a small bottle of apricot-colored liquid. *It certainly looks like a fair quality,* he thought as he examined it.

"Where do you get them?" he asked.

The girl laughed. "Maybe I find 'em."

"May I, ah, hold it?"

"Are you crazy?" she demanded.

"Only for a moment," he insisted, unhooking an additional three white-odd from his arm ring and placing them on the counter. He pushed them towards her, out of his own reach. "For security. Please."

The girl picked up the counters and stared at him incredulously. She shrugged and handed him the potion. As he took it, Elof felt its contents through the glass. *It's Knit, after all,* he realized, *Genuine, and good quality too. This is no easy concoction.*

"You made this," he said, respect clear in his tone.

"Well...yeah," she said, "how'd you know? Most people don't believe me even when I tell 'em."

"It's, well, you might call it a, ah, talent," he said dismissively. "And it seems you have a talent as well, only yours is far greater."

The girl put her hands on her hips. "Huh! Well, I already knew it, but it's nice to hear it from someone else. So, are you gonna buy it?"

"No."

She stared at him, outrage building. "Why not?" she said through gritted teeth.

"Because I can make it better," Elof replied, then he smiled craftily. "Furthermore, I can show you how to make it better too."

The girl couldn't restrain her curiosity. "How?" she asked.

"Come with me to the Temple at Enton," he offered. "Enroll as an Alchemist Apprentice."

Her nose wrinkled with distaste. "Shaefini?" she asked, seemingly annoyed by the concept. She crossed her arms and thought about it for several long moments. Then she shrugged. "Okay. It's not like I have anything here to stay for."

Elof laughed. "I know the feeling," he said.

"Lemme just pack up my stuff," the girl said. "My name's Kettil, by the way. I gave it to myself, 'cause I'm so good at potions." She looked off and rubbed her neck in embarrassment. "Well, it was 'cause I'm so good at soup, actually," she admitted, "but it works for potions too."

Elof smiled at her and extended a hand. "I am Alchemist Elof. It's a pleasure to meet you, Kettil."

***

The memory was a pleasant one, and Elof clung to it as he and Ulf walked. He recalled wheeling the potion cart to the orphanage Kettil had lived in. He recalled officially adopting her on behalf of the Staffkeepers of Shaefi. He did not recall the name of the orphanage, but he did recall how excited and proud she had been to gain a family name: Kettil Shaefisdottir, now a part of the same family as Elof Shaefisson.

"Ah, Kettil," he sighed, adjusting his spectacles, "I do hope you are well."

He heard footsteps rapidly approaching and strained his ears. They were still several minutes away, but he recognized the gait as Sage Runa's. He laid a hand on Ingrid's shoulder and indicated the direction. Ingrid stared at him with confusion but remained still in deferential silence. Eventually, Runa appeared before them.

"Alchemist Elof, Sage Ingrid," she greeted them, "I bear good news: Alchemist Apprentice Kettil has been found, and in good health."

Before she had finished speaking, Elof was running past her, back to Flamebud Village.

22

The boy began to stir as Hrafn released the spell holding him. He shook his head drowsily, looking about the room with bleary eyes. Despite the room's heat, he shivered. Hrafn allowed him time to reorient and thaw as he poured two cups of tea with a steady hand. The boy attempted to rise, found himself unable to, and instead used his shaky legs to push across the floor to the wall opposite the Elder Sage. Hrafn approached slowly, leaving Mischief on the far side of the room as a gesture of non-aggression, then sat on the floor several feet away and offered him a cup. The boy glared at him, still shivering, yet after several moments he could resist the comfort no longer and leaned forward to snatch the tea from Hrafn's hand, spilling several drops as he did so. The Elder Sage sighed, his age wearing on him terribly.

"I am Hrafn," he said. "It's good to see you awake. I never had my doubts; you seem a healthy lad. Yet I have been wrong many times before."

His surly companion slurped his tea in silence.

"Your name is Hakon?" Hrafn asked rhetorically. "Would you like any milk or honey for your tea, Hakon?"

Hakon scoffed at the suggestion and made no reply. Hrafn shrugged good-naturedly.

"You have become accustomed to the taste of bitterness quite young," the Elder Sage remarked. "It took me far longer. Even now, I almost can't drink it without a dash of milk."

"Just because it's easier to swallow doesn't make it better for you," Hakon said, breaking his silence at last.

"True," Hrafn agreed.

They sat quietly for a while, drinking their tea as Hakon's shivers gradually left him. When they had finished, Hrafn took up the teapot and poured himself another cup. Hakon held his own out reflexively, and the Elder Sage filled it without question.

"Where's my staff?" demanded Hakon after a few sips.

"Safe," Hrafn assured him. "Staffkeeper Baggi is minding it."

Hakon bristled. His jaw tightened and he looked away with shame in his eyes.

"Your staff will be returned to you," Hrafn reiterated, "of that there is no question."

"Then why take it in the first place?" asked Hakon. "You'll understand my disbelief."

"Yes, I understand," said Hrafn, full of sympathy. "I merely wished to speak with you first, and there are other legal matters to be settled before either of you can be released. But I assure you, I have no wish to see you incarcerated."

"So you're going to let me go after we talk?"

"I will allow it," said Hrafn, "but it is not solely my allowance you need." He met Hakon's rebellious gaze. "You are a clever boy, I can see, so I'll be direct with you. When you clashed with my Staffkeeper, you made an attempt on his life." He held up a gentle hand as Hakon opened his mouth in indignance. "No need to defend yourself; I don't hold it against you. But you see, my boy, this has incurred certain consequences. Staffkeeper Baggi has been granted honorary citizenship in this village in exchange for his services, and this boon has been granted by the Chief of Flamebud Village himself. You have, in effect, tried to take the life of one of his villagers. I imagine Flamebud will desire punishment."

Hakon remained remarkably composed. "I'm not afraid," he said.

"You are brave as well as clever, then," smiled Hrafn, "but I knew that much from the account of your expulsion from the Temple at Enton."

The boy's face snapped toward him. He frowned, a malicious display.

"So you know about that," he scoffed. "I shouldn't be surprised. For all the Shaefini talk of love and understanding, you have no patience for what you call mistakes."

Hrafn shook his head sadly. "I was away from the Temple at that time," he said, "but I first heard the tale when I returned, and then again an hour ago from Baggi. Had I been present, I promise you I would have opposed your exile with all my might."

Hakon laughed. "It's an easy thing to say," he replied bitterly.

"Yes. And I know that it matters not what I would have done, only what I did and did not do. I did not defend you from such an extreme course of action. Ove was a passionate man, but his passion made him reckless at times. He made a mistake in casting you out. I hope you can forgive him."

Hakon remained silent.

"The tea is gone," said Hrafn to dispel the dour mood, "so I shall now cease with my pestering. I'm glad we could talk, Hakon. This will be your lodging until it comes time for your trial. Should you need anything," he indicated a cluster of wooden chimes hanging next to the door, "simply sound the chimes."

With that he left the lad alone, a lock sliding into place behind him. Hakon glanced at the window, quickly ascertaining that breaking it to escape would cause too much noise. Then he spotted a small stack of tomes left for him on the bedside table. He picked one up.

"*The Legal Conduct and Judicial Processes of Various Staffkeeping Orders, by Aeskettil the Generous,*" he muttered aloud, then snorted in mild amusement. "Cheeky old man."

Hakon flipped it open and began to read.

***

"It wasn't as amazing as all that," said Baggi, only half-engaged in the conversation.

He kept his eyes on Hakon's staff, lying dormant in the center of the table. It was a surprisingly friendly thing, light wood with a knobby crown and six flat sides covered in runes. Baggi had expected a Staffkeeper of Death to carry something grimmer, a tool that emanated darkness and suffering, or at the very least something carved from darker wood. It unnerved him how normal it looked; he wouldn't have thought twice if he had seen it in the hands of one of his own fellow caravanners. *What is your name?* he probed, trying to establish a connection with his opponent's partner. Unsurprisingly, no answer came.

"Nonsense!" declared Amund, drawing him out of brooding. "Your victory was worthy of praise."

He shot his friend a significant look from his seat beside him and nudged him with an elbow. Baggi glanced surreptitiously toward Torny as she leaned over and dispensed drinks to the newly returned search party. She was gazing at him with an admiration that made his heart boil over. He blushed, unable to restrain himself from enjoying the attention. An amused but stern pulse from Compromise reminded him to contain his ego. *You're right,* he thought, and tried half-heartedly to rebalance his emotions.

"So you must be really good at magic," said Torny, a little too casually. She brushed her unruly hair behind an ear.

"I do my best," he replied as coolly as he could.

Amund choked on a laugh, hiding his smile behind his mug as he took a drink. Kettil returned to their stump-table, her hair thoroughly frazzled from the onslaught of hugs and affection Elof had bestowed upon her. Most of the Shaefini were happy to greet her with warm words and allow her space to recover, but her mentor had lacked such restraint.

"You'd think I died or somethin'," she grumbled, but her annoyance was clearly disingenuous.

"Well, you might have," said Baggi. "Can you blame him?"

"Not really," she admitted. "I bet it was pretty scary for everyone, being without me for a couple of days."

"It really was!" asserted Guthini.

They all laughed, glad the immediate danger had passed. As the laughter died down, however, an unspoken tension took a seat among them. Their gazes conjoined on the staff betwixt them. Guthini glanced toward the rooms.

"What are we going to do with him?" he mumbled.

"We will put him to trial," answered Amund immediately, "and there his fate will be decided."

"But he didn't actually do any wrong, right?" asked Kettil. "He didn't kidnap me or anything; I went with him on my own."

"I'm afraid it's not that easy," Baggi sighed.

"Why not?"

"Because of me."

Kettil scrunched her nose in confusion. "What do you mean?"

Amund answered for him. "When your caravan first arrived and healed Talia the tailor, I granted Baggi the title of Friend of Flamebud, as apology for misjudging his character as well as thanks for his service."

"I helped too," Kettil grumbled.

"This title grants certain limited rights," Amund continued, ignoring the interruption. "Put simply, Baggi is a legal resident of Flamebud Village. He is one of us in the eyes of the law." He bobbed his head thoughtfully. "Though he may not open a business here."

"That's still pretty generous," observed Guthini.

"Aha," sighed Kettil, "now I get it."

"Yes," said Amund, "Hakon is to be tried for attempted murder of a villager of Flamebud."

"Amund," asked Baggi, "what is the format of these trials?"

The Chief of Flamebud leaned back in his seat with his arms crossed. "It is similar to the council meetings. The accused is placed on stage, and those that wish to speak in condemnation may be granted their say by the chief. Afterwards, those that wish to speak in defense may be granted likewise. The chief may also call upon those who do not volunteer to testify, should they possess relevant information. Afterwards, all present council members cast votes, guilty or innocent. If guilty, the chief decrees an appropriate punishment."

He spoke by rote, clearly having been made to memorize the process and laws governing it long ago. Baggi frowned.

"And if none speak in defense?"

"Then," replied Amund, "it shall be an easy vote."

Baggi fell silent, thinking it over. *Doesn't seem quite fair, does it?* He asked Compromise. It pulsed an agreement.

"You will all be present, as you witnessed the crime," affirmed Amund in a voice that brooked no argument.

Guthini and Kettil nodded agreeably.

Elder Sage Hrafn entered the common room and caught Baggi's eye, beckoning him closer. He excused himself and obeyed, taking Hakon's staff with him. Hrafn led him out the inn's back door and breathed of the fresh air, absorbing the smells of toasted spices and dust that were Flamebud Village. He leaned heavily on Mischief. *I've never seen the Elder Sage look so exhausted*, Baggi thought, *I suppose Kettil's disappearance must have stressed him most of all.*

"Baggi," he began, "I would first like to apologize for the unorthodox circumstances of your ascension to Staffkeeper. No doubt you would have preferred the traditional Marking ceremony."

"I would have," Baggi admitted, "but I understand that the situation didn't allow for it. I was too worried about Kettil to mind much, besides."

Hrafn smiled at him, silver eyes twinkling. His reliable joviality put Baggi at ease.

"Alchemist Apprentice Kettil has been found and the danger has passed," he said, "yet we now find ourselves facing another pressing matter with young Hakon." He chuckled, the laugh's tone somehow apologetic. "It's one problem following another lately, isn't it?"

The young Staffkeeper chuckled as well. "It is."

"I imagine the trial will be held tomorrow," reflected Hrafn, "which means tonight is free of obligation. Might you like to receive your Marking then?" he asked.

Baggi stared at him. *This is sudden*, he thought. *No, actually*, he amended, *it's overdue already.* He smiled and bowed.

"Yes, Elder Sage Hrafn."

"I am glad to hear it. Now go invite your friends!" he urged. "I haven't much time to prepare myself, and it's been many long years since I last conducted a Marking. I hope you won't mind if I'm out of practice?"

"Elder Sage," asked Baggi in disbelief, "you will be carrying out the Marking? Is that not unusual?"

"Everything about your ascension has been unusual, my boy!" Hrafn laughed. "Now get to it and be in the square an hour before sunset."

"Yes, Elder Sage," Baggi acquiesced.

He bowed once more and spun on his heel, all but galloping back to his table and friends seated there. When he had filled them in, Amund nodded his approval.

"I will be in attendance, of course."

"And me!" shouted Kettil, unnecessarily loud. "I wanna be in the front so I can see!"

The chief crossed his arms. "I will see to it personally," he promised.

"I'm going to let Hjordis and Elof know," said Baggi, "and anyone else I can think of."

He took leave of them, leaving Hakon's staff in Amund's care, and strolled at a brisk pace through the village. He informed Talia, of course, and she went with him to invite the blacksmith whom she insisted would be a respectful guest. When he assented, the tailor offered to go on Baggi's behalf to the bank and invite Audr lest a personal invitation from her former foe seem disingenuous. By that time sunset was rapidly approaching and regret was building as Baggi found he had squandered his precious time and only invited very few. Word spread quickly through Flamebud Village, however, and by the time he returned to the square, he found the better part of the village had beaten him there.

***

The town square was silent. Sunset blanketed Flamebud Village in benevolent orange light, warm and comfortable, but soon the glow would evaporate and they would be left in darkness. To combat this, the Staffkeepers of Shaefi had lit a ring of ceremonial torches around the well, a tradition meant to catch the waning sunlight in their own fires and sustain the day for as long as they believed it to be so. The torch hafts were decorated with engravings of boars and mountains, waterfalls and rock willows etched in silver flake. Baggi had seen them before, of course, but found that tonight he could not look away; the craftsmanship was remarkable, and besides, it helped to focus on something other than his audience.

Many had shown to observe the Marking, far more than Baggi had expected. The Shaefini had reported to the Elder Sage at the end of the day, as they did every day, and had to a one chosen to remain in the area around the well when informed of the evening's plans, but even beside them many villagers sat or stood near the inn's facade. The center of the square, the space where the Marking would occur, was clear. Elder Sage Hrafn stood there with one hand on his staff and the other closed at his side, his back straight, his expression solemn yet delighted. Baggi scanned the attendees as he waited in silence.

Amund stood beside him, naturally, as did Kettil. Torny had posted in the open doorway of the inn, her safe haven, watching him intently and not looking away when he met her gaze. Aghi beamed down from the rooftop where he sat, at the place where post and roof met, taking a break from lookout duty to offer his presence. His legs swung restlessly in tight circles. Hjordis and Elof stood nearby; she made an encouraging gesture with one fist, he waved excitedly. Baggi chuckled, pleased and embarrassed by the parental image. Elsewhere, Talia leaned on the blacksmith. Kalfr the carrot-farmer had joined up with Guthini and the apprentices. They dared not speak, waiting for the ritual to commence with wide eyes. The Sages stood behind Hrafn, ready to offer support. It seemed improbable they would be needed, with the Elder Sage himself performing the Marking, but their presence reassured Baggi nonetheless.

Finally, when he deemed the time right, Hrafn beckoned him forth in silence. *Are you ready?* Baggi asked his staff, *Am I ready?* Compromise answered in the affirmative for both. He felt a proud hand clasp his shoulder, then slide gently away as he took a slow breath and stepped forward. Before Hrafn, he bowed smoothly.

"Baggi, son of Helga, brother of Bjorn," began Hrafn, "you have been assigned three Tasks that you might prove your comprehension of the precepts of Shaefi. These you have completed.

"For your first Task, you stood beneath the night sky and felt the sun on your face. In doing so, you came to know the warmth of Shaefi. For your second Task, you mended a rift in the fabric of this community. In doing so, you came to know to peace of Shaefi. For your third Task, you sounded the bells of laughter throughout this village. In doing so, you came to know the mirth of Shaefi. Through these Tasks, you came to know the nature of the Lady of Life. Now I entreat Shaefi to come to you and know your nature as well. I, her humble constituent, entreat her to reveal your Blessing, to show you the gift that lies in your soul."

With great gravity, wearing a smile, he lightly touched Mischief to Baggi's forehead and invoked a rune.

"Yngwaz," he concluded.

Baggi felt a swirling mass of positivity enrobe him. He saw nothing around him but a blue and white maelstrom, grandiose and ecstatic; the gentle storm caressed him with loving fingers of cloud. *I'm in the sky,* he thought deliriously, *and it's a perfect day for it.* He thought for a moment of what a long fall he must be in, thought of how terrified he should have been. But he was not terrified; Baggi felt happy. He felt like laughing. So laugh he did, he laughed and laughed for longer than he could ever remember laughing, with no interest in stopping, and somehow he was never wanting for breath.

A figure appeared in the cottony cocoon, emerging and melting away faster than he could track. This did not bother Baggi; he could feel her presence all around no matter where she manifested. *Lady Shaefi,* he thought, still laughing, *it's a pleasure to meet you.* The figure in the clouds laughed with him, or perhaps it was her laughter that Baggi was allowed to share. She slowed down and became a woman in front of him.

She was vague in shape, much like the place he had clashed, but she had more life than that place, and a voice and a personality. She was made of silver, or at least part of her was. The rest of her was bright and warm as the sun. Baggi thought she might be the sun. Her hair fell and churned and bubbled like a waterfall. She was naked, but then she had no body to cover, not as a human did. *Maybe we don't either,* the young Staffkeeper mused, and that made him laugh all the harder. He felt her humor and goodwill envelop him as the clouds pressed in closer.

A sliver of the sky pierced the bubble of clouds, and through it shot an infinitesimal pinprick of sunlight. It landed neatly on Baggi's forehead and sent a wave of mellow heat through his being. Something opened inside him, as if she had unlatched a hidden pocket in the cloak he had been wearing for years. He knew not what was inside, hadn't even been aware of its existence, but still its discovery was a great triumph. Shaefi laughed once more.

"It is well to see you, Baggi," she giggled without words.

Her voice was made of a million delicate bells, smaller and more intricate than anything human hands could produce. In it Baggi heard the runes, melding in sentences and pitched with innovative inflections that changed their meaning entirely. It reminded him of how Hrafn had spoken to the man at the inn where Ove died, or Bjorn whispering in his memory before facing the woman in bones.

"You too, Bjorn and Compromise." Shaefi said, as if the boy's thoughts had reminded her of their presence.

She caressed Compromise affectionately, familiarly. *You've mixed us up,* Baggi thought, the assumption ridiculous but pleasing. Shaefi held a hand over her mouth, and the place rumbled with barely restrained laughter. Baggi copied her; it felt the most natural thing in the world.

Then the place was gently melting away and he felt himself slowly touch down, back in the world once more, still giddy and still laughing. Elder Sage Hrafn stood before him, and he, too, rumbled with laughter, gentle and proud. The smile on his face told Baggi that Hrafn, too, was privy to Shaefi's indefinable joke. Hrafn collected himself and stepped forward with a silver brooch in hand.

"Staffkeeper Baggi," he declared, "may this Staffkeeper's Mark forever remind you of what you have learned."

Baggi gasped for air only long enough to recite his acceptance. "You honor me, Elder Sage Hrafn. I accept it with joy."

The Shaefini cheered and hollered as the ceremony concluded. Baggi saw Amund glance askance at the commotion before hurriedly joining in, pounding his palms together like a challenge. Torny stared with an unreadable expression, but her hands, too, were applauding him. Baggi saw for a moment how absurd it was, these people cheering him as if he were a hero. *All I did was finish a few riddles,* he thought, still wheezing with mirth, *and even then, I had help.*

Then the wagons were opened, and instruments were brought forth. Ice-chimes, great free-hanging bells, long and narrow in shape and larger than a man, were hauled on many shoulders, their frames unfolded as various players took up positions at each. Smaller instruments, too, were brought forth by those that owned them and knew to play. Guthini took up a five-holed horn-flute, Hjordis retrieved her lyre and adjusted the pegs with effortless intuition, and more than one Shaefini held a lur to their lips. When all were poised and ready, the ice-chimes were struck and a rhythm was established.

Naefjan music was less organized than that of the other regions; whereas Kichishi songs tended to be fast and energetic, with two or more soloists exchanging verses, and Melennese tunes leaned toward simple refined songs, soft and contemplative with minor personal flourishes, Naefjan music was a largely collaborative effort. It all started with the ice-chimes, which would establish one of many themes and repeat indefinitely. These themes were well known to every Naefjan, as they grew up singing and playing with them on special occasions and days of ceremony. When the theme was set, each player would join in at the moment the theme looped, one at a time or many at once, it made little difference. These contributions were unpredictable and often denied conventional theory; indeed, such experimentation was encouraged. By the same token, practicing music to be performed later was frowned upon as insincere. It was well and good to practice in order to understand your own style, but to bring a pre-manufactured melody to performance was nothing short of dishonesty.

The result was a style of music both consistent and discordant, recognizable in theme and rhythm yet unpredictable in melody. Baggi recognized the theme now: "Avalanche of Tusks," it was called, and as far as Naefjan music went it was rather frenetic. For this reason, it was often used in times of rejoicing. The newly marked Staffkeeper grinned and stomped Compromise's foot in time with the music. At the first refrain, Guthini's horn whistled along, all but overshadowing the other additions with comfortable enthusiasm. He played on time, yet ever so slightly behind the beat. *It sounds just like him*, Baggi mused. As the theme repeated, more instruments joined in, the song becoming rapidly more complicated and discordant. Compromise pulsed in time now, urging Baggi to join. *Yes, I should retrieve my flute*, he agreed, jogging to the door of the inn and slipping inside before he could be crushed under congratulations.

He went to the Staffkeepers' room, where he and the apprentices had relocated their possessions to accommodate Hakon, and took the wooden case tightly bound to his bag. The knots were tighter than he anticipated, and he struggled to loosen them. Outside, the music grew louder.

"So it's official, huh?" said a girl's voice behind him.

Baggi looked over his shoulder and saw Torny leaning against the doorframe.

"You're a Staffkeeper now?"

Baggi felt a nervousness come upon him. It was not his own nervousness, though that was certainly present as well; no, it seemed to be someone else's feelings. He checked with Compromise and confirmed that neither did his staff provide the intruding emotion. *Is it Torny?* He wondered. The innkeeper tossed her head and raised an eyebrow. Baggi felt her impatience stir in him and realized he was staring without speaking.

"Oh, yes. That's right," he said.

He stood and approached her, fishing in his pocket for the silver brooch. As he did so, twin heartbeats quickened in his chest. They stood close together, alone in the inn. *Almost alone. Hakon is just next door,* Baggi thought, then wondered why he was thinking it at all. He held his hand out and slowly uncurled his fingers, offering the silver to Torny. She looked at him strangely.

"You're giving it to me?" she asked softly. He nodded. "I wouldn't know what to do with it."

Baggi sensed uncertainty and joy swirling in him, no longer able to discern where his emotions ended and Torny's began. Instead of trying, he reached out his other hand, shaking, and took hers. He opened the fingers and placed the Mark in her palm.

"You'll figure it out," he said, "If anyone can use it to take care of Flamebud, it's you."

For a moment, Torny looked like she might make a retort or scoff. She felt a pleasant fear, a feverish discomfort, and because she felt it, Baggi felt it too. *So that's my Blessing?* He considered. *I suppose it's a good one. Not too flashy, but that's preferred, isn't it?* Compromise puffed in proud agreement. Torny's impatience bubbled once more in Baggi. He met her gaze and didn't need his newly refined empathic sense to see she was waiting for him.

"Um, Torny?" he mumbled.

"Yeah?"

"Can I kiss you now?"

Delight flowed from her to him even as she rolled her eyes and pretended to be unfazed. She opened her mouth to reply, but Baggi had felt her answer already. He leaned forward and kissed her. It was not graceful, or sweet, or particularly romantic. He moved too fast and bumped painfully into her face, and as her mouth was already open, their teeth knocked together and jarred the both of them. But their lips did meet, if only briefly, and Baggi figured that counted for something. *Perhaps not a kiss the skalds will sing of,* he thought ruefully, but somehow the clumsiness of the exchange made it feel all the more real. It felt genuine. Torny giggled slightly as she rubbed her jaw. Baggi, too, laughed at his own fumble.

"Give me a second next time," she said.

Baggi smiled, dopey and embarrassed but happy despite it all.

"I will," he agreed.

"Well, you know..." Torny said, trailing off and looking askance with her arms crossed. "I'm ready now." She blushed beguilingly.

So he kissed her again, slower this time, and much more carefully. It still felt clumsy and just a little silly, but the sweetness between them blossomed beautifully and filled Baggi's senses. *Yes,* he thought, *this is a good Blessing.* Afterwards, they stood in silence, smiling at each other and suddenly unsure of themselves.

"So what were you doing in here anyway?" she finally said.

"I was fetching my flute," replied Baggi, "to join in the music."

"You play flute?" Torny asked, stifling laughter.

Baggi would have taken offense, but he felt her affection behind the laughter and warmed to her reaction.

"A little," he replied, jokingly defensive. "Why, is that not allowed in Kichishi?"

"It's allowed," Torny teased, "if you're a child. Adults play stronger instruments."

"Then it's a good thing I'm only fourteen," Baggi quipped.

Torny laughed at that, and because she was tickled so was he. *I'll have to learn to control that,* he noted, *so that a stranger's anger or misery doesn't pollute me as well.*

His hands were still shaking from exhilaration and nervousness, but even despite this he managed to untie his flute case. He took the wooden instrument out and sounded a few appraising notes, then nodded in satisfaction. *Good that the road hasn't damaged it,* he thought. Then he turned back to Torny and made to leave, pausing at the doorway and indicating she should precede him. She did so graciously. As they made towards the back door, the duo passed the room housing Hakon. Baggi felt a melancholy seep through the locked door and penetrate him. *He's lonely,* Baggi realized. Compromise agreed, though somewhat dispassionately. Another feeling came to him from Hakon, a yearning for times gone. *And nostalgic too, it seems.* He heard a faint tapping from inside the room, in time with the music outside. Baggi remembered then that Hakon, too, was Naefjan, had undoubtedly learned the songs just as he had, just as they all had.

"Everything okay?" asked Torny.

She stood with one hand on the exit knob. The aroma of curiosity and concern wafted over to him.

"I wish he could come celebrate too," said Baggi, a little ruefully.

Torny snorted. "I don't think he would want to," she assured him, but Baggi shook his head.

"He does," he said simply. Then he sighed and went on, back to the celebration.

The joyful affair overwhelmed his senses near instantly, and in moments Hakon was forgotten. Instead of ruminating on the lad's fate, Baggi played his flute as well as he could and as happily as any. He felt Amund clap him on the shoulder, felt his friend's pride and saw with his own eyes proof of the Chief of Flamebud's claim to be the best dancer in the village. He endured many hugs and many congratulations and many ruffles of his long auburn hair from many other Staffkeepers and alchemists alike. And when the sun had truly gone down and the torches began to burn low, then more torches were brought forth and candles were lit wherever they could be placed as the Shaefini and Kichishi collaborated in cooking a great feast. Torny assured him, with some smugness, that she had already prepared many of the dishes earlier in the afternoon to celebrate Kettil's return. She even went so far as to open her last jar of preserved plums from the previous summer. These she guarded zealously from eager mouths until Baggi had been allowed the honorary first taste. They were sweet and juicy and turned to near liquid in his mouth, but mostly they tasted of care and determination and hospitality, just like the innkeeper herself.

After hours of music and food and some dancing from the Kichishi and the most confident or intoxicated Shaefini, the caravan began to disperse. Baggi lost track of how many good nights he was made to bid, but eventually even his closest friends parted and left him sitting on the front steps of the inn. He looked up to the stars and sighed happily, a sigh that turned into a laugh as he recalled the otherworldly mirth Shaefi had shared with him. He collected himself soon enough, but a euphoric smile lingered on his lips. He thought of how Shaefi had greeted him and Compromise and Bjorn as well. *I was too enchanted to put it together then,* he thought idly, *but she confirmed what I was already thinking.* He held Compromise across his lap. *You're still here, aren't you Bjorn?*

The door creaked slowly open behind him. Baggi did not turn to see who it might be. *They'll come around if they need to,* he thought serenely, and so they did. Hrafn approached beside him and sat on the same step, groaning as he did so. They existed in comfortable silence for several minutes.

"You know I'm very proud of you," said Hrafn. It was not a question.

"Yes," Baggi replied. "Elder Sage Hrafn, I was wondering about something."

"What is it, my boy?"

"Can a soul remain alive after the body is dead?"

Hrafn gazed at him carefully. "Perhaps," he said. "It depends on what you call 'alive'. Is it truly life if you cannot hear the pulse of music, cannot taste the sweetness of plums?"

"I suppose not," said Baggi, "but what of those who are deaf, or blind? Are they less alive?"

"They say that the blind can hear what to us is inaudible, that the deaf can spy what escapes our sight," answered Hrafn. "They are no less alive, only living outside of our perception."

"Then what if the soul without a body can feel what the senses cannot? Would it not be living too, only differently?" Baggi pondered.

"I sense that these questions are not hypothetical," prompted Hrafn, sidestepping the query.

Baggi found that he could not read Hrafn's emotions, not like he had Torny and Hakon. With them, it had been effortless, accidental even. *I suppose Hrafn is just too composed,* he thought. The idea impressed him. *I owe it to him to be direct, after all he's taught me.*

"I believe Bjorn's soul resides in Compromise even now," said Baggi casually.

He waited for a shocked reaction, but its absence caused him no surprise.

"I had a similar suspicion," the Elder Sage confided.

"And is that not worth sharing?" asked Baggi. "If one can live on after physical death, should that not be a skill taught far and wide?"

"Do you think so?" asked Hrafn. He stared intensely at the Staffkeeper.

Baggi smiled slightly as he realized Hrafn had seen through him. "No, I don't," he admitted.

There was a long silence. Baggi began to wonder if he had offended or upset Hrafn with his answer. *He wouldn't revoke my Mark, would he?* he wondered. *That's not done. And I gave it to Torny already anyway.*

"Neither do I," Hrafn eventually said. He turned his face upwards, toward the stars. "Life has no meaning without an end. What is sweetness without bitterness for comparison, what is a beginning and a middle without an end?"

"I don't know," replied Baggi.

"Of course you don't," said Hrafn congenially. "That is not the way of our world. No one could know such a thing." He paused, as if a sudden thought had occurred to him. "Did you know that I learned the runes from Shaefi?" he asked, far too easily.

Baggi balked at him. "What do you mean? She taught you herself?"

"Yes, me and many others," he nodded. "You know that Shaefi lived among the first Naefjans for some time, teaching the progenitors of our people how to tame magic and understand her language. She taught us to carve our staffs with her name and so guide the world on her behalf. These were the first Staffkeepers."

Baggi nodded. "Yes, I know. But you were one of them? I knew you were venerable, but that would make you...well, ancient," he marveled.

His words sounded more insulting than he had intended, but Hrafn nodded gravely.

"Although we teach the history at the Temple, not many apprentices glean the most crucial lesson. Why do you think she taught us the runes, bid us carry out her will, rather than simply remaining here in Solabell indefinitely?"

Baggi touched his lips thoughtfully. "To teach us death," he concluded.

"Yes," Hrafn agreed, "it was her time to leave. She knew that she could stay, could remain here and persist in physical form forever, but to do so would be a mistake. To be human is to endure many partings and many endings. Although we were saddened to see her go, we understood on some level that it was natural. Our own elders were approaching the end of their lives; we could feel it, yet we knew not what would happen, for there were no deaths before then to prepare us. We did not understand, until Shaefi showed us what it was to bid an eternal farewell."

As he fell silent, Baggi reeled. *So Shaefi herself embraced death? Or wants us to, or both? Then why do we fear it? Why didn't we listen? What went wrong?*

"Hrafn," he said softly, "why do we fight death?"

The Elder Sage sighed, and finally a sliver of his emotions came to Baggi. As he identified the emotion, Baggi felt his own fear and shock join it. *Hrafn is guilty? What of?* He wondered.

"Because Shaefi's lesson was not perfect," he granted. "When she left Solabell, she shed her physical life in a great deluge. The silver drops that rained from this storm came to be called the Water of Life, and they are essentially the same as her blood which we were born from, albeit diluted by the mortality of her physical form."

"And they fell upon you," Baggi realized.

Hrafn nodded. Baggi saw tears in his eyes and fright seized his heart.

"We were told to remain in our village and watch the Great Peak where she would depart. Back then, we only knew of the one Great Peak, you see. But I was unable to accept the loss of our Queen of Peace. I disobeyed and went to the mountain, thinking foolishly as only a young man can that I would convince her to stay. Instead, I saw the bliss on her face as she accepted the end of her time. I felt her blood rain upon me, and from that day onward time all but forgot me."

Baggi remained quiet as the Elder Sage collected himself. His breath was ragged as the memory strained him.

"I did not know how to let go," he eventually concluded, "but over the years, as I lost friend, spouse, and child, more times than I care to remember, I learned. Of course, I was not the only one who struggled with her lesson, but I alone had the longevity to learn. And so the Order came to misunderstand our Lady Shaefi."

He smiled at Baggi. There was a usual joyful twinkling in the silver irises, but now Baggi felt a weariness, the sadness of centuries emanating from his gaze. He didn't know whether it was due to his Blessing or simply a natural empathy. *I suppose they're the same thing in my case,* he realized.

"I know I have kept you, and the hour is late," he said in a lighter tone, "but there is one request I must make of you, Staffkeeper Baggi."

"Anything, Elder Sage," replied Baggi fervently.

"The Staffkeepers of Death will be coming for Hakon," he said, "if not tomorrow night, then the night after. They will be coming for me as well."

"For you?" asked Baggi, "But why?"

"You know why," chided Hrafn.

Yes, that's why he told this story, Baggi reluctantly acknowledged. *It's his time, isn't it? After all these years, it's finally his time.* He nodded.

"Let them take me," the Elder Sage said gently, "let them grant me my ending. But then stop them."

"Let them kill you?" asked Baggi, his voice weak.

"Baggi, that isn't the important thing," said Hrafn. "It's true that death is not something to be feared or avoided, but neither is it something to be enforced. You must make them see that."

"That's a job for the Sages," the boy protested desperately. "I'm only fourteen!"

"Precisely," smiled Hrafn. "You are still young, yet you have learned a lesson I denied when I was your elder by a decade. Your mind is open and your soul considerate. My time is long overdue, but yours is only beginning. And when years have passed and your own time approaches, I can trust you to face it with serenity. You are the reason I can find my ending. You can guide your people now."

Compromise hummed with pride and nervous energy. Baggi stroked it reassuringly, feeling the cold and watching the aura seep out of the runes in a constant stream of pale blue. *What do you think, Compromise?* He asked. *Can we do it?* For a moment his staff shared in his unease, but then it shook and vibrated in defiance of its own doubts. He smiled as the stubborn ambition filled him.

"Staffkeeper Baggi, will you do this?" asked Hrafn.

Baggi bowed his head.

"Yes, Elder Sage Hrafn. I will."

23

The trial was beginning to drag. A mild morning sun had long turned suffocating, and all those in attendance wore clothing damp with sweat, yet relief was rapidly approaching. Chief Amund excused Guthini from his testimony and the apprentice scuttled back to his bench in the front row next to Baggi. The only Shaefini in attendance were those that had witnessed the clash, the rest of the caravan withdrawing from the proceedings out of respect for the local judicial process. *We're next,* Baggi thought, fidgeting with Compromise. He invoked Ansuz in a whisper, just as he had during the previous council assembly, and prepared to be called upon. Amund allowed those present to reflect on the previous account before nodding to him. Torny, seated on his right, briefly squeezed his hand for encouragement. He stood up and formed the Sign of Flame.

"I now call upon the Staffkeeper, Baggi," he announced, returning the gesture.

Baggi took the stage and a deep breath as well. Hakon sat in a ceremonial throne of dark iron, bound in chains. He glared straight ahead, refusing to acknowledge any pain from the hot metal on his skin. *Are we sure we want to do this?* Baggi asked. Compromise nervously responded in the affirmative. *Alright then.*

"I wish to speak in defense of the accused," he said loudly.

The crowd scoffed somewhat affectionately, as if he were an infant demanding an extra serving of sweets. Baggi glanced at Amund and ascertained with runic eyes that he had expected this of him. His face remained passive save for a small twitching of the jaw. Baggi felt his frustration, but his trust as well and, surprisingly, not a shred of doubt. His friend's emotions were strong, discernible even amongst the mass of confusing responses flooding into Baggi via the council. He held up a hand for silence, and his people obeyed.

"Then speak," he said, voice neutral and resonant.

"People of Flamebud," Baggi began, "you know me and, I hope, trust my judgment as well as you could trust any outsider. I made a promise to you all last week, a promise to offer my Staffkeeper's Mark in order to cover the costs of our caravan's lodging. This I have done, as the innkeeper Torny can attest."

Torny turned around, holding the silver boar high in the air for all to see the proof of his words.

"I say these things not to boast, but to entreat you all," he continued, noting mixed reactions and not wishing to overextend his approach, "This attempted murder was made against me, and me alone. Should I not also be alone in determining his sentence? You know I would not make such a decision lightly; you know that I stand by the consequences of my decisions."

Talia stood up slowly and formed the Sign of Flame. Amund granted her attention.

"Staffkeeper Baggi," she said, "I respect you and appreciate the work you have done for us. I do not think this is in question."

Several heads nodded in agreement. *She's very brave,* Baggi admired, *speaking for all those too polite to do so.* Ansuz and his Blessing made clear her intentions. *They don't wish to seem ungrateful, but someone must voice their disagreements. I'm glad it's her.*

"Yet," she continued, confirming his assessment, "when the safety of the village is in question, the village as a whole must determine the response. Is it not so?"

As intended, her peers now warmed to the idea of speaking. Baggi felt their hunger for justice meet him onstage. Yet Talia did not sit down. He saw she meant to make another statement, one that was causing her great discomfort.

"I also must inform you," she said, voice quavering a bit, "that your argument is flawed. It is incorrect at the core."

"Please elaborate," he entreated, brow tight with concern.

"You say that he has attempted only to murder you, yet the scar on my collar says differently."

She pulled the neck of her tunic down to show the village the skull sigil on her collarbone, healing yet still far from forgotten. *Could it be?* Baggi wondered, turning to the accused. *Was it really him? If so, he truly is lost.*

"Are you quite certain it was this boy who attacked you?" he managed. "I have no doubts of your honesty, but it has been some time since that incident; is there any chance you are mistaken?"

Talia's expression hardened and Baggi felt a sense of betrayal pierce him.

"I am certain," she spat.

Suddenly, a sort of impatience filled the Staffkeeper. He looked to Hakon and saw the boy struggling to speak through the gag in his mouth. Baggi looked to Amund for approval as he made to remove it. He nodded.

"Ech," Hakon retched when his mouth was finally free. He took a moment to enjoy the release, breathing deeply and stretching his jaw.

"What have you to say?" demanded Amund.

Every face in the forum latched onto the accused. They remained perfectly still, not wishing to miss a single syllable of the damned boy's doomed defense. Yet when at last he spoke, it was not a defense that he issued.

"She's right," he finally sighed, "I'm the one who did it. About two years ago, we came through to take those whose times had come, and I thought she was among them. Even so, I should have killed her before starting on the sigil. It was a mistake, and I shouldn't have done it, but I did it and I know you won't believe that I regret it."

An unspeakable rage filled Baggi, from the audience and Amund both. His hands shook and he barely restrained himself from lashing out with his staff at the young man in chains. The impulse frightened him.

"But even if you don't believe my regret," he continued, "believe that my people didn't approve of that. I was punished for it severely; this scar is the proof."

He craned his neck to one side, displaying a grisly network of silver scar tissue on his neck and jaw. It was on the left side, just like Talia's own wound.

"We're a matched set," he grinned at the tailor, but there was no happiness in the smile.

"We share nothing," she snarled back.

Talia steadied herself on the blacksmith's shoulder and fell to her seat once more, shaken and drained by the confrontation. Regardless, her testimony had fulfilled its purpose. Baggi used all the strength of his being to burn away the rage in his inner fire, taking advantage of the mental exercise taught to him by Amund. It was exceptionally difficult; as soon as he exhaled the ashes of his anger, the villagers' wrath filled him once more. He tried to maintain Ansuz, but the bombardment of emotion was too much. In the final moments before he lost attunement, Baggi glimpsed Hakon's intentions. *He's given up on life already,* marveled Baggi, *the absolute idiot. He's desperate for control. This didn't have to happen.* But he saw an exhaustion in his eyes, too, a shame and hopelessness from which Hakon sought escape.

"I could have gotten you out of this," Baggi sputtered, reeling from the breaking of his spell.

Hakon smiled at him, an expression devoid of hope. Yet neither did it hold despair.

"You didn't," replied.

Baggi made to respond again, his own irritation now compelling him. But Amund stepped between them and shook his head. For all the fury Baggi felt inside his friend, the only expression on his face was one of disappointment and grief.

"Sit down, Baggi," he said softly.

He obeyed, took his seat, numb, and listened to Amund call for the vote. When he called for those who voted in favor of guilt, Baggi did not raise his hand. When he called for those in favor of innocence, neither did he raise his hand then.

"You should have remained silent," remarked the Chief of Flamebud as the outcome made itself obvious.

"Valdis didn't teach me to be a liar," replied Hakon.

Amund sighed, a rare display of weariness, and replaced the gag.

"I declare Hakon guilty of the attempted murder of Staffkeeper Baggi and the assault and attempted murder of Talia the tailor by his own confession. I sentence him to execution, to be carried out at sunrise by my own hand." He made the Sign of Flame. "The trial is adjourned. All present are dismissed."

The people filed out slowly. Baggi felt their myriad emotions swim through him as they passed, not a one optimistic. Torny remained by his side long after the rest had gone and Hakon had been taken away.

They held hands and cried quietly, neither sure quite what to say or how to feel.

***

The sun was setting, and Hrafn was frightened. He sat on the stage in the empty forum, Contemplating and enjoying the last flecks of sunlight as they mournfully retreated. Mischief was in his hands and his heart was in his throat. A comforting swell from his staff soothed Hrafn somewhat, but still he could not shake the fear. He had witnessed his last sunset, and now all that remained before him was twilight.

"It was a beautiful day, wasn't it?" he whispered to his companion. "And how long it stretched."

He felt Mischief's bittersweet resignation in his bones. The staff could be inherited, of course, bonded to a new Staffkeeper and so renewed with youth once more after Hrafn had departed, but it had no desire for that. The Staffkeeper's bond was alike to marriage; some remarried after they were widowed and found new happiness, while others never took another partner and were content with what love they had once had.Mischief would be among the latter. Although Shaefini would never dream of sundering a staff, much less the staff of an Elder Sage, Hrafn knew its wishes would be respected. He knew Baggi would see it done.

The sky began to purple; she would be coming soon. Kettil's reports indicated that the leader of the Staffkeepers of Death was an imposing woman wearing black garb and bones. It would be impossible to mistake her. Hrafn trusted her to find him, trusted that her position entailed a certain sense for death. So he waited now, in the darkening forum, knowing his end was approaching and knowing it was the best thing and feeling scared despite knowing.

He held a hand before his face. It was hardly visible, but truthfully, he had no need for his eyes. Hrafn had reflected on his hands countless times over the course of his long life, noticing each line and wrinkle accumulate as the years passed by. They were tarnished hands, notched with scars and calluses from a life on the road and the dangers of such a fate. Yet beneath these mementos were the same fingers and same palms, and beneath those flowed the same magically imbued blood. He barely felt its strength now. When he had been a young man, and even when he had been older than any human alive, the blood had been so hale, but the centuries had eroded even the vitality of Shaefi and now he was simply a tired old man. Hrafn chuckled quietly; he finally felt his age.

It was dark now, black all around him. His dark vision, too, was weaker than it had been once. His vision in general was weaker than it had been, though that would not plague him for much longer. Hrafn desired a light, desired the warmth and comfort of Sowilo. Mischief almost provided it for him without his input, but the Elder Sage recognized that the light would only make it harder. Besides, he was beginning to acclimate. He closed his eyes, inviting a yet deeper darkness, and began to meditate, preparing himself to feel nothing.

He could not say how long he meditated, in the dark on the stage with the pale light of the stars above shedding their tears over him. It was a long time. Toward the end, he really began to feel as if he were nothing at all. That was not alarming, or comforting, or anything. It was how he knew to open his eyes. Standing before him was the hazy outline of a black-clothed figure. Her face stood out, pale and grey beside the black, but her bones stood out even more so. They were polished and pure, clean white skeletons of varying sizes stitched to her garb that outlined her own frame like a homunculus shaped by clumsy hands. She clutched a staff in her left hand, but Hrafn could not see it. He only saw the finger bones wrapped around something in the dark.

"Hrafn," she said, and her voice was not so harsh as he expected, "it is time to stop running."

Hrafn nodded. He didn't know if she could see the gesture, so he also said, "It is."

"Final requests?" she asked.

"No," replied he, "my life has been too long and sweet to ask for anything more."

She paused for only a moment. "Would that all Shaefini were like you," she said.

There was a touch of wistfulness in her voice. She pulled off her glove and revealed her fingers, put her hand to her mouth, and then brushed the hand on her staff. The runes glowed an intense crimson, casting her face and Hrafn's in half shadow.

"Algiz," she invoked, and her aura cloaked Hrafn in a numbing mist.

She drew a long knife and stepped around him. Hrafn stroked Mischief one last time. *Goodbye, my beloved friend,* he thought warmly. Then the knife moved across his throat, and he thought no more. He hardly felt the blade, and certainly no pain. There was only a slight pressure, some apprehension, and then a wet sensation on the front of his robes. That was Hrafn's end.

Valdis wiped the blood from her knife, savoring the flavor of his death. It was extraordinarily rare for a Shaefini to retain their serenity when she came for them. His end tasted rich and full-bodied, like a fine wine, complex and surprising with its wealth of depth. She stood over him for several moments, eyes closed in appreciation. Then she heard measured steps descending from the benches toward her.

"Sowilo," said a boy's voice.

Soft, warm light emanated from the staff of a child approaching the stage. It illuminated only far enough to guide his way. He wore not the Shaefini blue-and-white cloak, nor the silver brooch they used as marks of status. Instead, his cloak was burned and ashen, and fastened with a wooden ring. His staff appeared restless, and he spoke comforts to it as he approached the stage and walked up the steps. Valdis watched him with her knife in one hand and her staff in the other.

"I'd like to honor him before we start," the boy said.

Valdis nodded. She would not stop funerary rites unless there were some attempt to undo what had been done, and clearly no risk of that was present. The lad did not appear to be Shaefini, after all. He kneeled over the body which still churned fresh blood and pinched some ash from his cloak. He held it in his fingers over the corpse and closed his eyes.

"Hrafn," he said softly, "was a wise and kind man. I knew him only for a short time, but that is the nature of life. It's short, and it's sweet, and then it's over. His life was long, longer than it ought to have been, and I know he felt guilt for that. But he used that long time to teach others what he struggled to learn, and by doing that, he guaranteed that new life would always succeed over stagnation."

Tears rained from his cheeks, and he sniffled loudly as he struggled to contain them.

"I will miss him so much. His people will miss him so much. All those who ever felt his love will feel his loss just as strongly. Yet we remain joyful because we were privileged to feel his love at all."

He began sobbing fully, unable to continue speaking. He released the ashes over the body with an uneven flick of his hand. After he had cried for a long time, his breathing returned to normal. He wiped his face on a sleeve and stood up.

"Those were not Shaefini rites," Valdis observed.

"No," he agreed, and then, without further pretext, "I'm ready."

"You wish to clash?" she asked, though his intentions were already clear.

"Yes," he replied.

Rather than bowing like a Staffkeeper of Shaefi, he stood tall as he brought his staff to his forehead. Its runes began glowing powerfully.

"Very well," said Valdis.

She cut her thumb and attuned to Relief, then sheathed her knife and held her staff before her.

Respectfully, the crimson and the ice-blue swam forth and met.

***

Baggi was alone. He looked around for the woman in bones and saw no one, only a plateau and a cottage with a barn beside. Compromise remained alert, but his staff shared in his confusion. *Where is she?* He wondered. He shifted from one foot to the other, unsure of how to proceed. The edge of his vision was blurry, like when he had clashed with Hakon, and this reassured him that he was, indeed, clashing once more and not simply dead or dreaming. Perplexingly, though, the similarities ended there. The buildings were sharp and well-defined, and he felt a sadness permeating not only his flesh, but the swell of the plateau beneath him as well. Baggi scanned his surroundings once more before shrugging and walking up the gentle slope to the cottage.

He smelled firewood and sensed the presence of bravery. Baggi knocked on the door and waited. Soon enough, it opened of its own accord. He stepped meekly inside and took in his surroundings. The cottage was humble yet comfortable: its wooden floors were stained a port-red that somehow reassured him, several quaint teapots hung from pegs in the small kitchen to his right, and two chairs, one small and one big, were positioned before the blazing hearth directly in front of him. A woman sat in the larger of the two. Baggi approached from the side of the short seat and took it for himself. He looked to his right at the woman, no longer dressed in bones and black, but instead wearing the humble goatherd's garb of the Eastern Great Peaks.

"Welcome to my home," she said dryly.

"I know you," said Baggi, "or I thought I did. Looking at you now, I'm not so sure."

The woman said nothing for a long time as she stared into the embers. She held a lyre in her hands, but the strings remained still.

"We have met once before," she finally said. "I know the staff you carry. Your name is Baggi."

"Yes," agreed Baggi, confidence returning, "when you came to Jolk. You recognized Compromise?"

She nodded. "We traveled together for several weeks."

Compromise pulsed uneasily, then reached deep into its memory and provided Baggi a name: Valdis.

"You slept most of the way," she said, apparently addressing the staff now. "Still I remember you."

Baggi could not feel her emotions; it made him hesitant to contin-ue. *What is this?* he thought. *Why aren't we fighting? Is this a trap? Does she only intend to lull me into defenselessness?* With a sudden surge of manic energy, he stood before her and gripped Compromise in both hands. *I should strike now,* he decided, *before she has the chance.* He raised his staff and swung it at the seated woman, focusing like before on Amund's style and hoping to borrow his skill. Valdis parried easily and rapped him on the forehead even without rising.

"Do not try to overpower me that way," she said dully. "I have far more experience. I will kill you."

Baggi rubbed his head and felt a sliver of his life leave him for Valdis' staff. The pain was hardly noticeable.

"It worked on Hakon," he said stubbornly, but he sat back down.

"Hakon is naïve," she answered, "easily surprised. I am not."

Baggi felt a slight headache coming on, whether from her calm, decisive speech or the blow to his head, he could not say. He wondered why she didn't simply beat him to death if it were as easy as that. It would apparently be a trifling matter, yet she made no move to strike him again. Anxiety crept in and he began to feel truly out of his depth. *We must stay relaxed,* he reminded himself and Compromise. *It seems the only way to win this is to stay calm and fight with well-composed words.* His staff assented to the strategy, but also sent a query his way. *I don't know,* he admitted, *I'm still not sure what we're going to be debating.*

Valdis remained silent as the boy's mind raced. Unexpectedly, she plucked with a single controlled finger and an out-of-tune note rang out, resounding in the still air. Baggi noted a swirling movement in the corner of his eye and turned to see a grey, ghostly image of a man in a cot with a girl not much older than Baggi kneeling over him. He heard their voices but not their words. They spoke with affection and grief in unequal measure, and finally the girl sobbed, took up a knife, and cut the man's throat. Silver liquid poured onto the floor and coated the planks beneath, then the figures and the liquid faded away and were gone. Baggi looked then at Valdis and saw that she, too, had been watching. He felt a faint nostalgia emanating from her now.

"That was you?" he asked.

She nodded.

"And your father?"

"Yes," she said, "Njal."

"You killed him."

"Yes."

"Why?"

She fixed him with an inscrutable expression.

"Because he was ready."

Baggi chewed on that for a moment, then said, "But were you?"

A vague relief met him then.

"You are thoughtful," she said, and almost sounded impressed. But then the faint feeling stopped. "Yes," she answered.

Baggi touched his lips as he pondered his next approach. *I thought we had her there,* he thought regretfully. *What now? She must have showed us that for a reason. We need to figure out why, what point she's making, before we can refute it.* He wondered if, once they ascertained her intentions, he would want to refute her at all. *But what's the alternative?* He mused. *Staying here forever?*

"Why didn't you send for Staffkeepers of Shaefi?" he asked.

For a sobering moment, he realized how comfortable he was, how easily the conversation came. *This is a clash,* he reminded himself, *you don't want to be comfortable here.* Yet he could not force a sense of urgency.

"We did not trust them," she said, "and I still do not."

Aha, thought Baggi triumphantly, *here is stubbornness, and stubbornness is a fault. We can exploit this.*

"Yet they may have given you more time to be together," he chided, "more memories."

A faint wisp of blood began to trickle from Valdis' staff.

"Or they may have prolonged his pain," she replied, "as they did my mother's."

"Is it not worth taking the chance?"

"No," she retorted, "not when he and I were ready. There was no gamble to be made in that decision."

The trickle stopped, then reversed flow and returned to its host. Baggi sighed, slightly frustrated. It felt like they had been talking for hours. Perhaps they had. Valdis had a slow, thoughtful way about her, a habit of speaking without haste that perversely reminded him of Hrafn.

"I suppose Elder Sages all take their time," he said aloud.

"I am no Elder Sage," she said, without waiting this time, in the manner of one who has spoken the words many times before. "Rank and titles are Shaefini nonsense."

"They are acknowledgments of one's contributions to the world," argued Baggi.

"Then their contributions, rather than their pretentions, should speak for them."

This admonishment extracted some blood from Baggi. Still, it was a trifle, and his only pain was an ignorable headache. He thought of Hrafn's body, lying gracelessly on the forum even now. *He will always be remembered as Elder Sage,* reflected Baggi, *yet how many will truly appreciate all that he was as a man? Most will only say, 'that was the Elder Sage who lived so many years.' How many will say, 'that was Hrafn, who loved his family and always spoke with gentle tones and valued joy above all else?'*

"Perhaps you're right," he granted, "the titles are a distraction."

With that admission, what little blood he had lost returned to him. *This clash will be long,* he thought. Baggi looked around and settled in for a long stay. As his gaze fell upon the teapots hanging in the kitchen, he rose and went to the sink. *A snow-melter,* he thought, impressed with the luxurious contraption. *Unless we made it for her – and I doubt we did, based on her distaste for Shaefini – this must have cost a fortune.* He wondered if it had been a part of the cottage to begin with, or a wishful liberty formed from Valdis' subconscious. *Why are we here, anyway? With Hakon, we were on a mountaintop. It felt like Naefja. That must have been a combination of our minds and our innermost comforts. But I have no connection to this place. Is it simply that Valdis' mind and soul are stronger than mine? Could she have overshadowed my presence so completely? That would explain why she remains so calm; I'm no threat to her.*

As he ruminated, Baggi retrieved water from the snow-melter. He wasn't sure how it worked, but in the dream-place he needed only to know what he intended to do with the device, and then it was done and the kettle was full. He couldn't remember how it had happened, but he did not dwell on the subject. He found tea in the first cabinet he tried and found the water was already hot. Baggi wasn't sure if it was ready because he though it ought to be, or whether he had simply lost all sense of time in the dream-place. It made no difference either way. He filled the teapot and returned to his seat.

Baggi handed a cup to Valdis and she took it with a grateful nod. Her eyes remained fixated on the hearth.

"Where are your bones?" Baggi asked after they had drunk.

"The deaths are with me," she answered, "even when I leave the objects behind in Solabell. Here I need no reminders. The memories are all within reach." He detected a tenderness in her as she spoke.

"I wonder if you might show me one such memory," said Baggi after a moment's hesitation.

"You wish to see Bjorn's death," she stated.

"I have seen it once before," he said, "but I would like your perspective."

They finished their tea as Valdis considered the request.

"Why?" she asked.

"Because I want to understand," answered Baggi solemnly.

It was quiet for a while. Baggi noticed that the fire crackled noiselessly, devoid of its most energetic and vital trait. The realization excited him. *She misunderstands fire,* he thought giddily, *she watches so closely and wishes to understand, but she doesn't realize it has a voice.* He smiled. *She's not infallible after all. We have a chance.*

"Very well," Valdis said. She stood and bade him follow.

24

The Flamebud Inn was silent, yet tension filled the void which lack of noise imparted. Torny sat at her bar and sipped her tea, then rubbed her eyes aggressively. The day had started with intense sparring and only become more exhausting as it progressed, from the trial to its aftermath and now her overnight vigil, but she could not sleep. She had a responsibility to uphold.

Aghi stood at the door to Hakon's room in the back hall, yawning every few minutes. This was supremely irritating to Torny, but she restrained her temper and focused on the front door. The plank had been dropped and the lock secured, but who knew what use such mechanisms would be against a Staffkeeper? Magic was a strange and intimidating force of which she understood little. Even her relationship with Baggi and time spent housing the Staffkeepers of Shaefi hadn't done much to diminish her apprehensions. She spun her knife shiftlessly on the counter and waited.

She wondered if Amund, too, would be tiring, at his guard post outside the back door. Then she snorted at the ridiculousness of such an idea. No, he was far too riled up to lose focus and risk Hakon's escape. The other villagers at trial may only have seen a stoic chief passing judgment on a criminal, but she knew him better than that. Indeed, Amund was filled with fury. He would hardly chance blinking before morning had come and his chance to exact justice upon the foreigner had arrived.

Torny had finished her tea and nearly glazed over as completely as the bar beneath her cup when a shifting of wood caught her attention. She watched as the iron-banded plank across the door lifted of its own accord. Swiftly but quietly, she picked up her knife and crept around the corner into the hall, held a finger to her lips, and signaled to Aghi that someone was upon them. He nodded dutifully and tiptoed into the common area. The lock rattled irregularly on the door, agitated by unseen hands full of impatience. It seemed whoever had unlatched the bar could not use the same method on the lock and had resorted to more conventional means. Aghi took up position by the door on the side of its hinges so he would be concealed when it swung open. Torny raised a glass bottle in her left hand as she gripped her weapon in her right. She didn't dare retrieving her cousin from out back lest the door open before she returned. All they could do now was steel their hearts and make themselves ready.

Her heart beat fretfully as she waited for what seemed ages. Torny thought for a moment of Baggi, out there in the dark with Old Man Hrafn. She wondered if their plan to lure the Staffkeepers of Death to the forum had worked. But then she wondered why someone would be surreptitiously entering her inn if their plan had worked, and her heart sank. Aghi looked at her, licking his lips nervously and gripping his metal-capped club with both hands. His knuckles were white as snow. At last the lock clicked, and the door creaked open.

Torny's first feeling was relief, for only one woman entered the inn where Kettil had described two remaining Staffkeepers. Furthermore, this woman was dark and young and slight, not tall and scarred like the leader should have been. That meant that they must have split up. Her second feeling was fear, for it was also possible that Baggi and Hrafn and the leader had all died and this last one now came to free Hakon. Then the woman spotted her and Torny had no more time to think. She threw the bottle with all her might at the intruder.

The Staffkeeper twirled her staff, in truth more a spear with an insidious obsidian head, and smashed the bottle out of midair before it struck her, breaking the glass and silence both. Still, the shards flew into her face and she instinctively closed her eyes for half a moment. In the ensuing opening, Aghi rushed forth with a crazed and fearful shout and swung in a high downward arc at her back. His manic battle-cry betrayed him, calling the Staffkeeper's attention behind and allowing her to sidestep with uncanny speed. Her spear fell upon him like a bolt of lightning, piercing his throat. Aghi gurgled, fell to the floor, and went limp.

Torny weathered a wave of sickness and took the advantage Aghi had afforded her. She rushed close as the woman struggled to dislodge her spear, swiping and spinning in a blur. Somehow her opponent evaded nearly every strike, using the haft of her spear to block that which she could not avoid. Aghi's body lolled about on the floor as she did so, the desecration of his corpse further driving Torny to expend her wrath upon the woman, but still she could not strike her. They danced in a circle around the spear, pivoting and backstepping and lunging with the post between them affording the woman just enough protection. Then, in a sudden reversal of motion, the Staffkeeper snapped the haft forward into Torny's nose, driving her backward two steps.

She swung blindly in front of her as she reeled, conscious of the possibility that her opponent would press the attack. Yet as she caught herself and locked eyes upon the woman once more, she saw that the Staffkeeper had instead used the time to wrench her spear free from Aghi and held it now in a relaxed grip, her body low and the tip swirling in tight, unreadable circles between them. Torny retreated, pirouetting desperately at the first thrust and then swatting the second aside as she tumbled over the bar and crouched low. Now her opponent's weapon would work against her; she would be forced to approach from the direction of the bar's opening to strike her, and even more crucially, that position put the hallway at her back. The Staffkeeper came around the bar just as predicted and traced her spearhead in the air as she prepared to strike once more.

A sudden hiss of leather alerted her to movement from behind as Amund appeared and chopped smoothly at her arms, hoping to relieve her of the ability to fight. This time, the woman had no space to dodge; instead, she was forced to drop her weapon in order to avoid a mortal wound. Still, the blur of steel and blood indicated it had not been an entirely futile attack. The woman retreated now, back toward the front door, and drew a short sword in her left hand. The right hung at her side, blood dripping from a gash near the wrist. She flexed the fingers experimentally and grimaced.

"I felt death in the air," she said seriously. "I felt it stronger with each step closer to this place. I see now why: three are ready to die here tonight."

Torny clambered atop the bar. Her adrenaline was robbing her of restraint, and she couldn't help snapping back,

"Didn't you think it might be your death you were getting closer to?"

The woman shook her head.

"I am Myrgjol, Master of Poison Dart Style and warrior of great renown. None will-"

"Shut the hell up," snarled Amund derisively, and attacked.

He danced around her swings and thrusts, swaying almost drunkenly as she tried in vain to pin him. Her strikes were fast, precise, yet the Chief of Flamebud evaded them all without blocking a one. Even Amund's skill was not boundless, though, and although he was unable to be hit, neither was he able to move forward within striking distance. Indeed, he was having great trouble finding space to retaliate with his own blade at all. He remained composed, but Torny saw a hint of frustration on his face, and she gathered that Myrgjol was a great enough fighter to notice his tells as well, sooner or later. So before she had the chance, Torny reached beside her, seized another bottle from the bar, and threw.

Myrgjol saw it coming this time, and rather than try to block the missile, she simply leaned back several inches to avoid it. As she did so, the tip of her sword raised just as many inches. It was the smallest of openings, yet Amund was unwilling to let it slip. He stepped in quickly, but Myrgjol was not so easily undone.

She dropped the blade again as Amund advanced, impaling him through the shoulder. He roared through gritted teeth and seized the blade with his left hand even as he swung his own sword with the right. Her leg arced upward and, in an amazing display of speed and flexibility, snared his arm before the strike landed. She jerked her leg backward and headbutted at once, disarming him. Free from threat, Myrgjol attempted to regain control of her own weapon, pushing and pulling and drawing blood from Amund's hand with each attempt, but he would not allow it. He planted his stance firmly and restricted her from moving entirely, raising his other arm to guard his head and face. Unwilling to surrender the offensive, the Staffkeeper finally released her sword and used her good hand to punch him repeatedly in the stomach and liver. Amund grunted with each excruciating blow, yet still he did not fall.

Myrgjol pulled back for another strike, but before she could renew the assault a sharp slice split her leg at the ankle. She collapsed to one knee, eyes wide with surprise and pain, and in the interim felt her good arm seized as a knife blade pierced her wrist. Torny released the woman, now without a single arm to fight with and only one leg to stand on. The Staffkeeper panted heavily as her lifeblood left her in several places.

"I lost focus," she said, her tone self-deprecating, "a beginner mistake. Shameful."

"Yes," managed Amund. He winced, leaned heavily on the bar, and could say no more.

Torny looked to her cousin for approval. He gave it with a somber nod.

"At least it was a battle-death," sighed Myrgjol. She did not close her eyes.

Torny plunged her blade into the woman's heart, pulled it out, and stood in respectful silence for several moments as she died. Afterward, she approached Amund. His wounds were serious, but she had confidence that he would live with the Staffkeepers of Shaefi's treatment. The short sword hung from his shoulder like a dart on the wall, and his hand was freely gushing. Torny huffed at him as she retrieved bandaging from behind the bar.

"That was pretty stupid, grabbing her sword," she said as she treated the wound.

"You have no cause to complain," he grunted. "It worked, did it not? And what are these bandages for, if not barfights?"

She laughed softly at that. Her hands were shaking, and after she had staunched the bleeding, she stared vacantly at the bound wound. The thrill of battle had left her, and she now stood feeling scared and alone. To look away from the bandaging would be to face the corpses on the floor of her home. To look away would be to face what she had accomplished: her first kill. Amund cleared his throat.

"You fought well," he said.

There was pride in his voice, but it was slight. Mostly she heard melancholy, and resolve, and an acceptance of guilt for what they had done. She heard in the three simple words a wish for a life where she hadn't been faced with such a terrible task, much less been so well prepared for it. She heard a yearning for a different world where killing was not something to become accustomed to and wondered if she would become accustomed to it as well, just like her cousin had at only nineteen.

Torny nodded and began to sob.

***

Her memory must be sharp, Baggi marveled. He had never been down in the Melenno Valley proper, the caravan having turned back to Naefja after Ove's death at their first stop in Geluwam. He had, of course, seen artistic renderings in tapestry from the Soft City and imported paintings from the eastern-most tribe, Fumvoir, yet the vibrance of the wetlands around him was full of detail and texture and could not be properly emulated even in their mastery. He looked up and saw that the canopy overhead was lacking for this same level of definition, assumed Valdis had not spent much time looking up, and turned his gaze back to his own level. The green of this forest was deep and verdant unlike anything he had ever seen. The woods in Naefja were barren and white save for their berry bushes and shrubs, those of Kichishi lush in their own right yet dry and dusty, but this land was soaked to its core. Mud pulled at his boots as he walked, an identical slumping suction sounding out with every step. It seemed the memory only accounted for one such noise, without variation.

Valdis walked before him, and a ghost of herself walked before her in turn. They tromped through the mud in single file, one after another, the wet, earthy aroma of Melenno thick in Baggi's nostrils. His stomach was uneasy; he knew what he saw would be unpleasant. The urge to distract himself by focusing on the intense purples and blues of surrounding flora was not easily overcome, but he forced it away. *I mustn't avoid this,* he resolved, *or I'll never understand.* A foreign flavor was on his tongue, bitter and sour but not unwelcome. At first he had assumed it to be a result of their environment, but as they traveled the flavor intensified and became more distinct, and eventually it filled his mouth as surely as an eagerly awaited meal.

"What is that taste?" he asked, mouth numb with the sensation even as he spoke.

Valdis did not look back as she answered. "It is death. You taste it because I tasted it at this time."

"Do you always taste it?" Baggi queried. "Is that how you find new Staffkeepers of Death?"

"I taste it when it is present," she replied, "near or far."

Baggi thought on this as they walked until Valdis surprised him by adding, unprompted:

"We are The Conclusion. Only the ignorant call us Staffkeepers of Death."

"I thought rank and titles were Shaefini nonsense," he frowned. "What difference does it make what you're called?"

"'Staffkeeper' is the title," she said, and a note of spite crept into her voice, "We use a name that minimizes our own importance. We are only an effect, not ones to be raised up or singled out. We have no titles, no superiors, and no ranks. We are simply The Conclusion."

She seemed not to notice, or perhaps not to care, as a thread of silver lifeblood trailed behind her and joined Compromise. *She knows this isn't quite true,* Baggi thought. He took no pleasure in the opening, but pressed nonetheless.

"The Conclusion then," he conceded. "But Kettil tells me you are their leader. They listen to you, they obey you. You are the leader of The Conclusion, you are the superior."

As he spoke, the thread between them thickened slightly. She abruptly stopped walking and stood stock-still.

"Here," she said.

Baggi stood abreast and peered under a humble overhang of branches with a treated animal skin lashed tight above to provide respite. Beneath it stood a family, four members, two parents and two children. The youths were about Kettil's age, but a fear had made its domain in their deep-green eyes, a fear that he had never seen in hers. They peeked around their parents' legs. The adults wore wide hats with channels carved in to guide the rain off their faces. If they had been in front of a tree, Baggi may not have noticed them, as their skin had the appearance of bark and their hair that of leaves. His fascinations were forgotten in an instant as he noted one more figure standing between them and the grey-Valdis.

"Bjorn," he whispered.

His brother looked familiar save for a patchy beard on his face. His hair was slightly longer than when Baggi had last seen him as well, falling just to the shoulders, but the tone was unchanged: dark and warm like mahogany. He slouched a bit, always had, and it seemed his time on the road with a pack on his shoulders hadn't done much to address the issue. His nose was narrow and a bit pronounced, and the impression of a smile, lop-sided, was present even in such a moment. Compromise was in his left hand, and Baggi's right.

"There is death here," came Valdis' voice from the grey memory construct. "Do not fight it."

"I'm a Staffkeeper of Shaefi," Bjorn replied, smiling weakly. "I have no intention of fighting."

"Then lay down your staff," commanded the echo.

Bjorn looked back at the family, heaved a sigh, and squared his shoulders. He turned back.

"My life for theirs," he offered. "Doesn't that suit you better?"

Valdis, the real Valdis beside Baggi, breathed deeply as her remembered self paused.

"He misunderstood," she said. "I never intended to take the Melennese."

"And why not?" said Baggi softly.

His attention was barely on her words as he soaked in every detail of the scene and made the memory of Bjorn's last moments his own. She turned to him, forcing him to tear away his gaze and face her.

"Because the taste of death was not on them," she said meaningfully. "It was his to begin with."

Baggi looked again at the scene before them and wondered what difference it made. "Why not tell him that? Why be dishonest?"

Valdis winced. It seemed he had struck a nerve, as a sizable splash of blood was his reward.

"Because his bravery came from a place of sacrifice," she said gently, "and I was willing to compromise my integrity if it meant an easier death."

"Very well," declared the memory of her. "It is an acceptable exchange."

"Will you return my staff to my family in Jolk? Compromise knows the way."

"As you wish."

Bjorn cradled Compromise close and began whispering. The words were unclear in the memory, but Baggi had heard them before. After he had finished, he raised his head.

"I'm ready," he said.

Baggi's heart pounded and his lips trembled as the grey thing that had been Valdis approached his brother. It procured a knife, the tool visibly defined, much more so than the woman herself, then invoked Algiz and stepped behind him. Baggi forced himself to watch as she gently placed a hand on Bjorn's shoulder. He acquiesced and dropped to his knees, then closed his eyes as if Contemplating. Perhaps he was. Then the knife fell across his throat and there was silver flowing from the wound into the mud beneath.

Baggi suddenly experienced a dizzying double-vision. He was kneeling, and his blood was pouring out, but his life was not in it; instead, his essence separated and flowed into Compromise, slowly and steadily, in equal pace with the blood. He felt body-death, felt his limbs go weak and his torso falling decisively into the mud even as his consciousness remained active. An unwelcome sense of triumph filled him for a moment, and then he was returned to merely an observer as he watched Bjorn's body collapse, empty.

A whirlwind tore through his chest, emotions wobbling and toppling and being rebuilt in a turmoiled flurry. His head pounded, and he doubled over as a tortured groan escaped his lips. His blood flowed in a thick stream to the crook in Valdis' hand. *This is too much*, he thought desperately, *I wasn't ready. I wasn't ready to see this, and it's killing me.* But then Compromise rushed into him and swept a cool reassurance over his panic. A silent voice in his staff told him to be calm, to remember himself, and Baggi focused on that command over all else. He breathed deliberately, not out of necessity, for in the place of clashing Baggi had come to know that such things as breathing were not required, but out of habit, for comfort and familiarity. It eased his confusion, and when he had calmed slightly, he risked building a fire in himself to feed his frustrations to. The flames smoldered inside him, warming him, washing out his anxiety and grief, his resentment of his brother's forsaking that he hadn't known he carried before this moment. When they were all burned away, he stood up straight and exhaled a great breath of ashes. They were visible in this place, they were real, and in the grey flakes he saw his brother's smile, his approval, his guilt, his mistakes. Finally, the flow of blood began to ebb, and then it ceased entirely. Baggi felt weak, but his resolve was unbroken.

"Thank you for showing me," he managed to say.

Valdis nodded. She looked at him, appraising.

"You are weak. You will lose this clash. Will you accept death so bravely as he did?"

Baggi locked eyes with her and struggled to maintain his posture.

"No," he said, "not like he did. I'll accept it without provision."

An emulsion of regret and pride flowed from Compromise, and Baggi knew it came from Bjorn. Valdis looked at him uncomprehending. Some blood returned to him, enough to steady his shaking body.

"I have a memory to show you, too," he continued. "Will you come?"

Valdis took a long time to answer as the forest melted to grey around them.

"Yes," she granted.

***

The village of Jolk was, quite literally, exactly how Baggi remembered it. He procured from his mind the cottages arranged in a semi-circle around the shrine to Shaefi, added the smoky chimneys and smell of wood burning. He assembled the glasshouses behind his family cabin and two others, erected the pens and sheep houses and populated them with his good friends Fleecy and Frosthoof, then coated the entire village in deep pillows of powder. From this layer of snow, he carved the footpaths between each building, topped with sloping wooden overhangs that minimized their necessity for shoveling. The insides of each were carved with intricate depictions of local folktales and painted sky-blue, white, and cherry-red. Some portions had been touched up more recently than others, resulting in a rustic, uneven charm. When he had recalled these, Baggi established the road out of town, curving out of sight as it hugged the smooth ravine floor. Baggi thought of the smells of Jolk, spices and ginger, and winter vegetables and fresh mutton stewing in the hearth. They permeated the village, intoxicating and pleasant, but even more comforting than these aromas was the cold. The chill of Naefja was inescapable, and many foreigners found this to be a harsh, uninviting experience. Natives felt differently. To many Naefjans, cold was a companion, ever-present and familiar, bracing and invigorating even if it hovered a bit too close at times. Baggi had missed it greatly.

It's all so clear, he thought happily, *but then, how could I ever forget Jolk?* He felt the absurd wish to rush inside his family cabin and visit his mother. *She wouldn't be there,* he knew, *not really. Just my memory of her. But that might serve just as well.* Still, he had a purpose here, and it was not merely to reminisce. *It was snowing a bit on this day, wasn't it?* He thought, fine-tuning the memory. A light snow began to fall.

"I have been here," remarked Valdis beside him.

"Yes," said Baggi. "You showed me your home; now I'm showing you mine. This is Jolk, and you're due to arrive soon."

The door to his cabin opened and a child, ill-defined in the same way the memory of Valdis had been, trudged out into the snow. *I was building something,* Baggi recalled, *a hideout. Or, yes, it was meant to be a hideout, but I lost patience and left it as only a single wall.* The memory-Baggi carried out his recollections before them. *And then, when I felt so secure behind my wall, that was when you came.*

"Right about now," he whispered, his words creating mist in the cold, "watch."

He gestured to the road out of town. Usually, travelers were a welcome sight. They would bear goods for trade, or stories from the other realms of Solabell, or magic and healing and joy. This, however, was not a usual day. As Baggi and Valdis watched, a swarm of black came warbling into town, spraying dirt and snow as spiked horseshoes pounded the trail. There were several of them, though how many could not be counted. It was Baggi's memory, after all, and he could not truthfully say how many there had been. His younger self peeked over his pathetic fortification as they filled the square. A creature of darkness and malice sat atop the lead saddle, scanning the near-empty village beneath a cap of great twisted horns. Baggi looked askance at Valdis and noted she appeared alarmed. He smiled sadly.

"Compromise?" whispered the remembered Baggi as he set eyes on his brother's staff.

The memory became darker then. The luster of Jolk was suddenly pressed beneath a heavy fear, stealing the shine of the sun and smothering the smells of home and hearth. The rider spotted the child and cantered over. He fell backwards and slipped in the snow, then became frozen solid as the ice beneath him. Slowly, horribly, the woman reached into a saddlebag and retrieved a skull. She tossed it to him, and the child caught it instinctively with both hands. At that, the memory of Jolk was gone. All was gone except the child and the skull in his hands and a detached, unreal terror.

"Bjorn?" he mumbled with lips numb not from cold, but shock.

Then the village returned, and the monster was peering down at him dispassionately. Compromise was lodged upright in the snow beside him. Baggi had not seen when she had put it there. He watched the riders seize their reigns once more as his mother came forth, shouting his name and rushing forward to wrap her arms protectively about him. The evil things left then, riding out just as they had arrived, silent. The memory faded and Baggi, the present Baggi, the clashing Baggi, found his hands gripping Compromise a bit too tightly. He relaxed them and allowed the place to dissolve.

He and Valdis stood, or perhaps only were, in a place that no longer had definition. He did not see himself or his opponent, but he knew at least that he still held Compromise.

"You think me a monster," observed Valdis. Her voice reached him from nearby, though of course she had no body to produce words with either.

"No," replied Baggi, his words soft and honest. "I did then. But I know now you're only a person."

"Then you concede that you were wrong," she said.

"No!" he shouted back. "You were wrong! You still are wrong! And you don't even see it!"

Shining blood began to flow into him from somewhere else.

"You think you're helping? You think a brave death is what you're giving people a chance at? Look at yourself!"

He conjured once more the image of Valdis, how he had seen her that day: not a human being, not a misunderstood altruist, not even an opponent. She was a being of darkness and fear, a force that existed solely to impart grief and seize hearts in predator's talons. The bones she wore showed them what awaited all those who lived. The bones bade them surrender.

"You go around taking lives and saying it's so they don't suffer!" he continued, screaming with unabated fury. "I promise you it doesn't work. How could you look at that boy and say he's not suffering?"

The monstrous Valdis dissipated and was replaced with Baggi at the Shrine of Shaefi in the center of town. He was praying, it seemed, but after mere moments he collapsed under his sorrow, falling to the cold stone in a heap of sobbing wails. He cried, and the crying was ugly and terrible. His grief, his hopelessness, filled the space they watched from. The older Baggi nearly cried as well. Yet he did not; he was too wrathful for that.

He grasped for Valdis' emotions and was thrilled to feel her own fear and grief join his. *Yes,* he exulted, *you've been a terror. You've done this.* All at once, the crying young Baggi became a girl in her teenage years, stained with blood and standing before a great pyre. Her eyes were dry and filled with satisfaction.

"You endured such pain because you could not let go," said Valdis. Her voice was gentle, nearly apologetic. "Until you learn acceptance, you will never understand."

All the lifeblood Baggi had earned began to leave him in a rush and her emotions became closed off once more. He felt himself weakening, felt life leaving him as Valdis claimed her victory with two simple sentences. *She's right about that, at least,* Baggi admitted sadly. A delirious determination echoed in his bones as he made up his mind for one last defense. *It's easy to say I've learned to let go,* he told Compromise, *but we have to prove it, don't we?* His staff pulsed sadly, and there was some fear in it as it knew what came next, but it bravely gave its assent regardless. At the same time, Baggi felt a comforting hand on his shoulder that quickly became a tight embrace full of joy and sorrow both. *Goodbye, Bjorn,* he thought, *and this time, I mean it.*

"Then I'll let go now," replied Baggi, "and let this be proof."

He raised Compromise far over his head and sundered it in two.

25

He awoke in sunlight, and his first feeling was warmth. His second feeling was confusion, and his third feeling was not his own, but it was concern. Baggi blinked hard and slowly raised a hand to rub his eyes, yawning softly as he did so. *Something is wrong,* he thought, *something is missing.* He tried to place the feeling, a hole in his chest that couldn't quite be pinned down, then in a sudden panic he threw off the blanket covering him and checked his body for external injuries. When he found none, Baggi breathed a little easier. He wondered briefly at the clothing he wore, a tan sleeveless shirt and violet knee-length skirt in the Kichishi style, and why he had been changed at all when he was uninjured. All at once, he remembered what he had done. *I destroyed Compromise,* he thought. A hollow feeling pounded in his heart; he smiled weakly despite it. *I let go. I said goodbye to Bjorn. I won.*

He sat up and took note of his surroundings. The room he was in looked to be of familiar construction to his lodgings in the inn, but he did not recognize its furnishings. There was only one bed, for starters, beneath a window, and a nightstand beside it piled high with all sorts of books written in Sparktongue. A chair was seated by the bed; apparently someone had been keeping vigil there. A desk squatted in the far corner under another window, overpopulated with papers and inkwells. Beside it was a wardrobe, huge and plain. The center of the floor boasted a fine, circular rug woven in patterns of scarlet flowers, presumably flamebuds, and a low table merely a foot high resided atop it. A small chimney was beside the door, but judging from the ashes inside, Baggi reckoned it hadn't seen much use lately. The ash reminded him of his cloak, and as he looked around, he spotted the garment hanging from a free-standing rack within arm's reach.

He stood, limbs stiff and weak, then went to the peg and donned his cloak. It felt a strange combination with his colorful Kichishi garments underneath. Baggi took one last look around at the room, searching for any indication of how to proceed, then shrugged and opened the door. The sensed concern led him forward. He found that his initial instinct had been correct; he was in the hallway of the Flamebud Inn. But the rooms the caravan had been renting were on his left, the doorway to the common room at the passage's opposite end. *So I was in... Torny's room,* he reasoned. The thought made him flush, though he couldn't quite say why. *I was sleeping in Torny's bed. That's nothing to dwell on. I'm sure she was staying elsewhere. Unless...* he hurried onward before his imagination could become ungovernable.

He stepped into the common room of the inn and was greeted at first by...nothing. It took several moments for anyone to notice him standing in the doorway. Guthini and Kettil were sitting at a stump-table; she seemed deep in thought, almost frustrated, as he leaned back with his arms crossed in triumph. Torny stood behind the bar, mere steps away from him, polishing a glass and staring vacantly into the air. The inn was otherwise empty. Baggi felt the concern from before, closer now, and knew it came from these three. He cleared his throat politely.

"Good morning," he said, "at least, if it is morning. I haven't been unconscious for the whole day, have I?"

All three faces shot toward him, and in a flash Torny was upon him, her arms around his shoulders and the polished glass shattering on the floor.

"Baggi!" shouted Kettil, rushing forward and hugging his left side.

"Oh! You're awake! I knew you'd pull through!" Guthini gasped, then joined them and embraced from the right.

"Yes, I'm fine," laughed Baggi, "just a little shaken. Where's everyone else?"

They pulled back slightly and exchanged unsure glances.

"Come sit down," said Kettil.

He did, nervousness building as they all settled into their seats. Torny poured each a mug of pepper-cider.

"So...um..." began Guthini, then stopped. He tried again, "So, you remember your Clash, right? With the leader? The, um...Staffkeepers of Death?"

"They prefer to be called The Conclusion," replied Baggi, "but yes, of course. It just happened; how could I have forgotten?"

"Oh yeah, you haven't had to wait around," said Kettil. "It probably feels like you just fell asleep and woke up, huh?"

"Wait around for what?" he asked nervously. "For how long?"

"For you to wake," said Torny, uncharacteristically soft-spoken, "for months now."

Baggi's eyes went wide. *How could it have been that long?* He thought. *Why didn't you wake me?* He asked Compromise. There was no response. *Oh yes. It's just me now.* His heart was sore with loss, the loss of his friend and of the time that had passed around him. He looked closer at his companions and saw now the passage of time on them. Guthini's Sparktongue was much easier now, he noticed, and he had been speaking without fear to Kettil. Kettil had apparently hit a growth spurt; she was now several inches taller than when Baggi had last seen her, perhaps even taller than Guthini. Both were leaner than he remembered, or perhaps that was only his imagination. Torny's eyes were glassy and bore heavy purple weights beneath them. *She must have had many sleepless nights,* Baggi thought, *so many days filled with worry.*

"Perhaps I'll just listen while you tell it all," he said sadly.

"Well," said Guthini reluctantly as the other two stayed quiet, "we were all locked up in our rooms that night. The day after Hakon's trial, I mean. And there was some noise outside, but we were under orders to stay in our rooms, from Elder Sage Hrafn and Chief Amund, so we didn't know what it was, but-"

"It was a woman, here to break Hakon out," interrupted Torny. "We fought, Amund helped, I killed her." She gazed into her mug with a far-off look. "But not before she killed Aghi."

Baggi remained silent, appreciative of the watcher and the few precious times he had had the opportunity to speak with him. *He was kind,* he thought, *and brave too.* He thought of the misplaced terror when he and Kettil had joined him uninvited in the lookout post and smiled a bit. *In his own way.*

"Yeah," Guthini resumed, uncomfortably, "so, in the morning we all came out and found out what had happened. And nobody knew that you and the old Elder Sage hadn't been in one of the rooms. I guess he didn't tell anyone about your plan because the Sages would have objected."

"And so would I!" declared Kettil. "Everyone lost their minds when I ran away for two days, but having you square off with the leader of...'The Conclusion', I guess...that's insane! She's terrifying!"

"So we all went and searched the village for you two," said Guthini, "and we found you in the forum. And Hrafn was..." he swallowed hard.

"He was dead," completed Baggi, "I know. I saw it happen."

There was a tentative silence.

"Right, he was dead," the younger lad continued, "and you were laying there on the stage too, and Compromise was next to you, but it was..." he paused and averted his eyes, "broken... so we thought you were dead as well, for a minute. But you weren't, obviously."

"We took you back here," Torny jumped in, "and I put you in my room to rest. The Staffkeepers took a look at you and said you weren't gonna die, but that you must have absorbed a lot of energy or something when your staff broke and the magic exploded out. Right?"

She looked to Guthini for confirmation.

"Basically," he agreed.

"They said we just had to wait and take care of you until you woke up, and that's what we've been doing," Torny said. "But after a week, the Sages said they couldn't wait anymore."

"They went back to Enton to pick a new Elder Sage," clarified Kettil, "but me and Guthini stayed to make sure you're okay, just in case something weird happens. I've been feeding you a new elixir to help your body reset. It's called Balance, and it's really amazing, even if I do say so myself! See-"

"Tell him about it later, Kettil," said Guthini. "He needs a moment to collect himself."

His courage shocked Baggi, but she only huffed and fell silent. The Staffkeeper sat and allowed the information to settle. Torny poured him another drink, and he felt their apprehensions intensify with each passing moment. Eventually, he nodded and sighed.

"Where is Compromise?" he asked.

"Amund has the pieces," answered Torny. "He wanted to keep them safe for you. Real stubborn about it, actually."

Baggi grinned despite himself. "That sounds like Amund."

His friends chuckled, relieved that he seemed to be taking the news so well.

"And Valdis?"

Torny and Guthini stared at him blankly, but Kettil knew to whom he referred.

"We don't know," she answered. "She wasn't there when we found you. But..." she hesitated, "there was a pile of bones."

Baggi balked at her. He thought of the grotesque version of herself Valdis had seen, that he had forced her to see, and then the pieces fell into place and he smiled.

"Not hers," he said, visibly relieved.

The others looked at him strangely and he felt their conflicted feelings, disappointment and relief in one. They sat silently in the sweltering heat of the inn's interior. *It's so hot, even for Kichishi,* thought Baggi. *I suppose it must be summer now.* Somehow, that was the most jarring part of it all.

"So, uh, what now?" asked Kettil, "I mean, should we go home to Enton? That's what the Sages told us to do."

Baggi felt Torny's yearning seize him, but she remained passive.

"Now," said Baggi evasively, "I'm going to see Amund."

***

"Halt!" shouted the Chief of Flamebud to the approaching wagon.

They obeyed, boars slowing to a stop as they pulled up alongside him. Their driver, a weathered man with a wrinkly face, doffed his cap politely.

"Greetings, sir," he said in passable Sparktongue.

Two sweaty little faces stood and peeked at Amund from the back of the wagon before a woman, perspiring even more heavily, stood and forced them back to their seats. They were pale, but their hair ranged from black to ruby. *Half-Kichishi,* he ascertained.

"Greetings," he replied. "What is your business in Kichishi?"

"We're returning to our homeland," beamed the man. "My parents brought me to Yngmuth when I was just a baby, looking for work, but the work's all dried up 'cept for the Guild stooges. So I thought to myself, 'why not take the family back to where we came from, eh?' Heck of a lot warmer here, at the least!"

Amund grinned. "A wise choice. Though the flames burn hotter when you stand before them."

The man smiled back as he recognized the Kichishi proverb.

"We'll adapt," he said.

Amund reached into a pocket and handed him a slip of paper.

"This carries my seal as Chief of Flamebud," he said. "It will take you as far as Ehkag if you wish. Present it at any further checkpoints. Welcome home."

The man thanked him, and his family waved happily as the wagon stumbled down the path and out of the mountains. *How generous I have become,* thought Amund mildly. As he watched the wagon descend, a single traveler approached the opposite direction, coming towards him. *And who is this?* he wondered. *They do not seem laden for a journey into Naefja.* The figure came closer, and all at once Amund recognized him: even in Kichishi clothing, his pale complexion gave him away. The approaching traveler waved overhead.

"Baggi?" said Amund, perplexed, then, as confusion turned to joy, "Baggi!"

He ran forth to meet his friend halfway, embracing him before even a word could be exchanged. The newly awakened lad laughed as the sudden approach nearly bowled him over.

"It is good to see you awake, my friend!" he gushed. "I was beginning to fear the worst!"

"Then your fears were misplaced," Baggi replied. "All I needed was a bit of hibernation."

"Ha!" laughed Amund. "A summer hibernation; bizarre, yet it suits you. How do you feel? If you are able to walk this far unassisted, it seems Kettil's potion kept you well after all."

"I feel fine," Baggi assured him, "just a little winded. It's not easy trekking without a staff to lean on."

Amund's face darkened. "Of course. I offer my condolences."

"Thank you," he replied sincerely. After a moment of silence, he said, "I'm told you have the pieces?"

"I do. None else could be trusted to guard them."

The Naefjan snorted. "Guard them from what? Staff-thieves?"

"You joke," replied Amund seriously, "but such a thing has been known to happen."

"Perhaps, but only if the staff is not already broken."

"True enough," he granted.

"Still, I'm glad you have held onto it. I wouldn't have chosen anyone else for the job. I assume you carry them with you?"

"I do."

He took off his *korta* and carefully extracted two staves with splintered ends, expertly hidden among the fabric. The runes that had before always glowed with cold power now were dark and empty. Amund relinquished them. Baggi held them, one in each hand, and smiled sadly as he held them close together. He nearly looked like he might try to rejoin the pieces, but then he stopped and held them apart once more.

"Thank you," he said. "I may not have any use for them anymore, but I'm glad to have them all the same."

"Will you still be a Staffkeeper without a staff?" asked Amund.

It seemed inconceivable to him that his friend could be anything but a Staffkeeper, so suited to it was he, yet that was not Amund's choice to make.

"Yes, I think so," came the reply. "I am a Staffkeeper; there's no sense denying that. A Staffkeeper of Shaefi, though? I don't think that's quite right. Either way, I suppose I'll need a new staff, but I'm not sure where to start. I've never crafted one before." He grinned weakly at Amund. "This one was never really mine to begin with, you know."

Amund put a comforting arm around his shoulder. They looked out over Kichishi below them, heat waves shimmering beautifully in the sky over the forest. Just on the edge of their vision, towards Ehkag, they could see where the forest ended and the grasslands began. It was a compelling contrast, the two landscapes so tightly pressed against each other.

"I think," he said eventually, "that I can assist you with this."

They went back down to the village on the hidden short path rather than the main road, talking the whole way of what had happened during Baggi's slumber. Apparently Kalfr was shaping up to be a promising martial artist, approaching others in skill who were years older; he accompanied Amund to the pass some days to prepare to assume the duty himself, but that was yet years off. Audr and Vigi were engaged and would marry at summer's end, and with the banker's wealth, the ceremony was apparently to be quite lavish. Amund's ancestral garden was producing phenomenally, and, inexplicably, so was the banker's; it seemed the hunger crisis had been averted after all. Of course, there was also less cheery news: neighboring villages had begun to lose sympathy for the town of children and now some turned hungry eyes toward what seemed a vulnerable opportunity for expansion. The flamebuds lived well in the woods, but their presence in the village proper was still sorely missed.

"And Hakon?" asked Baggi. "What became of him?"

"I carried out his sentence," said Amund evenly. "He is dead."

Baggi was quiet then.

"You grieve him?" prompted Amund.

"Yes," he agreed, "but not for long. It was his choice, after all. He decided he was ready, and he was not afraid to die. I know this."

Amund nodded. They walked the rest of the way to the village in silence, stopping many times along the way, partially so Baggi could absorb the news and partially because Kettil's potion hadn't been foolproof and the staffless Staffkeeper tired far easier now. Eventually they reached Flamebud Village, and with each villager they passed, the duo was forced to stop and entertain their well-wishes and exclamations of gladness for such a miraculous recovery. Still, it was not unpleasant.

When they reached their destination, Amund pushed open the gates to his mansion and led Baggi to a much smaller structure with gaping, paneless windows and a partial curtain hung over the otherwise open door frame. Inside, in the exact center of the marble floor, lay a smaller version of the offering space atop the mansion. Before it was a single cushion with incense burners on either side. Incense burned long ago somehow still lingered, filling the air with a pleasant musk and the texture of solemnity. A workbench with tools for wood-carving and metallurgy stood against the far wall.

"This is where my mother used to meditate," said Amund, "and a place where a Staffkeeper may craft their tool. It is a very special place."

He needn't have added the last; judging from his friend's expression, the shrine's gravity was not lost on him.

"I'm honored to be here," Baggi said.

"I am opening this place to you so that you may meditate in it when you wish. I will guide you in our method of constructing a new staff when you are ready," the chief continued. "Do you know what material you wish to use?"

Baggi thought on this for some time, staring at the pieces of Compromise in his hands.

"I'll need some time to decide," he said.

"You have it," stated Amund. "Now, come. You must be hungry. Even if not, I am. Let us go to the inn, yes?"

"Yes," said Baggi, all but drooling, "I haven't eaten in months."

***

The meal was excellent as always, Torny's cooking full of spice and passion and the pepper-cider sweet and refreshing. Baggi felt a strange tension between himself and the innkeeper, a resentment he couldn't explain. *What could I have done?* He wondered. *I haven't even been conscious.* The conundrum of his new staff, however, occupied most of his attention. Compromise had been carved from apple-wood, and that had seemed to him a good fit, but the metallurgy tools in Amund's shrine implied his new partner could be forged from metal if he so desired. He thought and thought and wondered if that were something he wished at all, and through it all he felt a strong guilt for leaving Compromise behind. *I can't abandon it,* he resolved, *not after all this. I can't turn my back on all I learned with Compromise by my side. Yet*

I can't cling to the past, either, or that would disrespect what its sacrifice meant.

Baggi retreated to his room, Torny's room, and stared into the cold chimney. The ash inside reminded him of the flamebud ceremony. *That was months ago in the village,* he reflected, *and mere days ago in me.* He took up ash in his hands and remembered what he had felt then, why he still wore his scorched and ruined cloak even now. *The old makes way for the new,* he pondered, *yet the new rises from the old. Like life and Death: one could not exist without the other. They're not black or white. They're grey. They're ash. But that's not how Shaefini see it, is it?* He thought of what Hrafn had said, about the Staffkeepers of Shaefi misunderstanding their own goddesses' final lesson. *Their core doctrine is in direct opposition to her principles. How could I expect them to change so fundamentally, based on nothing other than one boy's urging? Trying to reshape an Order that's so far gone is an act of desperation. Insisting otherwise is just the same as clinging to the past.* An idea began to form in his mind, but the noise of the common room kept it from fully developing. *Perhaps some time alone would help.*

He left via the backdoor, not wishing to incur further well-intentioned distractions, but a sense of hurt came upon him even before a familiar voice stopped him in his tracks.

"Where are you going?" Torny demanded.

"Out for a walk."

"That's not what I mean," she snapped. Her emotions hurled themselves at him: confusion, anger, grief, affection. "You love me, don't you?"

He smiled a bit. "Yes."

"And I love you," she said, "so are you staying here or not?"

Baggi was quiet for a while. It had been on his mind, too, but he hadn't been ready to decide. There had been so many surprises, after all. He had been overwhelmed. He had been nervous. Now he slowly approached and wrapped his arms around her.

"I'm going," he said, making the decision in the same moment. "But I'm not going far, and not for a while yet. I promise."

Torny's anger suddenly melted into sheer sorrow. She cried on his shoulder and violently pushed the tears away and then cried again.

"I've been worried," she admitted. "I thought you might never wake up, and here I was taking care of you and telling everyone it was gonna be any day now and every day believing myself a little less. And now you're awake, you're finally awake, and you're leaving? After all of that, you're just going back to Naefja? It's not fair!"

He hugged her tight and shared her grief and worry, felt the months that she had weathered all tear at him now. It was nearly unbearable.

"I'm not going back to Naefja," he whispered after her cries had quieted, "but I can't do what I need to in Flamebud Village. I'll be close, very close. It's important, I promise."

"I don't care how important it is," she sniffled, "if you're close, that's fine."

Baggi chuckled softly at that. *She's so direct,* he thought affectionately. Then the true impact of how close to dying he had been finally settled in his mind and he heaved a shaking breath. He pulled back slightly and took note of each speck and crease on Torny's face, committing them to memory but, more importantly, seeing them now. He kissed her. She wiped her face and then pushed him playfully away.

"Alright, go off on your mysterious lonesome," she teased, "but you better come back right after. And I'm sending you with some food and a lantern." He began to protest, but she silenced him with a finger. "Don't even think about arguing. You don't have any magic anymore, remember? How were you even planning on seeing out there in the dark?"

I was going to use Sowilo, Baggi admitted to himself, *except that I can't.*

"Okay," he consented.

She went away, keeping her eyes fixed on him until the last possible second, as if suspicious that he would violate his word and run off as soon as she turned, and after a few moments returned with a lantern in one hand and a basket in the other. He took them and walked through the streets of Flamebud Village, nibbling on the food she had packed despite his already full stomach, pondering whether his choice to leave the Staffkeepers of Shaefi was the right one, and, for that matter, if making such a choice marked him as a lunatic.

***

In the morning, he and Torny shared an early breakfast as she continued to catch him up on those proceedings which Amund had neglected to mention. After months of lying comatose, Baggi naturally felt quite weak, but for all that, his physical ability was remarkably well preserved by Kettil's new potion. He remarked upon this observation to the innkeeper.

"It's good that she found a new project to work on," he said, "after the Water of Life debacle. You see, she was attempting-"

"Oh yeah, I know all about that," Torny interrupted. "She told me a few weeks ago."

Baggi was stunned. *Of course,* he thought, *they must have grown close over these months. I imagine Kettil and Guthini are more at home here now than I am.*

"Ah, right," he said, "well, as I said, it's good that she moved on from that."

"I don't know if she moved on from it, so much as modified it."

"What do you mean?"

Torny made a hands-off gesture to absolve herself of the topic.

"Look, you better talk to her about it. I don't know the first thing about alchemy, so whatever I say is probably gonna be at least half wrong."

"Hm," nodded Baggi, worried now more than ever that Kettil may have persisted in her attempt to do away with Death. "It's strange that she and Guthini aren't here now. Do they take breakfast elsewhere, or have they simply gotten into the habit of sleeping in?"

"Hah!" she snorted. "No, they're right outside."

"I see," he replied, not quite understanding. "Then shall I invite them in?"

"Only if they're done. Usually I'd be out there too, but someone needs to make breakfast when there's an invalid in house."

His confusion only growing with each word, Baggi went to the door and pushed it open, a wave of early morning light rushing in to greet him. Outside, the villagers were standing in rows, training in combat. Amund stood before them and led them through form drills; based on the perspiration coating each student, Baggi assumed they had been at it for some time. Finally, their instructor allowed them a short break to drink from the well and bid them stand aside from the square, single file. In doing so he caught sight of the Naefjan on the porch observing.

"Baggi," he called out, "just in time to witness your friends' progress. Guthini and Kettil! You will be first to spar!"

To his amazement, Kettil skipped forward into the center of the square, garbed in cuffed pants and a sleeveless tunic. She waved at him and took a fighting stance, bobbing energetically even before

Guthini had stepped forth. Though similarly garbed, his arrival was more reluctant and his stance somewhat stiffer.

"Are you sure I can't partner with someone else?" he squeaked. "Like, for example...anyone?"

"You wish, baldy!" Kettil taunted.

Guthini narrowed his eyes and sighed as Amund gave the command to begin.

The scuffle was brief and graceless. Kettil was a born scrapper, and as Baggi recalled she had been brought up an orphan on the unforgiving streets of Yngmuth. By comparison, Guthini had no natural predilection toward fighting. Still, he gave his best effort. Unfortunately, his best effort was not enough to stop the frenzied ball of aggression that was his opponent. In under half a minute, he was on his back with a bloody nose, Kettil standing over him and jumping up and down in tasteless celebration. Beside him, Amund glanced over with some embarrassment.

"They are still new," he said apologetically. "I am teaching her restraint."

The Staffkeeper was too stunned by the entire scene to respond. Even as the rest of Amund's pupils carried out their own spars, he struggled to reconcile what he knew of his friends with their new pursuit. *I would have thought this to be the first thing he mentioned when we were catching up. It seems I'm not the only one Flamebud Village has changed,* he thought. Then he grinned. *Perhaps I won't need to bid them farewell after all.*

Finally the training session was dismissed and Kettil and Guthini approached him.

"What'd you think?" she demanded. "I'm pretty good, huh?"

She rubbed a bruise on her chin that Baggi hadn't notice before; it seemed Guthini hadn't been so completely helpless as he had appeared.

"You were remarkable, that much is certain," he replied. "I thought fighting was not allowed for Shaefini?"

Guthini looked guilty behind the bloody rag at his nose.

"Well, it's not real combat or anything," he said. "We're not actually trying to kill each other or anything. At least, I'm not."

He glared pointedly at Kettil. Baggi bit off a grin.

"A wise friend once told me that is a foolish distinction to make," he said.

"Aw come on, are you really gonna give us away?" Kettil whined.

"Far from it. Actually, there's something I want to ask of you over breakfast."

When they were seated at a stump-table and breakfast had been served, Guthini balked at his suggestion.

"You mean just...not go back?" he asked.

"That's the least of it," Baggi clarified. "The most being that I plan on starting my own Staffkeeping Order, and I want you both to be a part of it. It's clear that you disagree with at least one part of Shaefini doctrine, so why remain with an Order that doesn't represent your ideals?"

"And what are the ideals of your new Order to be?" the younger lad asked, conflicted feelings fiercely contesting in his features.

"Rebirth," he answered, "renewal. The cycle of life and death, one thing ending and making way for another. The grey place between each where the cycle begins anew, the place where extremes melt together and become something different born of both. Just like our world, this Order will be one of compromise and complications: the Staffkeepers of Ashes."

His friends were quiet for a long time. Guthini avoided looking at him, and Baggi could feel his indecision and resentment from where he sat. *It's to be expected,* he accepted, *I'm asking much of them. Quite likely too much.* He opened his mouth to assure them of their continued friendship regardless of what they decided, but Kettil spoke first.

"Okay," she said.

She pinched a bite of stewed spinach between her flatbread and chewed without hurry.

"Are... are you certain of this?" Baggi asked, surprised by her decisiveness. "I'm glad for it, of course, but this is a big decision to make on a whim."

"Yeah, well, I was barely even Shaefini to start with," she replied through a full mouth. "So long as I can keep being an alchemist, I don't care where I'm doin' it."

"And you're okay with leaving Elof behind?" muttered Guthini.

Kettil waved a dismissive hand without bothering to face him.

"We've been writin'. I'll just send him a letter tellin' him what we decided. It's not like I'm never gonna see him again. He can visit us, or we can visit them."

"If they'll have you," he scoffed, "after you've betrayed the kindness they brought you up with."

"Look," she snapped, "I'm not makin' war with 'em! I'm just not workin' for 'em anymore!"

Guthini sighed. His emotions were a maelstrom, desire for freedom grappling with an instinctual defensiveness of his upbringing. *He was raised at Enton from a baby,* Baggi thought, *meant to be a Staffkeeper of Shaefi his whole life. His won't be such an easy choice as Kettil's.* Even so, he had hope for the other lad; his months in Flamebud had obviously done much to shake his stalwart belief in the rigid ways of the Shaefini. The apprentice stood up from the table.

"I need some time to think," he said.

He left them then, leaving behind an untouched bowl of breakfast. Kettil raised her eyebrows.

"Welp. Mind if I take his?"

Baggi grinned, glad to have her on his side no matter Guthini's eventual decision. Yet his stomach still growled with the hunger of his hibernation.

"We can split it," he said, "while you fill me in on your new project."

"Sure thing. So I gave up on the Water of Life – not when I told you I did, but later, after I ran away – 'cause it ended up makin' something really disgusting when I tried it, so now I'm just tryin' to make something that fixes people while they're alive, but it's a lot harder without bein' able to use blood as an ingredient, you know..."

26

Hjordis took in the ramshackle house, mold and moisture in her nostrils. It was a reasonably large building, with four rooms on the second story and the kitchen beneath, but clearly the structure had seen better days. She turned an eye toward the gaping hole in the roof through which rain and sea spray fairly poured. *Suppose that's the first thing we fix,* she thought. Scanning the room for a bucket or a trough with which to catch the worst of the drip, she located a tin tub that did a serviceable job. Already her cloak was heavy with water, but she didn't much mind. *I'll have to get used to the damp,* she resolved, *that's just how it is by the sea.*

"Ah, Hjordis, could you lend me a hand?" came a voice at the door behind her.

She turned to where Elof was struggling through the threshold, arms full of luggage and construction materials, and rushed to relieve him. Between the two of them, they managed to stockpile their supplies in the kitchen beneath the stairs, deciding on the spot by virtue of its being the driest in the house. Their hoard consisted of two rucksacks containing their own personal belongings, as well as waterproofed wood to board up holes, stone-gum to seal cracks, several crates of carefully packed alchemical supplies, and stack after stack of literature from the archives at the Temple of Enton, all covered up neatly with a waterproof tarp.

"The tarp was a good idea," Hjordis said, catching her breath.

"Yes, well, it's the first investment one should make in Yngmuth," he replied. "There's always something that needs covering up."

They stood embracing each other, absorbing their new lodgings as the water dripped into the tub and the summer winds howled through the gap. *Even at this time of year,* thought Hjordis, *it's pouring like winter. I can't say I'm looking forward to the cold months.* Satisfaction, slung on her back, indicated its agreement, yet offered an optimistic reassurance as well. *I know, it'll be worth it. This will be a good place.*

"Oh," she said in sudden remembrance, "what about the sign?"

Elof hummed agreement and bade her follow him back outside. A latticework of tracks and trails carved through the mud in the lane, footprints and boar-tracks and neat lines made by wheels all overlapping and being splashed and erased and reprinted again the moment the next traveler came along. *The road will never look the same for longer than a moment here,* she thought, and it made their situation seem suddenly unstable. She breathed slowly and rebalanced her emotions. *Maybe that will become comforting in time.* They were close to the harbor; from the small yard behind the house, one could perhaps throw a stone into the ocean, if their arm were strong. Even such a short distance, however, was packed with two rows of homes and storehouses, blocking their view without shielding them from the mist or the roar of Yngmuth's bestial waters. *How anyone manages to sail in that – or is willing to, for that matter – is a mystery,* Hjordis marveled as the waves thundered.

Her partner went to the far side of their humble single-boar cart and raised one side of the expansive sign lashed to the back, bound tightly with a second tarp. She took the other end and together they hauled it inside to join the rest of their supplies.

"I suppose I had better start lacquering it right away; in these conditions it will take quite a while to dry," said Elof.

He fired the oven to dispel some of the cold and humidity, then donned his gloves and opened a crate full of alchemical ingredients. When he had assembled the necessary materials, he removed the tarp to reveal the sign, a grand display of fine painted oak that read:

ORDER OF THE STAFFKEEPERS OF SHAEFI, YNGMUTH CHAPTER

Hjordis kissed him on the cheek and filled her pockets with nails and a hammer, then hauled several planks upstairs.

"I'll take care of the roof," she said as she went. "Can't have the children living underwater."

She spent some time simply assessing the structure, finding a rusty iron staircase fixed to the exterior back wall that allowed her roof access and then cautiously testing her weight atop each tile lest she create another undesired skylight and injure herself in the process. When this was done, she took measurements and went back down to cut the wood to proper dimensions. Finally, she returned above and nailed the planks over the gap, sealing the remaining cracks with stone-gum. It was a clumsy job, but it would do until they were settled and at liberty to make touch-ups. *Maybe we could even hire a professional,* Hjordis entertained. *Not sure where we would find the odd for that, but you never know what could happen.*

She returned downstairs as Elof finished applying a coat of his personally formulated clear lacquer. She noted with delight that he had spent the time between applying coats mopping up pools of rainwater and marking which floorboards were dangerously rotted. He set their sign by the oven so that it might dry faster and sat across from it in the cramped kitchen. Hjordis sat too, stretching out her legs on the floorboards beside him with their backs against the cupboard and the enormity of their mission settling over them.

"You know," she yawned, "the Staffkeepers of Brathus think that the constant rainfall here is from the Prime Water."

"The waterfall that filled the ocean," he nodded, catching her yawn. "They say it's one of many, actually. That Brathus keeps them pouring so that the water lost over Solabell's edge is replenished and the ocean isn't dried up."

Hjordis snorted. *Of course, he's from here. It figures he would know all about it already.* It was common knowledge among the educated that Solabell was convex, yet for it to have an edge, where the world simply fell off into nothingness, seemed unbelievable even for all that.

"Do you believe that?" She asked.

She leaned her head on his shoulder and pulled her cloak, soaking wet and smelling of salt, over the both of them.

"If you trust men like Einar Sharpaxe," he shrugged, taking a sarcastic tone "it has been seen. According to them, it's not a question anymore; they've sailed to the edge and back, with the help of the Staffkeepers of Brathus to keep them falling off. And I always trust in the assurances of a pirate."

She chuckled.

"I love you," she said.

"I love you too."

It had been a long day of travel, with several hours of work tacked on as well; the overcast grey light of day was dying out. They kissed while the oven's heat fell upon them, and promptly afterwards drifted off to sleep. Hjordis dreamt that night of falling into the harbor, and from there being swept off the edge of the world. She fell through darkness, an endless fall with only gallon after gallon of black water for company. She reached in the dream for Satisfaction and awoke to find her staff in hand. She hugged it to her chest, snuggled closer to Elof, and fell asleep, dreaming no more.

***

The next few weeks passed in much the same way, Hjordis tending to the larger structural concerns and Elof taking on interior work and planning for the logistics of how their new chapter would be run. Over supper, on the floor in front of the oven, they would discuss the day's triumphs and shortcomings and talk of how delightful it would be when they were ready to house apprentices, of what a difference they would make in providing the hopeless unseen children of Yngmuth an alternative to the Alchemist's Guild, a place where they would be provided for, respected, loved as if they were blood. Gradually the house became habitable; they spent the odd allowed them by the Sages at Enton on furniture and other necessities, making the rooms as comfortable as they could and even taking the liberty of purchasing some decorations for the common area. Elof planted a garden in the back yard and potted more delicate flora inside to brighten the place.

Then, on a day wherein a rare few hours' sunshine pierced the cloudy harbor's skies, a courier came to deliver a letter in a wax-sealed tube. Elof took the tube and paid the man; it was a steep sum, four yellow odd, yet he did not hesitate, for the pattern adorning the tube made clear its origin was Kichishi. It could only have been a letter from Kettil, updating him on her extended stay in Flamebud Village and, perhaps, bearing news of Baggi's condition. Hjordis peeked over the rooftop where she was hanging the sign, its lacquer finally dry.

"What is it?" she called down. "More instructions from Elder Sage Runa? Or even better, a bigger allowance?"

"It's from Kettil," he replied as he scanned the contents. "She's still quite enjoying her stay in Flamebud Village, and it seems...oh my! It seems Baggi has awoken!"

Hjordis rushed down the iron staircase and through the house to the front yard, hovering close as she read over Elof's shoulder.

"That's amazing!" she gushed. "Such a relief! I was beginning to worry..."

She trailed off as they both continued to read. It seemed he had disagreed with his elders' instructions to return to the Temple at Enton. It seemed his disagreements hadn't stopped there.

"I suppose we won't be seeing them any time soon," Elof mumbled.

Hjordis clenched her jaw and took several breaths, attempting to rebalance her emotions. It did her little good.

***

Baggi inhaled the incense, filling his lungs with its sweet-burning cinnamon smoke, then pictured the ashes its sweetness would be reduced to and let go of the breath. It had burned his lungs a bit, yet it had also filled his senses with pleasantness. He could not smell the sweetness without inhaling the smoke, and he would not have inhaled the smoke if not for the sweetness. *Existence in pure symbiosis*, he thought. The incense was an apt representative of his new philosophy, of his new Order. He took another breath and repeated the cycle until the incense had burned down and was no more. When it was gone, he opened his eyes and looked around the shrine. He was alone, always was in the hut behind Amund's mansion, but as usual he felt a presence with him that he couldn't explain. He made guesses, naturally: that it was Sawtor's presence he felt, in the shrine dedicated to her; that it was Amund's mother, the presence of her own past meditations and convictions as a Staffkeeper; that it was something else entirely, perhaps the awareness of his new role as a Staffkeeper of Ashes. In the end, he decided it was likely something of all three, and many other things he hadn't thought of as well. *That's the way of our world, isn't it?* He thought. *It's never just one clear answer.*

He unfolded his legs, stretching before he rose from the cushion. The ashes of the breakfast and he had offered in the pit before him lingered, accumulating higher and higher with every morning that he spent in the shrine. Amund had instructed him not to sweep out the offering space until that which he meditated upon was resolved, and now, after a month had passed in such a way, the pile was rather sizable. He fastened his cloak and went out to greet the day.

As he pushed back through the wrought-iron gate, Baggi pondered that question that had occupied him since awakening from his clash. *Willow? Oak? Yew? Perhaps the tree of a local fruit, like needle-pear? Wait, no, that would be a cactus.* He sighed as he made his way to the inn, scratching his head and straining his mind and ultimately reaching his destination, but not a decision. He went inside and entered the kitchen, donning a stained apron and pausing for a moment as he watched Torny at work. Her pace was exceptional, knife flying as she chopped vegetables and seasoned by the handful without stopping to measure. He stood, smiling and admiring her, for as long as he dared. Eventually he cleared his throat to announce himself.

"About time," she teased, only glancing his way for half a moment before returning her full attention to her cooking. "Go ahead and get started on the flatbread, will you?"

He stood at the counter opposite her, facing the common room, and began to weigh the flour and water on the scale as she had taught him. When they were combined, he set to kneading the dough, occasionally adding a pinch of flour when it got too sticky and clung to the countertop. Baggi was glad that Torny had put him to work as soon as he was fully recovered; without a staff, he had no way of earning his keep, and had worried his lack of contribution would make him a burden upon Flamebud Village. The innkeeper had made his fears irrelevant by demanding he assist her in running the business. With Aghi gone, she had been sorely overworked and was glad for even his inexperienced hands.

"How was your morning?" she asked over her shoulder as they worked.

"It was nice," he replied. "Any excitement here?"

She scoffed at the very idea.

"I was meaning to ask you," he continued after a moment, "what type of wood your people use in funeral pyres."

"You ask the strangest things," she remarked. "I dunno, probably birch. There's plenty of those around. We get a lot of wildfires, because of the flamebuds and the creeping kindling, and birch is always the first to sprout afterwards."

"Is that so?" he asked, a wide grin growing on his face.

"Yeah, it is."

Some time later, lunch was prepared, and they had a chance to take a break in the common area. Occasionally a villager would come in for a brief respite from their business, and either he or Torny would attend to them and pour their cider or serve their meal, but Baggi had come to understand that afternoons were usually slow at the Flamebud Inn. They sat and chatted and ate the lunch they had prepared, and eventually Kettil came through the door and joined them. She was sweating profusely and carrying her alchemy box, which she slammed down on the counter in a dramatic display of exhaustion.

"Am I imaginin' it," she asked, "or do folks get way sicker now than when we first showed up?"

"It's summer," offered the innkeeper, "much more likely to get sun-sickness."

"Don't I know it," Kettil grumbled.

"Any progress on your panacea?" Baggi asked.

"Haven't had any time for it!" she complained. "And even when I did, it wasn't goin' too well. Makin' a potion that cures every wound and every sickness without stopping aging or sprouting an extra limb or somethin' is a lot harder than it sounds."

"I'm sure it's exactly as hard as it sounds."

"Don't get clever, Baggi," she said, laying her sticky face on the bare bar and wagging an admonishing finger at him.

The door creaked open once more and the trio turned to see an unexpected visitor: Guthini stood in the doorway, rubbing his arm awkwardly. He waved at them but made no indication to come inside. Torny, luckily, had no patience for such discomfort.

"Come in already!" she yelled. "It's been long enough. Kinda stupid to stop coming around just because you and Baggi had a disagreement. Where have you even been eating? Want some cider?"

"That sounds great," he said after a moment's hesitation.

He approached the bar and made an unclear noise in his throat. Then he coughed and tried again.

"Um, Baggi, I want to talk to you about, you know, the whole..."

"Of course," he answered.

Torny deposited two mugs of pepper-cider on the bar before them and tactfully requested Kettil's help in the kitchen in order to give them privacy and set the lad at ease. Guthini was quiet and appeared to be deep in thought. Baggi reached out with his Blessing and felt embarrassment, yet beneath it laid a deep resolve. *A resolve to join me,* he wondered, *or to oppose?*

"So you've come to a decision?" he prompted.

"I have," Guthini replied.

There was a long silence as he allowed the younger boy to gather his thoughts.

"We've been in Kichishi for a long time now," he continued, "nearly five months. But I'm not complaining at all! I really like it here. There's lots of things I like about it. I like the weather, how you can take your clothes off outside without even worrying about frostbite. I like the food, how it hurts at first but when you get used to it it's so full of flavor that you never want to stop eating. I like the people, and how they're all so confident and loud."

He looked over and made eye contact with Baggi, a previously unseen determination in him now.

"And I like how they fight," he asserted, "how they protect each other and how they protect themselves, and how they're not afraid to admit when something can't be solved by fighting with words."

"I like that too," the elder boy smiled.

"But I also like the way we are in Naefja," Guthini said. "I like how we always try to talk our problems out, even when it's obvious it won't work. I like how we laugh so often, and always stay calm, and I love how the cold back home wakes you up and reminds you to be alive. And I tried to decide which way I like better, but I couldn't. So, well, if your Order is all about the middle ground, and being a little bit of both things, then...I think that makes more sense to me than choosing one."

Baggi wasted no time with words. Instead, he pulled Guthini into an embrace, the apprentice squawking in alarm, and patted him affectionately on the back. After several moments he released his friend.

"I hoped you would see it that way," he said.

*****

"You are certain this is what you wish?" Amund asked.

"I am certain," Baggi asserted.

"Very well. Let us chop."

They alternated swinging axes at the base of the birch tree in the woods outside Flamebud's walls, hacking away at the trunk with as much reverence as could be afforded such a violent action. It took longer than the Staffkeeper anticipated, and he was glad that his strength had returned to him over the past month as Amund had coached him in conditioning his body. He hadn't been fit to train in combat, only having just returned to his previous level of fitness, but Baggi didn't mind. He had enough on his plate already. *Perhaps someday, but as things are now, I never would have managed,* he thought between strokes, *and for that matter, I may not have managed this either, not without Amund.* Indeed, the chief's swings cut deeper than his friend's by far, yet this seemed unimportant to him. His face was flushed with excitement, and he seemed to revel in each stroke. *Some people thrive on exertion,* Baggi thought. Finally, after the better part of an hour, the tree was felled and their task complete. They bound it with ropes and hauled it back together, Amund once more shouldering more than his own fair share of the burden.

When it was back in the yard behind the mansion, he turned back and clapped his hands together.

"And now, once more into the woods," he said.

"Again? Isn't this more than enough wood?"

"To craft a staff, we do not require wood only," Amund answered, already making for the gates. "We will need flamebuds as well."

"What for?"

"You know that before Shaefi made humans and animals, Sawtor created the land we live on, all land and all plants in Solabell?" Amund asked. "She took special care with the flamebuds; they are special to her. This is why they are special to us. When we burn them in the tempering flames, she will accept the significance of our offering and our undertaking."

Baggi nodded and forced the weariness from his mind.

"Then we'd better fetch quite a few," he said.

The next nine days were spent at work on the staff. Under Amund's instruction, Baggi carved the birch wood into a rod half the length of Compromise. He spent hours meditating on each rune as he carved, infusing their essences into the tool and bringing the staff to life piece by piece. When this was done, he took one piece of Compromise and bound it to the new wood with the roots of the flamebuds he and Amund had retrieved. Then he repeated the initial process as he renewed the runes already present on his old staff. Life inhabited the piece, not Compromise or Bjorn this time, but a new presence entirely.

They finally tempered the staff over the heat of the flamebuds. As the roots burned away, their impression scorched onto the joining place of the old and new wood, fusing them together. Baggi was in awe of the process; he had felt the need to pepper Amund with questions throughout, and his friend had answered even as he insisted he focus on the task at hand.

"The flamebuds' fire will bring it to life," he had said. "Its roots will keep the pieces in place, and when we offer them to Sawtor through the flames she will bind them together permanently."

The Naefjan took the completed staff in his hands, two halves made one. The runes on the top half, the birch wood, glowed orange; the runes on the bottom glowed ice-blue in remembrance of Compromise. All over, the blackened root pattern of where the flamebuds had embraced the staff persisted. *It's beautiful,* he thought, then remembered that the staff was alive. *You're beautiful,* he told it. *I suppose you'll need some time to get to know me.* Yet the connection was strong already; not as strong as that which he and Compromise had shared, perhaps, but certainly stronger than where they had started. This attunement was more personal; it was not Bjorn in the staff, but something like himself. He felt its energy, curious and thoughtful, and grew excited for the road ahead.

"So?" asked Amund, wiping the sweat of their labor from his face. "What is it called?"

Baggi felt the staff in his hands, felt the intentions he had imbued it with and the receptiveness with which it had taken them. He smiled.

"Acceptance."

EPILOGUE

"**A**re you ready?" asked Baggi.

Guthini nodded.

"Kettil?"

"Yep."

Acceptance probed through its partner's eyes, devouring each new sight and sound as it had been doing since birth. *Pay attention now,* he gently told the infant staff. *Partings and new starts are always worth remembering.* He chuckled as it eagerly took his advice, honing its focus on the farewell committee.

"You'll be back soon," commanded Torny, embracing him and kissing him before locking eyes. "Or I'll come after you."

"I know," he smiled.

"I will visit you often," said Amund, likewise embracing him. He pulled back and placed his hands on Baggi's shoulders. "Or as often as my duties permit. When they do not permit, then you come back to visit us."

"Of course," he said. "We won't be far. The border is less than a day's journey, after all."

The rest of the villagers came forward and embraced the trio in turn; some of them, like Talia and Hallsteinn and Audr and Vigi, were easily recognized. Others, he was embarrassed to admit, he could not recall meeting. Many had come to bid Guthini and Kettil goodbye rather than him, apparently having formed strong friendships with the duo during their stay in Flamebud. Even so, they all seemed at least to know Baggi, and they all wished him well. By the end of the farewells, the Naefjans' cart was heavily laden with parting gifts and provisions. *It's not a thankless job, being a Staffkeeper,* he thought, and laughed.

They left Flamebud Village, traveling up into the mountains and toward the border of Kichishi and Naefja, at the place where two seeming opposites met. They would return, and not after long, but still they were sad to go, and the villagers, too, were sad to see them leave. Yet when the travelers arrived hours later at a grassy, rime-frosted plateau tucked between three peaks, with a waterfall running down the farthest, excitement bubbled up in each of them.

The longhouse can go there, Baggi thought, already envisioning their new home, *and there's enough room for a great glasshouse in front, and a shrine beside.* He turned to his companions.

"What do you think?" he asked.

"It'll do," Kettil remarked.

"I like it," said Guthini.

Baggi grinned.

"Good. Then let's get to work," he said.

About the Author

Austin Scarberry is an author and pastry chef based in Portland, Oregon who largely writes fantasy, science fiction, and poetry. His debut book, "The Bumbling Heroics of Bolliver Hoopsleeve," is a collection of comedic cozy fantasy short stories published by *Wyngraf* in April 2024. This is his first novel. You can find his other work in Oprelle Publishing's poetry collection "Matter: Volume II," or in the award-winning *Sci-Phi Journal*. Follow him on social media @ScarberryWrites.

www.ingramcontent.com/pod-product-compliance
Lightning Source LLC
Chambersburg PA
CBHW061855310726
48972CB00004B/1038